# RECKLESS THIEF
## 82ND STREET VANDALS
### BOOK EIGHT

## HEATHER LONG

Reckless Thief/Heather Long – 1st ed.

ISBN: 978-1-956264-35-7

*For every risk you were willing to take.*
*Even the ones that didn't work out.*
*You're worth it.*

# SERIES SO FAR

# FOREWORD

Dear Reader,

Welcome to book eight of the 82nd Street Vandals series. If you have not read the first seven, stop. Do not pass Go. Grab book one: Savage Vandal, and start there.

Seriously.

This is a series that really must be read in order.

Speaking of reading in order, let's do a little previously in the 82nd Street Vandals. Merciless Spy opened following the revelation at the end of Dangerous Renegade from Bodhi that her mother was in a facility much like Pinetree.

Aware of the threats from multiple sides, the Vandals sent Em on the road with Jasper to keep her a moving target, while they dealt with shoring up security at home. They were also investigating the rats because they *know* they have a spy somewhere. Bodhi has been hanging out, but the guys are also missing Em.

In the meanwhile, Emersyn takes the time to read Jasper and Liam (separately) into the dark history of her relationship with Fuckbucket. For Em, it's both cathartic and terrifying to tell them, but Liam and Jasper both rally in different ways to comfort and protect her.

Freddie and Emersyn flirt closer to the edge of deepening their relationship, particularly since Freddie asked Em to push him. He has a moment that causes him to bolt, the PTSD of his own history coming back to sack him. Bodhi follows him as does Jasper. They help keep him grounded.

Needing time to get his shit together, Freddie goes to stay with Doc and work in the clinic. It's a challenge, cause he's a little embarrassed about freaking out, but he wants to be what his Boo-Boo needs. Doc points out that maybe he already is and he should trust her. Em gives him time even if she's missing him.

They celebrate Ms. Stephanie's birthday in and around getting Moira Sharpe, Emersyn's mother, from the facility. She's not all there when they bring her back. The level of drugs she was kept on doesn't help her clarity. Doc steals a very hot kiss during the birthday and tells Em to make him work for it, he is all in. Freddie teases her after but they are all right.

Em and Liam are also summoned to meet the king for the first time and that's a revelation about his identity and the fact he's no one that Em or Liam know. So that just adds to the confusion, especially when he makes it clear he considers Emersyn one of the Bay Ridge Royals now. Ezra backs their plays but it's just adding to the tension

Finally, we get to the opening night of Liam's club that was closed due to damage after the ambush in Ruthless Traitor. Em dresses up for the occasion in a sheer black outfit that teases her vulnerability as well as her confidence. The gang has a great time at the opening, she demonstrates her trust in them and they celebrate together.

It's only at the end of the night as they are heading back that everything goes sideways. An explosion at Kellan's auto shop, a fire at Vaughn's tattoo parlor, and a blowout for Jasper's car are just the beginning of the chaos as a body is dumped at the warehouse...

The war is only just beginning. Please be aware this book contains content with dark themes and intense situations intended for mature audiences only, including but not limited to: sexual assault, flashbacks of grooming, underage/childhood sexual assault, physical violence, emotional and mental abuse, as well as kidnapping, stalking, manipulation, addiction and other potentially triggering topics.

And now, as always, the housekeeping notes:

For those of you who have never read a why choose, or reverse harem before, first let me thank you for picking this up and giving it a shot. Second, the heroine will not make a choice in this book or any other between the guys in her life. It may take her a while to reach that conclusion, but it's the journey that drives it. There are many ways to frame this kind of relationship, currently why choose fits it very well.

Also, this is the eighth book in a series. While there may be no specific happy endings at the end of each of these books, there will be one to the whole series, that I promise you. Some of these books will have cliffhangers, largely due to the size of the story, but the happy ending has to be earned.

Finally, I want to add one last note. Books are not written in a vacuum. Worlds are not created in silence. There were some deeply challenging moments as I worked on this book, and thanks to some of the most wonderfully supportive people and the best girl gang ever, I made it. We made it.

Happy reading.

xoxo

Heather

# THE VANDALS

82nd Street Boys
 Jasper "Hawk" Horan
 Kellan "Kestrel" Traschel
 Rome "Hummingbird" Cleary
 Vaughn "Falcon" Westbrook
 Liam "Mockingbird" O'Connell
 Freddie "Unknown" Cleary
 Milo "Raptor" Hardigan
 Mickey "Doc" James aka Vandal
 Emersyn "Dove, Sparrow, Starling, Swan, Little Bit, Boo-Boo, Hellspawn, Ivy" Sharpe

**Other Characters**
 Elaine "Lainey" Benedict
 Adam Reed
 Ezra Graham
 Ms. Stephanie

# CHAPTER 1

*MILO*

Disapproval clung to Kellan, disapproval and maybe disappointment. But I'd been right to cut Mayhem loose. I needed to be here. She needed to be there…

Kellan pulled into the lot just in front of the auto body shop. Leaving the car running, he slid out. "I'll just be a minute."

"Need backup?" The alarm going off wasn't unusual. It probably had a short. Could also be kids breaking in to make their bones—they'd learn pretty quickly it wasn't a good idea.

"Probably not," he said as he shook his head. "Just keep watch from out here."

I didn't smile, but the idea of kids cutting out of the back and trying to "escape" only to find me in the lot? Yeah, that image entertained me. I studied the shop, and despite the cracked pavement in front of it and the damaged curbs in the area—the shop itself was in great condition.

They'd repainted at some point, and there were hints of

Rome reflected in the art on the building. We'd all lived a hard life, but the guys weren't letting it stop them from wanting more, building more—and they didn't change who they were to do it.

I really did see Ivy fitting in here. She fit all of them so damn well. Shoving the door open, I slid out. "Hey, Kel."

He pivoted to face me, and I spread my hands. No weapons. Not physical ones or ones hidden in my words.

"I know I sound like an asshole talking about sending her somewhere she doesn't want to go. I'm working on that."

"I know you are," he retorted with a grin. "You being an asshole is really not news to me."

Laughing at his smart-ass response, I would have flipped him off, but a spark behind him attracted my attention. What the—

The thought didn't finish as a conflagration ballooned outward in a wash of hot air. The force of it propelled Kellan forward, pitching him onto his face and slamming me back into the car.

Fuck. Sound had come with the blast that left nothing except silence in its wake. My chest hurt from the impact of the metal, but I shoved off the car as the heat rushed back. I hit Kel and rolled him, snuffing out the flames crackling along the back of his jacket.

Glass burst somewhere, followed by a high-pitched whistle shrieking. Covering Kel, I braced as a second explosion ripped through the darkness and the quiet. The roar punched through the silence, stuffing my ears. Heat scorched the air, making it almost too hot to breathe.

This had to be what it was like when a dragon breathed on you. Something popped and sizzled. The sting against my back had me rolling. I got the flames out on me then made sure Kel's were still out before I flipped him over and dragged him backwards.

Another pop and fire jetted out from somewhere in the back. I checked Kel's breathing. Blood coated his mouth, so I turned his head to keep it draining out and ensure his airway remained open.

He was gonna have a hell of a shiner. There was blood trickling from his forehead. I went for my phone. Hopefully, Doc was still at the clubhouse...

Blue and red lights flashed and sirens screeched, blotting out what noise I could hear as two patrol cars ripped around the corner. One bounced over the curb closest to us and stopped abruptly.

The patrolmen getting out both had their guns drawn. All I had was a phone in my hand as the guy's lips were moving, but I couldn't make out shit beyond the popping in my ears.

I stayed facing them, palms forward, showing the phone in my hand. The guy kept talking as he moved toward me even though I really couldn't hear a fucking thing he said.

The sound of a cell door slamming echoed inside my head. Guards moved through the throng, ordering us back to our lines. The horn blasted as they rushed the yard to separate inmates locked in a brawl.

I knew the drill.

Kellan was still out of it. However, he was also still breathing, so I moved to my knees carefully, dropping the phone so I could interlock my hands behind my head.

Cold steel locked around my left wrist, then my arm was twisted down, followed by the right where it was secured to the left.

The pat down wasn't gentle. They moved me away from Kel as an ambulance arrived along, with fire trucks and more flashing lights. Fortunately, I didn't have a gun on me.

Kel did—but he also had a carry license. The cops secured his weapon and wallet as I watched from the curb, handcuffed and deafened.

Meanwhile, the shop kept fucking burning.

*ROME*

"Call 9-1-1," Vaughn said as he threw the car into park before launching out the door. The fire consuming the tattoo shop was spilling out of the roof like some evil demon intent on swallowing the whole building.

People were fleeing the buildings on either side. Across the street, people had phones in their hands as screams erupted from inside. I called the emergency line.

"9-1-1, what is the nature of your emergency?"

"Fire, tattoo shop in the village. People need help. Trace the call." I left the phone connected as I went to help. Vaughn had his shirt off as he tried to get the gating up. Above, a window opened, like the whole building sucked in a deep breath.

Then it belched fire like the dragon exhaling. Hot, still-burning debris rained down. Vaughn covered his head, but it didn't save him from the fragments catching him in the head. He staggered, and I intercepted, dragging him away from it.

"Stay," I said, before cutting across the street and into one of the still-open clubs. My ears were already ringing from the explosion and the shouting outside. The music inside was too loud and it just added to the ringing. The bouncer tried to stop me, but I caught his thumb and twisted. The guy went down and I quickly shoved him away.

There was a glass in case of a fire break that I'd shattered with my elbow. I pivoted to head back out with a fire extinguisher in one hand and an axe in the other. This time, the bouncer just raised his hands and backed off. He stopped the second guy coming to intercept me, too.

The screams were even louder when I got out there with

sirens slicing through the night in the distance. Vaughn had already staggered back to the gate and dragged it up.

"Catch," I said, and waited for him to face me before I tossed him the extinguisher. "Move."

After adjusting my grip on the axe, I swung. It took three hits to knock the lock off the door. It pushed out but jammed again. Shoving the axe into the small opening, I wedged it open farther. Flames licked out to get to us, and Vaughn sprayed them with a fire extinguisher.

"The sprinklers aren't turning on," Vaughn said as we got the door dragged wider. Smoke bellowed out. The air tasted of heat, burnt flesh, and chemicals. The scent retched. A body was on the floor just inside. "Get her out," he ordered, taking the axe.

I hauled her up and out. The feel of her pulse was barely there, although she was still breathing when I got her to the concrete. Patrol cars, fire engines, and more pulled up. I didn't look at them as I went back for Vaughn.

He was farther inside. Flames spilled over counters and furniture, flowing like liquid. The walls were blackened, scorched from the blaze. The heat was unbearable. When I came across another, I hauled and carried them out.

Firefighters were going in now. I followed, even as the cops and other firefighters tried to protest. A hiss and gasp from above preceded the first frazzled spit of water from the sprinklers. More followed. The drops sizzled as they hit the ground. The water, like the air, was hot.

Didn't matter. Nothing mattered. No, as long as Vaughn was in that building—I would be too.

*FREDDIE*

.   .   .

5

"Was tonight weird for you?" It had been the first question I asked when Jasper and I were in the car.

"No," he said, lighting a cigarette after he started the car. "Put your seatbelt on."

"It wasn't?" I dragged the seatbelt over and clicked it into place.

"Nope," Jasper said, lowering the window to let the cooler air in as he blew out a stream of smoke. It was much nicer out here, even with the chillier weather. "You looked like you were having fun."

"I was—I mean, I did have fun. Still having it. Just—"

"It was weird?" Jasper checked as he pulled out of the private lot and then over to the side to wait for Liam and Boo-Boo.

"Yes," I said. "And no. Boo-Boo looked so fucking good. And she was happy. She looked happy to you, right?"

My knee was bouncing, but Jasper didn't comment on that. "She was happy, Freddie." He bumped my shoulder. "Take a breath. She's doing okay."

Happiness had wreathed her, filling her smile with magic and her eyes with confidence. The transformation had been... I laughed. "She really is kind of a swan, coming into herself."

"Not that she was ever an ugly duckling," Jasper retorted with an amused smile.

"No, never." Leg bouncing, I twisted back to see Liam's headlights come on. Probably making out with Boo-Boo. Lucky bastard. It made Boo-Boo happy. We were all gonna make her... "Jas?"

"Yep?" He cut a glance at me as they passed us, then accelerated out to follow. We were sticking with Liam and Boo-Boo as escorts.

"She told you." It wasn't a question. We hadn't talked about it directly. I hadn't discussed it with any of them, not straight out. I'd spoken around it, yet never said anything about what she told me.

Confession had been for us, and I'd take it to my grave for her. But...

"She told you what her uncle did." There was no beating around the bush, no second-guessing, or pretty words to soften the blow. "What the mother fucker did to her."

The air in the vehicle went volcanic as Jas took a noisy inhale. I gave him a minute to exhale. "Yes," he said. "She told me."

"We're going to kill him, right?"

"Eventually," Jas said, his expression darkening. "A one-way trip to hell might be too good for him. I want him to hurt first."

Hurt for every single thing he'd done to Boo-Boo. "I'll help."

A faint smile touched Jas' mouth. "I don't doubt it. Just remember—don't kill him quick."

I had no problems remembering that... *at all*. In fact, I flexed my hands and forced my knee to stop bouncing. "I think—"

The next words died unspoken as the whole car bucked. I jerked around to look. Had someone hit—

"Fuck," Jasper swore. "Brace."

The words barely left his mouth as a plume of fire shot out and the car bucked again. This time, it definitely felt like *something* hit us. We were on four wheels and then we were airborne, or at least flipping.

The car landed on its roof, skidding and throwing up sparks. All the blood rushed to my head. Lights blurred outside, and there was the shriek of more metal, then brakes squealing. We finally came to an abrupt stop.

Hanging, I tried to suck in a breath, but the force on my

chest was like a giant's fist crushing me. What the—more screaming tires outside and the crashing of metal.

There was a huge truck bearing down on Liam's car as he swerved and then whipped backwards, driving through traffic in reverse. The truck didn't slow in its pursuit, forcing other vehicles to slam on their horns and jerk out of the way.

A series of crashes rippled through the night.

"Out of the car, Freddie," Jasper ordered, verbally kicking me into action. I tried to depress the seatbelt lock except it was jammed.

Damn thing. I flicked out my knife and sliced it, barely catching myself from landing on my head. A gunshot ripped through the night. Then another.

I pushed out of the car in time to see Jasper and Liam striding through the wreckage, firing.

Where the fuck was Boo-Boo?

# CHAPTER 2

*EMERSYN*

The too-bright headlights filling the car blinded me. Liam swerved, then slammed the car into reverse. The world slowed from the moment I'd seen the plume of fire behind us and realized it had been Jasper's car.

Freddie and Jasper had both been in the car when it flipped. I barely twisted back as the sound of a horn filled the interior and the intense lights brought tears to my eyes.

Tires screaming, Liam retreated through oncoming traffic. The truck slammed into three cars, knocking them aside as it pursued us like some monster in a horror movie.

"Hold on, Hellspawn," Liam ordered, and I flexed my hand on the oh-shit handle even as the whole car spun. The truck was going to hit us, then—it passed by so close that sparks exploded off the side where the vehicles ground against each other.

I could see Jasper's car now, even as the cacophony of sound suddenly silenced. We lurched forward and spun again, smoke from the tires kicking up as they squealed against the pavement. This time when we came to an abrupt stop, Liam put the car into park.

"Gun." Liam handed me a weapon. "Out of the car. Moving target. Get Freddie and go."

Even as I closed my hand on the gun he passed me, his mouth fused to mine in a fierce, hot and bruising kiss.

"You better come back to me," I ordered against his lips.

"I will," he promised. "Now get moving. Keep moving. Trust no one." *No one that wasn't us.* The unspoken command resonated.

It wasn't a hard command to obey. I needed to make sure Freddie was all right. Freddie. Jasper. Everyone. Wrapping my hand around the grip of the gun, I was out of the car three seconds after Liam emerged.

Gunfire added to the nightmarish soundtrack of crackling flames, hissing water, metal groaning, people screaming, and guttural shouts. In the distance? Sirens.

Too far away.

I stayed low as I made sure of where Liam had moved. My heart was in my throat as Jasper appeared much like Liam had, both on their feet, both firing systematically as they approached the crashed truck.

There would be no questions for whoever was inside. They wanted to hit us. We hit back. A wild kind of joy kicked to life at the image. Jasper was okay. I pushed away from Liam's car and hurried toward Jasper's overturned vehicle.

Freddie collided with me, and we went down as the car itself exploded. Freddie rolled to take the impact of the landing. The blast of noise threatened to deafen me even as he pushed his hands over my head and rolled again to put himself between me and the explosion.

Heat ballooned upward. Sound rushed back in to the vacuum as I stared up at him. He was already standing, hauling me upward. My left hand was in his right, and I still had the gun clutched in my right hand. Light shimmered off his blade that I noticed he had in his free hand.

I turned to look past him to where Liam and Jasper were trading fire with someone else. Bullets whined through the air, the thud of them hitting metal galvanizing us both into motion.

Two hit the front of the car, and another skipped off the road not far from us. Yet another seemed to kick up dirt and rocks. The scatter of stones jumping included one bouncing off my hip. It stung, but I ignored it.

"We need to go," Freddie said, tossing a look over his shoulder to where Liam and Jasper were. "Still got on flats?" He looked at my feet.

"I can run," I promised. Even in the dress, I could run. I could tear it if I needed...

"Stay with me," he said, his expression fierce in the shadows as he cut a look behind us and then we were going. Hand in hand, he led me across the street and passed wrecked cars.

I made the mistake of glancing inside one. The blood all over the steering wheel and windshield promised if they weren't dead, they would be. The car had impacted other vehicles on the street. But it was the cracked glass radiating out from a single hole that said *why* the car crashed.

"Don't look, Boo-Boo," Freddie ordered, even though it was hard not to trace the path of destruction around us. There were more wrecked cars and shattered glass as a figure loomed up out of the darkness, and I had to swallow a scream as Freddie shoved the guy into a wall.

A gurgle escaped the figure as air whistled out and he clasped a hand to his throat. The arc of blood splashed across the damp concrete, and it wasn't until a gun slid out of the guy's hand and skittered across the alley that I recognized the threat.

"Don't look," Freddie repeated, tugging my hand to urge me along. I cut my gaze past the soon-to-be-dead man and down the alley.

"We need to get the gun," I told him, and he let out a breath as I pulled free to snag it.

"Yeah, yeah," Freddie said. "C'mon, Lara Croft, stay with me."

I glanced at my pair of guns then at Freddie. A laugh bubbled up from me, and his grin was a slash of light in the darkness. It was ridiculous and delightful—a morbid kind of levity. Something I needed desperately, even as adrenaline pounded through my veins with every squeeze of my too-rapid pulse.

Freddie navigated the network of alleys like an expert. The sound of running feet would echo behind us. We took shelter in recessed doorways more than once, trusting the shadows to shield us.

The further we went, the quieter and steadier our steps were. Liam wanted us out of the line of fire. Even under-standing the desire, I hated leaving them behind. At the same time, I stayed close to Freddie. Because the guys were safer if they could fight without worrying about us.

Freddie lifting up his hand to motion for me to wait, stopped me in place. He wasn't moving either, just—listen-ing, I thought. His head tilted like he could track a sound I wasn't hearing.

Not arguing, I gave him the time he requested. Two fingers. He wanted two minutes. I nodded even if he wasn't glancing at me. He made it five steps. Five. Before a shadow loomed up out of the darkness and caught him in the chest.

The blow knocked him into the wall. He crashed into the brick, hitting it with a kind of meaty thump. I raised the gun

Liam had given me, sighted the guy as he turned toward me and rushed forward.

Breathe. Wait for the beat of my pulse. Squeeze the trigger on the exhale. The gun had a kick, but I was ready for it, and I squeezed off two shots in rapid succession. He jerked with the first bullet, but the second halted him entirely.

The shock on his face burned an imprint into my brain as he stared at me, slack-jawed. Then he collapsed. There was no time to enjoy the victory because a blow caught me right in the crook of my elbow. The sharp jab sent pain skittering down to my fingertips.

The gun fell from my nerveless fingers, even as my new assailant gripped my left wrist, jerking it up and back to twist my arm behind me. Tears sparked in my eyes at the pain radiating up to my shoulder. I never got a shot off with that gun as he took it from my hand and shoved me against the brick.

It scraped at the lace of my dress, tearing it. Worse was the hot breath on my cheek and a very hard erection pressed against my spine. He gripped my ass with his free hand.

"I like a little fight in my whores," he whispered against my cheek then he licked me. Disgusted didn't cover it as I slammed my head back against him.

The bite of his fingers tearing at my clothes couldn't compete with the meaty crunch of his nose or his howl of pain.

"You fucking—" The next words died unspoken as he let out a strangled sound. The weight on my arm slacked off, and I yanked away. I met Freddie's gaze over the guy's shoulder as Freddie plunged a knife into him over and over.

He wasn't dead yet—so I slammed my knee into his nuts. All the air seemed to leave him as he collapsed. When

Freddie would have followed him down, I gripped his blood-soaked hand.

"We can go..."

"He hurt you." He was incensed, and the pain radiating from my shoulder and sending fire shooting down my arms was a testament to that.

"He can't touch me." It wasn't a lie. The guy was dead. His brutal contact already forgotten. If I had bruises—I didn't care. I was safe, and so was Freddie.

Gaze locked on mine, Freddie dipped his eyes from where my dress had torn, then down to the man below. He was still alive—barely.

"He's losing those fingers." It wasn't a request. I squeezed Freddie's hand then dropped to my knees to grip the guy's arm and yank it straight.

Flattening the offending palm to the ground, I cast my stare up to lock with Freddie's again. His lips pulled back from his teeth in a snarl of a grin. "You got him, Boo-Boo?"

"I got him."

"Which fingers?"

Three sparks of pain radiated from my ass, so I chose three fingers. Freddie severed them with brutal efficiency. The first one barely registered with the guy. The second one made him howl. After the third, Freddie kicked him in the head to silence him.

Finished, I reclaimed my gun. Instead of leaving the muti-lated digits there, Freddie scooped them up and carried them down the alley with us to toss them into a grate.

Yeah, I didn't want to think about that anymore. Clasping our sticky hands together, we took off through the network of alleys. I could almost tell we were getting closer to the water. The scents changed, and the breeze shifted.

When we would have emerged from an alley right on the

road, Freddie drew me back into the shadows. "We wait here," he said.

"In the open?" It wasn't so much a question as a confirmation. Freddie nodded once.

"This is where we wait. The guys will come for us." Absolute certainty. There were zero reasons to expect anything different. Jasper and Liam would come for us.

Or they would send Rome or Kellan or Vaughn. I shuddered as I tried to catch my breath. Freddie tugged me to him.

"Are you cold?"

Head tilting back, I studied him. This close, there was no mistaking the blood spatter on his face or hair. Another reason to not go any closer to the streetlamps. We were a bloody mess—literally.

The shivering wasn't from the cold but the reaction. I got that, and still, I didn't want to put too much pressure on Freddie. "I'll be okay."

"C'mere, Boo-Boo," he murmured, tightening an arm around me and inviting me right up next to him as he turned his back to the wind and shielded me from the worst of the draft.

"I don't want to scare you," I whispered.

"Not scared," he said, almost like a prayer. "Only scared when I saw that guy trying to hurt you."

"You stopped him."

His grin was breathtaking. "You stopped the son of a bitch who hit me."

"Never letting anyone hurt you again," I told him. It was my promise. "Not if I can help it."

"Well, same, Boo-Boo." Then he dipped his head, his nose brushing against my hair. "Can I kiss you again?"

I didn't bother with a verbal answer. Tugging my fingers from his, I raised my free hand to his face and my lips to his.

He fused his open mouth to mine, and the sweep of his tongue was a heady experience. My pulse hammered as I held on tight to him. Freddie squeezed me gently and then nuzzled my lips before he tangled his tongue with mine.

Intoxicating and delightful, I wanted more, but I still held a gun, and he had a knife. We were also covered in someone else's blood. When he dragged his head upward to gaze down at me, I couldn't slow my panting breaths.

"Don't run away," I whispered. "Please." I didn't want to put pressure on him, but I couldn't bear it if he had to flee right now.

"Not running, Boo-Boo," he promised. Then he kissed me again—this time, slow and deliberate. The pressure pushed me right up against the wall. Brick scraped against my back, but I didn't care. The softness of his lips was a temptation, as was the husky chuckle he released before he nuzzled kisses to my throat.

When his chuckle turned to laughter, I shifted my hand into his hair. The light tug brought his head up.

"What's funny?"

"Just pictured fucking your tits, Boo-Boo. Kind of want to do it—you know—eventually."

I opened my mouth, then closed it again as I considered it. "My tits?"

"Yep," he said with a grin. "Too weird?"

I shook my head slowly. "I don't think so—but I would think you'd want—"

"More?" Another flash of a grin. "I want more, Boo-Boo. But I really wanna fuck your tits. Like—not right now, but later."

"Whenever you want," I offered. "Just not sure I have a lot of tit to fuck."

"You got plenty of tits, Boo-Boo. Prettiest pussy I've ever seen and the sweetest tits. You'll see…" He shifted against me and glanced behind him before tucking me more firmly into his body. "You know where else I want to fuck you?"

The comment beckoned to me to play, so I nipped a kiss to his jaw before I said, "On the washing machine while it's doing the spinning cycle?"

It was a ridiculous comment, but I'd heard stories, and Freddie's expression lit up. "Let's add that to the list—we're gonna make a fuck-it list, you and me, Boo-Boo—all the places we're gonna fuck after we finish this shit."

I liked this plan.

I liked it a lot.

"Do I get to add to that list?"

"Hell yes, where do you want me to fuck you?"

Delight curved through the darkness and the crazy. We might be battered, bruised, and bloodied—but we were also together.

# CHAPTER 3

*KELLAN*

"*M*r. Traschel?" An unfamiliar voice spoke, accompanied by an inflating pressure on my left arm dragged me out of the abyss. Pain greeted me when I opened my eyes and it was a fight to not just shut them again.

Strobe lights sliced through the darkness. The taste of metal filled my mouth. The tight squeeze on my arm roused me more, and I fought to focus on the woman leaning over me.

"Take it easy, Mr. Traschel, you've likely got a concussion and you lost consciousness."

Did I?

When…?

Memory rushed in to fill the gaps. I tried to sit up, and the woman put a hand on my shoulder like she was going to make me lie down again. Yeah, not happening. The world swam when I twisted my gaze back to where the shop was still burning.

Engines from the local fire station, an ambulance, and cop cars were the source of the strobing lights. Bits and pieces floated to the front. Coming to check the alarm. Giving Milo shit and him responding. Turning to say something... did I say something?

The thoughts slipped away before I could fist them. "Where is Milo?" The words came out rough and raw. The paramedic stopped trying to make me lie down, which was good. I wanted the blood pressure cuff off.

"Sir?" This time it was a cop talking to me. "Mr. Traschel?" His tone was nowhere near as solicitous as the paramedic's. While it wasn't hostile, it definitely gave me something to focus on.

"Officer," I said, lifting my chin to meet the guy's gaze. The fact he was still standing didn't do me any favors.

"Can you answer a few questions for us?"

"Once my attorney is here," I said, not even trying to sugarcoat it.

"If you didn't do anything..."

"Yeah, don't try that with me. Innocent or guilty, everyone has the right to an attorney. I also have a concussion, according to the paramedic here."

Pointing her out to the cop seemed to remind him she was there. Yes, we have a witness, don't be a dick.

"Which means I might have some cognitive impairments that could lead to confusion in answering your questions. It's better for all of us if I call an attorney and have them here. I should probably get cleared by a doctor too."

The longer I spoke, the more sour the cop's expression turned.

"I'm going to get my phone out." Before he said anything, I added, "I'll also want my gun back. I have a license, but you know that since you also have my wallet."

Genuine surprise flickered over his face. "Look..."

"Pete," another cop called as he strolled up. "I got this."

Vasquez.

Pete scowled, then jerked his thumb to the side. "I'll deal with him then…"

Following the gesture, I frowned. "Him" was Milo. "Why is he in cuffs?"

"I'll take care of it," Vasquez said in a firm voice. "Neither of these guys are—"

"He just got out of jail—" Pete argued, interrupting Vasquez, and there was something to be said for the fact that Vasquez rolled his eyes.

"He finished his sentence and was released," Vasquez cut him off. "He's not on probation, so let it go and walk away."

The last seven words were delivered in a cold, brusque tone of a man who was done. I caught Milo's gaze as Vasquez dealt with his friend and the paramedic removed the cuff from my arm. The hospital debate was coming, but I'd skip that. Doc was back at the clubhouse.

He could handle the follow-up.

"Mind if I get my wallet and gun back before you go?" I asked before Pete could take off. I wasn't getting a friendly vibe from him. The fact he passed both over to Vasquez rather than me was fine. As soon as the irritation was gone, though, I glanced at the paramedic. "I'm good."

"You should go to the hospital…"

Raising a hand to stop her, I shook my head carefully. The world wasn't quite swimming but fuck the pound in my head intensified. "I've got a personal doc. I'll go see him. Promise. Give me what you need me to sign off on for choosing against following your medical advice. And thank you."

Her sigh spoke volumes. "Can you persuade him?" She looked to Vasquez for help, but Dan Vasquez had known all of us for a long time and shook his head.

"No, I know his physician friend. He'll be in good hands."

That seemed to persuade the paramedic more than anything else. She wrote up something on a clipboard and another on a digital tablet.

I scanned both items then signed them. After standing, I glanced at the shop. The world wasn't doing me any favors with the sway, but I got my shit together to remain on my feet.

Then I looked at Vasquez. "Why is Milo cuffed?"

"I'm taking care of it," he told me. "Let's answer some of *my* questions. After that, I can get you two out of here."

When I checked on Milo again, he just lifted his chin. The fact he was seated on a curb with his hands cuffed behind his back pissed me off.

"Uncuff him," I told Vasquez. "I'll call my attorney…"

"Really?" He eyed me. "This will go faster…"

"If you just stop trying to use your authority to intimidate us, that would be best. It didn't work when I was sixteen," I reminded him. "It's not going to work now. Uncuff him."

My shoulder stung as I shifted. However I'd deal with whatever that was later.

"Yeah," Vasquez sighed, then passed me the wallet. "The gun you get when we're finished."

Not open for negotiation. Fine. Whatever. I followed him to Milo. We needed to wrap this shit up because nothing about this felt accidental.

"Hey, Dan," I said quietly. "Thanks."

"Glad you're okay, kid."

Yeah. Me too.

Only the deliberate nature of the call and the subsequent explosion set off alarm bells for the others.

*VAUGHN*

The shouts from deeper in the building were growing fainter. The dense smoke made navigation difficult and breathing almost impossible. I'd slapped a damp cloth over the lower half of my face, but it wasn't helping.

I'd already hauled a few people out. Rome appeared out of the smoke like a wraith as I stumbled. He also had a mask on and caught me—then steadied me before he handed me a mask as well.

"Fire engines are here," he said just as the sprinklers kicked on. The scream of water whistling through the pipes was a sound I didn't know I'd missed. The spray was a little dank and warm. It sizzled once it hit the hot wood and soaked me where I hadn't already sweated through my clothes.

My foot hit a body on the floor, and I squatted to lift the prone form. Lauren's dark hair covered her face, and I swore, coughing as I tried to get her up. The fact that I staggered just added to my need to curse.

"I have her." Rome pulled her from me. "Go."

Coughing so hard my eyes watered made it impossible to answer. Rome had Lauren, shifting her until she was over his shoulder, then he gripped my arm. Right. I let him pull me toward the exit, trusting his navigation.

Outside, the cooler air was a punch in the face as we emerged from the hellish swelter inside. Fire trucks were everywhere, along with ambulances and shouting from the lookie-loos lining the road.

Someone took Lauren from Rome and then I was seated abruptly with an oxygen mask over my face.

"No," I said as I fought to remove the mask. "There are still people in there."

"Keep it on." Rome shoved the mask back into place and

blocked me when I tried to get up. One minute I was staggering to my feet, and the next, he parked me on my ass. I tried to glare at him, but it was hard to make him out.

"Rome," I snarled, but it came out even harsher, making me cough more. "The people—" My friends. My co-workers. Fuck, my clients.

"No," Rome said again, then shifted and pointed to the line of bodies on the sidewalk.

Bodies.

A couple were on gurneys heading for ambulances, but the rest were just—covered bodies.

Shuddering, I sagged downward and stopped fighting the paramedic strapping something around my bicep as they put the mask back in place. Rome stared at me when they offered him a mask, but he didn't pull the strap over his head, just pressed it to his face.

Yeah, he wasn't moving in case I tried to go back in.

Bodies.

I stared past him even as the burning in my eyes intensified the wavering. The coughing didn't help, and the tears that splashed out onto my face were as much a product of the smoke and the fire as the line of bodies.

"Lauren?" I croaked.

Rome pointed to the gurney being loaded into the ambulance. Not dead.

At least not yet.

That was—something.

A shout came from the direction of the shop, and I twisted to see a section of the roof collapse. Flames shot upward as smoke billowed and the crash of brick, wood, and metal left a gaping black hole into what had been the upper floors.

They had evacuated the buildings on either side. Although there were more people scattered around, like

Rome and me, on oxygen, just sitting there as witnesses to the destruction of it all.

Grief was a fist in my gut, harsh and unforgiving. I didn't know who'd been on shift. Sometimes guys came in on their days off. We didn't keep a schedule like so many other businesses. Most of us were independent. We rented the space, and shared the cost of the receptionist and the building. Then we all did our thing...

The weight of a hand on my shoulder steadied me. Rome held my gaze for a long moment. No, this wasn't my fault. Didn't make me feel better, however. We sat together, watching the building come down as the firefighters worked to keep the fire from spreading. The space itself was a lost cause.

The room where I did Dove's first tattoo. And her second... where I'd been building my business... where I'd been building toward our future. Hers. Mine. The guys. It was just gone.

More shouts sounded in the distance, and I shifted in my seat to drag out my phone. The screen was cracked and dark —a somewhat mournful metaphor for my current situation. Rome held out his and the message on the screen made my blood run cold.

LIAM:

Ambush. Check in.

Ambush.

We needed to go. Rome shook his head as he tapped out a message on the screen then showed it to me.

ME:

Same. Tattoo shop burnt down. Starling? Everyone else?

I barely managed to suck in a breath while I waited for the three dots to resolve.

LIAM:

On my way! H with F. J going to them. No word from M or K.

Liam was on his way. He was alive. So were Jasper, Freddie, and Dove.

"Raptor and Kestrel are fine," Rome said. The determination and faith in those words were something I needed right now.

"Too stubborn to be anything else," I managed to push out between coughs. That was an idea I needed to hold onto.

Someone was going to pay for this shit.

I glanced at the bodies on the sidewalk.

Someone was going to pay for all of them.

*JASPER*

I put two bullets into the last guy on the ground. We'd dragged him off the street. There was no cleaning this mess up. The wail of sirens approaching echoed down the canyon of streets. We weren't going to be able to stay here long.

"Son of a bitch," Liam swore, and I caught him glaring at his phone.

"What?"

"It wasn't just us," he said, showing me the message from Rome.

"We knew that, though." Suspected, maybe, but we'd both been aware of it. "Go—get to them. I'll get Freddie and Swan."

"You know where he'd take her?"

"Yep. A block from the clubhouse. Close enough to get to

it, far enough away to avoid any other ambushes." I glanced to where my car had been. "Leaving the scene of an accident."

"My attorneys will take care of it," Liam said without an ounce of irony or arrogance. "Take care of Swan and Freddie."

"What about Milo and Kel?"

"I'll get them after I get Vaughn and Rome. Head down."

"Watch your back," I told him, and we bumped fists. I didn't wait for him to give me a lift; I headed across the street and down an alley. If any of the cameras on the street picked up on the firefight, we were going to have other problems.

Nonetheless, those could wait. Right now, I needed to see that Swan and Freddie were in one piece.

I found the first body just inside the mouth of the alleyway. The guy was dead from a slashed throat. The second body was three blocks over and down with at least two gunshots to the chest.

The third guy was groaning, head moving from side to side as he let out whimpers of sound. Blood soaked the area around him and he was sans three fingers.

Three fingers.

"Touched our girl, did you?" I said, staring down into the shocked eyes. The rattle of breath was him drowning in his lungs.

Brutal way to go.

But the sirens in the distance meant someone *might* find him. Someone *might* get him help.

I shot him in the head.

I'd rather he suffered. Protecting Freddie and Swan from possible retaliation took precedence. Open war was bloody and reckless enough. Someone held this dog's leash before they sent him after us.

After her.

We'd carve that pound of flesh out of their hide.

Seven minutes later, I found them huddling together in the dark alley. Freddie appeared, knife in hand, before he recognized me and lowered it. Blood spatter covered him, and when I pulled him in for a hug, he returned it swiftly then turned us both to Swan.

Her dress was shredded in places. Like Freddie, she was also covered in blood, even though her smile was as fierce as she was.

I held out an arm, and she collided with us. Freddie didn't pull away as we cradled her between our bodies. The smell of sweat, gunpowder, and blood clung to them. I let myself have the moment.

They were safe.

However, we only got a moment.

Backing off, I stripped off my coat and held it open for her to slip on. Freddie took her gun, then passed it to me after she was wrapped up.

"Stay with me," I said to her, then flicked a look to Freddie. "You got her back?"

He nodded once.

"We're going around to the back, then straight inside. Don't slow down for anything."

Swan's hand slid into mine, and not for the first time did I marvel at how tiny she was compared to the rest of us. The sharpness in her eyes and the strength in her grip told me our little Vandal was more than ready for whatever came next.

Good.

"Liam?" was her only question.

"He's okay," I promised her. "He went for Rome and Vaughn. We'll know more soon."

She shuddered, then nodded once before she raised her chin. "I'm ready," she said, the barest of quavers in her voice.

I leaned down and pressed a kiss to her lips. Just the one.

A reminder to both of us that we were alive and a deposit for more later. "Yeah, you are," I whispered. "You have this, Swan."

Her tremulous smile lit me from within, and she squeezed my hand. "I have you both, too."

Hell, she had all of us.

# CHAPTER 4

*DOC*

he ride in the ambulance seemed to elongate time. I'd left the rats on full lockdown. Moira Sharpe was out and secure. The sedative I'd given her would keep her out for a few hours yet. No one else could get into the clubhouse. There was no waiting for the others to return; Steph needed a hospital, and she needed it now.

Across from me, the paramedic worked in tandem with me to stabilize her. An oxygen mask was on her face, helping to push air into her lungs. A pulse ox monitor on her hand— her bloody, broken hand. The alarm went off as her blood pressure dipped. Internal bleeding...

Had to be.

"Hanging another bag."

I registered the words but kept moving, looking for any open wounds. Hoping I could find something I could stop. There were gouges to her palms from her broken nails.

Scrapes on her knees. The clothing was one of her suits—she'd been taken while working.

How long had they had her?

Her shoes were gone. One of her toes had been broken. A slice down the center of her foot oozed blood. Her knee was turned out slightly.

Dislocation.

Another alarm went off, yanking me from assessment mode.

"V-fib."

I shifted my attention to compressions immediately. Her heart wasn't getting enough blood flow. The ambulance screeched around a corner as the paramedic, Megan, sliced open Steph's shirt. The bruises visible along her chest sent a wave of violence through me that had no outlet.

Mickey J had no place here. Steph's brother couldn't be treating her.

The Vandal in me wanted to gut everyone involved. He didn't heal; he broke.

Doc—I had to be Doc. I'd fucking embraced Doc for years, and that was who Steph needed. Megan got the pads attached and the machine hummed as it charged up.

"Clear," she warned, and I lifted my hands. Steph's whole body convulsed up as the charge hit her.

"Still V-fib," I said as I resumed compressions.

"Charging," she warned even as she reached for the radio to update the hospital. Another corner, and like Megan, I braced myself to keep from falling as I kept on with the compressions. One eye on Steph and the other on the monitor. "Clear."

Hands up, I focused on the heart monitor as Steph arched up off the bed.

"Sinus rhythm." I nearly sagged in relief, and the paramedic nodded as we went back to checking her wounds.

"Two minutes," came the warning from the front. We were almost there. Those two minutes stretched out as Steph opened her beautiful eyes and looked up at me.

When she raised a broken hand to me, I clasped it gently. "I'm here," I promised her. "I got you."

Then we were there, and the doors flew open as a trauma team rolled out to meet us. I helped lift her gurney out.

"Doctor James," the ED doctor said as she nodded to me. "Doctor Adler. Fill me in."

The thing about an ED was you didn't stop moving for the brief, so I filled her in while on the move. We were heading straight into a trauma bay.

"On three," Adler said, then we were transferring Steph onto the hospital bed. Bloody gauze fell away. "Get me the portable x-ray in here, and let's get her out of these clothes."

I worked with her to get Steph situated.

"Doctor James, you need scrubs if you are to remain in here." It wasn't critical, just firm advice. I backed off as a nurse took my place.

"I have you, Doctor," another nurse said as she hustled over to me and directed me to another room. After cleaning my hands, I stripped out of the clothes and into the scrubs. Then I was back out to see that Steph was still in the bay. They passed me an apron as they shot x-rays.

The images began to populate on the screens and I lost count of the number of broken bones.

"Jesus," one of the nurses whispered, and I was right there with her. Even if I hadn't already recognized the signs of torture, they were evident on that screen.

Breathing grew difficult, the rattling sound a warning. Adler was already doing a chest tube, her movements swift and efficient as blood spilled down onto the tile below.

"We're gonna need next of kin," Adler warned. "Someone call up to the OR."

"I am," I told her, and the doctor paused where she was securing the chest tube. "This is my sister." The word came out harsh and husky.

Rough sympathy filled the other doctor's eyes. Thankfully, she didn't try to chase me out, even if there was no way they'd let me do more now that they knew. She also didn't try to sugarcoat this. "Does she have a medical directive?"

"No," I said, with a sharp shake of my head. "And, yes, I want all life-saving measures taken."

"Understood."

A surgeon walked in, his darker scrubs, cap, and mask a sign that he'd probably just stepped out of another procedure. "What do we have, Adler?"

She went clinical as she detailed the wounds we'd identified, including the damage to Steph's heart. The blood loss, coupled with the internal injuries, was doing a job on her.

"Get Dr. Ortega," the surgeon said. "And let's move her up now." They were gearing Steph up to move, locking the sides up as they shifted wires and moved the IVs. "I want Peterson up there too."

A nurse thrust a tablet at me for permission. I glanced at the surgeon. "I want to be there."

He narrowed his eyes.

"I'll stay out of it. Your OR, your rules. But I need to be there for her..."

I hadn't been there, and look where she was now. I thought he'd say no for a moment, but then he just nodded once. "Come with me."

Time ceased to have meaning once we were inside the OR. The team moved efficiently as they got her onto the table. The anesthesiologist was working on her levels and they had blood already hanging because of the loss she'd suffered.

The second surgeon arrived, a general one. The doctor working on her already was a cardiothoracic surgeon. They conferred as they scrubbed in and stepped into the surgical theater.

Periodically, they shot questions at me. Allergies? Prior injuries? How long had she been in V-fib? Otherwise, they did their work. A call went out for an orthopedic surgeon for her knee and brutalized fingers.

I'd spent years trying to clean the blood and destruction off my hands. Years working to atone for the stupid mistakes I'd made when I'd failed to listen to the one reasonable voice in my life.

Steph had given up a lot to take me on and try to keep me out of trouble. She could have cut bait and let me go into the system. The age difference between us had always made her more parent than sister. Yet, not once had she given up on me.

She never gave up on anyone. With the biggest heart I'd ever known, she'd not only fought to keep me on the straight and narrow, she'd also fought for every single child in her charge. Even for those who were adopted or found their way out of the system, Steph had always been there for them.

It would have killed her if she'd known about Little Bit and the trauma she'd faced. How many nights had she sat up with Freddie? Or went with Vaughn when his mother was dying? Even going so far as to ensure he got to go to the cemetery regularly.

The thoughts filtered through my mind like images flashing on a slideshow. Even as I tracked every move they made, they were in a fight against time to keep her stable while also repairing the internal damage.

"I can't find this damn bleeder," the surgeon said, jerking me into the present. "Get me another bag up there."

Every team had its own shorthand. The machines had begun to beep again as blood pressure dipped. They fought to get it up, and then it would tank again.

Too many bleeders.

Too many.

One by one, they cauterized or tied them off. Flying stitches couldn't keep up with the damage. Then she was in V-fib again. And they brought her back.

Sinus rhythm. Bleeding under control.

Another hour and we were back in that same trench again.

It was like for every grueling inch we gained, we lost another one somewhere else. Never had I felt more helpless than standing there as they waged war to bring her back from that edge.

"Looking good," the one surgeon told me. "We're going to close her up and give her some time before we go in again."

"Fuck," the other said at the same moment as the alarms went off. Blood began to spurt from inside the incision. They went to work with lap pads and tried to create a visual.

She was blowing stitches. They weren't holding. I tracked it to the way her heart rate slowed. It wasn't V-fib, for it was genuinely slowing. Her blood pressure dipped.

*Goddammit, Steph,* I wanted to scream at her. Don't fucking do this.

Still, I said nothing. Did nothing. I didn't move. I might as well have been stone, locked into place as I tried to will her to keep fighting. Anything she needed, fuck, they could take it from me.

Hypovolemic shock.

I recognized it even as they tried to stop the bleeding. Four bags of blood, and she was still losing it too fast.

Flatline.

They kept going. Extraordinary measures. New bags of blood hung. Manual CPR while they tried to get those bleeders clamped and stopped.

No sooner did they get one closed when another would rupture.

CPR wasn't buying us much time. At ten minutes down, the surgeon looked at me and I understood. Doc understood.

Mickey J wanted to shout at him to keep going. Vandal wanted to threaten his life. Only Doc understood the futility of it.

She was already gone.

I shifted my gaze to the clock on the wall that had started the minute she'd flat-lined. My heart was a rock in my chest; as still as my sister's.

He was waiting for my answer—an answer I didn't want to give. Finally, I nodded once.

"Time of death…"

Everything slowed. The work, the hands trying to save her, all because it was done. She couldn't be saved, and the surgeon backed off, as did the nurses as I walked forward.

Steph's eyes were closed, her expression so peaceful it didn't belong in this place where a hellish battle had been waged to keep her with us. Her features blurred as my eyes went hot. Carefully, I reached over to lift the mask from her and the anesthesiologist helped.

Stroking her hair back, I pressed my lips to her forehead. I wanted to weep, but the tears burning in my eyes refused to fall. The petrification of my heart left a dead weight in my chest.

One of the doctors put a hand on my shoulder. One by one, they cleaned up some but then left me with her. Giving me time. Time I didn't know what to do with as I stood with the final remnant of my family.

The woman who never gave up on anyone. Mickey J wanted to rail against the world, to yell and break things. He wanted to grieve and to mourn. It didn't matter if the level of traumatic damage had doomed her before they dumped her in front of the warehouse.

A warning?

A threat?

A punishment?

I didn't fucking care what the intention had been. Doc stayed with her so Mickey J could beat himself bloody inside me. I wasn't ready to leave her.

Nevertheless, when I was… when I walked out those doors, Vandal was going to find every single fucker who put a finger on her, and I was going to tear them apart.

They were going to feel every ounce of her pain.

Steph never gave up on anyone. She loved with her whole heart. She would tell me that vengeance didn't help anyone.

Maybe it didn't. However, it would hurt those fuckers, and that would have to be enough for now.

A tear sloshed down on her cheek as I pressed another kiss to her forehead. "I'm sorry," I whispered. I should have been better.

I should have been faster.

Eyes closed, I lingered there for another beat and then made myself go. I made myself leave the operating room. The nurses moved to take care of things as I continued sightlessly down the hall. It wasn't until I cleared security that I saw them.

My Vandals.

They stood there, a disheveled wreck of bruises, and stinking of smoke. Even my little bit was there, the bruises in her eyes the first thing to punch through the numbness.

I didn't have to say a word. Milo turned and slammed his fist into the wall, and then Little Bit was there, and I picked her up as she wrapped her arms around me. I had no business even touching her. Only I didn't care about those arguments anymore.

Steph was gone. I'd lost her when I wasn't looking.

Over my dead body was I losing Little Bit.

# CHAPTER 5

*LIAM*

The calls to Mom's phone just rang repeatedly before going to voicemail. Dad's didn't even ring, it just clicked over to voicemail. A call to security didn't get me any closer to answers. The flashing lights, smoke, and chaos sucked me in as I pulled onto the street a block away from the tattoo shop.

They were diverting traffic, so I called Rome.

"I'm here," I said as soon as he picked up. "One block south. Need me to fight up there, or can you guys get to me?"

"Coming."

The call disconnected, but those two syllables settled some of the acid boiling in my stomach. Then the text came through to help assuage the rest of it.

JASPER:

Have them. Going to the clubhouse now.
She's bruised but okay.

Bruised.

The singular syllable lit a match to my temper. I wasn't the one who typically burned hot. Jasper was the rash, impatient one. I was the cold, calculating one.

JASPER:

Status?

I narrowed my eyes as soon as I saw Vaughn and Rome heading toward me. My mirror looked like hell, and Vaughn actually looked worse.

I was beginning to see the value in just letting my temper boil over.

ME:

Got 'em. Taking them to the hospital.

Normally, I'd take them to Doc, except you didn't fuck with fires. He read the message but didn't respond. He didn't need to any more than I would. The door to the back opened and Vaughn sagged inside, coughing. The reek of smoke was so pungent it made my eyes water.

"You look like shit," I said, and Rome just stared at me. "Yeah, I look like shit too. You're going to the hospital."

Slipping back into traffic, I followed the detour around what was left of the tattoo shop. There were ambulances leaving the scene. They should be on one of those. The fact that neither argued had me cutting around traffic and accelerating.

The ER was chaos, a jam-packed waiting room, and I glared at it. We could go to a different hospital. I had the—

"We're good," Rome said as he climbed out, then peered back to Vaughn who was coughing. "Where do you need to be?"

Right here, only…

Fuck.

"They called me from Mom's phone."

The emotion draining out of Rome's expression had to mirror mine. He didn't have to ask me who "they" were. They were behind the attacks. That meant they had Mom, or maybe they were fucking with me.

I really wanted them to be fucking with me, but until I got ahold of them…

"We'll go with you," Vaughn said before another cough wracked him. I cut a look back at him then Rome shook his head.

"I'll stay with him," Rome said. "Go." Then he held up his phone. "Call backup. Don't get dead."

Yeah, our backup was a little thin at the moment. "You too…make sure a doctor looks at you too."

My other half just flipped me off. I stayed in place until they were inside, then I floored it out of the parking lot. Security called when I was a block from the airport.

"They aren't here, Mr. O'Connell," Billings said, his tone professional if tense. "Alarm was disabled. No sign of force. Everything appears neat and orderly. There is a note on the fridge addressed to you."

"Open it."

"Stand by, sir."

I tried not to twitch as I pulled over to the side of the road. Head on a swivel, I scanned everything around me. What the fuck time was it? It hadn't even been eleven when we rolled out of the club, and now it was four—no, five in the morning. Fuck.

Updates had hit my phone from Rome. He just ticked off the words the nurses and doctors told them. They were okay. Smoke inhalation and needed oxygen. Bruises. Scrapes. And Vaughn had managed to crack a couple of ribs in there.

Rome had some burns, though he didn't seem to care about those.

I'd check them later.

Hellspawn—

"Mr. O'Connell," Billings said. "I considered offering you the opportunity for reparations. However, after some thought, I decided against it. You and your friends took something of great value to me. With this in mind, you will all be repaid in kind. A loss for a loss.

"What you treasure, you will lose. What you value, you will see taken. Understand that this might be the first move, yet it is by no means the last. You made the mistake of stealing from me. There will be no mercy. No negotiation. No salvation. When I have destroyed you, I will take back my prize."

Billings cleared his throat. "There is no signature. Only an address."

"Give it to me."

I recognized the street name immediately—the old house.

"Bag the letter for evidence. Sweep the house, full breakdown. Get another security team to the hospital to keep an eye on my brother. I want a third set of teams on all the stores."

"Yes, sir. Should I send someone to this address?"

"I'll take care of it myself."

Whatever happened there was done. This wasn't so much a warning shot as a swipe to score first blood. He—and I had money on Bradley Fucking Sharpe as the culprit—wanted us to feel this loss. To suffer.

The tires squealed as I jerked the car around to go the other way. Tires screeched as other cars hit their brakes to avoid colliding with me.

My phone began to buzz as orders went out. More

messages were coming in. I kept my focus on the road. Rome was at the hospital with Vaughn. They had each other's backs.

Jasper had Hellspawn and Freddie. Kellan, Milo, and Doc would back them. That knowledge helped me ice over the cracks as I risked more than a few reckless driving tickets to get to the old house.

The driveway was a blur as I raced down it. I must have hit the gate access, but I drove right up to the circle in front of the house and pulled out the gun before heading inside.

Acid left a sour burn in the back of my throat. Inside the foyer, the house was quiet except for a hushed scratch and skip of the record player. It was dated, even though Dad had it in his old office. I'd just finished restoring it when I bought the house.

The interior was cold, colder than the air outside, if possible. Still, sweat dotted my skin as I crept into the home I'd claimed for myself. A home built and created by the two people I was here for. Moving on silent feet, I followed the hush and scratch from the vinyl down the hall to Dad's old office.

The pocket sliding doors were parted. They shouldn't be open at all. I had gotten into the habit of securing the doors whenever I was here, and even Adam had left them closed during his tenure.

A part of me half-hoped I'd push those doors wide to find Adam Reed sitting in there fucking off. It had been weeks since we had an update from him.

Another problem for another day.

The softest of sounds came beneath the hush and scratch. That—wasn't the player. When it came again, I shot down the hall and shoved the doors wide, gun ready.

Nothing could have prepared me for the sight of my

mother, tied to a chair that was on its side, tears rolling down her face as she tried to reach Dad.

His ashen face betrayed his status. For a suspended moment, I stood there, all but forgetting how to breathe. Then Mom made that noise again, and I quickly scanned the room before pocketing the gun to go to her.

She lifted her red-rimmed, wet eyes to meet my gaze as I pulled a knife out to slice through her bonds. Her hands were so cold and she let out little twitches of pained sound.

"Jonathon…" The way she whispered his name came out so utterly broken, it threatened to crack through my resolve. The ice inside of me shifted as I helped her free of the chair. There were bruises on her wrists and ankles. More bruises on her face. A handprint on her cheek.

I was going to tear these bastards apart. They were going to be alive for every single blow and slice.

"I'm here, Mom," I whispered, then reached over to touch my fingers to Dad's throat. Even as she clutched me, she trembled. The lack of a pulse seemed to make mine even louder.

Suddenly her sob split through the silence and I hugged her as we sat there on the floor of Dad's office, surrounded by the past and the cold invasion of death. While I wanted to close my eyes as I rocked Mom, I didn't.

There was no looking away from this. Jonathon and Mary O'Connell had given me the life I craved, the life I wanted, and they'd *loved* me. Loved my brother. They'd never second-guessed that choice, as far as I knew.

Not once.

And I'd brought this to their door. Mom's tears were like a dozen razor blades slicing through me. It took time and willpower, but I had to get her up. I had to check her for injuries and she needed a doctor.

Shock was a problem.

I pulled strings with the sheriff and had my own security do a full sweep of the house. The visual security inside the house had been trashed. Electronics ripped out, hard drives taken. The internal monitoring had been off during Adam's tenure, although I'd turned them back on after.

Whoever destroyed it knew what they were doing. There was nothing from the moment they arrived. When the ambulance came, Mom roused from her stupor and grew hysterical. She didn't want them touching Dad, or taking him.

It took me time to settle her back down, and eventually, she agreed to a sedative. Billings sent a whole team for her. I wanted them covered on all points.

Even more, because I was going to have to leave her, and I wasn't sure she'd forgive me.

"This looks bad," Ezra said as he stepped inside with one of the security guys right behind him.

"It's worse than it looks," I told him. "Give me five to get Mom squared."

"Yep."

He was there, a ghost in the background as I moved. Mom took some coaxing, but I got her into a second ambulance, this one with security in attendance.

"Those men are terrible," Mom told me. "I don't want you to do anything, Liam... promise me."

I would not lie to her, not about this. "I can't do that," I said, kissing her hand. "I will come to you as soon as I can. I need you to listen to the guys. They will make sure you are secure and keep you that way."

She made a face.

"Mom," I said, trying to keep my voice firm while also being kind. She deserved the kindness more than anything. "I'm sorry—I should have been here."

"Baby," she whispered. "I'm glad you weren't there, and so

was Jonathon. He didn't want anything to happen to you..." Tears welled in her eyes again. "I don't know how to do this alone."

"You're not alone," I promised. "We're going to get through this together. Will you listen to the security team? Let them make sure you're okay. Listen to the doctors, and then you're going on a quiet retreat for a bit—time to recover and to grieve. Then when it's safe, we'll bury Dad."

The last few words clawed at my throat as I said them, and she squeezed her eyes shut as she tightened her grip on my hand. "They wanted to scare you—they wanted to hurt you and then Dad—" She let out a lost sigh. "Jonathon's heart has been bad for a while. He didn't want you to know."

If only I could allow myself the right to close my eyes. Only I didn't. I kept them on hers.

"After...they just...they left." The weeping intensified but then slowed again as her eyes drifted shut. I glanced at the paramedic who was dealing with her IV.

"The sedative is hitting her now," she assured me. "Don't worry, Mr. O'Connell, she will be in good hands."

The paramedic was with the company.

"Thank you," I said, then pressed a kiss to my mother's forehead before slipping out and closing the doors.

Ezra walked up to stand with me as the ambulances pulled away. Security worked with the sheriff and the police. It was after eight in the morning and my eyes were pure grit at the moment.

Dad was dead. I didn't even know how to process that information. He wasn't waiting somewhere for a phone call. He wouldn't be giving me shit about not doing something for Mom. He was *gone*.

It was my fault he was gone.

My phone vibrated in my pocket and I pulled it out.

The messages on the screen were numerous, but it was Hellspawn's name that leapt out at me.

HELLSPAWN:

Ms. Stephanie...

# CHAPTER 6

*T*he silence in the clubhouse proved almost suffocating. It had taken a while to persuade anyone to sleep. I started with Mickey, coaxing him into my bed after he showered off the blood. His movements had been sluggish and he wasn't all there. Still, he let me tease him to sleep with slow strokes of his hair. After, I moved to Liam, who crashed in Rome's room, silent and grieving.

Jasper was next; like everyone else, he hadn't wanted to sleep. However, he was still healing and a little pushiness, along with curling up with him, got him to sleep. Freddie had zero interest in me persuading him, though. He finally drifted off in the room where I'd been watching over Mom.

Vaughn and Rome were both rough, but they were also both asleep—finally. Thankfully, I hadn't had to persuade them. They crashed on the big sofa in our suite, so I'd just left them both tucked in before retreating to check on Mom.

I didn't even know what time it was. It seemed years since

our night out at the club. Once Jasper got us back to the clubhouse, we learned about Mickey and his sister. Then word trickled in about the other attacks.

Vaughn and Rome had been at the hospital when we got there. Kellan arrived with Milo. The blood on Kellan's collar and the smell of smoke and char filled the air.

"You should be sleeping," Kellan said as I slipped into the kitchen. He and Milo were drinking coffee, their conversation breaking off at my entrance.

"So should you," I scolded, going to him when he held out an arm. He'd showered and changed, even though the burnt scent seemed permanently lodged in my nostrils. The curl of his arm around me pulled me in tight.

The squeeze bordered right on the edge of too much, but I leaned into him and let him pull me onto his lap. My hip protested when it impacted gently, but I ignored it. There was a cut there. I'd washed it out in the shower before the hospital. Freddie had found some liquid band-aid and helped close it up for me.

I could survive a cut.

Across the table, Milo watched us with dark, brooding eyes and I held out a hand to him. "I'm fine, Ivy," he said, his voice as gruff as his gaze. But when I curled my fingers at him and flattened them again, he sighed. "So stubborn."

Just a flicker of a grin before he slid his hand over mine, squeezing gently.

"You're not fine," I said, then cleared my throat at the emotion punching through. Exhaustion weighed on all of us. "None of you are."

The ambushes had left such deep, lasting marks. I had no idea how we were going to move past all of this, just knew that I needed to be there for them. I couldn't bring back Ms. Stephanie or Jonathon or all those people at the shop...

"I need to call the hospital in a little while," I said softly. "I need to check on Lauren." The only other survivor from the tattoo shop had passed in the time we'd waited for news of the surgery.

Milo's knuckles were bloody and raw. He'd hit the wall more than once earlier.

"And I need to clean these up…" I twisted to press a kiss to Kellan's jaw. His eyes were so tired, the twin shards of deep blue were almost glassy. "You need to sleep."

"You can bully me into bed in a bit, Sparrow," he murmured. "Right now, I need to think and I need to plan before everyone else is awake and alert enough to start striking out for blood."

There would be blood. No doubt existed within me. We would get retribution for all who had been harmed—for all who had been taken from them.

The words on the call earlier floated back up, and I glanced at Milo. "I'm fine, Ivy," he tried again and I wrinkled my nose at him.

"Shut up." I rose, squeezing his hand and Kellan's gently before I released them. "You're not fine. We already established that. None of us are. But you're oozing blood, and those look nasty. I can help clean them up. Hardly my first injury to treat, and I can do something about it. You can sit there and let me."

His lips pursed as he gave me a flat-eyed glare. Once upon a time, that look might have terrified me. Now? All I did was glare right back at him. Milo wouldn't hurt me.

Ever.

The exaggerated sigh of exasperation made me smile, and I headed for the first-aid kit they kept in the cupboard.

"Want me to—" He didn't finish the question when I hopped onto the counter and climbed to stretch up to the top cabinet where they kept the newer supplies. We'd already emptied out one of the kits when we got back after the road-side ambush.

"Apparently not," Kellan said in a fairly droll tone. I caught the flicker of his smile as I climbed down. Milo just shook his head.

I paused long enough to get a bowl of water, then carried it over to the table. "Hand," I said, flipping open the case.

For a moment, Milo looked like he was going to argue then held his hand out to me. I studied the broken skin over his knuckles. It was a mess.

A real mess.

I cleaned each one, careful not to reopen them but also to ensure I got out any dirt. The mark around his wrist made me frown; it was red and irritated.

"Cuffs," Milo answered, and I jerked my gaze up to meet his.

"What?"

"I'm getting more coffee," Kel said as he stood, and he hesitated momentarily, which pulled all of my attention.

"If you want to rest, I can get it after I finish." I wasn't the only one tracking his unsteady movements.

"I can get it, Sparrow," he assured me, before he pressed a kiss to the side of my head. "I know, I look like hell. I'll be fine."

There was still a pallor to him that had been present since he and Milo arrived at the hospital. If Milo hadn't pressed him to see a doctor when they got there, I would have.

"It's a concussion, Ivy," Milo said softly, and when I glanced at him, his lips barely seemed to move. "He doesn't want to rest until we're a few more hours past it."

"That's not what they recommended at the hospital…"

"I heard that," Kellan said before the grinder kicked on. After, he added, "You can fuss about me when you're done doctoring his knuckles."

A sigh escaped me. Concussion. Smoke damage. Buildings burned. People tortured...

Tears burned as I blinked them back and tried to focus on the wavering image of Milo's knuckles.

"Hey..."

The lump in my throat made breathing hard, and no amount of fighting the tears kept them at bay. One splashed down my face and Milo was instantly on his feet, his arms circling around me.

The sob came out a hiccup, followed by another as I lost the battle. They were all hurting so badly.

Took something precious to him—

Took something precious.

I hated him so much. This was my uncle. The guys came for me and then we got my mother, and now...

A hand pressed to the back of my head as Milo all but picked me up. I wanted the tears to stop. I was supposed to be looking after them, but I couldn't stop it.

Mickey had been so damn broken. The pain in his eyes would forever haunt me. Rome looked like hell. Liam destroyed. Then there was Vaughn—the agony radiated in the air around him. Milo, Kel—no one was safe from my uncle's retaliation.

"Sparrow," Kellan's voice penetrated the haze of tears as I cried against Milo. The firm weight of his hand on my back seemed to drag me back from the edge. "This is not on you..."

"Fuck, no," Milo said, his vehement growl provoking more tears. "Jesus, Ghandi, and Joseph, Ivy. This is definitely not on you. Ever."

Lifting my head, I glanced from Milo to Kellan. The understanding in his eyes threatened to break me. Yes, this was on me.

"No," he whispered, as if reading my mind. "This is not.

They might be striking back at us, Sparrow. But this is not your fault. It's their fucking fault. It's the son of a bitch who took Ms. Stephanie, who took Liam's parents, who set the explosives and came after you guys in the street."

He slid his hand down to my hip, the contact gentle and light.

"It's the bastard who put their hands on you and on Freddie, who tried to take out all of us. They wanted to hurt *us*, not just you."

"Because of me..."

"No," Milo said, wrenching my attention back to him. I still hadn't— "I don't care what that fucking family who adopted you thinks. This shit? This crossed a line a long time ago. What they did to your mother? What they're trying to do to you? Goddamn right, we're not going to allow it to happen. They want to scare you. They want to make you run."

Kellan stilled against my back as Milo set me down, then cupped my face. The smell of blood and antiseptic joined the scent of smoke, clogging my nostrils.

"That's what this is," Milo said, his expression darkening as his gaze locked on me. "It's all a gambit to make you run. To make you leave us so that we can't protect you..."

Had someone...?

"No, I don't know what is at the root of this. No one has revealed your secrets to me. Not the guys. Not Mayhem. No one. I want you to trust me enough to tell me, but whether you do or not is irrelevant. Because you're my baby sister, and what comes for you, is coming for me."

"For us," Kellan said in a steely tone, and Milo lifted his gaze to look past me. The wordless communication translated into a worried expression before his whole demeanor softened.

"Coming for us," Milo said, reinforcing Kellan's words.

"They drew blood. I'm not doubting that. I refuse to let them take you. We all will. I just need you to keep fighting for *you* and to trust us."

Curling my hands into fists, I sniffled. "I just—hate that you guys are all hurting."

"We know," Kellan said, then slipped an arm around me to tug me back against him. His chest was flush with my back. Milo didn't scowl or glare. If anything, he appeared almost indulgent, which seemed to underscore the moment. "We hate that you're hurting too. We do this together. They want to drive a wedge between all of us."

"Divide and conquer," Milo said with a long sigh, reaching for the cotton I'd used to dab his knuckles. He resumed the work with care. "It's a plausible theory. You put a wedge against one person, turn that person against the rest or put them in a position where they see only one way out..."

"Sacrifice the one to save the many," Kellan continued, then he pressed a kiss to the side of my head. "We're not sacrificing anyone."

"We already—"

"No," Milo said with a stern shake of his head. "They made a mistake in taking Ms. Stephanie. They compounded that mistake by taking Liam's parents. They just added salt to the wound by going after the businesses. They want us distracted, looking away, and they want *you* afraid."

A shudder went through me. What had I said? I told no one because everyone I'd ever told had died? The doctor. The nurse.

"Don't be afraid, Ivy," Milo said. His dark eyes held a threat of violence, but it wasn't directed at me. "A few years ago, someone put me in that position. They set me up—threatened the guys—threatened to pursue worse with them, and I went to jail for three years to make sure that didn't happen. I made a mistake..."

The shock from Kellan translated with how his arms tightened.

"I let fear dictate my decision. It was on me to protect my brothers. Just like right now, you are trying to put it on yourself to protect us. The problem is... I didn't trust them to protect me."

Milo focused on Kellan.

"Don't make my mistake," Milo continued as he stared at me again.

"I don't know if I can tell you," I said slowly. It wasn't fear holding the information captive. Well, not entirely fear. I didn't want to hurt him... but all of this was going to hurt him.

It was going to hurt all of us.

"You don't have to tell me anything except, yes, you'll trust us to protect you too. Trust us enough to stay *here* with us. Trust the guys who are more than willing to cut off limbs to keep you safe. Trust me...Let me shield you and be the big brother I always wanted to be."

Closing my eyes, I leaned my head back against Kellan's shoulder. His strength was right there, steadier than it had any right to be, considering the hell he'd been through the last few hours.

My lover behind me, my brother in front of me, and the family I adored everywhere in the clubhouse. They were all hurting so severely. Grieving. Raging.

Wounded.

Swallowing the tears, I glanced upward at Kellan. He met my gaze steadily. I didn't have to do this now...

But I did.

Milo's world had been battered. He deserved to know why.

He needed to know.

"Do you want me to stay?" Kellan asked, his hand flattened over my abdomen and I wasn't sure which of us was keeping the other up. He would stay without question. He was giving me the choice, though.

Did I want him to have to listen to this again? No.

Did I need him? Always.

But it was Milo I focused on. "I have a story to tell you about my family...this isn't a good time to tell it. Only, there will never be a good time." The raw ache in my soul cracked through the barely formed scab and began to bleed. "The one thing I need you to know—that I want you desperately to understand—if this isn't my fault, then it isn't yours either."

*Please, believe me.*

The air went still before it ballooned with all the things we weren't saying. Flattening his battered hands onto the table, Milo locked his gaze on me.

"Who hurt you, Ivy?"

The unspoken, *please, trust me,* hung between us.

I forgot how to breathe. My heart fisted in my chest, the pound of it against my ribs a staccato bruise expanding to squeeze out all the air.

"My uncle..."

# CHAPTER 7

*EMERSYN*

*E*very other time I'd told this story—*my* story—I'd done it out of necessity. The first time had been a cry for help. The second... the second time, I needed medical assistance. The pain and humiliation of that treatment had left its mark on me.

Each person I told wanted to help me to survive, to get help, to admit that I needed someone to know the darkness I'd inhabited all my life. No one had been able to take on my uncle. Not the doctors or the nurses or even my mother. I never told her. The reality that Uncle Bradley would take her away had haunted me.

Absolute freedom didn't find me until Freddie did in Pinetree. Until we sat back-to-back, holding hands. He told me his story. I told him mine.

Pulling out that brick had only been the first step. I'd had to chip away at the others, one at a time. First with Rome, then Vaughn, Kellan, Mickey...and eventually Liam and Jasper. Each time I had clawed back another piece of myself.

As much as I *never* wanted Milo confronted by this part of my past, I couldn't stand the idea of another ambush coming for him. Uncle Bradley was going to hunt me.

Or maybe he already was.

If he knew about Milo, and how could he not, then he would use whatever tools at his disposal to harm him. If he had to learn about this ugly piece of my past, he needed to learn it from me.

Excavating this part of my soul should be easy. I'd already dug down through layers of emotional scar tissue to get to the heart of it. But from the moment I mentioned my uncle's name, I had all of Milo's attention.

Kellan had urged us to sit and took the chair beside mine. He held fast to one of my hands, giving me a lifeline to push through this.

"For as long as I can remember," I said, my gaze fixed on Milo's, "Uncle Bradley has been the dominating force in my life. I spent more time with him than with my own parents, or at least it felt that way. When I met Lainey at school, he had me moved from sharing a room to being by myself because the Benedicts weren't good enough, and a Sharpe should never have to share."

Disgust coursed through me at that memory. I'd begged him—*begged* to not lose Lainey as my roommate. But he didn't want me to spend so much time with others.

"I didn't see it when I was younger," I said. "The way he would isolate me. No friends were ever good enough. He didn't want me to associate with people outside of the family but offered me an array of physical activities to keep me busy, and since my parents traveled so much, I was often left with him for weeks at a time."

The tense line of his jaw reflected the stoniness in Milo's eyes as he studied me.

"I'm telling you this part because—because this is the life I'd always known. Even when I thought it was wrong or wanted it to stop, I didn't know how to make it stop. I didn't have anyone I could tell...and before you ask me, no, I never told Lainey before I came back from Pinetree. She knew something bad was happening, except I never told her since I didn't want my uncle to take her away too."

I managed all but the last few sentences without emotion clogging my throat.

"The first time he touched me..." I began. Even as the shaking was there, so was Kellan. His hand never left mine and his strength never wavered.

Milo's hands clenched into fists, and when I got to my tenth birthday, the chair hit the wall and shattered. He rubbed a hand over his face as he stalked away then back again.

"Your whole life?" Three words. "He fucking did that to you your whole life." The last part wasn't a question. Then his expression emptied. "Ivy, when you went back..."

"Yes."

Kellan gave a little jolt next to me. The tension lacing through him seemed to draw taut. His attention was on Milo.

"That's what your mother was talking about." Again, not a question. The rage shimmering in the air around him seemed to take on a life of its own. He gripped another chair, flexing his brutalized hands on the back of it.

"Yes," I said simply. "And I'm going to assume that her finding out is why he put her in that place."

Why he'd hurt her.

"He always warned me that it was so easy for something to happen and that I should be careful what I said to her... I didn't want her last memories to be something awful."

The chair cracked and shattered into pieces. Milo stared down at the parts of the chair he held and then dropped them. His chest heaved with rapid breaths as he battled to calm down.

"All those times I thought you were safe…"

"You didn't know," I said with a shudder, finally easing up on digging my nails into Kellan's hand. There were going to be half-moon indentions for days. "No one knew. I protected his ugly little secret because it was *my* ugly secret."

The press of Kellan's lips to the side of my head helped to steady me, but even when I glanced at him, there was no escaping the wild heat in his eyes or the very real rage lurking there.

"It wasn't your fault, Sparrow," Kellan said. "You did what you had to in order to survive." Then he focused on Milo. "It's not your fault either. We all thought she was safer, better off in that world… none of us had any idea."

All at once Milo fell back a couple of steps, and if he hadn't hit the wall, he might have collapsed to the ground. "When I said you needed to go back…"

He was so stricken, I had to stand. I had to go to him. It didn't matter if my legs were unsteady or if the tears were wet in my eyes again. I'd hollowed out that dark corner of my past so many times that it was raw, yet I hated telling him as much as I hated seeing the hurt in his eyes.

"You didn't know," I reminded him. He kept flexing his hands, the violence swirling around him. When I reached out, he crushed me to him and lifted me right off my feet.

"I'm sorry," he whispered, the words muffled. "I'm so fucking sorry, Ivy. That was not what I wanted for you…"

"I know," I said, trying to offer him soothing. "This is why I didn't want to tell you. Me having a good life was so important to you."

Dampness hit my neck as I returned his fierce embrace.

He was crying. The fact he was shedding tears sliced right through me and the hot sting of wetness in my eyes spilled over.

"Fuck, Ivy." Grief and anger drenched his tone. "*You* are what is important to me."

He dragged his head up, the red rimming his eyes a brutal testament to how much this hurt him.

"You," he repeated. "You were *always* the important one. I wanted you to have everything… shit that our parents fucked us out of because Mom couldn't get clean and Dad was a fucking dick."

"Milo…"

"No," he said softly. "No, don't say sorry or try to comfort me. I think I need this right now…I need to be pissed off."

"You're not alone," Kellan said, and my brother peered past me to his friend.

"You knew."

"She told me."

"Thank you for protecting her." The genuine gratitude amidst the tumultuous anger made me want to hug him more. Then he focused on me again. "Mayhem knows?"

"Now." And she never told him; she wouldn't have, because it was my secret.

He settled his hands on my biceps. His grip was firm but not painful. "Is she in any danger with this knowledge?"

I swallowed. "I don't—know. I sent her a text from the hospital. If my uncle was punishing us for taking Mom, I wanted to warn her. She said she was fine."

Milo's expression went distant.

"If you want to go to see her…"

"No," he said once, shaking his head. "We should tell Liam's friends, though." That sent a muscle ticking in his jaw.

"Ezra and Adam?" I tilted my head. The names evoked a far less relaxed response from him.

"Yes," he said through gritted teeth. "They want to protect her. They can make sure she stays safe."

Despite all of that, indecision played out across his expression.

"I'll call Ezra," I said, and he scowled down at me. "Hey, I like Ezra most of the time, and I like Adam. Except when Lainey needs me to not like them."

That chased away his scowl and the corners of his lips quirked up.

"You get a pass because you're my brother, so I won't choose between you."

"Noted." He sighed. "Fuck, c'mere." He dragged me into another hug, and I gripped him as tightly as he held onto me. "I'm sorry, Ivy. So fucking sorry."

"I'm okay," I promised him, and when he gave a little startled movement, I pulled back to hold his gaze. "I really am okay...I'm not there anymore. I'm here. Where I am safe and cared for. Didn't I say going out in that dress that no one would touch me and get away with it?"

It was probably the most flippant of responses, yet it made Milo chuckle. "You did." Exasperation seemed to creep through the cracks of his temper for a moment. "You really do belong here, Ivy. You will always belong here. You always have...I know what I said. But that Milo was a fucking idiot."

"Hey," I protested, punching his shoulder. "Don't talk about my brother that way."

His grin was so real, genuine humor and warmth bursting free. "Gonna kick my ass if I keep it up?"

"Yes, and I'll get Liam and the others to help me."

"Seven to one, Raptor," Kellan said dryly. "You're toast."

Laughter rumbled out of him. It was rough but real. He pressed his lips to my forehead, lingering there for the longest moment. I closed my eyes to drink in the contact and the nearness. I broke his heart. He was a survivor, however.

He was trying to comfort me even as I wanted to comfort him.

"Take Kellan up to bed," he said finally. "Both of you get some sleep. I'll keep an eye on things here and on your mother."

"Are you actually sending me to bed with one of the guys?" I put a hand over my heart. "Have we reached that part where we can talk about how good the s—"

He covered my mouth with his hand, chuckling and shaking his head. "Nope. Just go to bed, Ivy, and I'll pretend all you two do is sleep."

"Milo," I said when he would have backed away. "Promise me you won't leave if I go to sleep?"

His eyes narrowed.

"Give both of us your word," Kellan said, his tone firm. "She doesn't want you going after him without us, and neither do I."

"For now," Milo agreed. "I'm not going anywhere. Too many wounded, and I need to be here for Doc too."

My heart twisted at the mention of Mickey.

"And Liam," Kellan agreed. "This is going to get worse before it gets better."

That was the part I hated.

"They started this," Milo said with a nod. "We'll finish it."

Then he dropped his gaze to me. "Now, go get some sleep and sit on Kellan if you have to. I'm sure you can find a way to keep him in bed."

I snickered, and he groaned.

"Yeah, no, that's not working for me. I will pretend I have no idea...and you two get some rest."

"Milo," I said, and he glanced down at me, the sadness tangling with anger and frustration in his eyes. "I love you."

Three simple but truly profound words. They bubbled up

right through me because he needed to hear it, and I needed to say it.

"Love you too, sweet baby," he whispered, putting two fingers to his lips before pressing them to my cheek. Then, when I gave him a hug this time, he collapsed into me. "Love you more than I can say."

"You don't have to say." He honestly didn't. "I know I was stubborn at first…"

"At first…" Kellan laughed softly behind me as he echoed those words with a scoff. I just shot him a grin as Milo set me back on my feet.

"Fine, I'm stubborn. Love me, love my damage."

"Done," Kellan told me simply, then lifted his chin. Warmth stole through me. "C'mon, Sparrow, put me to bed so I can drag you into it with me. Milo gets it."

"I do," he promised, then gave me another kiss on the forehead. "And I'll be here when you two get up. If your mother wakes up, I'll come get you."

One more hug. I just wanted it as much as I wanted to give it to him. Then Kellan caught my hand in his, and we headed for the stairs. Milo didn't follow, but the sounds of him cleaning up the shattered chairs followed us.

"You did good, Sparrow," Kellan soothed as we got to the top of the stairs.

"I hated telling him."

"I know, but you controlled it. You told him what he needed to know and you were there for him. We'll keep being there for both of you."

"We'll be there for all of us." Because we weren't the only ones hurting. We stopped to check on Mom and Freddie. Freddie was out on the sofa, and I covered him with a blanket and then kissed his forehead. Mom was still sound asleep.

In the suite, Rome and Vaughn were still asleep on the

sofa, though Vaughn snored a little louder than usual. Liam had folded around a pillow in Rome's room, sleeping on his side with a tense expression. Mickey looked similar as he slept in my bed, and finally Jasper.

I was worried about all of them. But Kellan tugged me into his room. We helped each other strip, and I frowned at the burn on his shoulder and the bruises. He scowled at the fingermarks on my ass and the cut across my hip.

By the time I crawled into bed and curled up into his arms, everything keeping me upright seemed to collapse. "I love you too," I whispered to Kel.

"I know, Sparrow," he murmured. "I'm damn grateful for it. Now sleep."

He didn't have to tell me again.

# CHAPTER 8

*EMERSYN*

*a* hand smoothed over my hip as another cupped my breast, and lips pressed against my throat. Warmth blanketed my back. The stroke of a tongue over my pulse point as fingers dipped between my thighs roused me from sleep in a pleasurable haze. The slow, soft grind of a very erect dick against my ass had my eyes fluttering open.

The scrape of teeth along my pulse beckoned me, but then fingers twisted a nipple and a shudder rocked me. I clamped my thighs on the hand cupping my cunt, then he thrust two fingers into me, and I turned my head. Rome gazed down at me as he swirled his fingers over my clit, then plunged them into me again.

His lower lip glistened, and I reached back an arm to curl around him. Then his mouth fused to mine as he increased the pressure against my clit. The heel of his palm ground against me as he added a third finger to thrust. The action mimicked the push of his cock yet lacked its full weight.

Another shudder went through me, knocking loose a moan. The tease of Rome's tongue against mine left me hungry for more. The position gave me no control though. Rome held it all. He stroked his cock along the seam of my ass as he fucked me with his fingers. The twist and pull against my nipples only increased the sensual torture, making me arch more.

When he pulled his touch from me, I damn near whimpered, but then Rome lifted his hand to my lips. With fingers slick with my own juices, he pressed them against my lips and I began to suck against them. His eyes dilated, and I was violently aware of him mimicking the stroke motion of his fingers with his cock.

Suddenly, I didn't want his fingers anymore. He twisted one nipple until the sting of pain rippled out and heat bounced from my breasts to my cunt and back again. Pulling off his fingers, I twisted and he fell back against the covers. A distant part of my mind registered Kellan.

I stole a look at him. His eyes were open and laser-focused on me. Like Rome, Kellan was also hard as a stone. The sheets didn't hide the thick tent forming over his erection. Dicks did that. I teased a hand down Rome's chest as I slid down him, and then I was nose to dick with his cock.

Rome's soft sigh was the heady response I hadn't even been aware of wanting. I traced my tongue along the underside of his cock. Hot, soft velvet skin, inked with my image... it was intoxicating. Even more, was the way he curled a lock of my hair over his finger, but he didn't press on my head.

Wrapping my hand around his base, I teased my tongue up and down until I could wrap my lips around the tip of his cock. The groan vibrating from his chest only encouraged me to take him deeper. While I didn't have to keep a hand on his hip to stop him from thrusting, another hand touched the back of my head.

"Swallow all of him, Sparrow," Kellan ordered in a rough voice. My cunt clenched at the command. "All the way."

I relaxed my mouth as Kellan pushed my head down and swallowed as Rome's cock pushed into my throat. His groan echoed my own.

"That's a good girl," Kellan praised. "Like how he feels in there? He likes it. Can you feel how hard he is?"

I could and sighed before raising my head, only to swallow him back down. The strokes were slow, and deep. When a new hand stroked over my ass, I tried not to startle, but the shock of hands touching me that couldn't be Kellan or Rome took me off guard.

"Just me, Dove." Vaughn. The hoarse whisper was a far cry from the soothing croon of his voice that enticed me so much from the beginning. He teased the pierced tip of his dick along my wet folds. "Fuck, you feel good, Dove."

I pushed back at his tease even as I followed Kellan's instruction to bob up and down along Rome's length. All I could smell and taste was them. The feel of them around me, the salty, bitter drop of pre-cum that I sucked down like a treat.

"Fuck her, Vaughn. Can't you see how much she wants us..." There was something in the way Kellan said that a moment before he twisted a nipple right to that point of pain. It pulled the tension even more taut within me, and then Vaughn pushed into me, a single relentless thrust that stretched me out over his cock as he braced my hips with his hands.

I wanted to cry, it felt so good, all the while being so much. Kellan released the nipple and the tingles spread out as blood rushed back into the tip.

"That's our girl," Kellan murmured before he scraped his teeth over that too-sensitive nipple, and I bucked. Only I wasn't going anywhere. Rome's hand steadied my head as he stroked his fingers through my hair. When I lifted my teary eyes to meet his gaze, he gave his hips the barest arch.

A question.

Oh, yes.

Please.

I relaxed my mouth again. Did I want him to fuck my mouth? Oh—I barely managed to keep it together when Vaughn began to move. The slap of skin on skin, the heavy weight of his cock filling me up, and the wild way his piercing teased into me was one thing.

Then Rome thrusted, the push of him sliding into my throat so intoxicating. I was drunk on the taste of him, and I wanted more. Warmth dribbled over my ass and then fingers were spearing into me. Kellan's lips formed around my nipple. I was just in a sea of sensations.

There was no way to fall into a rhythm because they shifted speed and depth every time I began to float away. Then there were four fingers in my ass. The burn and stretch matched the heat from the sharp sting of Kellan's teeth that raked over my nipple.

The shaking began somewhere in my core, and I couldn't focus on what I was doing. I held onto Rome, digging my fingers into his thigh as he thrust into my mouth, the dribble of pre-cum hitting my tongue steadily as Vaughn fucked my soul back into my body with wild, deep thrusts.

Kellan slid his hand between my legs, testing the edge of how much pressure I could take as he worked a finger in against Vaughn's dick, and the intensity triggered an orgasm.

Rome's dick choked off my scream as I came. Vaughn swore, slamming home deep as hot jets of cum warmed me on the inside, and Rome pressed my face down until the tight, springy hair around his base tickled my nostrils. I swallowed as he came. I was still shaking as we collapsed together.

Drool slid from the corner of my mouth as Rome slipped free and I whined as Vaughn pulled out, but there was already a fat head of a dick pressing at my ass as more warmth dribbled there.

A hand wrapped around my hair and Kellan tilted my head back. Tears soaked my face, and he studied me, his gaze intense. "You good, Sparrow?"

"Yes," the word came out on a trembling tone.

"You want more?" The spongy head of his dick pressed right up against the rim of my anus, the stretch already encouraging me to push back.

"Yes," I whispered. The little quivers and explosions were still detonating. I wanted more. Needed more. Even then, I wasn't ready for how he slid into my ass. I was looser than I realized and the pump of his hips pistoned his dick into me.

A low sound escaped my throat that turned into a sob of pleasure. Kellan tightened his fingers in my hair, keeping my head angled back. Rome leaned in and teased a kiss to my lips, then Vaughn eased his head to my chest and began to nuzzle around one of my nipples.

"She likes this," Rome said, more to Kellan than me, although his gaze dipped back to my eyes. "Kel likes your ass."

I laughed as Kellan gave a firm thrust, tugging my hair at the same time. My scalp lit up as the heat plunged into my ass. Vaughn and Rome took turns kissing me as Kellan rocked into me. It was a slower build this time, the pleasure elongating, stretching me thin between them.

And fuck me, I wanted more. When Vaughn wrapped my hand around Rome's steadily stiffening dick, I began to stroke him then turned as Kellan urged my head toward Vaughn as he teased his cock against my lips.

"Can you handle all three of us, Sparrow?" Kellan asked.

All three...oh...a shudder raced through me and I tightened my fingers around Rome. Could I handle them? Yes... Oh, yes, I could. But I couldn't answer because Vaughn took over, thrusting against my mouth and teasing my throat as he stiffened under my tongue.

"Shift," Kellan ordered. I didn't know what he meant until the guys all moved. I was on my back in seconds, on top of Kel, and Rome moved his cock to my pussy. I was a slick mess from Vaughn already, but he just pushed his way into me and then stretched me out between them. I writhed before they turned my head and I greeted Vaughn's cock with a kiss.

Thank fuck they took care of the movement because I was so full, and I couldn't do more than roll my hips. I had one leg up over Rome's shoulder while Vaughn held my other thigh open.

The friction of their legs moving against mine, the weight of Rome pushing me into Kellan, and Kellan's hands bracing my hips to help control our rhythm threatened to split me open.

"Fuck, I love your mouth, Dove," Vaughn whispered in his harsh croon. "I love everything about you..."

"You're taking us so good, Sparrow. I can feel you clenching down on my dick like you never want it to leave. This ass—it's perfect. Just like the rest of you."

Rome angled his strokes, stretching me further as he stiffened to a full erection. His strikes pulled grunts from me and from Kellan.

"So hot," Vaughn muttered. "I'm enjoying their dicks disappearing into you as much as I am feeling you swallow mine."

"Such a good girl," Kellan continued as he slid his hand up to where Rome fucked into me. It was like he wrapped his hand over his cock and around my cunt. The pressure intensified as Rome let out a low sound, and then there were no words. Just our bodies moving as Kellan began to torture my clit.

My movements grew far less graceful as I writhed between them. Sensual overload seemed to short-circuit my thoughts. It was all about the contact, the friction. The way their fingers tugged and pulled. How their dicks filled me up, and the sudden surge as Vaughn came in my throat.

Still choking on his release, Kellan shoved me right off the edge, torturing my clit, as Rome struck sparks inside me. The wild heat of Kellan's cum filled my ass.

I clung to someone's hand as Rome came, and we all shuddered together. Vaughn dropped onto the bed next to us as Rome draped over me. We had to be crushing Kellan, but he just kept rubbing his hands up and down my side.

Sore and trembling, I couldn't gather my thoughts. When Kellan turned my head, I kissed him, slow and steady. Rome nuzzled kisses down my throat to my breasts then up again. Kellan released my lips only for Rome to claim them, and then they were easing out of me.

A whimper escaped, but Vaughn was there, his kiss capturing the sound as he began to rub my sides. The bed shifted, and then Kellan was back with a hot washcloth. He ran it between my legs and then along my ass.

Sticky with sweat and cum, I shivered from all the contact. The shower turned on, even though I was content to float here, curled between Rome and Vaughn. When Kellan came back again, Vaughn slipped away. Then it was time for him and Rome to swap out.

"Oh, you're showering," I whispered as I drifted along, and Kellan laughed softly.

"Yes, we are." Then he pressed a sweet kiss to my lips. They'd also taken turns cleaning me up. I was sore in all the right ways. "Thank you, Sparrow."

"Yes," Vaughn agreed, stealing a kiss when Kellan was

done. When I opened my eyes, Rome gazed at me with such utter softness it threatened to undo me.

"I think I should be thanking all of you." My muscles were so warm and loose, I wasn't sure I could move.

"No thanks ever required." Kellan dipped his head to suck a bite against my breast. The sting just edged the pleasure still flowing in my veins. When he ran his hand over my abdomen and down to my cunt, I was aware of his fingers pressing cum back into me. "We made you a mess, Sparrow."

"Best. Mess. Ever." A yawn stole through me as he cupped his hand over my pussy like he was keeping Vaughn and Rome inside of me. The delicious thought sent another shiver through me.

"Sleep, sweet Dove," Vaughn urged, nuzzling light kisses against my throat. They were all touching me, the contact light but firm. As much as I wanted to linger right here with them, I was tumbling into the safe space they made for me.

The safe space they created just by being here. The soft rumble of their voices soothed even the grief right now, letting me drift. I needed to take care of them, but their hands kept brushing away the tension and I couldn't fight the battle anymore, tumbling headlong into darkness and dreams of flying, where it didn't matter if I fell.

Because they had me.

# CHAPTER 9

*JASPER*

id-afternoon had become night at some point. The phone said it was after five when I rolled out of bed and staggered into the shower. Hot water beating down on my head helped to clear the cobwebs. My eyes were sore. My chest hurt—the bruise from the seat belt had definitely left a mark—and then there was an ache in my soul.

Grief was an all too familiar companion. The day my mother died, my father told me to stop fucking crying and grow up. Crying had never been my strong suit. Even when the tears burned, they refused to fall.

Finding a bloodied, wounded Freddie after he'd been assaulted in that container had ripped something open inside of me. It was fury, not tears, that spilled out. And that rage translated into killing the son of a bitch who hurt him.

I'd always been a fighter, but rage was so much easier than tears. Protecting my brothers, our family, became the driving force within me. It fueled my drive whenever Freddie dipped into troubled waters with his addictions. Helped beat back those who would take what was ours.

Then Milo went to prison. Liam left. Freddie kept slipping. Honestly, looking back, those were not our best years. At the same time, everything had been a fight. Probably why I survived.

Then Swan came to town.

She came to town, and she was hurting. I couldn't walk away from that any more than we could have let that guy go when we found Freddie. She needed out and, fuck it all, I'd *needed* to save her.

I hadn't realized just how much I needed it, needed her, until she was here. She was an indelible mark on all of us long before we added ivy to the tattoos we all sported. Ivy to signify our promise to Milo to protect her.

Now, a promise to her.

Emersyn telling me what her uncle had done, gutted me. Even then, the tears for her hadn't fallen. Not until I got her the pound of flesh she so richly deserved.

Ms. Stephanie's loss echoed deep inside me. It didn't seem real. How could she be gone? If I picked up the phone...

Only she wouldn't answer it again.

If I went to her house to check on the landscaping... she wouldn't be there to laugh, smile, and wave me inside.

When I needed her...

While she had never become my mother, Ms. Stephanie had been the one true constant in my life outside of the guys. One of the very few adults I had ever trusted or wanted to please.

As an adult myself, her respect had been everything.

And she was gone.

Taking the time to trim my beard, I met my dry-eyed gaze in the mirror. I wanted to cry for her. I owed her so fucking much. What were a few goddamn tears? Yet, they wouldn't come. Not even now.

Finished, I braced my hands on the edge of the sink. I needed to get my shit together. The last couple of hellish days had bled one into the other. They had come for us.

Swan's so-called fucking family had come for us. The message Liam got, was the epic reach of the destruction they'd visited. It wasn't the places they hit—fuck, it wasn't even my car. That was all collateral damage.

We could rebuild places and things.

We couldn't replace people. We couldn't bring back the dead.

Leaving the bathroom, I finished getting dressed and headed out. The sitting room was empty and quiet. I glanced at Swan's room but left her for now. She might be with Doc. Or with Liam.

Hell, she could be with her mother. I'd find her when she emerged. As long as she was in the clubhouse and safe where we could protect her, I would be patient.

I paused to check in her mother's room. The woman in question was asleep. She still looked like hell; sooner or later, we needed her up and functioning to answer questions. Swan would need her for more.

Freddie glanced up from where he was flipping cards on the table. Though deep shadows were under his eyes, he didn't look too bad.

"Going down for coffee," I told him. "And food. I'll bring you up some."

"Not even asking me if I'm hungry?" A sliver of teasing entered his voice. It was so faint to be barely there, but he still offered it up.

"No," I said. "Cause I'm not hungry, either. We need to eat. If you want something specific, tell me."

He shook his head before he raked a hand through his

hair. It looked a little on the greasy side, like he'd done nothing except run his hands through it repeatedly. "I could use a shower."

"I'll be back to take over for you or send someone else up. You hanging in there?"

"Yeah," he said, his slight smile calling to the echo of pain inside me. "I'll live. Boo-Boo is safe. You guys all made it back."

We weren't going to talk about the ones who didn't.

"If that changes, tell me." It wasn't a request.

He saluted, the gesture a little mocking, but I got it. Leaving him, I headed downstairs. The wall across from the room had been half-leveled between the living room and kitchen. What had been separate areas now looked like someone had punched in a bar window.

On the far side of the destruction, Milo stood in the kitchen with bloodied and bruised knuckles and what looked like a sponge. Most of the debris on this side had been swept from the looks of it, but there was still drywall dust on everything.

"I'm not gonna comment on the fact we just renovated this place."

Milo snorted but didn't respond. The interior of the kitchen was a bit worse, what with blood spatter decorating the drywall dust. Worry spiked through me. The coffeemaker had been moved, though it was intact. The table was missing four chairs, now there were only two.

"Need a hand?" I asked before going to the pot and just starting a regular pot of coffee. I liked the fancy stuff too, but I'd been weaned to straight black coffee. I needed it today. The stronger, the better.

Then I needed to get food sorted for Freddie and me. Maybe for Milo, too.

"I got it," he said in a harsh voice that had me pivoting to find him staring at the damage and not moving. "She told me."

"She told you." Repeating the words made me sound like a dumbass. However, the neurons firing to make the connections weren't lubricated by coffee yet. "Shit." Reality settled into my bones. "She told you."

It was a fucking miracle there were still walls standing. More surprised he was still here. While I was glad he'd heard it from her, I hated that he knew.

I hated that I knew, even though I wouldn't change it for a heartbeat. Because she'd had to fucking live through it. My ass could handle the discomfort the knowledge brought me.

"Jas," he said slowly after wiping more debris off the counter and onto the dustpan. He pulled out a trash can and dumped it all in there.

While he hadn't turned to face me, I straightened and settled my stance. If he needed a fight to work off the aggression, we would take this shit outside. Swan didn't need it, but I wasn't remotely opposed.

Just needed to feed Freddie first.

"I'm—sorry." The two words jangled a discordant note in the current situation. Not only were they not the words I expected to hear at all—

"Fuck the wall. We can tear the whole thing down and rebuild it again if necessary."

Twisting to face me slowly, he wore the barest hint of a smile. "For going after you so hard because you took Ivy—for blaming you that Ivy was here…for not fucking trusting you with what was going on with me."

"Oh." That.

Milo dipped his chin and let out a gruff half-laugh. "Oh—I stormed back into everyone's lives and took out my rage on you. Blaming you for taking my sister, for seducing her, for putting her in danger, and…"

He stared at his hands.

"You didn't know," I said slowly. "None of us did."

"You knew." It wasn't an accusation.

Blowing out a breath, I went for the big mugs and filled them with coffee. I needed whiskey for this conversation, but that wasn't happening right now. "I didn't know about that."

Maybe if I'd paid closer attention...

"I knew she was afraid of her partner." Brass tacks. "That he'd been abusing her." The image of her as she slipped out of the venue and hid behind the door when Arlington crashed out after her. The guy had initialed his own death warrant right then and there. "I knew she was hurt."

Glancing down at my coffee, I studied the distortion of my reflection in the dark liquid.

"I wish like hell I'd known about the uncle. He'd already be shark chum and dumped somewhere by now." After a long and painful dismemberment. I'd have to cauterize each and every limb as they came off.

No sense in letting him bleed to death too early or to pass out from the pain. We could be patient, wake him up, and go again.

"I still—"

"Milo, did I like you beating my face in for a few weeks there?" I shook my head. "Did I understand it? Yes. Did I give you back what you served me? Also, yes. We didn't know. I hate that we didn't. Nonetheless, we know *now*."

"It's never happening to her again." That wasn't a question, but I understood why Milo needed to say it. Why he needed to lay it out there. "All I ever wanted for her...and she ended up in Hell. Then she gets here, and all I tried to do was make her leave..."

"I can tell you we didn't know a few hundred times, but even not knowing, you were still a dick about the last."

He snorted, then scrubbed his damaged hand over his face. "It's all so fucked up, Jas. Everything."

"Yeah," I said, exhaling a long breath. "Except as bad as it is—it's also better."

His sudden frown almost made me laugh, because right now? Yeah...

"Look, I know it sounds crazy, and maybe it is. A lot of bad shit has gone down—so much." Too much. "But one, she's here with us. Two, she trusted us by telling us what had happened. She's trusting us to hear her, to protect her. The fact she trusts us at all is a fucking gift. Three? We're together. Not only is she here. *You* are here. Doc is back. Even fucking Liam...maybe especially fucking Liam."

And Freddie was clean and sober, fighting to stay that way. Like Emersyn, he wasn't in this fight alone, and we'd back his every single step.

"The last forty-eight hours have been hell."

Milo and I locked eyes. I meant it. It had been hell, but it was better because we were together.

"No one's alone," Milo said finally, leaning back against the counter like he needed the help to remain upright.

"Exactly," I said. "And I know I'm the fucking hardhead in this group even if you've been really challenging for the title, but we're together. That matters. We'll handle this—together. For her. For you. For Liam. For Doc. For all of us."

"I keep thinking we're missing something," Milo said. "Why would her family commit her mother, commit her... why would they do these things?"

"Because Swan isn't their family." She'd never been their family. "She's a possession. One they want back—or I should say *he* wants back."

"What about the father?" Well, that was the ten-thousand-dollar question.

"Hopefully, her mother can give us an answer. If she can't—"

"I'll rip it out of his lungs myself if I have to," Milo said.

"I thought we'd start at the feet and work our way up. Go old-school. He doesn't need his limbs to live."

A cold smile creased Milo's face as he straightened. "You know, I always did like to watch you work."

"I'm more about participation," Liam said from the doorway. His expression was absolute granite. "I don't care who gets the last blow, but I want blood and answers. If it takes a lot of pain to get to the answers, I'm really fucking okay with that."

"We're going to need a plan…and I need to get Freddie some food."

"I have a plan," Mickey said, his voice rough as hell like rocks tumbled with every word. "We'll start after I look at your hands." He nodded to Milo, then focused on me. "Where is Little Bit?"

# CHAPTER 10

*DOC*

$\mathcal{T}$he world had indelibly shifted. Waking in Little Bit's bed without her the day after Stephanie died, I could genuinely say I wasn't sure which way was up. The landscape had shifted—the field of battle, a morass of foggy swamp.

Danger, and our choices, had come for us.

They'd taken victims along the way. Cataloging every bit of damage Steph endured would haunt me until the day I died. Although I would make sure those who did it felt every single sting, every lash, every broken bone.

Taking my phone off the charger, I dialed the number for their anonymous voicemail from memory. When they were busy, it could be a few days. Still, they could access it from anywhere in the world. As soon as the option for a message came up, I selected it.

"I need help," I said, not bothering with codes. "Call me when you get this." Then I rattled off my number.

Pushing off the bed, I headed into the bathroom with the phone in hand. I hadn't spent that much time in Little Bit's space, yet there were touches of her everywhere. Her old room had been generic, save for the painting Rome made for her and the bear—I glanced back into the bedroom.

The bear was sitting on the nightstand right next to the bed, lovingly placed. The ratty old thing was probably one of Rome's most prized possessions. The fact he'd given it to her the day she arrived said a lot about his feelings even then.

The organic splashes of color against the softer shades made the room feel more like an artist's palette. There were touches for her dancing, for films, and touches like the bear. The photos on the dresser were another personal touch. While the shower heated up, I walked over to study them.

The one from Steph's birthday raked right through my soul—everyone was in it except Little Bit. She'd taken the photo. It was Steph in the middle, surrounded by all of us making various faces. My gaze fixed on the happiness shining in Steph's eyes though. It practically beamed out of her.

Surrounded by her success stories, the kids had always meant so much to her. She lived, and—I closed my eyes, sucking in a deeper breath. She lived, and she died for them.

For me.

With care, I put the photo back into place. There was one there of Milo and Little Bit when they were children. That had to have come from Milo. That baby...fuck, I'd carried her out of that place and taken her and Milo to Steph.

She'd been such a gregarious baby, sunshine to Milo's more somber temperament. The sunshine was still there, hidden under layers of muck the world had flung upon her. That her uncle had tried to suffocate her under.

Eyes aching, I straightened it and then frowned at the one tucked into the back. It was of me. I had no idea when she snapped it, but my arms were crossed and I appeared less than impressed.

If I had to guess, this would have to be me listening to Jasper threaten me or rail on about something. I couldn't even tell where we were in the photo, but I could imagine the exasperation and me shaking my head.

"I see you, Little Bit," I murmured as I set the photo down. I saw her in all the images. Including the one of her and Freddie with their cheeks pressed together as they crossed their eyes and stuck out their tongues.

Absolutely ridiculous. But perfect for them both.

Despite the urge to look further, I forced myself into the shower. I needed to wash off the last couple of days. I needed to clear my head. I needed the plan forming in my head to coalesce.

Stripping down, I rubbed the left side of my chest. The rough layer of scarring under the tattoo hid the ache as I stretched the muscles. The nerve damage left some areas sensitive, while others were deadened to stimulation.

The shower didn't take long. The shampoo and soap smelled like Little Bit. It soothed some of the jagged ends that couldn't quite close over the gaping wound in my heart.

A part of me couldn't believe I hadn't bled to death from it yet. Trauma response. It didn't matter how familiar I was with it. The trauma response kept me moving. Fight or flight.

Fuck, I wanted the fight.

There was only one toothbrush, so I used my finger to do a sketchy scrub with the toothpaste before rinsing out my mouth. Towel around my hips, I slid back into her room and glanced around.

Clothes sat on the dresser. A note sat on top of them. "Jasper had some stuff that should fit. We can go get your things later when you're up for it. E."

I dragged on the jeans, followed by the shirt. My leg

protested. The muscles ached and so did my knee. The lack of regular exercise the last few days was throwing me off.

I needed to get to some liniment and stretch before I was too stiff to be useful to fucking anyone. The phone rang in the bathroom and I picked it up on the second ring.

"Hey, Doc," Alphabet's familiar voice was a welcome sound. "When and where?"

Bracing my knuckles against the counter, I bowed my head. "You guys have the time?" They had their own jobs, their own work.

"We're making the time," Bones said. It had been a while since we talked. Didn't change the notes of the challenge as he spoke. Whether they had a job or not was irrelevant. They made their own schedule. Bones had always disliked authority. Not a great quality in the Army—or so they said.

"You said you needed help." This was Lunchbox, his Irish accent more pronounced. Growing up a military brat, he'd lived all over the world but spent seven years with his grandmother in Ireland. The Irish stuck. "Tell us where, and we're on the way."

"Already would be there," Voodoo threw in on the edge of a yawn, "but someone just said call and didn't give us coordinates."

Dropping my chin, I leaned back against the wall. I'd known they'd come. Known they'd back me. That was what we did.

"Braxton Harbor. Come to the clinic. Call me when you're ten minutes out and I'll meet you."

"Calling ahead, Doc," Alphabet said. "It's like you want us to be civilized or something."

"Or something... Depending on when you get here, if I don't answer, I'll leave the details on the line."

"We'll be there in twenty-four hours," Bones said. "We just need to make some arrangements."

"She won't like it," Voodoo commented, but Lunchbox chuckled.

"You not liking it isn't the same thing, man." Lunchbox had moved, and he sounded closer to the phone. "Doc?"

"I'm here."

"How bad is it?"

"They killed my sister."

Absolute silence greeted my statement. It stretched out for a full minute.

"We'll be there in twelve hours," Bones said. "Don't move without us."

Then the call ended, and I lowered the phone. My guys were coming. The kids needed to know.

Leaving the quiet suite, I headed downstairs. I'd hoped to find Little Bit with the guys, except it was just Milo, Jasper, and Liam. Anger buzzed in the atmosphere like a live wire had been cut.

I felt for the kids, I did. Liam had just lost his father and his mother was a wreck. He should be with her, yet I understood why he wasn't. I understood why he had to be here too.

Jasper ran food up to Freddie. Little Bit was still sleeping, or so they thought. Milo said she'd gone up with Kellan. So she'd made sure we were all resting before she went to rest.

I could appreciate it, even if I itched to lay eyes on her right now. I could be patient. Milo didn't bitch while I cleaned out the disaster he'd made of his hands. They were covered with bruises and cuts.

"So, what's the plan?" Liam asked, making up a massive batch of scrambled eggs while bacon cooked in the oven. When you fed a huge group, it was the fastest way to go. I cleaned up from dressing Milo's wounds, then went to brew another pot of coffee.

"My team is coming," I said, keeping it brief.

"Your team?" Milo said, straightening.

"Four guys who were part of my squad." The only others to survive that last engagement. "They were the guys who got me out after the firefight." I didn't talk much about that battle and had zero intentions of doing it now.

The weight of Jasper's stare had me glancing over my shoulder. "I'm assuming you wouldn't call these guys in if you couldn't trust them."

He still wanted validation. Some other time the caution might have amused me. Jasper lost trust in me a long time ago, that he'd begun to regain any at all? Yeah, I got the need to trust but verify.

"No, I wouldn't. They can help. They also have access to heavier munitions, intelligence, and the benefits of not being one of *us*."

"Anyone who did deep background on you would get them," Liam pointed out. Milo said nothing, his jaw tense, and his lips flattened as if he was still stewing over all this. I left him be—for now.

"Possibly, but we don't have a lot of public contacts and haven't in the last four-plus years. They've been to Braxton Harbor all of twice, and once was to pick up the cargo you guys needed relocated."

Calling people cargo would never sit well with any of us, but the important part was they'd taken possession and gotten them out. Then helped relocate them somewhere safer.

"That said," I continued, pouring coffee into a mug for myself before moving to let Jasper get his own. "They know how to not be noticed until they want to be. They also won't hesitate to act should we need it, and if we needed to stash Little Bit or someone to get her out of here—they'll bleed anyone who comes after her."

Milo jerked his head up, and Liam turned off the heat on the stove as he faced me. I tracked each of their stares.

"*You* want to send her away?" Jasper tested the words like he couldn't believe them.

"No. I want her safe. This is open war. She doesn't need to be in the trenches."

"She won't go," Liam said, his tone flat before he served eggs onto each plate. "I won't force her." He paused to look at Milo. "No one will force her."

"No," Milo said slowly. "We won't."

That shocked the shit out of me. "This is going to get worse before it gets better."

"It's already worse," Jasper said, then he clasped a hand to my shoulder before passing me a plate. "Sending her away... I like the idea of her being safe. I don't like the idea of her not being with us."

"Agreed," Liam and Milo said in the same breath. Any other time I might have laughed at the looks they shot each other, like they were surprised they agreed. This wasn't funny, in any case.

"Look," Liam continued as he settled against the counter to eat. The lack of chairs around the table didn't invite anyone to sit. "We lay it out, we work out a plan, we take this whole thing on, and we do it with her. She *is* one of us. If she goes for it, we also make evacuating her an option."

"We could send Freddie with her," I said. "That gets him out of this too."

"No," Jasper said, before Liam could say anything, earning him narrow-eyed looks from the others. "I get it," he said, sweeping us with a stare. "I get wanting them safe, but here's the thing—*she* is the target. We take her out of play, and there is every chance we will have to keep her out. 'Cause all they have to do is go quiet, go deep, and we know that mother-fucker has the money to do it."

"Then there's her mother," Milo said as he straightened. "We still don't have a firm grip on her mental status. And I don't want Ivy out of reach. Here—here, we can look after her. We can protect her back. We know who we trust, and no offense to your friends—they aren't us."

"Agreed," Liam said. "I was just going to go with, no, she isn't going. Although I like their reasoning, too."

"So do I," Little Bit said, and it twisted all of us around. She stood in the doorway with Kellan, Rome, and Vaughn lined behind her. They were all freshly showered, her lips were puffy, and there were definite hickeys on her neck. But it was the dark sobriety in her eyes that arrested me. "If it protects all of you for me to go—if it is the only option—we can discuss it. However, I don't want to leave. I want to be here...this fight is coming for you because...because my uncle is coming for me."

The steadiness in those words had me flick a look at Milo. His lips compressed, though his expression held. She'd told him.

Setting the plate aside, I held out a hand to her. To my absolute gratification, she came straight to me and I pulled her close, hugging her. "I don't want to ask you to leave," I told her. "I never want that, but I do want you safe."

"Then let me help," she said against my shirt, and I sighed as I tucked my face against her hair. "Let me do what I can. I've gotten pretty good at following the rules."

"And she's a damn good shot," Kellan added. "We will take it under advisement, Doc. We get it. We really do."

I just lost Steph. I could not lose Little Bit. None of us could. Squeezing her, I sighed. "We'll keep it as a fallback plan."

When she leaned back to look at me, I cupped her cheek. She leaned into my palm and it settled some of my restlessness. "Fallback plan."

Her eyes brightened a fraction.

"Someone want to tell me where the fuck all the chairs went?" Kellan asked. "And why are we remodeling that wall?"

"Percussion therapy," Milo deadpanned his answer without missing a beat. "I'm working on my feelings. It's taking some practice."

The corners of Little Bit's lips twitched, and she wasn't alone. Laughter, a little wild and a little disbelieving, surged around the group, even as she wrapped her arms around me again and I cradled her to me.

No. I refused to lose her. We couldn't send her away. We just needed a more efficient and brutal plan.

# CHAPTER 11

*EMERSYN*

*I*t was raining the day of the funeral, like we were in one of the movies we'd watched. The debate over the service had been tense, from the location to the burial. They discussed everything from the investigation from the cops, the security, and whether we risked anything by being out there.

Ultimately, everyone had focused on what Mickey needed. Milo was hurting. They were all hurting. The day before the funeral, I'd gone with Rome and Liam to check on Liam's mother, but he hadn't wanted to linger. She was not ready for a funeral for his father. Despite the fact she was heartbroken hadn't been lost on me.

Rome settled into the chair next to Mary O'Connell's, and he'd pulled out his sketchbook while she spoke to Liam. I'd sat with Liam, with his hand clasped firmly in mine. Halfway through, Mary broke off her reminiscing to stare at the sketchbook.

"Is that…"

He held it up so she could see the sketch of Jonathon standing behind her where she sat. It was haunting and elegant. "I can stop," Rome offered.

"Sweet boy, no, that's—that's so beautiful."

The soft smile he gave her had Liam gripping my fingers so hard it hurt for a moment. His brother was comforting his mother, and in his very particular way, Rome was offering comfort to Liam.

"Thank you…"

Rome nodded, then went back to his work. Before we left, the sketch had been framed and sat next to her bed. Security around Mary O'Connell was impressive. They were taking Jonathon back to Florida.

The funeral would take place there in a few weeks. He'd always wanted to be cremated she said. They would do whatever she needed, Liam promised. The service could wait for her to be ready.

"Thank you," she murmured to me as we prepared to leave.

I hated myself in that moment. I was part of the reason her husband was dead.

"Thank you for loving my boys," she said, then gave me a hug that should have been awkward. Except it wasn't. I wrapped her up tight, returning the ferociousness of her embrace.

"I know they aren't telling me everything," she whispered in a hushed voice. When I pulled back, she gave me a gentle smile. Her eyes were still so sad a hint of light gleamed within them. "He always kept his secrets, and Jonathon said we had to let him, but this is dangerous. I need them both to be okay. Take care of them for me?"

His mother knew far more than I thought. Even Liam would be happy realizing she knew. "With every breath left in my body," I promised her. She sniffled once, then gave me another tight hug.

"Take care of yourself too."

That whole interaction stuck with me as we left. The weirdest part wasn't going to see his mother in the secure facility, but more the security escorting us.

Mickey's friends had arrived the previous day, and following a brief introduction, he'd left with two of them. The other two had stayed at the clubhouse with a girl who looked strangely familiar. She didn't say much, though I caught her watching me the same way I watched her.

When we left this morning, two of them had escorted us. Neither said much. The fact that the tension ratcheted when they said they were escorting us had both Liam and Rome eyeing them.

But when their gazes tracked to me, the twins had relaxed. They were coming with us because of me. As it was, Mickey had asked me to check in with them or him if I planned on leaving—even if I was going with the guys.

Between his comments about sending me away, and the wild tension padding every single movement or syllable from him, I didn't want to argue. "For now," I promised him. "While all of this is going on…we'll work it out. Nevertheless, the guys have to have some say too."

Kellan hadn't disapproved of the idea, but he'd wanted to meet these guys first. Something we'd all agreed with, then we met them, and I couldn't tell you what I thought of them.

For the funeral, the guys were all in suits. Not everyone wore jackets, but they were all in ties. It was probably tacky to admire how handsome they looked. Three of Mickey's friends were going with us. One—Alphabet, remained at the Clubhouse with Grace.

Mom had woken earlier that morning. While she'd been a little groggy, she seemed clearer than she'd been since they brought her back. Had it been almost a week already? It was beyond surreal.

A week.

So much had happened in that week.

The service took place in a church located not far from the group home Rome said they'd spent so much time in. Like so many other parts of the neighborhood, it had cracked sidewalks, dingy walls, and an air of too much use, but there was a warmth inside them.

The minister, Roland West, introduced himself as a Unitarian and a friend of Steph's. He and Mickey seemed to know each other well enough. Affection had been present as they'd shaken hands. When he wanted to pull Mickey aside to speak to him, I intended to give them privacy. Although before I could step away, however, Mickey had taken my hand.

"You didn't want a graveside service," Roland said as he studied Mickey.

"Steph never liked them," Mickey explained. The roughness of his voice made me ache for him. There were unshed tears, anger, and something indefinable coloring every single word. "Particularly when the kids were involved. Too hard on them."

"I remember. What I thought we would do, since you want to keep it simple is begin with a welcome and reading. Then you can speak if you'd like at the beginning. If not, we can open it up to her friends and others in the neighborhood who knew her. Let them have their say."

Mickey's hand tightened.

"We can take as long or short as you'd like. We'll pass the candle to each person as they speak. Keep it informal but also open. When the last person has spoken, you can have your chance again if you'd like. If not—I'll finish up, and we'll go from there. Sound good?"

Pulling at his tie, Mickey nodded. He never seemed to be a man given to fidgeting. Then again, I could hardly blame him for the present restlessness. "I appreciate it, Roland."

"After the service, would you like company to go with you to the cremation facility?"

"Appreciate it, but…" Mickey glanced down at me. "That one's a little more private. If you can handle the food and drinks after…"

"Darla's already gotten everything ready. The neighborhood came prepared, too—everyone loved your sister."

"Yeah," Mickey said with a sigh.

Roland gave him a sympathetic smile before clasping his shoulder then moving away. The guys weren't that far away. They'd taken an entire pew near the front, but no one was seated. Mickey's friends had taken different points around the room, with two near the doors. Everything about their postures said they were on high alert.

Pivoting, I tilted my head to look up at Mickey. We hadn't had much time alone at all since everything happened, but he continued to stay at the clubhouse. He'd even slept in my room again. I'd curled up with him, just wanting him to sleep, except he hadn't said much.

"Can I do anything?" I asked, hating how fucking helpless I was to do anything right now. The grief in the air was palpable. Every single one of them hurt, and I hurt for them.

"You're already doing it, Little Bit." Gruff as it came out, his expression softened some. "I'm gonna be a miserable bastard for a while. You being here and just—not letting me send you away is a good thing."

Head tilted, I summoned a smile for him. "If I thought you truly wanted me gone, I might pick a fight with you. But I get it. You want me safe."

"Yes." He lifted my hand and pressed a kiss to it. "The kind of people who can do this…I don't want to risk you."

Shifting my stance, I focused on Mickey wholly. We stood near a wall, and he'd more or less moved to block me from the whole room. The tension lacing him seemed to have a visceral force to it. Like I could pinch it and pull it away from him as if it were some kind of nylon.

"You're not risking me." When he would have protested, I raised my eyebrows and he exhaled a long breath even while keeping my hand against his chest. "You're not. I know the risks. I'd say better than all of you, except—the last few weeks have taught me that there are no limits to how far Uncle Fuckbucket will go."

Mickey blinked. "Did you just…?"

"Yeah, Lainey called him that, and I think she's right. Every time I call him my uncle, it's like I'm claiming him or embracing that relationship. I don't want to anymore." Before I actually said Fuckbucket, I hadn't realized how fucking true it was. "I don't want to claim him. He's a brutal, unkind, selfish fuckbucket who deserves to pay for every horrible thing he's done to all of you."

And to me. But I survived him. Survived to find my real family. That was what mattered. I survived. My mom survived.

"You… amaze me," he said, his voice dipping. Then he shifted his stance and peeked to the right.

"Sorry, Doc," Freddie said as he joined us. He fidgeted with his tie. "I—Boo-Boo, can you fix this? It's strangling me."

Mickey squeezed my hand. "It's fine, Freddie. Thank you for dressing up for this. Steph would have appreciated it."

"She'd have been in shock and then wanted to know what I blew up," Freddie said without an ounce of self-recrimination. The corner of his mouth kicked up. "To be fair, I only ever wore ties when I had to see a judge."

A chuckle escaped Mickey as he moved around to block

us from the rest of the room and let me turn to Freddie. The knot he'd done had gotten too tight and wasn't aligned properly.

"I'm going to undo it first," I warned him, and he nodded. "I like this tie, actually." It was black and gray, with sharp color blocking. Freddie deserved more color, but the monochrome effect gave him a somber air. He'd pulled his hair back into a tie at his nape.

He looked quite dapper.

"Thanks, Kel loaned it to me." Freddie made a face. "Not really a suit and tie guy."

With care, I reset the knot before fixing his collar. "No one is a suit and tie guy. They say the suit makes the man, but that's not true."

"No?" Mickey asked, his tone a little lighter, even shaded dark with sadness.

"Absolutely not. You can dress up monkeys in suits and ties. We did that one year in a show I did. Adorable creatures and kind of hilarious. They look great in tuxes. However, they are adorable and entertaining, not powerful."

"Not really seeing how that applies to me," Freddie teased, a faint spark in the storm of his blue eyes. "Unless you're saying I'm adorable and entertaining. Which I would totally accept."

Chuckling, I smoothed down his tie and collar again, fixing it so it was all comfortable for him. Then I rested my hands on his lapel. "You are absolutely adorable and entertaining, but the guy in this suit is amazing even when he's in jeans and a ripped t-shirt. He's not so bad in scrubs either."

A flush touched Freddie's ears. "Thanks, Boo-Boo." When he caught my fingers lightly and raised his brows, I lessened the distance and hugged him. The contact was light, but he squeezed me gently. The faintest of tremors went through him. "I hate funerals," he whispered.

I could understand that, even though I'd never actually been to a funeral. Not once. Not even those few formal ones held for others in Uncle Fuckbucket's social circle. He never wanted me at those. I would attend the receptions after, if I went at all.

"Hey, Doc," one of Mickey's friends said as he approached us. I hadn't memorized all their names yet, but I thought this one was...

"Yeah, Bones, thanks. Stick close to Little Bit if I get pulled away?"

The man flicked his dark-eyed gaze at me. He nodded once.

"We got her. We got you, too. The minister guy said we're close to full, so he's getting ready to start unless you want to take a few more minutes..."

Mickey hesitated. Everything about him went tranquil as he gazed around the room then up to the front. There would be no casket, not here. There was a picture of Ms. Stephanie at the front, though. Everyone who came in tracked their eyes to it. Even now, I caught Jasper staring at it, his expression brooding. Then Milo put a hand on his shoulder and the pair shared a small smile.

I hated that they were hurting.

Hated it so much.

"We're good," Mickey said finally, turning to hold out his hand to me. I took it, then held out my free hand to Freddie. He clasped it easily, and I walked up to the front with them. Mickey would sit in the first row while the guys took the row with us, along with the one directly behind us.

It didn't escape me that Milo had Mickey's back or that Liam settled on the far side of Freddie or Jasper took an outer row seat.

"Good morning," Roland said, heading to the podium in the front. "It always seems odd to say good morning, good afternoon, or even good evening when we gather for a memorial or funeral service. Like saying *good* is somehow anathema to why we are here..."

He paused for a moment, his gaze going to Mickey.

"Losing someone we care about is always difficult. Few, if any, words can soften that loss. What is good, however, is sharing that loss with others. Coming together to remember, to support, to love... Stephanie James touched many lives. She changed the lives of nearly every person in this room..."

Mickey's hand tightened around mine, as did Freddie's. I held onto both of them as I listened to Roland speak. I wish I'd gotten more time with Ms. Stephanie. More time to know her as they all did. I loved her because they loved her, and more—because I'd seen just how much she loved all of them.

# CHAPTER 12

*DOC*

$\mathcal{T}$he next two hours passed almost too swiftly. One by one, every single one of those boys got up there and said something about Steph, even Rome. They shared their memories, their affection, and their loss. More than that, they shared their hope.

Every single one except Milo. I understood. I wasn't sure I could get up there and talk, either. Having the kids here helped. Having the guys here helped. Having Little Bit *right here*? Helped.

Didn't change the fact Steph wasn't here. All in all, more than a dozen others came forward with stories or tributes. The slimmest fraction of the lives she'd touched. Yet, I appreciated them all. It was hard to resent the fruits of her life's work when they were sharing how much she'd meant to them.

When Milo finally stood, Little Bit's hand tightened on

mine. He walked up to the front. Instead of facing us though, he stared at Steph's photograph.

"I don't have to look at the faces in this room to know who Ms. Stephanie touched," he said, straightening as his shoulders went back. The weight of the world had been weighing him down for so long that it left his throat scratchy at how much of a burden the world had been to that kid.

A kid who'd grown into a man. Maybe not the man the kid intended to be, but a man, nonetheless. Milo had taken a wild hit that knocked him off course. But he was rebuilding himself, one day at a time.

"I wish I had better words to describe what she meant to me. Or all the things she taught me. She never made a promise that she didn't do her damnedest to keep. She taught that one polite word was better than a hundred rude ones. She reminded us that we were human and that it was okay to screw up. Forgiveness and acceptance were her love language. I wouldn't have survived without Ms. Stephanie. I'm going to miss you."

Closing my eyes, I dropped my chin. Missing her was like missing a limb. Little Bit dropped her head against my shoulder and I cracked my eyelids to look down at her.

I didn't deserve this comfort, either. Not when I'd pushed her away so hard. A part of me agreed that she deserved far better than me. I was too fucking old for her. I'd held her as a baby. Only I didn't see that baby when I looked at her.

Nor did I see Milo's baby sister, or even that broken, abused girl that a far too impulsive for his own good Jasper had stolen and then they'd brought to me at the clinic. The brown eyes gazing up at me steadily housed a maturity and a strength I couldn't have imagined.

Didn't deserve her. Shouldn't want her. Wasn't letting her go. Obsessed. I'd drag myself over shrapnel and broken glass if it kept her with me. Kept her with us.

Eventually, the service ended. Roland took the time to speak to everyone. There was food and drinks laid out as more people came in to share memories and time. I avoided the well-wishers and the sympathizers. Instead, I stayed to the side, tracking the movement in the room.

Little Bit was never alone, she floated between us. For a time, she was with Milo, comforting him. She went to Freddie, teasing a smile from him and then rewarding him with a soft kiss to the corner of his mouth. With her presence alone, she chased away the gloom and lightened the air around us.

"You got this?" Bones asked as he moved to lean against the wall next to me. I'd spoken to a few of those present, but most were giving me distance. Then again, I was now what most of these guys and some girls had been for years: an orphan.

Didn't matter that I was in my thirties. We'd lost our parents a long time before. Older than me by a decade, Steph fought to keep me with her, and she'd fought to keep me on the straight and narrow. I'd been a little shit and Steph had been my family.

Not willing to lie to Bones, I just shrugged. "Another hour. Max. Then I want Little Bit out of here." Out of public scrutiny. We all had her, Liam and Jasper alternated with who had her back. Kellan kept her in his sightline, and Vaughn was her shadow. Freddie and Milo took most of her attention at the moment. Where the fuck was...

Rome ghosted along the edges of the room. His twin moved in the other direction. They were both scanning the space. Everyone took a different position, a different angle— no one was left with their back exposed.

"We taking you two back to the warehouse, or you want to go somewhere else?" Bones was about as much into conversation as I was, but Lunchbox and Voodoo were also positioned so that one of them was always within reach of Little Bit.

"Warehouse."

I wanted a lot, but she needed to be where it was safe. Even if I wanted to take her far, far fucking away from all of this, I wouldn't. I wouldn't take her from them or them from her.

"Alphabet's working on that location you requested." Those words pulled my attention, and I finally shifted my gaze from Little Bit to Bones. His expression was neutral, his eyes cool, and his whole demeanor almost perfectly ice.

"Is he getting closer?"

"Not before we left," he said, checking the message on his watch. "Not yet. He'll narrow it down."

Patience was not my strong suit at the moment. In the field? In practice? Even in surgery—the image of Steph's surgery flashed before my eyes, and I blew out a shaky breath. "I need a minute."

Not waiting for his response, I kept to the edge of the room and out a side door. The door closing behind me muted the sound of conversation. The darkened hall was calm, quiet, and isolated. I reached the end of the hall and leaned against the wall.

Head down, I flexed my hands, curling them into fists then forcing them to relax. The service was for Steph; the coming violence was for me.

All I could see was the bleeding in the operating room. All I could hear was the beeping of the machines ticking away her life. All I could taste was the sterile air...

Cool hands framed my face and I jerked my head up. Adrenaline spilled into my system, hot and furious. I closed my hands on Little Bit's biceps, barely managing to not yank her away.

Her eyes widened. "Sorry," she murmured. "I didn't mean to startle you."

I searched those honey-brown eyes in the low light of the hall. They were wells of darkness, relaxed and inviting.

"You didn't seem to hear—" I dragged her to me, the need to kiss her a pure, primitive need pounding in my blood. As gentle as I desired to be, the first press of my lips to hers was anything but. I devoured her mouth, and she opened to the first thrust of my tongue.

The curl of her arms around my neck and the arch of her body invited me to pick her up, cradle her slender—sometimes too damn slender and fragile—body to me. Her weight against my chest was negligible compared to the liquid heat spilling into my system.

Chocolate with a hint of strawberry burst across my taste buds, along with hints of coffee and the sweet vanilla scent that I identified with her. The smell of her shampoo. The conditioner. With every thrust of my tongue, she opened wider to me.

I wanted to touch her. I wanted skin under my hands. Some distant part of my brain recognized we were in a hallway. Lifting my head, I broke the kiss long enough to track a door, open it, and close us inside. There was a deadbolt, so I threw it and then quickly searched the room.

Empty.

Closet, empty.

There was a desk and a little leather sofa.

I ignored both.

Focusing on the woman before me, I cupped her chin and stroked a finger along her lower lip. "You are so fucking precious," I told her because, goddammit, she deserved to hear this. "You are remarkable, courageous, fierce, and so fucking strong."

Her lips parted and her breath came in explosive little pants to match my own.

"I know nearly every inch of this body," I told her, trailing my fingers to her throat where her pulse beat frantically. "I looked after your bruises and your wounds…"

"Helped with my PT," she whispered, the huskiness of her voice going straight to my cock. "Looked after me…sometimes, I think you know me too intimately."

"No such thing, Little Bit. I was a fucking fool to push you away. I want you," I said, not bothering to sugarcoat it. "I want whatever part of you you'll let me have."

Wanted her so fucking bad.

"Need you…" I admitted, and I wasn't proud of the way my voice broke on those two words.

I needed her. The world was full of incendiary devices, and they were detonating all around us. I needed her. Needed to feel her. Needed to make her come. Needed to lose myself inside of her.

"Fuck," I swore. "You deserve so much more than a quick and dirty fuck in this goddamn office."

She pressed her fingers to my lips, and I sucked them into my mouth. Her eyes darkened further, if possible.

"Anything," she whispered, and my cock turned to iron. The want of her had been there from the first time she lifted that chin as she dared me to treat her like the queen she was. "What you need—what you want—if I have it, it's yours."

I dipped my head to her dress. It was a simple black dress that hugged her sweet figure. "Turn around," I told her, the command sending another pulse of lust through me. I was going to come on her like a fucking teenager if I didn't get a grip, but she was right there…

When she turned to face the door, she placed her hands against it and then pushed her ass back toward me. I slid my hands to her hips and gathered the skirt, pulling it up.

Beneath it, she was bare save for a simple thong that did nothing to hide the sweet globes of her ass.

Bruises decorated one cheek, faint and fading, though clearly fingers... Dropping to my knees, I pressed my lips to the first bruise, then the next. Glancing up, I found her looking down at me as I nudged her legs further apart.

"I'm going to make this up to you," I promised. "My beautiful, sweet little bit. "

She swallowed once as I glided my fingers up to hook into the thong and drag it down. I could leave it on. I could tug it aside and fuck right into her, but I wanted a taste.

The first glimpse of her pretty pink pussy lips had me smiling. They glistened, damp and swollen. Someone else had already fucked her today, and if that didn't make me even harder...

After she stepped out of her thong, I pressed it to my nose before shoving it into my pocket. A shuddering breath escaped her as I pushed her thighs wider, then pressed my mouth right up to her wet cunt. The sweet treat of her filled my mouth as I teased my tongue over her folds, then pushed inside of her.

Slow and deliberate, she deserved hours of praise as I kissed and made love to every inch of her.

"Soon," I whispered against her pussy, savoring every lick as she drenched my face. "Soon, my beautiful girl, I'm going to worship this body until you only know pleasure."

She shivered, goosebumps rippling over her skin.

"Except right now..." I pressed one more deep, carnal kiss against her cunt, licking her up as her muscles spasmed. "Right now, I'm going to fuck you with my cock. Not your fingers. Not mine. Just me and my cock filling you up..."

"Please," she whispered, and I found her pupils were blown as she looked down at me. Her whole body trembled. Or maybe that was me. One more kiss as I unbuckled my belt, then unzipped my pants. I shoved them down as I stood.

My dick ached as it slapped against my belly. I was leaking pre-cum as I teased it along her slit. This could be so much fun, to edge her until she sobbed from needing me.

But *I* needed her right now.

"Hold on, Little Bit," I whispered against her ear. I nudged my cock to her entrance, having to bend my knees a little, even with her ass pressed out toward me. I looked for a better angle. Gripping her hips, I lifted her as I straightened and then I was fucking into her. The hot velvet glove of her cunt was the sweetest goddamn feeling.

Her gasp as I shoved into her immobilized me, but not until I was already balls-deep. The trembling in her thighs communicated to my own. Grabbing the chair, I dragged it over and put it in front of her, never once pulling out. I liked having her impaled on me.

"Such a good girl," I whispered. "Little Bit, on your knees, hands on the wall…" Every command she obeyed, and then I flexed my hands on her hips. "I'm going to fuck you now."

"Yes," she said, and the single syllable dragged down my back as if it was her nails.

"You're going to know who's fucking you, aren't you?" Keeping her still, I pulled all the way out then slammed back in. She gave a little grunt and a low keening note came out.

Oh, that was a sound I wanted again. I rocked my hips back and then thrust deeper. She let out another soft sound, like she was trying to contain it.

No, I wanted every scream. I wanted to feel her come. I wanted her to shout out how good it felt.

My little bit.

There was little finesse in how hard I fucked into her. I managed to not dig my fingers in and bruise her hips, but when I reached around to tease her clit she began to spasm and her cries escalated. I pumped into her, the cries urging me to fuck her deeper even as my balls dragged up.

"That's it, Little Bit," I murmured in approval as she began to cry out. I teased and tormented that little nub until she practically bucked against me. "That's it. Give me everything. You're going to take my cock, and I'm going to fill you up right now."

It was more syllables than words at this point, and I didn't care; my balls were so tight, that the liquid heat split me in half as I came. I surged into her, holding her as my release filled her up.

I pressed against her back, the softness of her ass, the ripple of muscle beneath it tucked against my groin. My cock twitched like I was a fifteen-year-old, but fuck I wanted to do it again.

Rather than pull out, I kept her sealed to me while I nuzzled kisses against her throat. "Thank you."

She laughed, the sound almost as musical as it was breathless. "I think I should be thanking you."

No, she never needed to thank me. Sooner or later, I would soften and slip out of her, but I was right where I wanted to be and when she leaned back into me, I cradled her tighter.

"I'm here," she promised, and it took me a minute to realize tears were sliding down my face as I kept nuzzling her throat. "I'm here, Mickey."

# CHAPTER 13

*FREDDIE*

*F*unerals sucked. I'd only ever been to two of them before, and I'd never been to one for someone I *knew*. Someone who was…

Emotion clogged my throat and I dug out that little package of tissues that Boo-Boo had hidden in my pocket. Blowing my nose, I stared out over the bay. The view from the top of the warehouse offered a different perspective on the world of Braxton Harbor.

From the gentrified areas to the north spreading into our neighborhood, to the abandoned ones to the west where it bordered the harbor itself, to the endless yards of storage containers.

Standing up here, I could look out over the world—the beautiful and the dirty—and none of it could touch me. I dug around in my pockets for the half-crushed pack of cigarettes. They were Jasper's. I'd found them sitting in the main room of the suite.

Finders, keepers, and all that.

Besides, there were like three left in it so he wouldn't care. Pulling one out, I eyed the crumpled, kind of off-center state of it and laughed. It was a lot like me. All messy and bent, but there were no nicks in the paper. Just as I set the filter to my lips, the hatch to the warehouse flipped open.

Twisting, I almost lost the cigarette as I grinned. Boo-Boo poked her head out to look at me. Her hair was pulled back into a ponytail, but the whole day seemed a bit brighter with her smile.

"Do you mind some company?"

It had been two days since the funeral. Two days. That seemed an impossible amount of time on the one hand, and not remotely long enough on the other.

"I can go—" she offered, and I shook off the melancholy to cross over to the hatch. She was balanced on the ladder. Rome was on the ground not far away, his gaze fixed on her. When I lifted my chin, he nodded.

"Don't go," I said, holding out a hand to her. "You're always welcome. I just didn't expect to be caught so quickly."

Her laugh was worth being caught. She clasped my hand easily and held on as she finished climbing up. Still holding onto me, she leaned back to wave to Rome then blew him a kiss before we closed the hatch.

"Rome is on guard duty today," she informed me. "Not that you guys are calling it that."

"Nope," I said, as she took my lighter and held it up for me, and together we blocked the wind then lit the cigarette. It tasted like ass as it burned my lungs, but I still took a long drag and ignored the cough when I released it. "You want one?"

"Maybe," she said. "Mostly just came to hang out with you."

I jerked my head to where the chairs and fire pit were.

118

Someone had been up here recently, it was swept clean and two of the chairs had been fixed. There were new chains in place to keep the chairs locked down from the wind.

A peek in the fire pit showed fresh wood. It wasn't really that cold, but the wind could be brisk. Still, she curled up in the chair next to mine as I settled in and stretched my legs out.

"How are you doing?" she asked, and I shrugged.

"I should be asking you that." The day of the funeral, she'd been almost ethereal, untouchable in a way. A word, a smile, or even just holding a hand, she'd been everywhere as she tried to take care of us.

When Doc disappeared after the service, she'd gone after him. They were gone for a while, but she'd definitely been a little more disheveled when she returned.

"I'm fine," she said with a shrug. "Or as fine as I can be while all of you are sad."

"Yeah," I said, blowing out a stream of smoke. "I know you're hurting too…hurting for Doc and for Milo…hurting for me." I stole a look at her, and the corners of her lips quirked up.

"It's my fault Uncle Fuckbucket came after all of you…"

"Nope," I said, before taking another drag.

"Freddie."

"Boo-Boo," I countered, holding up my fingers one at a time as I ticked off the points. "I know three things. None of this is your fault. Uncle Fuckbucket is a walking dead man. And we're going to be the ones who end his tyranny over your life. By we, I mean the Vandals."

The quirk at the corners of her mouth saved my soul. We were talking about the fucker who abused her repeatedly, and yet she could smile. I'd do just about anything for that smile.

"I hate that he has caused pain to so many people just to punish me."

"Although it's not your fault, Boo-Boo. You know that, right?"

"I want to," she admitted. "But that's a little harder."

Yeah. "I know."

The sun played hide and seek behind the fat white clouds decorating the blue sky. As far as days went, it was really pretty. Though I should have brought sunglasses up here.

Quiet swirled around us, kind of like the smoke from the cigarette before a breeze brushed it away. I lit a second cigarette from the first and coughed as it burned my throat. As irritating as it was, it satisfied the other craving itching under my skin.

"Are you okay?" The soft question pulled at me.

"No," I told her. "But you know that."

Another flicker of a smile, one I had to answer with my own.

"Been dying for a hit all day," I admitted. "To be honest, been dying for a hit since the car flipped that night. Then that fucker touched you..."

"You took care of him." Absolute faith. The kind of faith I didn't deserve...

"Yeah, I did. I just wish I'd gotten to him before he did that."

Her shoulders lifted in a graceful shrug. "I had some bruises—everyone has been very determined to make me forget them."

Yeah, I should have made it hurt more.

"And you cut off his fingers." There was that smile again.

"You know what I adore about you, Boo-Boo?"

"My taste in coffee and donuts?"

A chuckle escaped at her response. "I will never argue with your taste in either. Though I may ask to share."

"You don't have to ask," she said, her voice dipping a fraction with emotion. "Whatever I have, I'll always share it with you."

"What about when you get mad at me?" Playing with fire right now? Yep. I flicked the ash off the end of my cigarette.

"Hmm...even then. Though I haven't been mad at you yet, so I'll reserve the right to change my mind. Maybe I'll make you watch me eat a donut first, then I'll share."

She looked so damn serious that I couldn't help but laugh. "I'm not the easiest guy, Boo-Boo."

"I hate to break this to you," she said, her expression barely shifting. "None of you are easy."

"Well..." She had a point. "But I'm particularly difficult."

"I'm a brat," she tacked on with a shrug. "I bet I can be more irritating than you are if I set my mind to it."

Huh. That was a thought. "How about a bet?"

"A bet?" When she straightened up, I reconsidered the offer for a heartbeat.

No, I wanted the bet. "Yeah, which of us can be more difficult and irritating to the others."

"That feels like a trap," she murmured, but it didn't seem to dissuade her. "I don't know if they need to be dealing with us being difficult right now..."

I laughed. "Maybe. Maybe not. Sometimes, giving them something else to think about can be fun—" Then again, I sighed. "Then again, maybe not *now*."

"But we could bet on it for later."

We could. I rolled the cigarette between my fingers before I took another drag. My eyes watered and I sputtered another cough. When she reached over to pat my back in sympathy, I turned my face to blow the smoke away from her.

"What are the stakes?" If we were going to bet on anything, we needed to have stakes.

"What do you want?"

I stared at her, then reached over with my free hand to tuck an errant tendril of her hair behind her ear. The tilt of her head, the dark length of her hair—even pulled back into the ponytail—appeared to have grown so much longer over the last year. That was what hair did, obviously, even though it fell nearly to her ass at this point.

No answer seemed to come easily to me. If anything, all I wanted was this moment. "More moments like this."

Confusion filled her eyes. "Just hanging out with me?"

"I like hanging out with you." Loved hanging out with her. Boo-Boo didn't mind it when I was quiet. She laughed at my jokes. She let me have my little lies when I needed them. When I wanted more...

I wanted more.

Holy shit, I really did want more. I wanted to make her smile and I wanted her to be proud of me. I wanted...I wanted to be the person she needed. I wanted to take the risks she took...

"I haven't forgotten about our date," she promised. "I'm actually excited about it."

"Might be a bit," I grumbled.

"I can wait."

"What if I don't want to?" The irritation was immediate, but I winced because I didn't want to lash out at her.

"Then don't," she countered, leaning back and pulling her legs up to sit crisscross in the chair. "We can be creative."

Creative?

"What? Do our date here?"

At the Clubhouse? With the guys? I mean, I liked the guys, but... I wanted to take Boo-Boo out. Like when Jasper and I took her to the movies. Granted, I invited myself on their date.

"Why not? I mean—we have rooms that we don't use."

I frowned.

"We have my studio—"

Scratching my jaw, I turned that idea over.

"There's the warehouse itself. If we get rid of the rats, we could probably play laser tag out there or something..."

I snickered.

"There's the pool table and darts..."

She was offering up so many excellent suggestions.

"We also have that huge sofa in the suite and a television."

"That all seems kind of... boring for a date, Boo-Boo. I want it to be special for you."

Head tilted, she smiled. "It will be special, because it's with you."

That squeezed all of the air out of my lungs. I crushed out the cigarette. "I don't know if I'm worth that much."

"Freddie," she said, sliding out of the chair. She knelt in front of my seat, and I shifted my leg so I didn't have a knee in her face. "You are worth everything."

No, I wasn't.

"Yes, you are," she said, as if arguing the thought I hadn't spoken aloud. She covered my hand with hers, and there was a question in her eyes. When she started to pull her hand away, I clasped her fingers. She could touch me; I liked it when she did. "You are worth it to me."

I opened my mouth then closed it again. How the fuck did I argue with that? She was worth it to me, too...worth so much more. Dropping the dead cigarette into the fire pit, I squeezed her hand and then pulled out my phone.

Boo-Boo didn't pull away. She just watched me as I skimmed through my apps and pulled up the music one. Finding the version of the song I wanted took me a hot minute. When I had it, I stood up slowly, still holding her hand, and tugged gently.

Graceful as always, Boo-Boo rose to stand with me. Fear

fluttered in my stomach, like acid burning its way out. "Will you dance with me?"

Surprise flickered over her face. "Up here?"

"Yep," I said, then pressed play on the music and tucked the phone into my shirt pocket before I could lose my nerve. The soft piano version of "Infinity" by Jaymes Young drifted out, almost too soft with the breeze but more than loud enough for us. Her eyes brightened at the first couple of bars.

She put a hand on my shoulder as I settled one on her hip. I didn't know much about fancy dancing, but I could do this. For fourteen perfect seconds, she drifted with me and the world narrowed its focus down to just the two of us.

At the sixteen-second mark, I began to sing and it came out a little broken and rusty at first. Fuck knew singing right after I smoked probably wasn't a great idea, but Boo-Boo's eyes grew so wide. Surprise and delight filtered across her face and every single fear I had went to ash just like that cigarette.

I sang for her, and she danced with me.

# CHAPTER 14

*EMERSYN*

*D*isbelief and joy were the most tightly wound emotions. No matter what anyone else said, they were the ones that often seemed to appear together, at least for me. Not sure what it said about me that being happy was not often believable in my life.

Actually, I knew exactly what it said about me. I didn't trust happiness, not when it was explicit or genuine. Instead, I was far more comfortable with darker emotions.

Pain and I were longtime companions. Misery and loneliness made up the rest of my circle. When I followed Freddie up to the roof, it had been more about worry for him disappearing on his own when he'd been facing so much hurt.

That was the thing about soul-deep injuries; they left scars no one could see. Scars that smarted like bad joints did in the cold or in the rain. Scars that flashed with fire when new injuries managed to touch too close to them. Scars that, by their nature, couldn't be erased.

I traced my fingers over the scars on the inside of my forearms. They were hardly gone, even if my awareness of them had faded some. I could forget for a while. Become so used to their presence I didn't see *them* as I had before.

That didn't make them go away. However, it did dull the memory of what caused them to a point. Softened the harsh reminder of what they were—the result of a choice I made to protect the men I loved.

Love.

That word was almost as alien to me as was happiness. Yet, both were daily companions. I used to keep everyone and everything at arm's length. I learned to not make friends, for isolation was safer for me. Safer for others. My one guilty indulgence had been my best friend.

Speaking of which, I glanced down at my phone. There was still no response from her. The app where we still talked whenever we could was open and my last three messages hadn't been read.

ME:

> The funeral was hard. I know I said I wouldn't interfere, but I think Milo could use a call if you can.

ME:

> I miss you. Let me know you're all right.

ME:

> If I don't hear from you soon, I'm calling Ezra.

Again, nothing.

Unease slid through my system. After the night of terror, Ezra had let Liam know she was all right. She was safe. That was the only reason I hadn't freaked out. At the same time...

The door to the bathroom opened, and Mom stepped out. Steam billowed out of the room since she'd been in there for nearly an hour. Hopefully, there was still hot water left now that she was done.

Her hair was wrapped up in a towel, and she wore the thick robe Liam had delivered along with a selection from the store. I hadn't even realized he'd bought clothes for her at first. I adored him so much, especially since he'd planned for this in the middle of everything else.

"Sorry, darling," Mom said as she walked across the room to where I was sitting. I would have gone to help her, but she waved me back to my seat as she eased onto the sofa with me. This close, it was hard to miss the trembling. "I had to take a break during the shower."

"If you needed help, I could have come in there..."

"I thought I would be fine," she said, slowly pulling the towel from her hair. The long mass fell dark and wet against her shoulders. For the first time in my life, there were streaks of silver scattered amidst the dark hair.

She still seemed so pale and shaky. The vivacious, sometimes larger than life, woman with immaculate cosmetics and hair was utterly absent. In her place was a reasonably attractive, if fragile, woman with her nerves on full display.

"Can I get you anything?" I offered, preparing to stand, but Mom shook her head.

"No, darling, I think you and your friends have done a lot for me. I just need to get my strength up. Showering shouldn't take every ounce of energy I have."

While I agreed with her on many levels, I'd also been completely worn out before, not to mention drugged, and Mickey hadn't told me everything they subjected her to, either.

Then again, Mom had said very little. She slept, a lot. After the first few days, Mickey hadn't had to give her more sedatives. She didn't rally, not at first. If anything, she seemed to sink deeper into depression.

"Mom…" I leaned forward, but she glanced away and then stood. Almost fumbling with her towel, she moved away. "I know you haven't wanted to talk about this."

"Darling," she said, not entirely turning to face me. If anything, she only let me see her profile and there were tears on her face. "I—I don't want to make you talk about any of that."

Before I could say anything, a firm knock struck the door. There was no mistaking her flinch as she jumped nor the cautious look she threw at the door. The sense of panic bruised my heart. I understood that fear.

"It's a friend," I promised her. No one who wasn't a friend would just knock on the door. To get to this one, they needed to get into the warehouse and then into the clubhouse. We'd hear it if it weren't a friend.

But Mom took the clean clothes we'd set out and vanished into the bathroom before I even reached the door. Swallowing a sigh, I opened the door to Milo.

The quick once-over he gave me was enough to make me smile. They all did it in distinctive ways. It was like they had to scan me for injuries and verify for themselves that I was alright, at least physically.

"Hey, Ivy," he murmured, putting a hand on my bicep before he shot me a quiet, questioning look. He always waited for me to come forward a little and then he'd press a kiss to my temple. The one-armed hug was always there, but if I stepped into him then I got a full one.

Right now, I needed the hug. Milo and I were still working our way through this relationship thing. The easy affection he had for me, especially if I needed it? It was magical.

"Hey," I greeted him. "Everything good?"

"I came to ask you that," he said, giving me a little squeeze before he scanned the room behind me. "How is she?"

"Honestly? I don't know," I admitted. It was almost awkward right now. Was it because she was getting cleaner and clearer? Was her own guilt and self-consciousness playing into it? I wasn't sure. "You want to come in?"

After another searching look, he nodded. The guys had been very cautious with Mom so far, but there had also been enormous distractions. The time was coming when we needed to ask her questions.

They needed to ask her. They were being gentle with her for my sake, but the swift withdrawals were as much a fear and panic response as anything.

Sometimes, I was the same way. If I didn't talk about something, then I could pretend it wasn't happening to me. Folding my arms, I retreated toward the sofa again. "Mom is getting dressed."

He nodded slowly, tracking my path until I took a seat before he followed me and took the chair closest to me. He'd barely sat when the bathroom door opened again and he rose to his feet.

Mom slipped out like a wraith, dressed in a pair of leggings and an oversized tunic. Both were more suited to me than her. She looked—so normal in the clothes. It was hard to wrap my mind around it, around her.

Weirdest of all, her nails were bare of any polish. Outside of pedicures and manicures, I couldn't think of a time in my life when her nails weren't some fun color. Moving slowly, she glanced from me to where Milo stood. Her movements were excruciatingly careful, like she was hurting.

I needed to talk to Mickey to see if she might be having some kind of side effects or lingering consequences of the meds they'd had her on.

"Mrs. Sharpe," Milo said as she stopped behind the opposite armchair and faced him.

Mom studied him for a long moment, the silence stretching so thin it felt like it would snap.

"You're the little boy," she said abruptly, surprise fluttering through the words like pages flipped in a book. "The brother."

Dipping his chin, Milo nodded once. "Yes, ma'am. I remember you too."

The air practically crackled with all the things they weren't saying. This awkward history—*my* history. "Mom, this is Milo. Milo, this is my mom."

She flexed her hands against the back of the chair, like she wasn't sure what to do. The discomfort stained the air around her. The indecision weighed on me even as she seemed intent on fighting her own responses. Letting go of the chair, she circled it and held out her hand.

"I'm Moira," she said. "It's lovely to meet you again."

I bit my lower lip as Milo studied her hand for a moment, then reached over to accept the handshake. "Yes, ma'am."

They hesitated, both of them. Finally, Mom took a step back. She rubbed her hands against her sides, then folded her arms. "I suppose you both want to talk."

She didn't quite look at Milo, just at me. My mother's unease and fidgetiness translated to my own nerves.

"If you're up for it," Milo said deliberately, the gruffness in his voice more poignant to me than hostile. "Ivy would prefer that you rest though, if you're not."

"Ivy—" Her gaze flickered to me, and I raised my brows. "That was your name when we adopted you."

"It's still technically one of my names," I told her. "I'm still Ivy Hardigan." The weight of Milo's regard washed over me. "I'm also still me," I continued. "Yes, we have questions and need to talk, but Milo is right. I want you to rest if you're not ready yet."

Nothing we said or did would make this any less difficult. Not for me. Not for her. Not for Milo.

"But if you can handle it, I need to talk to you about Uncle Fuckbucket." I managed to get those words out almost steadily. "And Milo has questions about—"

"Uncle Fuckbucket?" Mom repeated the words, shock punching up the syllables. "You're calling Bradley a Fuckbucket?"

She didn't wait for my answer before she started laughing. Sitting down abruptly, she covered her mouth with her hand as though struggling to contain the sound. Except, the laughter kept escaping.

Only the lack of mirth in her eyes and the hysterical notes to her humor kept me from being upset. Tears escaped and she swiped at them, but then she shook her head as she pressed both of her hands to her face.

"I'm sorry," she exhaled, voice still shaking with over-wrought emotion. "It's not funny at all. At the same time... dear God, that is the perfect title for him."

She lifted her head to meet me, her tear-filled eyes shimmering. "My sweet baby..."

"You didn't know," I reminded her.

"I should have..."

"Yes," Milo said before I could. "You should have."

I swung my head to face him, but he wasn't looking at me at all. He stared at Mom, and rather than wilt under that hard-eyed stare, she lifted her chin.

"You promised me that you and your husband would love her and take care of her and *protect* her."

Mom swiped at a tear.

"What happened to that part?"

I wanted to protest and defend her. At the same time, I

cut my gaze back to Mom, who kept wiping at the tears escaping. I wanted to know what she would say... I didn't blame her. Right? I didn't think I did, yet at the same time...

"I—have no excuses. I always thought we were doing everything perfectly. I didn't know as much about babies." Now she looked at me. "But you were such a happy child, so easy, and then...you grew more somber and distant as you got older. I thought it was...just that you wanted to do other things."

Now it was my turn to look away. Not because I was ashamed of my choices or even of what I wanted to ask her, but because... "You were always gone," I said finally, then peered at her. "You and Daddy always had work, travel..."

She closed her eyes and dropped her chin. "I know, baby, I wish I could—"

"I just want to know why you adopted me if you were never going to have time." Licking my lips, I lifted my shoulders. "Did you actually want me? Or did you want a photo opportunity?"

Mom flinched like I'd slapped her.

"Of course, I wanted you," she said, her voice cracking. "We did. Daddy did want you...I can't have kids. I always wanted to have them, and Daddy wanted an heir. Maybe he didn't want you as much as I did or..."

"Or?" Milo asked into the quiet and she jerked, turning to face him as if she'd forgotten he was there. "Or what?"

I studied Mom as she went almost mute. The tears were still streaming down her face, which was unusual enough to keep me riveted. Whatever she wasn't saying, she was terrified to say it. That happened to me when a truth was too close, too right there, and hanging on me.

Then it was easier to say nothing. If I didn't admit it aloud, it wasn't true, right?

"Or it wasn't Daddy who had to approve."

The way her shoulders dropped and her eyes closed again answered my question.

"Uncle Fuckbucket was the one who wanted me." I was going to throw up. Pivoting, I headed for the door.

"Baby—Emersyn..." Mom had followed, but Milo cut her off. "Bradley controlled the money. He controlled the business...he controls your father—sometimes. Yes, he had to approve. I just—always thought it was because you would be the heir. He'd shown no interest in ever marrying after..."

"After?" Milo prompted again. "Stop editing yourself. Keeping secrets already hurt her. The truth is just showing us the teeth that have been digging into her."

I twisted to look back at Mom, who stared at Milo with such haunting misery.

"After I rejected him and chose his brother..." That seemed too easy, and then her weary gaze sought mine. "Two days after our wedding, he sent your father away and spent the next week raping me every single day."

Ice slammed through me.

"I got pregnant, but I lost that baby, and the...damage was considerable. He accused me of choosing to get rid of his child. So if I ever wanted another...I had to get his approval, and your father..."

"What about him?"

"He didn't know," she said, tears streaming. "He couldn't have known."

Only she didn't believe that. It was like someone cut her strings and she just sat abruptly.

"You don't know that for sure," Milo said, an ounce of kindness creeping into his cold voice. "And you aren't positive he didn't know what that son of a bitch was doing to Ivy..."

The horror on her face said it all. Yeah, I needed to go. I couldn't—

Leaving her room, I was down the hall and trying to get into the suite when the door opened.

"Hey," Kellan said as he pulled it wide. "What's wrong?"

I didn't have the words. When he tugged me to him, I just buried my face against his shirt. Deep breaths drenched me in his scent, even as the tears I was holding at bay burned in my eyes.

"I got you," he whispered, his voice soothing as he picked me up.

"What happened?" Vaughn asked.

"I don't know," Kellan whispered. "Whatever it is, we got you."

Then another hand was on my back. Rome. He pressed a kiss to the back of my head and bracketed me. Then Jasper and Vaughn were right there too.

The dam broke and the tears spilled over.

"Damn right, we got you," Jasper promised, and Rome echoed the sentiment with a gentle touch.

"We're here."

# CHAPTER 15

*EMERSYN*

"*D*id it help?"

"*The water? Yes.*" Exhaustion weighed down on me. Every single one of my muscles was too heavy. "*Thank you.*" Manners were so crucial to every situation, whether it was to the maid who cleaned my room or to the waitress who brought coffee at two in the morning.

Rome snorted softly, and I glanced over to find him shaking his head. There was a hint of a smile on his face as his pencil continued to scratch at the paper. "I meant telling you my name."

Oh. I'd said that it could help, and now he wanted to know if it did. As uncertain of that answer as I was about my location, I said nothing until he verbally prodded me again.

"I don't know." I wanted to turn away but it hurt to twist, so I had to settle for just closing my eyes.

\* \* \*

*I WAS STILL SITTING ON THE FLOOR READING WHEN KESTREL arrived.*

*The door thudded down the hall, and I glanced up from the page in time to see Kestrel arrive at the top of the steps. He stared at me and then at the closed door as he approached.*

*"No sign of him?"*

*I shook my head. "I don't even know if he's in there." The thought had actually occurred to me a couple of hours earlier. "I might have been sitting out here reading aloud for just myself all day."*

*Leaning over, Kestrel hit the door with his fist in a rapid beat. "Freddie, open your fucking mouth and tell Sparrow thank you for spending her whole day sitting on this hard, fucking cold ass floor for you."*

*Mouth agape, I stared up at Kestrel as he extended that hand to me. I clasped it and let him pull me to my feet. I ignored the soreness radiating up my butt from where it had gone numb again down my legs, which also protested the absolute lack of movement all day.*

*A few seconds later, the door opened to the near pitch-dark room. I couldn't see Freddie, but I could smell him, and the scent of sweat and body odor was a little strong.*

*"Thanks, Boo-Boo," he said in a raw voice. "I really liked you reading."*

*"There's a sandwich here for you. A couple of them."*

*When I would have picked them up, Kestrel tugged me back from the door. "He's a big boy. He can get them. You've looked after him all day. Let's look after you, shall we?"*

* * *

*"ARE YOU HIGH?" THE QUESTION SLIPPED OUT BEFORE I COULD swallow it back as I shot a look at Doc. "I don't have a brother." The*

*soft, lazy good mood from the night before vanished. Dread-infused anger iced in my system as I went hot and cold all at once.*

*What the hell was going on?*

*"Dove," Vaughn said quietly, and I cut a look away from the pained expression on Doc's face to the measured one on Vaughn's. There it was—in his topaz eyes—worry and sadness. His face, like Kellan's, was also marked up. Neither of them was bleeding though, not like Jasper.*

*That didn't mean they hadn't been bleeding.*

*I jerked a look back at the bruiser in front of me. He was huge. Big, like they all were, yet there seemed to be something much more dangerous about him. Dark brown eyes locked on me and I shook my head.*

*"I don't have a brother," I repeated slowly. "Trust me, I would have known."*

* * *

I SWALLOWED AGAINST THE BURN IN MY THROAT AND IN MY EYES. *"I don't remember a time when my uncle didn't touch me." It was so hard to utter those words and I stared at the darkness of the room, terrified someone would hear it. Hear me.*

*Worse, they would hear me telling Freddie.*

*His back stiffened against me.*

*"He used to dress me up, or he would have his staff do it..." I licked my lips even though there was no spit. "He liked to take my clothes off, pet me, and dress me up again."*

*The bile from earlier just seemed to sit there, and one of the tears slid free.*

*"He calls me his princess."*

MY EYES SNAPPED OPEN, AND EVERY MUSCLE TENSED AS MY heart hammered a staccato beat. Where was I? The room… this wasn't my room. Movement next to me had me shifting to the side, and I turned to meet the storm in Jasper's gray eyes.

Recognition, quickly followed by relief, trickled through me. I sank back into the pillows. Thanks to the fairy lights around the ceiling, the soft glow they gave off chased away the darkness. Some of their bedrooms still felt so new.

The soreness around my eyes had me rubbing a hand over my face. There was dampness on my cheeks. Had I been crying while I was asleep?

Jasper rolled onto his side, cupping my cheek gently. With care, he used his thumb to wipe away the tears.

"You're safe."

"I know," I whispered, rawness crackling in my voice. Even if I had to keep reminding myself. "I know," I repeated, and it came out more assertive this time. His whole expression gentled.

"What do you need?" The soft question soothed over some of the rougher places. My throat was sore, my eyes ached, and the fact I'd been crying hadn't been lost on me. My nose was still a little stuffy.

"I don't know," I admitted, wrapping a hand around his nape. The heat radiating off his body had me curling toward him even as he blanketed me. The weight was what I wanted. All at once, I twined my arms around his neck even as he settled into the cradle of my legs.

Jasper nuzzled kisses over my face, then down to my throat. The butterfly light, barely-there contact, more than what I realized I needed. Each brush of his beard against my face or throat had me clinging tighter. The tension cording my muscles alternating between fire and ice.

It must have communicated because he nipped at my

earlobe; the sharp little bite of pain grounded me. Then teased his tongue in whirls over my earlobe. "I'm here, Swan. You're safe."

*Uncle Fuckbucket was the one who wanted me...*

The chill skating under my skin threatened to slice through. Jasper lifted his head and searched my features. I had no idea what he was searching for, but then his mouth crashed down onto mine. Yes, *this* was what I needed.

*Jasper* was what I needed. The glide of his skin against mine, where my legs wrapped around him, pulled my focus to the present. Moreover, the contact drowned out all those voices in my head.

"I'm here," he repeated over and over in between kisses. The tears slipping from the corners of my eyes turned the kiss salty. Digging my fingers into his shoulders, I held on tight.

"Jas," I whispered in between biting kisses. He lifted his head, his stormy eyes holding me captive. "I'm—" What was I? I was... Why did words have to be so hard? "I love you," I said, finally. It didn't seem like much to offer when he was blanketing me in warmth and strength. Even less when compared to how he seemed firm to stand between me and the rest of the world.

I barely even knew what time it was or when we came in here. I remembered the tears and hugging Kellan so tight. I remembered all of them being there, though at some point, I collapsed into sleep and woke up here.

Safe. Safe and not alone.

"I love you," he whispered like a sacred promise. "I love you, and I have you. No one is taking you. You are not alone..."

So many words I needed to hear. I traced my fingers over his face. "How do you know what I need to hear?" How did he always know the right things to say?

He chuckled. The sound was dark and tempting even as he pushed his hips against the cradle of my thighs. Half-dressed as we were, it didn't disguise the weight of his cock pressing against me or stop me from soaking through my panties in anticipation.

"I don't always know the right things," he teased, nuzzling another kiss to the corner of my mouth. "I can be a real bastard, remember?"

A giggle escaped, tear-drenched possibly, but still a laugh. "Oh, I have some experience with your bossy, asshole side."

"Yeah, you do," he said, nipping my lower lip. "Didn't scare you. You just got right back in my face."

Adoration filtered up through me.

"As for the rest, Swan..." He braced himself up on his elbows before tilting his head to kiss a path down my throat. The soft bristles of his beard tickled as he licked, bit, and sucked in between bites. My nipples went to painful tips. "Being alone...being abandoned...it's the worst fucking feeling on the planet. We've all been there."

The words arrested me.

"We've all lost."

Tears burned anew in my eyes.

"We've all been burned by those meant to protect us."

He bit down on my pulse point, and the pain was sharp and incandescent as he sucked a hickey into place. I didn't even have to look to know it would be there.

Running my hands down his back, I slid them under the band of his boxer briefs. His ass clenched at the contact.

"You are not alone. No matter how much it hurts or what happens, we will always come for you. We will catch you, and if we can't, we will fucking jump right after you." Head rising, he fixed his gaze on mine as he gripped the collar of my t-shirt, then it ripped right down the middle splitting it open.

The cool air on my nipples sent a fresh bolt of need right through me.

"I have you," he whispered, dipping his gaze to my chest. Shifting my hand around, I tugged his briefs down until his cock was free between us. Pre-cum beaded along my hand as I stroked him. "Have me," he continued. "However, and whenever, you want."

"Help me?" I was stroking his cock, fisting him from base to tip and back. I didn't want to let him go. He gripped the side of my thong and it snapped before he dragged it off.

I wasn't usually wearing thongs. However, Mickey had been so thrilled with the one he stole at the funeral, I'd decided to wear a few more just to see what the guys thought.

A shiver rioted through me as Jasper held it up and smiled. "Have I mentioned how much I like these? Though, I'm fine with commando...in fact, in the suite, I'd be good with you wearing nothing at all."

Despite the tears and the pain clenching in my chest, a laugh burst out of me. "If I'm always naked, you guys will get nothing done."

"Don't you worry about that," he mused as I guided his cock right along my slit. We both hissed at how wet I was. Wanting him was like an eager burn in my blood. "We'd get you done."

Yes, they would.

The bite of his teeth punctuated his declaration sharply as he slid a hand down to hitch up my leg. The weight of him pressed into me, his tip right there at the entrance. "You would have so much cock, you'd get tired of it."

Once upon a time, that might have been a threat. Now? It was a promise I found myself craving. "Impossible," I said as his back muscles clenched beneath my fingers. His dark gaze held me riveted as I kept teasing us. His dick was so fucking hot, and the skin velvet beneath my fingers. I kind of wanted to jack him off until he came in my hand.

At the same time...I wanted more. When only a breath separated our lips, I tilted my hips and angled him as he lifted his own. When he clasped my face and kissed me until I had no breath of my own left, he sank into me with one full thrust.

One of us groaned. Maybe both of us. The kiss turned deeper, more drugging, and I was seeing spots for lack of air, but I didn't want to let him go. I stole little gasps every time he shifted his head or moved to change the angle of the kiss.

With a growl, he surged deeper into me. His balls slapped against my skin as he rocked faster and harder. It was a brutal pace and I relished the challenge of meeting it.

The thrusts promised pain; they hit so hard, and I wanted more for pleasure was raking over my nerves. "You feel so good," I whispered, and he let out a growl.

"You have no fucking idea how good you feel," he uttered through gritted teeth. "Sweet, tight little cunt, taking my cock so fucking well. I want to fill you up, fuck you until you can't walk, then roll you over and fuck you again. Look at how good you take me..."

The litany of words acted like an aphrodisiac, and I writhed every single strike he scored. The scrape of his teeth, the burn of his beard, and the hot sucking kisses just added to the streaks of fire racing through my system.

What might have been languid heat when we first began to kiss had turned into white-hot tension, coiling tighter and tighter. The snap—it was right there, and when it finally burst, I came on a scream that he tried to smother in another kiss.

Only the brutal pace didn't cease. If anything, he lifted me, pressing both of my thighs back so he could hook my legs. Then hands to the bed, he shifted so he could rock into me at a furious pace. The angle let him watch himself slide in and out, and I dug my nails into his shoulders as I shuddered.

I wanted to watch, and at the same time, my vision white-edged as the pressure became too much, too intense… "I can't…"

"You can," he growled, twisting his hips with every thrust, which robbed me of speech. "Look at you fitting me like the hottest glove. Beautiful cunt, swallowing my cock with every thrust. You can take me, Swan. You can…"

Head thrown back, I screamed as I held onto him and he powered me right through the orgasm unfurling in my system. The force was beyond exquisite. Even when I thought I should beg him to stop, when it was too much, I struggled to hold on.

Fresh tears hit my cheeks as another scream broke free. He fisted my hair and slammed his mouth down, fusing his lips to mine as his hips stuttered. The first hot pulse of his release seemed to ignite another inside of me, new flames to lick up every last drop of passion.

How long we hung there suspended, I didn't know, and I didn't care. His kisses turned slower, lazier, but no less profound. We were bound together, his cock hot and tight inside me. Then he rolled us over and slid his hands to my hips, keeping me in place.

"Sit up," he ordered, and I rose on shaking limbs to look down at him. "Squeeze me inside you…" Trembling, I flexed around him. The spasming of my inner walls seemed to make it even harder, and I swore we were soaking his bed as cum leaked out around him.

He was still stiff, not all the way hard, yet still there. "That's my girl," he said, tightening his grip on my hips and then moving me. Pleasure was sharp and bright, almost overwhelming when I was still shuddering. "That's my girl, be good for me, take me more and we're going to get there again, you and me…you're going to come until you can't take it, and then I'm going to get you another cock to fill you."

The difference between flying in the silks and flying in his arms was all in the control. Jasper lunged upward, his mouth latching onto my breast as he sucked a nipple against his teeth. He thrust up even as he ground me down, and I let go. Flying in bed or in the air—it was all freedom, and he wasn't kidding when he said he'd catch me.

Still, I held on tight, because I wouldn't let him fall either. My cunt was clenching so tight, he had to really work us together to get the friction we both wanted.

"Mine," he whispered, kissing the Vandals tattoo between my breasts. The next time I shattered, I flew apart without a care in the world. I was absolutely his.

And he was mine.

# CHAPTER 16

*VAUGHN*

*a*fter Ms. Stephanie's funeral, the last thing I wanted to do was attend another. More than a dozen people died at the shop. Two more survivors weren't expected to make it. Of the fifteen inside, only one was hanging in there. The guys wouldn't let me go to the memorial services alone, nor would Dove.

While I didn't want to invite trouble, I had made an appearance and left flowers. I'd spoken to more grieving families and friends. I wasn't alone in my guilt over the incident, though I was responsible, unlike the other tattoo artists who hadn't been working that night.

The tattoo shop had been burned down because of me. Because I had a space there. A soft hand feathered down my back as Dove settled on the sofa behind me.

"You are really cutting into my brooding time," I teased, and her smile grew. A couple of days earlier, her smile had not been present. Her tears had threatened to break my heart. It had taken her time to rally and to tell us about what happened to her mother.

As much as I hated to admit it, we'd asked Milo if he thought she was lying after Jasper took Dove into his room to sleep. He'd won the rock, paper, scissors, but we'd all checked on them.

"You can brood," she said, sliding her arm over my shoulders. I slid mine around her waist and just towed her down into my lap.

"Yeah?" I said, curling my arms around her. I had burns in places, and they were itching where they'd begun to heal. I'd survive. When the skin was done healing, I could cover some up with new ink.

"Yeah," she said, tilting her head back to rest on my shoulder. She stretched her legs out along mine, using me as a chair, but honestly, she had more than enough room to sprawl. "I just don't want you to feel like you have to brood alone."

Pressing my lips to her temple, I rubbed a slow circle over her stomach. The ink that I'd put there needed more work. We'd talked about it. Talked about her arms too. I was going to have to get new equipment. Another long sigh escaped me. She didn't say anything, didn't push me, or even ask me any questions.

What she did was relax into me, and some of the tension leached out of my bones as I held her. The steady thrum of her heart, the faint floral of her perfume—or maybe that was just her shampoo. Her hair was soft and pulled into a ponytail that spilled over one shoulder.

The length of her hair was something I'd begun to enjoy, especially when she rode me and it spilled down over her breasts. That thought sent a bolt of lust right to my dick, and while I'd never not be turned on by her, I was also content just to sit here and hold her.

The television was on, but I'd muted the sound while I watched the news, which segued into daytime soap operas. I'd even forgotten those things existed. Dove didn't make any moves to change it, nor did I. She stroked my arm gently, her touch so light it was barely there and at the same time, it settled something in my soul.

We got about thirty minutes of just quiet, being together. My dick was getting increasingly interested in the ass pressing into me, when the door to the suite opened to let Liam in. Goddamn, he looked like hell.

"Hey," I said, leaning forward even as Dove did.

"Hey," he said, stripping off his jacket as he crossed to the sofa and dropped onto it next to me. "You mind if I..."

When he motioned to Dove, I opened my arms and she turned, already sliding over to straddle his lap and wrap her arms around him. It was like watching a decaying orbit as they collapsed into each other. Her strength in that tiny body was easy to overlook—if you didn't recognize the true power she wielded.

Dove could handle us—*all* of us. While I'd never once imagined that the love of my life would be the love of our lives, it made so much damn sense. My brothers loved her every bit as much as I did. She loved us. Not sharing her seemed anathema. Even if I still wondered how it would all work out in the end, I wasn't *afraid* of how it would turn out.

No, I was more curious.

"I'm here," she whispered. The words carried so much weight I shifted in my seat to put a hand on his shoulder. Liam's arms flexed as he held her. The lack of bruises on his hands and face were as telling as the way he held her.

We all had our coping strategies. Liam needed a fight. The fact he wasn't taking any on said a lot more about his worry for recent events. Collateral damage was a real thing, and we were moving targets.

Liam shuddered, then lifted his head to meet my gaze as he rested his cheek against her hair. The shadows under his eyes were pronounced, so was the red in them. Grief was a fucking bitch.

When he held out a hand, I gripped it and then Dove curled in his lap to put her hand over ours. I met the soft brown of her eyes as she stroked her thumb over my hand. The silence we'd been enjoying earlier wrapped around all three of us. The long sigh Liam released clearly echoed my earlier one.

Yeah, grief fucking sucked.

"Thank you, Hellspawn," he said in a gruff voice. She lifted her head, and that smile was everything. She combed her fingers through his hair.

"Can I do anything else?"

"Already doing it," he said, releasing my hand and dropping it to rest on her hip. "You're smiling, you're safe, and you're where I can reach you."

Couldn't really argue with the logic.

"I wish I could do more," she admitted.

"We all do," I said, even as the door opened to let Kellan, Jasper, and Freddie in.

I lifted my chin even as my phone buzzed. Before I could even pull out my phone, Kel said, "That's from me. Calling a meeting. Doc is checking on your mom right now, Sparrow. Milo is waiting for him, and they'll be down here."

She twisted in Liam's lap, her expression tightening even as she tensed. "Is Mom okay?"

"She's fine," Jasper said, his tone soothing. "Doc's doing what Doc does. You know he likes all his tests."

Unfortunately, the gentle words didn't settle her. If anything, they seemed to make her more anxious. Liam frowned as she climbed out of his lap.

"Maybe I should..."

"Boo-Boo," Freddie said, holding out his hand. I wasn't the only one who released a breath when she took it and let him tug her to him. "Your mother is fine. Doc will tell you if anything is wrong. So will Milo…"

"I haven't seen her since…"

He shrugged. "She's your mother, and she'll deal with it." Freddie's lack of fucks where Moira Sharpe was concerned was not an uncommon feeling. Milo had briefed us. I still didn't buy she knew nothing. Maybe she didn't want to know, and maybe she convinced herself.

Dove believed her though, and for that—

"Sparrow," Kellan said in a firm tone that demanded her attention. "You can see her after the meeting. Right now, I need your head here and in this discussion."

Fresh worry flashed over her face, and Freddie actually glared at Kellan. "Dude, there are ways to say we need to talk that don't involve doom and gloom."

"Yes," Kellan said, his tone still stern even if his expression softened. "I also promised Sparrow I wouldn't cut her out. There are things we need to decide, and that means I need her focused here and not on whatever—"

"Whatever her mother has to say right now," Jasper finished it almost smoothly, which was weird, and I wasn't the only one staring at him. He smirked. "What? Just because I'm usually an unreasonable jackass doesn't mean I don't know how to be reasonable."

"Uh-huh," I said, even as Kellan snorted.

"Who are you, and what have you done with Jasper?" Freddie demanded, his mock scowl adding weight to the question.

Dove laughed. The musical sound cracked some of the tension and pulled a swift, if sad, smile to Liam's face. Hell, even I was grinning despite myself. Her humor faded, however, when the door opened to let in Doc and Milo.

Her knuckles went white where she held Freddie's hand and I'd be damned, but he stood right there, bracing with her.

"She's fine," Doc said, clearly reading the room as he focused on Dove. "Little Bit...your mother is fine. She's still tired and undernourished. I'm worried about the depression, yet I'm not as worried about her mental state."

"That said, we've locked the door on her room." Milo folded his arms, his jaw set in a way that said he was ready for battle.

Son of a bitch, if Dove...

"Good," she said, and the single word jerked all of our attention. The severe melancholy and sobbing had come because of something the woman said, but I didn't think it had alienated Dove. "I don't want her to do anything fool-ish, and we need to focus on—dealing with Uncle Fuckbucket."

The name was funny, even though none of us laughed.

"Where is Rome?" Dove asked, and as if she'd summoned him, he opened the door. Paint spatter covered his hands and there was a bruise on his face. "What happened?"

Liam was up and across the room before Dove even got there. He eyed his brother even as Rome ignored him and turned to Dove.

"Rope slipped." He showed her his hand and I wasn't the only one who frowned. "Hit the wall."

She touched the side of his face, but Liam narrowed his eyes. "You aren't supposed to be running around by yourself."

When she wrapped herself around him, Rome just flipped his brother off. That actually pulled a laugh from Liam and the bubbling tension in the room dialed down.

"I'll get some ice," Dove offered, but Rome shook his head.

"Doesn't hurt." Then he looked at Kellan. "Why are we meeting?"

Kellan sighed. The rapid-fire shifts in everyone's mood

were a real testament to how fucked up everything was right now.

"Little Bit," Doc said, holding out a hand to her. "Maybe we should…"

"Nope," Kellan said, shaking his head. "She stays."

He and Doc essentially shared a glare, and it ratcheted the tension up.

"She doesn't need to discuss *this*."

"Man," Jasper said, swinging right into the fight. I scrubbed a hand over my face. "You don't just get to decide what she can handle or not. Kel's right. She's a Vandal, she stays. This involves *all* of us."

"Maybe it doesn't—"

A whistle split the air and pulled everyone around. Freddie lowered his fingers from his lips. "How about we stop bitching about what Boo-Boo does or doesn't get to do? This sucks for all of us. Kel said she needs to be here, and unless *she* wants to skip out, she stays."

"Agreed," Milo interjected, and even Dove twisted to stare at him. His expression softened for her. "You proved your point over and over. This is your life. We are your family. We do this together, or we're not doing it at all."

"That's not totally true," she said, giving Rome a squeeze before she moved over to Doc and just like she had with Liam and me, she leaned into him when he wrapped his arms around her.

Taking care of us by letting us take care of her. I admired that.

"It's as true as it needs to be, Ivy," Milo told her. "The uncle is dead one way or another. Your father is too. You don't have to do a thing."

Woah… "He knew?"

And I was on my feet. I wasn't the only one. That was the confirmation we'd been waiting for, but my gaze wasn't on

Milo but on Dove. Her eyes dipped before she closed them, and Doc tightened his arms around her as she sighed.

"We have confirmation?" That was from Liam. "Because we're still trying to track the fuckbucket down, but that dickwad is in Vegas."

She gave a little jerk at the description, but Kellan's aggrieved look shut everyone up. "One, we don't have *absolute* confirmation yet." He glanced at all of us before looking at Dove. "Your mother wants to believe he didn't know about what was done to her or you."

"I know," she said softly, almost too softly. It was Doc's expression that grew more foreboding.

"I think she's fooling herself," Milo said, and like Kellan, he gentled the tone down. "I think it's easier to lie to herself about it than admit maybe he knew and didn't care."

"However we don't know that for sure," she said. "And I don't know how to find out for certain."

"I do," I said, even as Liam, Doc, and Jasper echoed the same two words.

Dove glanced at all of us then focused on Kellan. "You want to go get him. You want to talk to him directly."

He nodded. "It might be simpler to put a bullet in his head." Gentle didn't mean he was going to softball the info. "But we need to know what he knows and what he did."

"He could know where Uncle Fuckbucket is."

Freddie cracked his knuckles. "He could know more than that, Boo-Boo."

This was why Kellan wanted her here. We were going to find this out, although she did deserve to have a say in it and if she wanted to face him.

Well, she got to have that call too.

"So, the first question," Kellan continued. "The most important one... how involved do you want to be in this?"

# CHAPTER 17

"Hold up," Lunchbox said, putting a hand up to keep from going any further. Granted, I was just coming out of the clubhouse and into the warehouse, but what the hell? "Sorry, Doc didn't say you were going anywhere today, and we don't have coverage."

We don't have…

"I'm not going anywhere. I just needed to get out of the clubhouse and walk around." That meant walking out here in the warehouse. I was fine with that. Increased security meant no leaving without at least two others and not leaving the clubhouse unarmed.

I wasn't leaving the warehouse, and I was definitely armed.

"Excuse me." Without waiting for him to agree, I circled around him and set off on a circuit of the warehouse interior. No trucks were being loaded or off-loaded. After what happened to both the auto body shop and the tattoo place, no one was allowed inside the warehouse who hadn't been cleared by the guys.

Mickey's friends were an exception. Though technically, he had cleared them so I guess the guys cleared them. Swinging my arms, I set out at a brisk pace to do circles. The awareness of being watched crept over me and the steady thump of shoes to concrete told me I had a tail.

Cutting a glance back over my shoulder, I eyed Lunchbox. "You can see me just fine without actually following me."

"Sure can," he said with the barest hint of a drawl. "I can absolutely see you. But I can't intercept anyone trying to get at you if I'm more than five feet away."

That almost made me trip. Who was going to—you know what, stupid questions got stupid answers. We'd already had one invasion. If someone busted in one of the doors and I was more than five feet away—dammit, he had a point.

With that, I just nodded and returned to my walk. Restlessness was like a fever in my blood. Inside, I had to deal with my mother, who had discovered she was not allowed to leave. I'd tried to talk to her, but that hadn't gone as well as I would have liked.

Milo and Kellan were both of the opinion that she was hiding something. I wanted to argue with them, fuck did I want to argue with them. I wanted to dispute every single thing. At the same time—

The slam of a door startled me and I pivoted, but it wasn't the door to the clubhouse at all. It was one of the outer doors.

"Gracey," Alphabet called, his voice almost aggrieved as he followed her inside. Honestly, I hadn't seen much of these guys at all. Instead of answering him, the dark-haired woman marched straight toward me—no, she was marching toward Lunchbox.

"Grace," he rumbled, turning to face her. She hit him hard

enough that the slap almost echoed in the warehouse. I winced for her, and he didn't do anything except look to the right after she struck.

Alphabet huffed as he caught up to them, but she darted around Lunchbox and stalked right toward me. "Grace Black," she said, sticking her hand out. "I know you. You're Emersyn Sharpe."

That was fantastic. I eyed her then her hand.

"Goddammit, Gracey," Alphabet swore, before he shot me a crooked grin.

"Ignore them," she said, determination in her smile. "I intend to." I took her hand and shook it slowly.

"Nice to meet you." It was hard to ignore the two men practically towering over us, and Lunchbox wasn't keeping a five-foot distance anymore. Letting go of her, I pivoted to walk again.

I wasn't sure what to make of Grace when she fell into step with me. The guys backed off a fraction, but their low conversation spoke volumes for their annoyance.

"Sorry to stage a raid on your—what exactly are we doing?" Like me, she was dressed in comfortable clothes, though I had on leggings and she wore jeans. She was also in pumps, but I had on ballet flats. It was more just to keep my bare feet off the warehouse floor.

"Walking," I said. "And I don't mind. I already had company." I glanced at her again, then focused my gaze forward. "I'm sorry if we met before or if I should know you. You look familiar, but…"

"We haven't really met," Grace said, folding her arms. Her long, raven hair had been pulled back into a braid, emphasizing her delicate cheekbones and porcelain features. "Well, we met briefly when we got here, but that was before the funeral, and it's been a little busy."

I nodded.

"I recognized you because I've been to one of your shows."

Ah.

"And I probably look familiar because I did the campaign for Enchanté last year." The minute she said the name, I could almost see the ads from the magazines that ended up in my dressing room on the road.

"You're a model," I said unhurriedly. "I never knew your name—sorry."

"It's fine. It's the face that sold." It was kind of funny that Grace shrugged rather gracelessly. "I guess you're not performing anymore?"

"Taking a break." Wasn't sure if I would tour again, really. Though the guys had said we could make it work. With everything else right now? Touring was the last thing I should be doing. "I'm guessing you're not modeling?"

"No, at least not right now. I might go home—eventually. Nonetheless, I want to find my sister, and these brutes are certain someone is looking for me."

Lunchbox sighed, though Alphabet said nothing.

"I'm sorry." We all had problems, but I was sorry to hear about hers. "Where is your sister?"

"I think she was taken by the same type of people who took—"

"Little Bit," Mickey said, the interruption stopping both of us. I spun, not having expected him but then caught Alphabet sliding a phone away. Eyes narrowed, I flicked a look from him to Mickey. "Can we talk?"

Well, the question was an improvement. I glanced at Grace, who was staring at Lunchbox and Alphabet with a quiet kind of fury. Neither of them looked remotely chastised by her anger.

"You okay if I step away?" Because, yeah, I didn't know

her, but I wanted to know if she was in trouble and if Mickey's friends were the source.

"I'll be fine," she said. "It was nice to meet you again. Maybe *next* time, some people can mind their own business and let us walk."

"You are our business, Sweet Cheeks," Lunchbox said. "And so is the little dancer. Now stop proving how difficult you can be, and let these two go talk."

As Grace rolled her eyes, there was almost a hint of a smile. She might be irritated about whatever was going on between them but was also having fun.

"I'd like that—being a little dancer and all—I need my little walks."

Grace actually grinned as Lunchbox huffed out a sigh. I just turned to join Mickey, and when he offered me an arm, I tucked my arm through his. He didn't waste any time heading back toward the clubhouse.

I stole a look back to where Grace faced off with Alphabet, while Lunchbox split his attention between them and where Mickey and I were walking. He probably wouldn't relax until we were back inside.

Mickey said nothing until we were in the kitchen. The debris from the fresh hole that now looked out on the living room had been cleared away. The guys had also taken the first steps toward framing it. It still served as a reminder of Milo losing his shit after I told him about my uncle.

Once we were in the kitchen however, Mickey hesitated and I studied him. We hadn't talked much since the funeral. He'd been trying to take care of things at the clinic, his sister's house, and a whole host of other tasks that were pulling him away.

With a sigh, he finally turned to face me. It wasn't quite resignation that crossed his features. If anything, it was more like he braced for a fight.

"If you're about to tell me I would be better off some-where else, just don't." Folding my arms, I leaned back against the counter. "Please. I don't want to have that fight with you, but I will."

Surprise flickered over his expression. The tautness of his jaw seemed to go to granite. "Little Bit…"

I raised my eyebrows, waiting. Because if he really intended to try and persuade me to run away and hide, we would have a problem.

While I agreed with the rules and the precautions, I refused to run away from them. I refused to run away from any of them. Not again.

Rather than continue his sentence, he raked a hand through his hair and stalked across the room to me. Cupping my face in his hands, he dipped his head and then his lips were on mine. Hunger and heat swept through me at the sweet possession in his kiss. Even as I pushed up on my toes, he gripped my hips and lifted me to sit on the counter so we were more eye to eye.

The kiss demanded everything and gave more. We were both panting when he rested his forehead to mine. "You make me crazy, Little Bit."

"Hmm, I think you were crazy long before I got here," I said, keeping the teasing light. "You just can't hide it from me."

His snort pulled a real grin to my lips. "I want you safe, you know that, right? It's not about making you leave? Or sending you away? The last thing I want to do is put you so far away I can't see you…"

"And at the same time, it's exactly what you want." I locked my gaze onto his eyes. The light brown color held almost too much darkness, or maybe that was my imag-ination.

"I just lost Steph," he said, breaking my heart all over

again. "If something happened to you…" He shook his head, cupping my face. "That's why I called my team. It's why they're watching you."

I was aware of that, intimately, in fact. I couldn't go anywhere without one or, most of the time, two of them trailing me and whichever of the guys I was with.

"And I accept that you guys need to know I'm safe. It's why the others aren't fighting you on this, either." Not that they hadn't been giving his guys some severe stink eye. Liam didn't like them. He didn't *say* anything specific, but his level of vigilance rose when they were around.

Jasper was the same, while Kellan was more circumspect. Rome and Vaughn didn't seem to care one way or the other, but Freddie remained cautious and wary. Milo's reactions, on the other hand, held far more curiosity. Then again, his relationship with Mickey was a lot more fraternal than mine, so…

Flattening a hand on either side of me, Mickey tilted his head. "You're not going to bend on this, are you?"

"Nope. Unless there's a compelling argument for why I need to go." I pressed a hand to his chest, right over his heart. "We're still figuring some of this out and I know you want to keep me safe. All of you do, and I want the same thing for you. If I thought that leaving would protect you…"

His gaze leveled. "You going back to that monster wouldn't do anything except hurt you."

"I'm never going back to him," I said. "Not willingly." Had I said that aloud before? The words were sharp, new, and tasted acrid on my tongue. "I know I'm still figuring things out with everyone…though the one thing we've all agreed on —" I hesitated. "All of us except you, it would seem, is that you can't just hide me or send me away. I belong *here*."

That earned me a bland look.

I shrugged. "You're the only one who keeps talking about

sending me away..." And that hurt more than I wanted to admit. "You bring it up to everyone who isn't me, too." The guys weren't having any of it anymore, not even Milo. "They're planning how to get to Vegas and back, with my father... and whether any of us should go."

"Or if we use my guys for it," Mickey admitted with a sigh. "Little Bit, putting aside that last piece...I don't want to send you away."

I would have protested, but he pressed a finger to my lips.

"I don't *want* to do it. I worry that if I don't fight for it, fight for you, something else will happen." He moved his hands to my wrists, lifting my arms so we could both look at the scars along them. "You have suffered so goddamn much...these are just the scars we see."

"But you've seen the other scars." The ones inside.

He nodded, and I sighed. "I think you're one of the strongest people I've ever met, nevertheless it would kill me if something happened to you again. Especially if we could have prevented it by not being selfish with you."

"How is it not selfish to put my safety above yours? Or theirs?"

"What if I could persuade Freddie to..." Thankfully, he didn't finish the question. "That isn't going to work, is it?"

"No," I told him, even as I licked my lips. "They're my family. This is my home." Goddamn, those words felt so good to say. "I want you to be my family too."

Surprise flickered over his face.

"But I won't be hidden away like some victim who can't lift her head or take the light. I've been a victim my whole goddamn life." Even before Milo's and my mother died from the sound of it. I was helpless to protect my brother; he sacrificed everything for me. "I refuse to be a victim anymore. Was I raped? Yes. Was I molested for years? Yes." Every word burned in my throat. "Have I tried to escape before? Yes. Am I terrified of what he will do to all of you in his sick little quest? Yes."

Mickey's eyes fixed on mine as I raised my hand to touch his face.

"The scars say we survived, Mickey, so stop looking at me like a victim." I needed this from him if he could offer me nothing else. "Please stop treating me like that. Please—let me be your family and your partner and a Vandal...just like you. I need to protect you too."

Eyes closed, he leaned into my palm. "Goddammit, Little Bit." Then his mouth was on mine, burning me up from the deeper possession. Dragging his head away, he stared at me again, and I was gasping for another taste. "Do you trust me?"

Did I? It had been rocky for a while. I could admit that. His rejection and the harsh words had driven the wedge that the time with my uncle and Pinetree had blown wide and left me raw.

I had forgiven him. I adored him. But did I trust him?

Unnerving as it was, the answer was right there. "Yes."

"Will you come with me?"

"Right now?" I blinked. We weren't supposed to...

"Yes. We'll have backup, and the guys won't have to worry. I promise."

"Will I be able to come back?" Please don't be a trap. Please don't be a trap.

"You can go wherever you want," he promised. "I'll kick down the damn doors myself if I have to. I won't cage you, Little Bit. No matter how damn much I want you hidden and safe, I won't."

"Then I'll go with you." The words were barely out before he crushed me to him in a hug that squeezed out my breath. He leaned away and palmed his phone before he gave me a once-over.

"Jacket, heavier clothes. Something to hide the hair."

"Sunglasses?" I teased, and he grinned.

"That too, and Little Bit," he said as he lifted me off the counter and touched the gun I had tucked into the holster at the small of my back, "armed is good."

I grinned. "I can handle that."

"I know you can. You're my best girl."

Okay, that wasn't fair because a delicious shiver went right through me. "Oh, does that come with a reward?" I couldn't help the tease. Course, then he gave me the slowest smile that threatened to strip me right out of my clothes. If Milo caught me fucking Mickey in the kitchen, he might never get over it.

"Go get what I told you to get, and we'll see." Oh, that sounded good. I pressed a hand to his chest and nuzzled a kiss to his jaw. He cupped my nape and held me there for a moment, before giving me a gentle shove. "Go. Or I'll be delaying us by eating you out on that table and the guys might get the idea I want company with you."

Whew. I blew out a breath because that was a most tempting threat. "I'll be right back."

The scorching heat of his gaze followed me all the way to the stairs and lingered over me as I took them two at a time. Kellan and Jasper were in the suite talking when I let myself back in...talking and planning.

"Hey guys," I said as I dropped a kiss on Kellan's lips before turning to Jasper. "I'm heading out with Mickey..."

# CHAPTER 18

*DOC*

*V*oodoo and Bones followed us when we left the warehouse. I wasn't in my truck but in a car Alphabet had secured for me. The fact it was a muscle car and had a standard shift helped settle my nerves. I liked having the control. As with the other vehicles Liam had been bringing in, the car was armored and reinforced with bullet-resistant glass, among other fun features.

The kids understood conflict and protecting the territory we'd claimed, as well as protecting each other. My guys understood war and that we were already in the middle of several engagements. Blood had been spilled, and we would be spilling more before this was over.

"Tell me you're not taking her somewhere to stash her," Kellan commanded when he came down while she changed. "If this is an end run to do what you wanted to do with her, that's not going to fly."

I sighed. Irritation rifled through me, though I could hardly fault him. "I thought about it," I told him and ignored the cold-eyed stare. Kellan had every right to be protective. They all did. He was every bit as in love with her as the others were...

As I was.

So I could respect his need to ask the question. Even the need to remind me that this wasn't my call. He was a damn good leader, but I would never take my orders from him.

"As I said," I continued before he could rip into me on the subject, "I thought about it. Little Bit will never go for it. While I might be able to live with her hating me as long as she was alive and in one piece, I can't live with hurting her."

Sending her away would *hurt* her.

No matter how much I wanted her as far away from the hell coming for all of us—coming for her. That was the point. It was coming for *her*. To *take* her.

"So no, I want some time with her." Time to talk to her— to really speak to her in a way that I hadn't. "You guys also *need* some time to hammer out the plans. Lunchbox and Alphabet will be here. Talk to Alphabet about what you need. He'll get it made."

"No questions asked?" Kellan said, observing me. His prior tension seemed to have eased at my admission, but I shrugged.

"He'll ask what he needs to know. They're aware of the sensitivity of the situation," I said, casting a quick look up the stairs, "as well as the risks. If he can't do it, he'll let you know. If he needs more, he'll tell you that too."

He nodded once. "If you plan to keep her out all night, text me. I'd prefer you had backup for both of you, even if you want privacy."

Rubbing the back of my neck, I tilted my head to stare at the ceiling. "I'll let you know."

"Doc…" Kellan said, a glimmer of sympathy in his eyes. "This isn't forever."

"No, it is forever," I told him as I straightened. "She is forever."

That was the admission I'd been avoiding for months. Pushing her away had seemed the thing to do for her and for Milo. In the beginning, before I knew who she was, I'd been willing to deal with their reactions to getting her away if that was what she wanted.

In all of this, I'd been fighting them, fighting her, and, most of all, fighting myself. I locked gazes with Kellan.

"If she is forever, that means we are." That meant we had to find a way to balance this relationship, all of us with her. He blew out a breath and then chuckled.

Of all the reactions I expected him to have, *laughter* wasn't where I would have gone. "You think this is funny?"

"I think you *are*," Kellan told me with an almost *smug* smile before he clapped me on the shoulder. "We already knew she was forever and that we would have to share. It works though, because it means we're all invested in protecting her from everyone—even ourselves."

That was a warning.

"You're a bit of a shit, Kellan Traschel."

His grin grew. "Yes, I am. Except remember—she comes first, Doc. I like you. You're family. But I *love* her." Despite the smile, his expression had gone deadly serious. "Don't do anything stupid with her again. You made your mistake where she was concerned. You don't get to do it again."

The warning I accepted for what it was. They would put her first like I needed to put her first and not the way I'd been doing it before. No, I needed to not only put her first but give her the say, even if it went against the grain to let her risk herself.

"Agreed," was all I said. He didn't need platitudes or

explanations. He wasn't asking for them either. What he wanted was for me to understand the rules.

I could live with it.

Any other conversation would have to wait because she descended the steps with a baseball cap over her hair and her braid sticking out the back. She also had on jeans, sneakers, and a sweatshirt that practically swallowed her.

The fact her lips were swollen and her cheeks flushed told me that Kellan's absence had been noticed, so the guys bought us some time. Lucky little bastards. She grinned at Kellan and paused to give him a kiss.

"We're all good?"

"Yes, we are," he said, turning her to check the gun holster under the sweatshirt. It was accessible, but the shirt could get in the way. I just needed to make sure nothing demanded that she'd need it.

Her huff of laughter drew my attention to where he pushed the shirt up higher. He adjusted the holster then the shirt. It would make it less likely for her to get stuck in the hem of the shirt. Then he pulled her back to him and murmured in her ear.

Amusement surfaced from beneath the irritation. Kellan wrapped an arm around her and murmured in her ear. The pointed look he gave me over her head reminded me that forever meant sharing her forever too.

Yeah. I got the message.

I nodded, and he grinned before turning toward me. "Be good, Sparrow. I'll see you and Doc later." The last was another pointed line. Just reinforced my opinion that taking Voodoo and Bones was preferable to the guys. I wanted the time with her, and they were right to protect her.

However, she didn't need to be protected from me.

"Where are we going?" The soft question pulled my attention back to the car. I had my head on a swivel, scanning traffic as we were en route to the apartment.

"My place," I said. "Sorry, I just wanted you to myself for a few hours."

"Why are you apologizing?" Curiosity filled her gaze, and I had to drag my attention off her and back to the road. We didn't need a car wreck and we were still in the open.

"Because—" I sighed. "You know, Little Bit? Can we wait to do this back at the apartment where I can hold you and talk to you?"

She settled her hand on my thigh; her touch was a brand I wanted to add to my ink. That side was bare. Maybe I'd start by inking her on me, making the change she'd already wrought permanent.

My phone rang as we neared the complex. I answered with one press of a button on the steering wheel.

"You're clear," Voodoo said. "Bones wants to sweep the apartment before you go in."

"Thanks, guys."

"You got it," Bones said. "You locking in for the day or until tomorrow?"

I cut a look at her. "To be decided, but the guys will feel better if we get Little Bit back tonight. We'll plan on that for now."

"Sounds good," Bones said. "Voodoo is dropping me off. Take a drive around the block."

"Copy that." I hung up, then glanced at Little Bit, who watched me with a small smile on her lips. "What?"

"I dunno, you're different when you talk to them. Kind of like you're different still when you talk to the guys or to Milo —though I think there are real differences in how you handle Milo versus the others."

"Probably because I have different relationships with

them." Kind of obvious, but she didn't comment on that. Instead, she squeezed my thigh. We'd almost completed the circle when the phone rang.

"Go," I said when I answered.

"You're clear," Bones said. "Alphabet swept the place for bugs when we got here, and I just did another electronic sweep. You're clean there too."

Little Bit gave a little start, but I covered her hand with mine. "Thanks, guys. Going radio silent unless there's an emergency."

"Enjoy yourselves," Bones said. "We'll be here, keeping watch."

They kept watch as I parked, and Little Bit waited for me to get out and circle the car to open her door. A soft smile flirted with her lips as I tucked her under my arm and got her inside. Weirdly, I hadn't been at the apartment much in the last few weeks.

Not since Freddie went home. As it was, a forgotten blanket lay on the sofa. The pillow he'd been using was also still at the head. The kitchen was clean and all the dishes were done. The interior smelled a bit musty, more from the air not moving.

I kicked on the air conditioner to get the fan on so the air would circulate. In the kitchen, I pulled out a couple of beers and popped the bottles open before heading back to the living room.

She wasn't...

"Little Bit?"

"I'm back here," she called. "I was going to use the bathroom, and then I got nosy."

The bluntness of that admission made me smile. But the sight of her sprawled on my bed wearing little more than her bra and panties stopped me dead. The gun was on the side table, and she was sprawled in the middle of the black comforter like it had been laid out for her.

Honestly, it probably had been. Crossing the room, I nudged the door shut with my foot and set the beers down before I unstrapped my holster and settled it on the nightstand.

Like this, I could see her Vandals ink and the ribbon of birds and words on her abdomen. I'd seen them before, but I hadn't really been in a position to appreciate them. And at the funeral, I'd been further interested in fucking her and giving us both a lot of pleasure than just admiring her.

"Hi," she said softly when my gaze reached hers.

"Hey," I said, then eased down onto the edge of the bed. "Comfortable?"

"Maybe," she said, then laughed. "You wanted to talk, so I thought about the few times we've really talked. Clothing was kind of optional."

Nodding slowly, I traced my fingers down her leg. The muscle rippled as she lifted her leg then slid it across my lap. It was easy to forget just how strong she was. Maybe too easy.

"Mickey..."

I flicked a look up at her.

"Whatever it is...I'm not going anywhere."

The corner of my mouth kicked up. "Even when you should cut me loose and kick me to the curb."

"Well," she said, curling her toes against the comforter before sitting up and reaching for one of the beers. "We tried that too. Then you changed your mind."

"Yeah," I said. "Have I apologized for being a bastard to you yet?"

"Yes," she said. "But I won't object to hearing it again."

"Good girl," I murmured as she drank her beer. "Make me work for it."

"You did say..." A blush touched her cheeks. "And a part of me genuinely does want to make you work for it..."

"Let's circle back to that in a minute," I said, running my fingers up and down her leg. "Let me say again how truly, deeply sorry I am for having been a raging jackass at you. Making you come in that bathroom was a moment I really enjoyed until I turned it around and used it to push you away."

Head tilted, she studied me.

"And my greatest regret is I didn't see how badly it hurt you. I thought—a little pain now would be better than a far worse one down the road." Blowing out a breath, I wrapped my hand around her ankle. "Milo had just gotten out of prison, and he was—not in a good place. It shifted the balance all the way around, and you were struggling."

"You chose to put Milo first." No recrimination existed in that sentence.

"Yes and no. Milo and I have a different relationship from the others. It's because I was the one who found you two after your mother died. Milo had been doing everything he could but was struggling, and this little punk kid..." I shook my head. "If you believe nothing else, never ever doubt how much he loves you. Because I have never known anyone as strong as he was back then. I thought I was a badass, but he was looking after you and trying to do all these really adult things while his mother was also dead."

Tears shimmered in her eyes, and I frowned.

"He never cuts himself a break. Even so little, he just...he put you first. You were what was important to him. Then I took you guys to Steph—" That sliced pain right through my chest. "Admitted to her what I'd been doing..."

Running drugs.

"The thing is...every choice he made from that point

forward always took you into account. For some reason, he trusted me. Even when he should have wanted to shoot me for being the guy who brought his mother drugs." Drugs that killed her. "Only he didn't. He trusted me. He listened to me. When he struggled, he came to me. The guy he was when he got out…"

Fuck, he'd been hurting.

"The long and the short of it was that Milo needed me, and the idea of me getting turned on by his baby sister was not something he ever needed to think about. I thought…I knew you didn't want to go home, but I also thought you had opportunities that you could get back to and for a while, that maybe you would go. It would be easier on you if you weren't attached."

"Too late," she whispered, and I sighed. "What about you?"

"What about me?"

"You hurt me to make me go away, to make me let you go…then you couldn't let go."

No. I really couldn't. "Honestly, if I was hurting, then it was my own damn fault and I deserved it."

She took another drink of her beer, then scooted forward until she was straddling my lap. The angle was awkward, but I braced her to ensure she didn't fall.

"You deserve a kick in the ass," she told me. "Then again, you don't deserve to hurt like that."

"A few months ago…" I pointed out and she shrugged.

"That was before. Things have changed."

Yeah. They really had. Or maybe they were how they'd always been, and I just had a sharper, clearer view of it all. Fuck, I had an armful of one of the most gorgeous women I'd ever known, and she was next to naked. The idea of flipping her over and fucking into her was so damn tempting.

"Little Bit…before we go another step, there are some

things you need to know. About me. About my time in the army. About the choices I made. About the choices I may yet make..."

Fearless little thing met my gaze without hesitation. "I'm listening."

# CHAPTER 19

The grooves at the sides of Mickey's mouth deepened as he studied me. This close, it would be hard to conceal even a well-kept secret. I hadn't been kidding when I told him I would fight him if he tried to send me away again. Understanding the need didn't make it hurt any less.

"I wish there were easier ways to tackle this," he admitted, and I leaned back against the arm he'd looped around me.

"Well, in training, if you aren't certain you can pull it off —you warm up and just go for it. You won't know until you try. How about a little motivation?"

I reached behind me and unhooked the bra. It slid down my arms effortlessly. His heated gaze went to my breasts then back up.

"Little Bit," he practically growled. "That is not motivating me to talk."

"I'm not done yet," I teased, and while he might have

wanted me to stay right there, I scooted off his lap before I slid my panties down and off. Since I never got my thong back, I held out the black lace to him. "For your collection."

A real laugh escaped him. Then I picked up my beer and walked over to the chair in the corner of his room. There were some clothes on it, so I picked those up and moved them before taking a seat and crossing one leg over the other.

Mickey tracked my movement then reached for his own beer. "So, my motivation is torture?"

"Well, you say potato. I say potahto." Either way, I grinned at him as I leaned back in the chair. It was oddly comfortable being completely nude while he wasn't, and the distance between us added a kind of erotic buffer.

Shaking off that thought, I focused on him.

Exhaling, I raised my beer to him. "Whenever you're ready."

"You know when I told you I wanted you to make me work for it," he said, with a hint of complaint.

"Too late to change your mind," I told him. "Unless you truly have changed your mind, and then I guess you can persuade me to come over there…"

"No." Shaking his head, he huffed out a laugh then moved to sit on the end of his bed where he could face me. "I want to tell you this. I need to tell you this. Although I don't want how you look at me to change."

"I get that." Maybe more than he realized.

Surprise flickered across his face.

"Telling you wasn't easy… telling any of you wasn't. It seemed to get easier toward the end, but maybe that was me ripping it open enough times to get all the ick out." Turning the bottle around in my hands, I divided my attention between it and him. "I didn't want all of you to look at me differently…"

Worry crept into his gaze along with a ferocious kind of anger. I'd seen that look in all of their faces.

"It did change how you looked at me," I said.

"Little Bit..."

"I'm not saying it changed in a bad way. Though it did change. I used to be able to pretend no one knew what had happened. That...I wasn't dirty or filthy or all the horrible things I've felt over the years. I could pretend that it never happened to me. I convinced myself that pretending was good. If I pretended long enough, it would be real."

"You know none of us think any less of you."

"I do know that...if anything, I see how much you all care about me when it comes up. Even if I didn't see it in your eyes, I'd feel it in how you are all tightening the circle around me. You're all letting me love you, and you're all drowning me in love...it's scary. Nevertheless. I think it's worth it."

He sat forward, bracing his chin on his hand as he stared at me. "You are your brother's sister."

"What?"

"You remember what I said about him being the bravest and the strongest kid I'd ever met?" At my nod, he smiled at me. "You have every ounce of his strength and bravery. Maybe even more. Maybe it's just how you Hardigans are made."

I laughed. "It could be in the name..."

That actually earned me a chuckle. The laughter eased some of the melancholy lingering in the air.

"Do you still want to tell me?" I said, "I didn't mean to make it about me."

"I know but thank you for trying to comfort me. I needed to hear that." Tipping the bottle back, he drained the beer and then stood. Moving to the dresser, he set the empty bottle down. "When I joined the army, I didn't do it because I wanted to save people or because I had any real interest in fighting overseas, or even going to school."

Arms folding, he both looked at me and seemed to be a million miles away all at once.

"I'd been in and out of trouble as a teenager," he admitted. "Once upon a time...my street name was Vandal."

Surprise fluttered through me.

"I was an arrogant, stupid little shit who thought I knew how the world worked. I made money running drugs, getting in and out of scrapes, controlling my little piece of the streets —" He shook his head. "I was just stupid. I didn't recognize that actions have consequences, not until you and Milo paid the price for my choices."

Our mother.

"I'd done a lot of dumb shit, although I'd never gotten anyone killed. Never robbed two kids of their only family... especially after Jeff left."

Jeff...

"Yeah, I knew your dad. I worked for him, too. He left when your mom got too deep into the product. Just walked away from his family, the prick. But the point was, I kept doing my thing and not worrying about who it hurt. When I ended up in front of a judge in the weeks that followed, he gave me a choice. Get my shit together, enlist in the military, and turn it around or face possible conviction and time in jail."

No-brainer on that one.

"Steph kept telling me it wasn't my fault, even if I had contributed. The thing is, I knew the truth even if no one else wanted to admit it. I got my shit together, finished school and headed for boot.

"The next couple of years, I was a model soldier, or at least as model as I could be. I had an issue with authority, but they kicked the shit out of me. I met Voodoo and Bones while I was in training. They came up with me. Alphabet and Lunchbox came along later.

"I discovered that, as long as I kept my mind out there, I wasn't focused on here. Only I still thought about Milo, and visited him when I had the chance. Took him to see that show of yours once when you were eight."

The poster at the clinic.

"But the thing is, no matter whether I was here or I was there, I was still running away. Running to not face what I had done. I could tell myself you were great. Look at you—superstar at eight, with a wealthy family. Milo, he was the kid with the plan. He was gonna be running this city before you knew it...I could keep running."

The tension winding up through me kept me on edge. I half-forgot my beer until the cold bottle touched my thigh and then I put it aside.

"Then came the ambush. I had convinced myself I had it together, and more than half my unit got wiped out in a series of bombings. Nearly got my fire team too. The last thing I remembered was the sound and the burning...pretty sure I screamed too, but that could have been someone else."

I couldn't have looked away if I had tried.

"When I woke up in the hospital, I had nothing, just pain. Burns can kill the nerves if they're bad enough. Except the thing about burns is you can't dress them, not at first, and you have to keep cleaning them so they don't get infected... no amount of pain medication will take that edge off."

I'd seen the burns on him, the scars decorated with tattoos as if to hide the reddened and mottled flesh. It was easy to forget that his scars were as much on the inside as the outside.

"I forgot what life was like without pain. Couple of times, I thought about killing myself. Eating a bullet would be easier, you know." He shrugged. "Never could do it though, and one day, it hit me...I was finally paying those consequences. I burned down your lives..."

"Mickey, no," I started to say, but he gave me a gentle smile.

"It's okay, Little Bit. Really. I wanted to pay that cost. I wanted to pay for the stupidity of my youth. Somewhere between the showers to clean off the dead skin and the treatments to help me keep my limbs, I discovered that I wanted to live. I *wanted* to be better."

Straightening, he stripped off his shirt. I'd seen the scars and the tattoos before.

"That's what these are," he said, motioning to his arm then to his side. The tattoos went all the way down his leg. "They are my commitment to the future, to helping people— to med school, to being a doctor, to stop running, and when I was ready, I came back here."

To Braxton Harbor.

Tossing the shirt aside, he crossed the room to where I sat. "I put away Vandal when I went to boot. I did my best to forget the streets here, to put it away, to bury it all." Once in front of me, he reached down and picked me right up out of the chair.

Sliding my hands around his neck, I leaned into him. The roughness of half his chest was a contrast to the seeming smoothness of the other. The heat spilling off of him wrapped around me, and I shivered as one of my nipples brushed against the rough ridges of the scar tissue.

"I came back here and was going to be Doctor James. No more streets. No more fights. No more crime...nothing. But even running toward something didn't mean I'd stopped running."

I frowned as he brushed his lips to my forehead.

"Then those stupid boys brought this wounded bird to my clinic. Bruised, battered, and so fragile. For the first time in years, Vandal woke up again, and I was ready to take on what hurt you. He wouldn't leave me alone."

"And you offered to help me even when they weren't interested in letting me go." I stroked my hand through his hair. "Then I got out."

"Yeah, and then you decided to come back, all on your own. I couldn't fathom it. Nevertheless, I saw you changing them, or at least them fighting to put themselves back together. I wanted to be near you...then Milo got out, and you know the stupid shit I pulled."

"I remember," I said slowly, marveling at how he stood there, gaze locked on mine.

"I'm sorry again," he murmured, kissing the corner of my mouth. "Because when you left...when you went back to protect everyone, I had no idea how bad it would be for you. When they brought you back..."

I glanced at my arms, and Mickey let out a low sound.

"When they brought you back, and you'd been brutalized and hurt all over again, there was no putting Vandal back in the past. No more running away from him. No more running from any of you—but especially no more running from *you*."

Tears burned in my eyes all over again.

"Little Bit, I'm still a doctor, but I'm also Vandal. I still want to give back, but I refuse to let anyone hurt you *or* them again. I'm in this fight—*all* of it. The guys are here because I needed backup. We needed it. They are going to do what we need them to do..."

Licking my lips slowly, I pressed a hand to his cheek. "I don't want you to do anything you don't want to do."

He turned, carrying me back to the bed. When he set me down, I wasn't quite prepared for the way he followed me. This wasn't the side room at the community church.

This was his bed and he was right there, larger than life

and all in my space. I couldn't glance anywhere that wasn't at him.

"Little Bit, when I say I'm all in, I'm all in. They hurt you first. Then they came after us to hurt you again. It will be my genuine pleasure to absolutely fucking destroy them for you."

A shudder twisted through my system. Those words were as dark and provocative as when Jasper told me they were torturing Eric.

"Has anyone ever told you that bloodthirsty is a good look on you?"

Amusement curved his lips again. "As long as it looks good to you, I don't give a fuck what it looks like to anyone else..."

I shivered.

"It definitely looks good to me."

"Good...now I have a question for you..."

He shifted his hands to my braid and began to loosen it but didn't take his gaze off me. When I licked my lips, he seemed to track the motion, and I half-expected him to kiss me, even though he didn't.

"Question?" I finally managed to push out. It was hard to think and he was undoubtedly getting hard as he pressed against me. The denim was a little rough, but it was also a distinction to the roughness of his skin. I lifted a hand to touch his chest and when I would have hesitated, he nodded.

"You may absolutely touch me, Little Bit." There was something sexy about that permission. I stroked my fingers over the tattoo there, studying the pattern as I teased my fingers over the twists in the scar tissue.

I was kind of petting him, but he didn't seem to be complaining. I lifted my head as he pulled my hair free and combed his fingers through it. "I thought you had a question..."

"How are you feeling right now?" He stared at me intently.

"Physically?"

"That and emotionally—mentally—how are you?"

Drained. Worried. Afraid. Elated. Terrified. Thrilled. Confident.

Safe.

"Loved," I whispered. "I feel loved."

# CHAPTER 20

*EMERSYN*

Shyness feathered through me at the intensity in his eyes. I indulged myself, stroking and petting his shoulders, then his arms. The texture of the scars versus the undamaged skin was so wildly different—his two sides; the healer and the warrior. The poetry wasn't lost on me, nor was the irony. I wanted to explore all of his tattoos. I wanted...

Stretching upward, I pressed my lips to the first image painted over the scars. It looked like armor, shaped over the skin, or maybe his body had become his armor. He slid a hand to my nape, almost supporting me as I traced the ink lines that followed the ridges and scars beneath.

The woodsy combination with his natural scent filled my lungs. I could see Mickey as a mountain man without trying. He had the size, the fierceness—his gentle hands disguised a deeper roughness. I loved all the layers. He let out a groan as I nuzzled kisses, continuing my exploration.

He finally rolled over, and I grinned as he settled me on top of him. Hands gliding down my sides, he chuckled. "I want to fuck you until you scream," he said. "Slide into that slick little pussy, fill you up, then fuck you again. You are so goddamn beautiful, Little Bit."

Heat scalded my skin at the compliments. "I want you to fill me up," I told him, tracing my fingers around his nipples. The one on his right puckered, but not the one on the left.

Nerve damage.

I dipped my head, pushing my hair out of the way so I could tease and lap at the responsive nipple before paying homage to the unresponsive one. The striations under his tattoos made my heart ache. More, this close, the individual nuances in the armor-like pattern made more sense, and I lifted my head to study it.

"It's a dragon..." There were the beginnings of a head there, eyes barely slit open as if the dragon was asleep. Although the pattern of the scales distracted you and steered your attention to the shoulder and his arm. When he cupped my face, I caught his hand and kissed the palm before teasing kisses along his arm.

His groan just made me smile as I followed the patterns laid over the scales of the dragon. A hidden rose, a vine of ivy that tugged at my heart, then a lily, and more. They were tucked in some places, subtle. While in others, they were open and more pronounced.

Life bloomed even in adversity. Or maybe even armor couldn't keep the hope from trying to take root. I made it back to his shoulder, then began to kiss my way down his side. I had to lift his arm to trace my fingers over the Samurai inked there.

It took me time to find it, even as he shifted to let me gaze at it. The Vandals tattoo was right there, tucked behind a shoulder blade on the Samurai. His bowed head looked like he was contemplating his state or maybe preparing for war. Armed with a pair of swords still in their sheaths, he might not be seeking the fight, but he was ready for it.

When I got to the denim, I glanced up to find his gaze riveted on me. "If you want those off, you have to promise to sit on my face."

Laughter bubbled up through me at that sexy offer. "You make it sound like that would be a chore."

"Might interrupt your looking…"

Possibly. "Then I'll just have to spend more time sitting on you naked until I've seen it all."

His eyes darkened as my fingers brushed over the button on his jeans.

"Why Alphen?" The lettering over his abdomen was so distinctive.

"Another word for Alfeim," he said, and when I shook my head, his smile grew. "It's the Norse realm for the elves. A land of light…"

"A promise." It clicked into place. The dragon, the armor, the samurai… "Access to the land of light." I was only teasing a little as I scooted back to undo the button on his jeans, then tugged down the zipper.

His cock was better than I remembered it as it strained toward me. The scarring on his side went down to his abdomen, and the skin at the base of his cock showed similar striations. I stroked it from base to tip. While one side still sported crispy hairs, the other was almost curiously naked. Maybe the hair hadn't come back.

Flashes of the pain he'd described scattered through me. Not thinking about it too much, I bent to press a kiss to the too-smooth flesh. His sudden inhale made me flick my gaze upward to where his eyes seemed locked on me. Mouthing little kisses, I traced every part of the area that had been wounded.

At the base of his cock, I tested the differences in skin texture. The scar ended just before the softer, velvety skin of his dick began. However—

"Don't think about it," he ordered, and I stared up to where he'd pushed himself up on his elbows. "And I told you if you wanted them off, you needed to sit that sweet cunt of yours right on my face."

Heat fisted in my chest then spread rapidly into my system. "What if I want to finish exploring first?"

"I'd remind you that you should have said that before you unzipped my jeans." The hint of a growl underscoring those words went straight to my cunt. The temptation to straddle him and sink right down was there.

The need to be disobedient swelled inside of me, kind of like how I wanted his cock. I shifted my stance to move a little to the side, then lapped at the tip of his dick. Droplets of pre-cum were right there, and I rolled my tongue over the head of his cock like it was my own personal treat.

His eyes narrowed, and his expression went stern, but his eyes—they darkened as his pupils seemed to dilate. I teased him with a little shake of my ass. "Little Bit—"

Whatever else he intended to say choked off as I swallowed his cock all the way down my throat. Pleasure suffused me at his groan. Then his hand came down on my ass, not a slap so much as a stroke of his fingers over one cheek.

"You're being a brat," he said, gritting his teeth, and I tilted my head so he could watch me swallow his cock down.

The lift of his hips as he pushed into my throat added another wave of smugness to me. His control unraveled with me. He wasn't pushing me away or trying to keep me from doing what I wanted.

"Right," he grunted, and I laughed when he lifted me up and then settled my knees on either side of his face. "Hello, sweet pussy, what a bad girl you belong to…" I could hardly comment when he licked me from entrance to clit and then sucked my clit against his teeth like it was his mission in life.

The tension ramped up so swiftly that I tried to pull back. But he kept his hands on my hips, holding them still as I lifted my head while he thrust upward at the same time. The pressure to swallow pulled him into my throat, and he scraped his teeth over my clit.

Pain and pleasure sparked in one continuous loop, increasing as he used his tongue and teeth. I moaned around his dick, trying to return the favor and then dragged my mouth off to scream 'cause the orgasm split me open.

He sucked and licked, lapping up all the moisture escaping me. It was embarrassing how much I writhed, riding his tongue at his urging. Then he went back to my clit, and the stimulation drove me right over again.

Submerged in the bliss, I didn't even try to fight the drowning pleasure as I stroked his cock. It was all I could do to keep myself up as I rode his mouth. The slap of his hand against my hip surfaced me.

"Up," he ordered, and I lifted my leg. Moving with more speed than I expected, he eased out from beneath me and then his jeans were gone, and I was left staring at his leg.

Pretty sure I gaped at the gorgeous lion on his thigh. A compass was visible against the line of his ass. And there on his thigh, I tilted my head. It was hard enough to focus through the sensual haze, but was that…

"Little Bit." The command drew my attention back up to Mickey. "Sweet, precious Little Bit." He settled on the bed then patted his thigh. "Come ride me, sweetheart. I want to feel that sweet pussy of yours wrapping around me. You still spasming? Can you feel me licking you up?"

The trace of his tongue over his lips sent another bolt of

heat through me. I scrambled right into his lap and straddled him as he fisted his cock.

"Good girl," he praised, resting one hand on my hip to guide me downwards, and then I was impaling myself on him. His groan was just another caress to my senses. "That's my girl. You're going to ride me until you make yourself come..."

Half-drunk on the softness in his voice, I met his gaze.

"Play with those breasts for me," he instructed. "Pinch your nipples then tease them again. Show me what you like..."

The earlier shyness came back. Was I truly rolling my hips, adding that twist to feel his cock inside me? Could I be so hedonistic as to play with myself...

There was a gentle pinch on my ass. "Now, Little Bit. Show me what you like, make yourself come. I want to feel you milking me. I want you to take every bit of pleasure I can give you..."

I cupped my breasts, rolling and squeezing the nipples. He watched as I met his thrusts. He was thick, but his length seemed to reach deeper into me. Every downward thrust felt like he was going to connect our pelvic bones and lock us together.

Head back, I kept massaging my breasts as he slid two fingers against my clit. The stimulation was almost too much and a little whimper escaped me.

"That's my girl. Let go...you can take this. I know you can. Look at how gorgeous you are. So goddamn sweet, taking my cock like you were made for it. Come here, Little Bit. Let me suck on those tits for you..."

He didn't have to ask again. I stretched over him, and he pushed up, locking his lips around one nipple. Then the other. The little spurts of pleasure increased with every stroke of his cock. Dragging his head back, he sat up fully and then his mouth fused with mine.

Wanting him—needing him—I increased the pace and his arms wrapped around me as he thrust up to meet me. He wasn't quite hitting my cervix, but holy shit, it was so close. The change in angle ground my clit against him, and then he was sucking on my tongue as the pleasure exploded outward. I cried against his lips as I came.

Fisting my hair, he tilted my head back, kissing a path along my throat. The whole time, he whispered a litany of praise.

"So, fucking beautiful. Strong. God, I love the way your pussy feels around me. These breasts are perfect. I want to suck on them until the only thing you feel is me. Do you know what you do to me, Little Bit? How much I want you?"

His grunts punctuated them and his voice broke when his orgasm burst. The liquid heat spurting into me prompted another needy little moan.

"Love you," he said, the declaration binding me up body and soul. "Love you so much, Little Bit." This time when I cupped his face and his lips met mine, the kiss held the same urgency, yet there was a far more seductive element present. "My bliss and my blessing," he whispered. "Mine."

Fuck yes, I was his. It did something to me to be claimed by them. To feel the brand of their affection settling into all the cracked and splintered places in my soul. They were taping it up, sealing them closed.

Was I broken? Yes.

I pulled my head up to meet his gaze, panting and unable to get my breath back. I was absolutely shattered and in a thousand pieces.

These men...my men, my vandals, they put me back together again. They showed me over and over again—broken wasn't bad.

"I love you." It was as much a promise to him as to myself. For Mickey was broken too. We all were. When I nuzzled a kiss to his lips, he opened to me and then we collapsed together, still shaking as he devoured my mouth—maybe trying to consume all the emotion we were sharing.

Perhaps he was just pouring it into me. The cum was slippery where we were still joined, and I bumped my hips to his. His groan answered my own.

"I love you," I repeated, not that I needed the words. I wanted them. I wanted him to know.

"My little bit," he whispered in between the kisses. "The things I want to do to you... to do with you."

"Yes," I answered. "Anything."

And I meant it. For them? For him?

Anything.

# CHAPTER 21

*ROME*

It was weird that I could keep playing without putting coins in. Apparently, Vegas had long since upgraded their slots and similar games. You just needed a card loaded with your cash and you could play forever.

Other than wasting money, it gave me something to do. Movement to my left was one of Doc's friends taking a seat. Alphabet. I wasn't sure about the names, but I didn't necessarily care. If that was what they wanted to be called, it didn't matter.

"No sign of him?" He slotted his own card and hit the button to play.

"No."

"Well, this is one of three."

I nodded.

"Makes it easier if we could get a bead on which was his favorite."

It would be easier still if he'd been at home with his wife or worried about his daughter. Though it didn't matter. I hit the button to play it again.

"Gambling has never been my thing," Alphabet said. The man seemed to have a need to speak. The chatter didn't bother me; it reminded me a little of Freddie. "Literally, all we're doing is pressing a button. There's no skill here. Cards are different. Then again, it's more about the luck of the draw. I prefer games that rely on my talents and my brains and not—"

His machine lit up, an alarm celebrating his cash win. It also attracted a lot of attention.

"Fuck me," he muttered. "Right. Off I go."

The next two days passed similarly. We staked out the three casinos Reginald Sharpe preferred. On day four of our hunt however, I hit the jackpot on the machine and on our mission.

Ignoring the obnoxious noise, I sent a message to the guys. I had eyes on him. I was following. They answered in variations of "on their way." Pulling the card from the slot, I slid it into my pocket.

Leaving the drink and the machine, I followed the man and his escort. Three men were with him. All armed. Interesting. They navigated the maze of machines and games. It made it a challenge to get to the elevators with all the distractions.

I had no such issues. Alphabet got to the elevator bank ahead of us. He was the first one into the elevator the four of them boarded. I followed, phone in hand, and ignored them. Twenty-fourth floor.

I hit the button above it for the twenty-second. Only music played for sound as the elevator rose. Sharpe's phone rang. He silenced it. A moment later, it rang again. He repeated the action. I kept my gaze on my phone even if I was aware of everyone else in the elevator.

The third ring had him swearing. "Goddammit." He put the phone to his ear. "I'm on my fucking way." The crude irritation didn't sound better in his cultured tones. It just broadcasted annoyed.

The doors opened on the twenty-second floor, and I stepped out. Glancing from left to right to orient myself even as the doors closed behind me. While I might want to hurry, I didn't.

Las Vegas had cameras *everywhere*. We'd made a point of doing everything casually. We didn't have as many contacts here, but we had some. Doc's team had more. At the end of the hall, I went into the stairwell and climbed up to the twenty-fourth floor.

Once there, I used the other keycard Alphabet had given me to get out on the twenty-fourth floor. You could only access a floor if you had a room on it. Fortunately, these keys opened every floor.

I made it just in time to see one of Sharpe's men getting back on the elevator. The other two were nowhere in the hall. After the bell dinged, Alphabet appeared from the other end of the hall. My phone buzzed.

*Room 2418.*

A second message popped right after it. Kellan, Voodoo, Vaughn, and Freddie were in the building. Milo wasn't here because none of us were certain he wouldn't just kill Sharpe.

Jasper and Liam had been left with Starling, along with Doc and the rest of his team. They would make their way up here.

A new message came in from Alphabet.

*Room 2417, all ours.*

I didn't ask how he did it; I didn't care. I got to the door and let myself in. A knock on the connecting door accompanied another message.

*It's me.*

I opened it.

"I set your guys up in 2420. They have a connecting door to 2418. It's booked, but not with a guest." He was pulling a strap over his head. The limp seemed more pronounced than downstairs, but he didn't comment, so I left it alone.

Instead, I moved back to the door to keep watch.

"Fifteen minutes to set up. One guard is out, two in with him."

Matched what I already knew.

"Best plan to get him out unharmed is to lure one or both of those guards first, then take him."

"We don't care if he's harmed."

The man in that elevator had not acted like someone missing his wife or daughter. He could suffer. We needed him alive. You could be maimed yet still alive.

It took an hour before Kellan was ready to make a move. In that time, the third guard returned with room service, then they rolled it inside. The third guard remained but the other two left.

Pity.

One guard would be easy to subdue.

"Transport is here," Alphabet said. "They're ready to do a pickup when we are."

I nodded.

Leaving the room, I crossed the hall and knocked on the door.

"Wrong room," the guard in the room said.

I knocked again and waited. A blank expression and no comments went a long way sometimes.

"Wrong. Room." The guard was closer to the door.

And annoyed.

I didn't smile, but I did knock again.

"Look, you stupi—" The guy swore as he started to open the door. I didn't wait for him to finish, just pushed in and cracked him in the face with the door. He staggered back but then lunged right for me, except I was already inside and I had a gun up and pressed to his forehead.

Across the room, Sharpe stood near the windows overlooking the city, cell phone in hand. He hadn't turned around yet, although there was no doubt I had his attention. Satisfied, I pistol-whipped the guard, using the butt of the gun to knock him out.

Crossing to where Sharpe stood, I nodded to his phone.

"Brad," he said slowly. "I need to put you on hold."

Sweat beaded Sharpe's forehead. I didn't care if he was uncomfortable. I waved him over to the bed and caught him in the back of the head with one solid blow. He crumpled face-first into the bed. Too soft a landing, but I dragged him over to ensure he was still breathing.

"Reginald," the voice on the phone said, "I am not done with you."

His name was on the screen. Good. We had the phone number. Impatience creasing every single word, he called to his brother again. I lifted the phone to my ear as I walked over to unlock the adjoining door.

"Your brother can't come to the phone, Mr. Sharpe," I said.

"Who the fuck is this?"

"You'll see." I could leave it there or add, "Maybe." With that, I ended the call and then powered the phone off. Kellan stared at me and then at Sharpe.

"This wasn't the plan."

"He'll live." I hadn't broken his nose.

Not yet, anyway.

Exasperation touched his expression, but Vaughn

grinned. He reached down and hauled up the guard into the other room.

Kellan walked over to Sharpe. He checked his pulse, then emptied his pockets. He tossed the wallet and keys to me, along with another phone. I also made sure it was shut off, then stuck it in my pockets with the other.

A knock at the door. "Housekeeping," Freddie called. "Sorry to disturb you, Mr. Sharpe. We've come to take care of the mess."

Vaughn let him in, his expression almost amused. To be fair, none of us were enjoying the experience... yet.

It was too serious, and we all wanted to be back with Starling and the others. Freddie was dressed like a hotel employee. He dragged a laundry cart inside, followed by Voodoo, who dressed like hotel security.

"We have a six-minute window," he said. "It's closing rapidly. Alphabet has eyes on the guards."

We split the tasks. I packed his suitcases, taking everything in the room, including his laptop, digital tablet, and more.

"What if there's something in the safe?" Vaughn asked as he dumped the man, not so gently, into the laundry cart after applying a judicious amount of duct tape.

"Leave it," Kellan said. "We're at five minutes. You two go. Everyone else in the other room."

We left the guard duct taped and secured inside the closet of the other room. Then we were wiping it down before we left, splitting up. Transport was here, so that meant going downstairs.

With Sharpe's suitcases stored in a trunk we'd brought with us, I left them with Vaughn to get downstairs. Alphabet would scan them before we took them anywhere in case they had GPS tags.

Downstairs, I strolled out of the hotel and headed toward

the back like I was out for a walk. It was dark outside. I hadn't even realized the time until I'd gone into a room and seen a window.

The hotels and casinos here were not interested in the outside. The air was dry and hot. There were also too many people. Kellan came out a different set of doors, catching up with me before I even reached the driveway that led into the garage in the back.

When we got there, Freddie was already wheeling the laundry cart out with Voodoo. A lean woman with eyes so pale brown they seemed practically golden waited. Dressed in a dark blue jumpsuit and sporting a hat, she was disguised as a driver for the linens company.

"Only two carts," Freddie said as he approached her. She wasn't alone. The other guy was tall, blond, and even if he wore the same outfit, everything about him screamed cop.

Kellan must have come to the same assessment because he raised a hand to Freddie. Voodoo shifted forward to take point, and the woman laughed softly.

"I told you that you can't sell this yet," she said over her shoulder, and the guy with her simply shrugged.

"Don't care. Rick's with Fletcher while he handles surveillance, and you aren't meeting these assholes alone."

"You're adorable," she said, before facing us. "Transport. Special delivery."

"I wasn't expecting you directly," Kellan said casually. A muscle ticked in his jaw.

It was her turn to shrug. "I read the request. It seemed to be a reasonable one. Are you sure you want delivery and not just disposal?"

"Yes," he told her. "We have plans, and they require the package to be intact."

"Very well. It will be no less than three days, no more than five." She held out a card. "In seventy-two hours, call that number and leave the address where you want to accept delivery." She seemed to study Kellan for a moment, maybe longer than the guy with her seemed to like.

"Done." Kellan took the card with a firm nod. "Thank you for your assistance."

"Of course, I love road trips." Then she flicked a look at me, and the guy with her actually growled. Freddie was gawking after he and Voodoo loaded up the two laundry carts. "Nice eyes."

Then without another word, she climbed into the van. The guy with her didn't get inside until she had the engine running. Kellan checked his watch as they pulled out and then looked at Freddie before he glanced at Voodoo.

"Your partner?"

"Already out."

The next hour was spent erasing our presence before we climbed into the car with Vaughn. I settled into the back and closed my eyes. It was a long drive, and Freddie was already wired.

"Tell me we're getting food," he said as Vaughn pulled out into traffic. Doc's friends would be right behind us.

"We're getting food after we're out of the city." Which meant at least a couple of hours 'cause we'd want to be well clear. "Grab a nap," Vaughn suggested. "You haven't been sleeping."

"Don't like being this far away from her."

Could hardly argue with that thought when I hated it too. Pulling my own phone out, I went to her contact and sent her a kiss.

The heart eyes she sent back made me smile. I turned the phone to Freddie. "She's all right. Now sleep."

He grunted, but he stared at the message for a long beat. "Okay, then. Wake me when we get food."

I nodded, put my phone away, then folded my arms before closing my eyes.

In a few days, we'd be back with Starling, and we'd have Starling's father strung up in the fridge. He would tell us everything he knew.

Then we would kill him.

# CHAPTER 22

*EMERSYN*

*T*he music began slowly, each note unfolding as "I Tried" came through the speakers. I stretched upward to the melancholy notes. Every movement was exaggerated and held for an extra beat. The slowness encouraged deeper extensions. The slow tempo let me flow from one position to another as the music transitioned to Thomas Day's "Not My Job Anymore."

Muscle memory took over. While I might not train quite as grueling as I once had, I needed this. I needed to empty the fear and the worry. I needed to let the grief, and the anger, choking all of us, go. Even if it was just for a little while.

I couldn't forget what had happened. No one could. I used to lie to myself that it didn't matter. After burying it all as deep as I could, the poison still spilled into my dreams, my soul, and my life. Pouring myself into the music, I submerged and surrendered to it. Every step lifted me, allowed me to shoulder those burdens, then slipped free of them.

From "You Put a Spell on Me" by Austin Giorgio to "Unholy" by Sam Smith, I graduated through the balladic lyrics. The playlist increased in speed and tempo until I was up on my toes, alignment perfectly placed, and then I made the leap. The silks were right there, and I had not flown since Rome and Liam took me to the fairgrounds.

Sharper motions were demanded as I climbed the silks, rolling and wrapping. I dropped when the notes fell and let go as I flew. It was like coming to life as the world melted away. All that existed was me, the music, and the silks.

Every stretch took me higher. Every twist added another layer to the dance in the air. The ballads grew fiercer. The loneliness circling around me shattered, releasing the vise around my chest.

Guitars and drums kicked in as I twisted and flowed. Every snap of the silks sharp and every drop sent my pulse soaring as I rocked out. There was something hilarious about matching the kicks and leaps on the ground to dancing in the air.

Controlled motion.

Miming surface.

Rolling up and the spins to drop.

The first time I'd taken to an aerial ring flashed through my mind. The absolute elation. The magic that always accompanied flying. Even as my arms and back muscles burned, I reveled in the fire. Soaked with sweat, I slowed the speed of transitions even as I craved the discomfort.

Coldplay segued to Queen, then back to a classical piece, and so on. Every single song meant to wring every drop of emotion out of me until I was bare. The fire consumed me, burning away the excess, leaving only *me* behind.

When the final song ended, I hung, curled into a perfect hip lock split knee drop.

The silence seemed even more profound as the present

rushed in. Every muscle trembled, and sweat dripped off me toward the floor. I didn't have to look up to know someone had arrived. The difference in the air had been there, yet I hadn't emerged from the zone until now.

Blinking slowly, I curled my abdomen to force myself to sit up, then caught the silk and rested, half sitting in the cradle I'd formed. In the mirror, I met my brother's gaze. He stood close enough to the door that I had to wonder if he stopped as soon as he came in.

"Goddamn, Ivy," he said, blowing out a breath. "That was…"

"Not my best work," I admitted, then uncurled myself from the silks and slid down until I could drop. It was taking too long to get my breath back under control. I needed to step up my regimen. "However, I've been down for a while."

"Looked pretty damn amazing to me," he said, and I shot him a grateful grin.

"You're my big brother, you're supposed to love everything I do."

He snorted. "Hardly. You do plenty of things I don't like." He held up his hands as if to stave off any protests from me. "And I'm learning to suck it up for the most part."

I grinned while grabbing my towel from where I'd left it with my phone and mopped at the sweat on my face. I pretty much stunk like hard work now. "You have," I said. "I appreciate that."

"Appreciate it enough to talk to me today?"

Despite the wariness in his voice and the caution in his eyes, I scooped up my bottle of water and grinned, "I talk to you every day." Then I took a long drink while he chuckled.

"Right, I walked into that one."

"Yep."

Looping the towel over my neck, I began to walk a circuit of the room. I needed the cool down as much to slow down the sweating as I did to ease my muscles. Everything was burning, only it was a good burn.

Arms folded, he leaned against the wall. "How are you doing?"

I glanced at him before I took another drink. The water was deliciously cool. I had no ready answer for him. "I don't know," I admitted, locking gazes with him as I paced in my circle. "Most of the time, I feel pretty good. But there are moments..."

Moments *and* bad dreams. I didn't sleep alone, that helped. But Mickey also had bad dreams the last few nights. More than once, he'd just gotten up and left. It was like once he jolted awake, he couldn't just stay there.

Once Liam had just come in as Mickey left and crawled right into the bed. With him wrapped around me, I'd been buried in heat and just went back to sleep. Nevertheless, Mickey wouldn't stay when the nightmares came, and I wasn't sure what to do about that *yet*.

"Then I can't get out of my head, and I start asking myself a thousand questions. At least Lainey messaged me back— finally." That was another irritation.

Interest lifted his expression. "How is she?"

"She says she's good." I believed her. To a point.

Worry stamped across his face. "You don't think she is?"

"I don't know, that—bothers me. I've been a shitty friend to her."

"No you haven't." His defense was instinctive and I adored him for it.

"I have been. Adam is off doing whatever the hell he is. She's back there dealing with their parents and trying to keep her little sister out of drama, and I haven't exactly been much help."

"You're safe," he said, as if I needed the reminder. "That's what Mayhem needs from you. She needs to know you're safe."

"She also needs to not be alone," I pointed out and he grunted. "Yeah, just dismiss my concern, but the point is—you two seemed to have something."

It was weird. But I kind of liked it too.

"She doesn't belong here, Ivy," he said, and I rolled my eyes. After draining the water bottle, I put the cap back on it and then flung it. It bounced right off his head and he blinked at me.

"Stop deciding where people belong. I swear, you were a damn hall monitor when you were a kid."

He retrieved the bottle, eyeing me with what looked suspiciously like a smile, even if he fought it. "Did no one ever tell you that throwing things at people isn't nice?"

"Nope," I informed him, popping the p. "I skipped that lesson with Ms. Manners. Didn't Liam tell you? I'm a hellspawn."

Laughing, he shook his head. "Tell you what, why don't you go shower and change. Then we can grab some food. Hang out for a bit."

"Everything okay with you?" Of course, it wasn't. Not being okay had been our reality for a while now. But I'd been managing to scrape together happiness because the guys took care of me. I'd hoped Milo had been doing that with Lainey, but he sighed.

"Yes and no," he said. "Go shower. I'll send a rat to get us some pizza. I feel the urge to listen to you bitch about how many carbs you're eating."

I flipped him off, and he laughed.

"I want a veggie lovers, please...with sausage...and pepperoni...and maybe some ham."

"Yeah, that sounds like a veggie lover to me," he commented as he opened the door for me and I grinned.

Just for that... "We know I love the meat lovers, so we could just order that."

His gaze flattened and he just stared at me. "Brat."

I grinned even wider. "Yes, yes, I am."

And proud of it.

His chuckle followed me up the stairs. Mickey wasn't here, he'd gone to the clinic and Bones had gone with him. Lunchbox, my normal shadow, was not present at the clubhouse today. I had to assume he was with Grace, whom I hadn't seen since that day in the warehouse.

I needed to ask Mickey about her and make sure she was all right. Mickey trusted his guys, I got that. Didn't hurt to verify, in any case. While she looked like she'd enjoyed slapping Lunchbox, I knew just how easy it was to hide what was really going on.

Jasper and Liam were not in the suite, which surprised me. When had they gone out? Everyone had been busy. I glanced toward the door to the hall. I hadn't seen my mother in a couple of days, and each time I considered it...

Pivoting, I headed to my room for a shower and change. The room itself was quiet, the bed made and neat, but the two huge bundles of flowers on the dresser hadn't been there when I left that morning.

Pink, orange, and yellow roses—one multi-colored stuck into the bouquets as well. There were Peruvian lilies. Daisies. Sunflowers. Baby's Breath. And ivy...

They were the largest group of flowers I'd ever seen, and they were *beautiful*. Even when I'd gotten roses for a performance or a new show or a closing show, they'd been a dozen long-stemmed roses at most, and that was it. Those had been beautiful too but not like *this*.

A card sat between them and I picked it up, taking deep breaths of the sweet fragrance from each colossal vase. The room was going to be like sleeping in a garden. That just made me smile.

Slitting open the envelope, I pulled out the note card and unfolded it.

HELLSPAWN,

*You brighten all of my days, especially these last few weeks when it's been so damn dark. Maybe it's because you've been in the dark and it doesn't frighten you. Or maybe it's because you survived the dark and appreciate the light. Maybe it's just that you're so goddamn stubborn, you remind me that I'm not alone and won't let me pretend otherwise.*

A LAUGH BUBBLED UP INSIDE OF ME.

*THE POINT IS YOU'RE THE PERFECT GIRL FOR ME. FOR US. YOU deserve to be told that, and often. You also deserve flowers, diamonds, and all the pretty things I can persuade you to accept.*

*I love you.*

*Liam*

TEARS FILLED MY EYES AT THE SIMPLE, DIRECT DECLARATION.

*P.S. THERE ARE TWO BOUQUETS 'CAUSE JASPER WAS BEING A LITTLE bitch about wanting you to have flowers too. I'm pretty sure it will be seven when everyone returns, but mine were first, and J can suck it.*

.  .  .

I BURST OUT LAUGHING, BECAUSE IT REALLY WAS SO THEM. TEN bucks says Jasper saw him write that and flipped him off. Their glares probably morphed into laughter. Taking another deep breath of their scent, I smiled.

Even after my shower, I was still smiling at the flowers. I got dressed in comfortable clothing and then opened the door to the sitting room when my phone rang.

Milo glanced up from where he sat on the sofa, his own phone in hand. I dug my phone out.

Lainey's name flashed up at me from the screen.

Hitting answer, I put it to my ear. "You're okay?"

"I'm fine," she said with a huff. "Sorry for the sudden silence on my part. I've spent the last two weeks stuck on Ezra's fucking island."

Ezra's family owned an island. I'd forgotten about that.

"But you're okay?"

"I'm fine," she repeated, sighing. "Are you guys okay? When I flew back today, he filled me in. Also, I have a new bodyguard, can't wait for you to meet him." The dry tone almost made me laugh.

"You know, for once," I caught Milo studying me. "I agree with Ezra. I wanted you safe, too, although I may punch him in the balls for not letting us know what he did."

"Honestly, being kidnapped is not at all as sexy as you made it sound." She almost managed to sound scolding, and I rolled my eyes.

"I'm pretty sure I never called it sexy, Lainey," I said her name on purpose, and Milo rose to his feet. "But the fact that you're safe and healthy is more important."

Some of the tension drained out of Milo's locked shoulders.

"Are you at home?"

"I'm at my grandfather's apartment in the city, hence the bodyguard. Andrea is back in school, so I don't have to deal with my mother or Adam's father. Grandfather had meetings this week, so I asked him if I could stay here. Tally is supposed to come for a visit, but…I can come to you."

"I would love it if you were here," I said, and Milo's expression went taut. "However, I don't want you right in the middle of this at the moment. Too many uncertainties, and we know Uncle Fuckbucket is gunning for us. But we got my mom."

"Oh," Lainey's voice dropped, concern etching a deep line beneath it. "How is that going?"

"I'm having a hard time with it," I admitted. "But Milo has been fantastic, and so have the guys."

"Can I do anything?"

"Stay safe," I told her and drifted close enough so Milo could hear her even if he didn't say anything. "What about you? What do you need?"

A little more was right with my world at knowing she was okay.

"You to be safe too. If that blockheaded brother of yours is there, tell him to look after you."

"I always have," Milo rumbled. "You be good, Mayhem."

"I'm very good at what I do," she retorted. "I have to go, but I am being cautious. I expect the same from you two as well."

"Love you, Lainey."

"Love you, Em."

Milo said nothing, but she didn't stick around for it. I sighed. "She's okay."

"Good," he said. "You ready?"

"As ready as I'll ever be. What are we going to do?"

209

# CHAPTER 23

*KELLAN*

The drive back from Vegas had been uneventful and downright boring. Freddie's penchant for chatter helped pass the time. We'd all avoided the one topic preoccupying all of us.

Sharpe. What he knew. When he knew it. What he did with the knowledge.

How painful his death was would largely depend on those factors. The two people entrusted with Milo's Ivy, with my Sparrow. One had been a victim herself. I felt for her, I really did.

Yet, she was well aware of what her brother-in-law was capable of and still left a defenseless child with him regularly? Yeah, she didn't get a fucking pass for that. Not from me. Not from Milo. Not from any of us.

From the day Sparrow left her mother's room—and whatever confirmation she'd given Milo and Sparrow—and collapsed in tears, she'd avoided additional time with the woman she'd wanted to rescue. I wasn't sure how aware of her choice she was, but there was no mistaking it.

Did I want to confront her about this? No. *Should* I confront her? I wasn't sure, and I didn't care for the idea of putting her on the spot. Currently, she needed all of us to be her port in the storm.

Trusting us with her secrets had been a boon, and an act of faith. Trusting us with her pain exceeded what we could have asked of her. She'd *suffered* for far too long, and she'd suffered alone. She didn't have to do that anymore. She believed enough in our *promises* and in *us* to let us take that burden for her and protect her.

It was a far too precious gift I would not allow *anyone* to diminish. If she needed the break from her mother, then she got a break from her. If she wanted the woman gone?

We could do that too.

In fact, maybe that was what we needed to do. Make arrangements to secure her *elsewhere*. The only issue with that was taking her had incited the uncle. That made Moira Sharpe a target.

How bad was it that I didn't mind the idea of dangling her as bait? A knock on the door dragged me out of my thoughts, and I raked a hand through my damp hair. "Come in."

When Sparrow poked her head in, her smile chased my dark thoughts away to a corner where they could admire her and plan. My darkness didn't scare her, and that...well goddamn, did we get lucky with her.

"Do I want to know where that expression came from?" she asked, slipping inside and closing the door behind her.

"You don't have to ask," I said as I crossed to her. She pushed off the door and walked right into my arms. I cupped her face, then dipped my head to drop a soft, nuzzling kiss to her lips. "Just thinking about how incredible you are and how much I love you."

Her eyes brightened as surprise flickered over her face. Yeah, I needed to use my words more often. She covered my hands on her cheeks with her own and then pushed upward to nuzzle a kiss to the corner of my mouth. It was light, effervescent. As I teased her lips apart, I sighed at the welcome in her smile and the soft sound of her laughter that turned into a groan.

"We're never getting out of here if I keep kissing you, Sparrow," I teased, and she lowered her hands to my arms then skated them up to my chest.

"I'm not really hearing a downside there," she said, before turning to nip one of my fingers. I wrapped one hand around her throat as I traced my thumb along her lower lip. She let out a little sigh, and I swore her whole body went liquid as she held my gaze. "Except…"

"You wanted to take me out on a date." The offer, the need for connection, all of it had bowled me over.

"It's not terrifically safe right now," she admitted. "Security is a concern."

Pride unfurled in me at the declaration. "It is very much a concern. We can wait for a real date, too. I'm not in a hurry. I'm happy to simply be with you."

"I can't tell you how much that means," she said, spreading her fingers out over my pecs. "And if you truly think it isn't safe to go out, well, then we get creative."

I had to laugh. She was so damn serious. "Sparrow, I'm fine with doing whatever you want to do. I am more than fine. Truly. If you want to go out, tell me where and we'll make sure to secure it."

Scraping her teeth over her lower lip, she flashed another smile at me. "I already made a backup plan."

Clever girl. I tightened my grip, just a flex around her throat, and she tilted her head back. Her eyes dilated and her smile grew. The steady drum of her pulse beneath my thumb just added to the inclination to take her to bed and keep her there.

"Did you now?"

"Hmm-hmm," she practically purred the acknowledgment. The sound went straight to my dick.

"Tempted to tease the information out of you." So tempted, yet... I drew little circles with my thumb before nibbling on her lower lip. "And at the same time, I want to enjoy your surprise."

Her eyes brightened and she twined her arms around my neck the next time I leaned in for a kiss. Her mouth softened and opened to the invasion. When her tongue curved against mine in invitation, I groaned and squeezed gently as I wrapped an arm around her.

"Sparrow." I would have growled, but she hooked her fingers into my towel and tugged it away before kissing along my jaw. Then she pulled back and stared up at me.

"I have a surprise for you right now..." She slid her fingers around the base of my cock, and it was already a rock for her, ready and willing.

Her pupils were blown and large. "Whatever you want," I promised her. "Not about to tell you no."

She grinned and nudged me back toward the bed. I sat when I hit it, and then she reached past me for a pillow. When she dropped it in front of me, I narrowed my eyes.

With a light finger, she tapped my nose. "You said you wouldn't tell me no."

Chuckling, I tracked her as she nudged my legs apart. Dropping to her knees, she ran her hands along my thighs up to my cock and away again. The movement teased and tantalized. The sensual look in her eyes as she held my gaze kept me riveted.

"Sparrow," I said on a sigh as she wrapped her hand around my cock. The first glide of her fingers was cool, and I was on fire. The contrasting sensations along my cock had me tilting my head back. "Fuck…"

"Not yet," she murmured. "Need to save something for after our date."

The soft tickle of her hair against my thighs added yet another layer to the sensuality she was treating me to. Then her mouth closed over the head of my cock.

The contact was almost too light, too gentle. Kittenish licks with light suction designed to drive me absolutely mad. She pulled back then ran her tongue along the vein throbbing in my cock. Then her mouth enveloped me again and I slid all the way into her throat.

At the first sound of her choking, I fisted her hair and gave the barest of tugs. She obeyed, pulling back but lifting her gaze to fix on mine. Need vied with desire, yet my need to protect her overrode everything else.

"Suck me off, for I will never say no to the feeling of your mouth on me or fucking your throat—but you aren't allowed to choke. Do you understand?" Fuck she was so beautiful with her lips around my cock. "Blink once for yes. Twice for no."

She rolled her eyes almost playfully, then blinked once. I stroked my fingers through her hair.

"Good girl," I murmured. "Now take all of me that you can."

With little encouragement, she dipped her head down to swallow my cock. The feel of her throat around me was the welcome home I didn't know I needed. Long swallows, hard pulls, gentle licks, then increased friction.

She held my gaze while I fisted her hair, and when her mouth relaxed around me I began to control the rocking motion. Tears shimmered in her eyes, and I eased back a little…

"Still good?"

One blink and a tear trembled on her lashes before it fell to glide down her cheek.

I loosened my grip, and she fisted the base of my cock before taking me all the way down. The thrusts grew deeper, and the pull fiercer. My balls were dragging up and I was going to come.

"You going to swallow all of me?"

Another single blink and another tear trembled out to join the first.

"You're so good for me," I murmured, stroking her hair as she resumed those deep-throating strokes that made me want to blow my load instantly.

I fought it, even as another tear joined the first two. The trickle of tears was so goddamn beautiful, especially when her eyes were so warm and filled with light. No pain for my sparrow—liquid heat boiled at the base of my spine.

Her movements maintained their pace even as mine stuttered, and no amount of control would keep me from coming right down her throat. I rode that pleasurable wave as she choked and swallowed.

A little dribble of cum escaped the corner of her mouth, and I shuddered as she maintained that intensity right there. The stimulation was almost too much, and my hips bucked. When she finally released me, she licked her lips and leaned back. Her little huffs for breath matched my own.

"When—" I had to take a moment to catch my breath. Fucking her mouth was almost as much fun as fucking her cunt. "When is our date?"

"We have time," she said, catching that dribble of cum on her finger then licking it up. That sent a bolt of lust right to my dick making it twitch. We might not be up right away, but I had lips, fingers, and a tongue. "Did you want something else?"

I chuckled, hauling her up and dropping her on the bed. I

wasn't too proud to hide the fact I was all shaking limbs, however I didn't need to walk to eat her out.

"Yes," I informed her as I peeled down her leggings. "I'm hungry, and the perfect juicy treat is right here…"

"This was supposed to be about you," she protested, though her legs went wide when I pushed her thighs apart. The perfect splits, and it bared her pussy to me. All sweet pink, wet flesh and the sweet bundle of nerves poking out from under its hood.

"Oh, don't you worry, Sparrow," I promised before licking her from entrance to clit. "This is definitely going to be something I enjoy, and so will you."

When I pressed my lips to the inside of her thigh and blew a raspberry, she let out a peal of laughter that was the balm to my soul. Once she started giggling, I went to work on making her scream.

I managed three orgasms out of her before I slid inside. She wrapped those beautiful legs around me, then tilted her head back to bare her throat. Sweat gleamed on my skin and on hers, and I gripped her throat as I rocked into her steadily.

"This time," I whispered to her. "We're going to come together. You can do that for me, can't you?"

"Yes," she sighed, arching those hips to meet every thrust. Neither of us rushed. The rock and grind as I pushed into her and rolled forward to meet and envelop me were heavenly. It was an eternity and no time at all before she spasmed around me, and I let go. We clung to each other, her breaths coming in fierce pants as we kissed.

I rolled onto my back, taking her with me and cradling her to my chest. She was shaking all over. Stroking her back, I closed my eyes and savored her nearness. The last few weeks had been hell.

The next few didn't promise to be much better—except

when we were done, everyone who had ever hurt her would be gone. Erased.

"We can't go to sleep," she whispered against my chest, her breath teasing my skin.

"We can do whatever we want," I answered. She laughed, but a yawn interrupted her. Lifting her head, she stared at me from beneath her tousled hair. Her eyes were shiny, her lips swollen, and her face deliciously sex-flushed.

My dick was already showing a valiant attempt at stirring again. Given another half hour or so, I could be balls-deep in her again.

"I want to take you on our date."

With a mock sigh, I said, "Fine, if you insist. Does it get to be a naked date?"

Her laughter filled the room, and I grinned. While she did want the date, we didn't have to get up immediately. We had time for another shower—eventually— and my stamina had me pinning her to the wall there too.

A couple of well-spent hours later, I let her guide me down to her studio where a table and chairs had been set up and a meal awaited us.

"Someone has been sneaky."

"A little calculated effort," she said, grinning. "Milo helped."

"Did he?" That amused me almost as much as her radiant expression.

"He did…Now, if you will take a seat, Mr. Traschel, and pour yourself a glass of wine. We'll get started." Only instead of sitting when I pulled out her chair, she backed away and shook her head. "Nope, that table is for you right now."

I tracked her movements, more curious than anything, as I took the seat. A date in her soundproof studio was a nice compromise. Especially since we'd reinforced the walls.

When she eyed me expectantly, I chuckled and poured myself a glass of wine. "Happy?"

"Yes," she said, before flicking on the music, then adjusting the lights. Five minutes later, she held me in rapt awe as she twisted and twined in the silks—dancing in the air, performing.

One particular twist had her angled in flight, and our gazes locked. It took me back to that night she invited me to watch her perform. The night everything changed. Our broken bird had reclaimed her wings.

# CHAPTER 24

*DOC*

"Thanks for coming, Stephen," I said to the doctor studying the charts in front of him. "I know this wasn't much notice."

"I owe you," he said, resting his knuckles against the desktop. "And you've got excellent records, but you and I both know the locals may have an issue with this transition."

"Maybe, for a little while, but I'm hoping it won't be more than a month. Two tops." Though it would take as long as it would take.

Wars always seemed to involve logistics, supplies, manpower, and luck. Plans changed, and the neighborhood was aware of the issues we'd been having. Maybe not the exact details, but the mechanic shop burning down the same night as the tattoo parlor and car explosions on the strip near Inferno?

Yeah, there was no mistaking that.

"The good thing is that the neighborhood is like a family. You'll get the grandmothers first. Make nice with them, and you'll be golden."

Stephen Butler chuckled. "Got it." He shifted his stance, then reached out a hand to shake mine. "I'll take care of the place."

Gripping his hand for a moment, I nodded. Stephen and I went back to basic. We'd both ended up in bad situations in the field, and we'd both ended up in medical school. After that, we'd taken some drastically different paths. But he wouldn't ask a lot of questions, and that was what I needed.

"If anyone comes looking for me..."

He grinned. "Sorry, Dr. James took a leave of absence, and we don't know when he's returning."

I clapped his shoulder. "Thanks again."

"No problem. Watch your back."

I paused at the door and nodded. "You too."

Then I was out in the hall. Leaving the clinic was a lot more challenging than I expected. This place was everything I'd poured my life into when I got back. It was where I'd begun to try and put right the things I'd fucked up.

Walking away felt a little bit like surrendering, even though I wouldn't risk the clinic or the people in the neighborhood to Little Bit's insane uncle or the people working for him. If it was just me, fuck it—let them come.

It wasn't just the guys or me. In fact, it wasn't really about *hurting* us, while that was definitely a part of it. No, this campaign focused on terror. The person he wanted to terrorize was the one he wanted to drive away from our protection.

Bones waited for me near the exit door to the lot in the back. "Good?"

"It'll do. Where's Voodoo?"

"Sent him to the car," he said. "His attitude has been annoying me."

That was new. "Do I need to care?"

"No," Bones said with a shrug. "He does. He'll get over it. None of us like having Grace here, yet the alternative isn't acceptable and it's his turn to be in the doghouse with her."

With that comment, he opened the door and scanned the lot before taking point. Voodoo was in the shadow of the car, his sunglasses shielding his eyes as he kept watch.

Good to know whatever the issue was, they had it handled—hence the "no" to my question about whether I needed to care. They didn't involve themselves in my personal life, I wouldn't intrude on theirs.

"Where to, Doc?" Voodoo asked as he slid behind the wheel. I got into the backseat and stared at the clinic for a long time. It was going to be a while before I got to come back here—if at all.

"Apartment," I said. "I need to pack up some shit."

It wasn't like I was going to stay there again. That night with Little Bit was the first night I'd been there in a while and was most likely the last.

"You ready to think about your sister's place yet?" Voodoo asked, barely tossing me a look in the rearview mirror.

Pain spasmed in my chest. I hadn't been to her house, not since she died. Jasper and Milo had gone for me to check on it. They reported no damage. I needed to go. I would go.

"No."

Not yet.

"Roger that."

I cut my gaze out the windows, scanning the streets as we drove the few blocks from the clinic to my place. I had a memory of nearly every street. I knew the people who ran the corner store, a three-generation family working in the grocery. The coffee shop on 80th. The bar at Prescott.

These people were part of my penance. Taking care of all of them. This was exactly what I'd done for the past four, almost five years. Until Hell decided to rain down once more.

I wouldn't risk anyone else.

"Alphabet still at the warehouse?"

"Yep," Bones said. "Your girl is tucked in safe and tight. She seldom comes out without one of you." No, she didn't. Alphabet had been on site the whole time as the guys made the Vegas run.

Acid burned in my gut. "Thanks."

"Yep."

My phone buzzed and I pulled it out of my pocket.

KELLAN:

Special delivery arrived. Stored in the fridge.
ETA?

Special delivery.

Her father was in custody.

ME:

30 minutes.

Kellan put a thumbs up on the message, and I leaned forward. "Special delivery arrived. Let's make this a quick stop."

"Yep."

It took us less than three minutes to get to the apartment after that. I spent fifteen minutes packing, mainly clothes, photographs, and some personal items. Everything else could wait.

"We can clear this out for you, if you want," Bones offered.

"I must be more than a little fucked up for you to make that offer." Bones was a good friend, and a trusted comrade. In a straight-up fight, you wanted him on your side. He was brutal but efficient. The thing with Bones was he had less interest in people's feelings than he did in women's fashion trends.

Then again, considering their charge's former occupation, maybe that had changed too.

"You're compromised," Bones said. "Happens to the best of us, Doc. You called us in for help. That's what you'll get. You've saved every single one of us, so we all owe you a few lives."

I wanted to argue the point, except that it required more energy than I had at the moment. "It's a favor I never needed repaid, but I'm grateful for the assist. So, thank you."

Bones just nodded, then said, "We don't have to hug or anything, right?"

I chuckled. "No. I'm good."

He gave me a thumbs up then grabbed the second bag. It left us both with one hand free. Voodoo remained with the vehicle and on watch. No more bombs on the vehicles. We'd all started double-checking any car we got into and we had mirrors to scan beneath them.

If the car couldn't be secured, then it had to have a guard —no more risks. Well, life was a risk, but minimizing them was good.

We pulled back into the warehouse at the twenty-nine-minute mark. Little Bit stood with Milo, her expression tense and her arms folded. That didn't look like a fun conversation.

"Voodoo, can you run the shit inside and check on Alphabet?"

"Yep. Gonna relieve him to get some sleep. I can handle surveillance for a bit."

Bones nodded. "Check in with LB too. See how she's doing."

Voodoo stopped dead and cut a look at Bones.

"Suck it up," Bones told him without sympathy. "You didn't have to be an asshole about it."

"Fuck," he muttered, then grabbed the bags from the back before stalking off. Ignoring that as not my current problem, I headed for Little Bit.

"I don't know if I want to see him, especially after what Mom said."

"You don't have to," I told her before Milo uttered a word, and she shifted her gaze to me. The intense darkness in her eyes called to me, but the flicker of a smile on her lips when our gazes collided made me open my arms. She slid right into them and wrapped herself around me.

Bones moved past us and headed for the office where Kellan and Jasper waited with Vaughn. I didn't see the twins or Freddie, but they were likely nearby.

Holding her tight, I rested my chin on her head and peered at Milo. His expression hadn't changed, though it relaxed some as she did. He rubbed the back of his neck.

"I know I don't have to," she murmured against my chest. "But I should."

Milo closed his eyes and blew out a breath. Yeah, she would make herself do it even if she didn't want to be anywhere near him.

"Little Bit," I said, pulling back and meeting her gaze. "There is no *should*. We know what we need to know. I'm not sure about what you need to know. However we can find that out, and you never have to see him again."

"What I need to know is if he knew," she said slowly. "If he knew and did nothing. I need to know if he was ever really my father or if I was just the toy they picked up for Uncle Fuckbucket."

Rage kindled in my gut, hot and wrathful. No child should *ever* have to learn their parent was such an epic fuckup. "Tell me how knowing will help you."

I needed one good reason to *not* stop her. Because every instinct I had said not a chance in hell did I let her walk in there, did I let her see the steaming pile of shit.

"Because if I don't see and hear it, I may always wonder... and I can't live with what-if or maybe anymore. I need to know. I need to know so I can put him behind me if I need to do that."

Fuck, if that didn't stop me cold. My anger was still there. So was my need for vengeance for Steph and for Little Bit. Only I wouldn't take this from her...

Milo tugged her hair gently and she twisted to look at him. "Will you promise me one thing?"

"If I can." Good girl, don't promise anything without hearing what it was first.

"If it gets bad, or you need to stop, just go. Don't explain to anyone or try to muscle through it. Walk out. Can you promise me to do that?"

"I can try," she said slowly, then let out a shaky breath. When she held up her hand to show us it was trembling, I wanted to drag her away from all of this.

"Just remember," I told her. "You're not going in there alone."

Milo didn't say anything, he simply nodded. Yeah, I didn't envy him right now. The urge to break someone over and over for what they'd done to her was right there.

"This is just the next step," I reminded them both as I tucked Little Bit under my arm. Focus and control were easier when I had them to look after. As much as I was looking forward to getting my hands on that asshole, Little Bit's feelings and needs came first.

We had time to take him apart.

Kellan's focus was on Little Bit as we approached. He studied her then flicked his gaze up. Vaughn and Jasper also zeroed in on her, with Vaughn giving her an encouraging smile.

"This is how we're doing this. We're starting with straightforward questions. We're going to keep it polite and entirely non-threatening."

Jasper snorted.

"Then we're going to rip out his liver and tap dance on his spleen," Liam said from behind us. Little Bit twisted as the twins and Freddie arrived. "Don't worry, Hellspawn. We aren't doing anything until he hangs himself."

Until he hanged himself. A when, not an if.

Bones leaned against the door to the office, his expression neutral. "If you want answers, I can get them."

"Thanks," I told him. "This is personal."

He nodded. "You need me, call me. I'll keep watch out here."

Kellan hadn't moved yet. He focused on Liam, then Jasper, and finally Milo and me. "Are we clear? Straightforward, polite, conversational… if you can't handle that, don't go in there."

"I want to ask the first question," Little Bit said, and everyone swung their gazes her way. The need to object, to send her back into the clubhouse or further from here, was there. Even Kellan, who seemed far calmer than the rest of us, gave her a measuring look.

But, "You sure, Sparrow?" was all he asked.

"I don't know what he'll say… I don't even know what I want him to say. But…I want to ask the first few questions, then if I can't handle it…" She glanced at Milo. "I'll go and let you guys deal with him."

That was a hell of a concession on her part.

"Thank you, Dove," Vaughn said softly. "But you got this."

"Yeah, you do," Jasper agreed.

"Freddie," Kellan said, switching his gaze to him. "Give your knife to Sparrow, please."

That startled everyone. For her part, Little Bit glanced at Freddie and he shook his head. "Knife an asshole once because they spoke out of turn and everyone thinks I'm a loose cannon."

"No," Rome said as Freddie passed Little Bit the knife. "Everyone *knows* you are protective and fast. We need to ask him questions and get answers, not kill him."

The unspoken "yet" hung off the end of his sentence. Little Bit closed her hand around the knife then slipped it into her pocket before holding her hand out to Freddie. He clasped it, and I let her go so Freddie could walk her inside. Kellan and Vaughn moved ahead, with Jasper dropping back to bracket her free side while the rest of us followed.

It didn't matter if I'd seen pictures of the man. Her father didn't look like much sitting chained to a chair in the middle of the fridge. He was still in a dress shirt and slacks, although he had no shoes, jacket, or tie. His hair was disheveled, and a huge bruise marred his cheek.

Shipping must have been rough. For now, I kept my distance, standing back and folding my arms as everyone filtered in. He studied all of us, defiance in his eyes as he lifted his chin. The moment he caught sight of Little Bit, though, that facade began to crumble.

"Emersyn?" Shock jerked through his voice. "What are you doing with—"

"I'm here to ask you some questions." She didn't answer his.

"Emersyn," he managed to sound almost commanding. "Let me go, and we can discuss this civilly, whatever this is."

"That's not negotiable at the moment," she told him, and the shock resurfaced on Reginald Sharpe's face. "Maybe if you're honest with me and answer our questions, we can discuss it then."

From this angle, I could see the white knuckles on her hand where she was hanging onto Freddie. He'd gone rock still, his whole focus on the man in that chair. It was a damn good thing he didn't have his knife, but Vaughn, Jasper, and Liam were framing them in a triangle form as much to protect them as to keep him from killing the son of a bitch outright.

"Fine, ask me your questions. You've been missing for months, and I thought you were in trouble. Instead I find you here whori—"

He never finished the statement, Kellan punched him so hard blood flew from his mouth and his head jerked before the chair toppled over.

Pulling a handkerchief out of his inner pocket, he wiped off his knuckles. "Let's be very clear, Mr. Sharpe. When you speak to her, you will speak in a respectful, polite tone, or you will be corrected. No one speaks to her like that. I don't give a fuck who you are."

Liam and Jasper picked him and his chair up and positioned him back in place.

"And people say I have anger management issues," Jasper quipped, making Little Bit actually laugh. It helped with the tension in the room.

Kellan gave her a soft look. "My apologies for interrupting, I didn't care for his tone."

"Thank you," she said, and I had to cover my own smirk as Sharpe stared from her to Kel and then back again. He had no definitions or understanding of the woman he was dealing with.

I hope she made him choke on it.

"You know, I was going to ask a lot of different questions, but I mainly only have two." She straightened and took two steps forward without quite closing the distance to him. "Did you know that Uncle Bradley raped Mom after you were married? And did you know what he was doing to me?"

# CHAPTER 25

*EMERSYN*

The earlier trembling seemed strangely absent as I stared at my father. Outside of some video footage on the news, I hadn't seen him in almost three years. If I tried to concentrate on it, we barely spoke. I received gifts and cards, the occasional sorry he couldn't make it back for my break, but that Uncle Fuckbucket would take care of me.

Right now, I couldn't recall the last time we sat down to a meal. Whether it was that harsh reality surfacing from years of denial or the violent one seated right in front of me, staring with empty eyes, I had no idea.

Worse, watching him—all I could see was the vague resemblance to his brother. It was there... around the eyes and the shape of his mouth. His chin wasn't quite as squared off, and his cheekbones weren't as sharp. The pun didn't even pull a smile to my lips.

More disturbing, the exhaustion on his face. The luggage beneath his bloodshot eyes. Scraping away the polished veneer left a far different man from the one who inhabited my memories.

"Answer her questions," Kellan said when Daddy didn't say a word.

He cleared his throat. "Maybe we could have some privacy…"

"No," I answered before anyone else could, squeezing Freddie's hand too much. He didn't pull away or say a word, however. "These guys are my family. What you tell me, I'll tell them. So no, they aren't going anywhere."

"They are not your family," Daddy snapped, sending spittle and blood flying. It was a little unnerving to see how gruesome the blood on his teeth appeared as he spoke. What was more unnerving was how unmoved by it I was. I'd seen bloody attack after bloody attack—I'd even killed a couple of people…

His bloody mouth honestly didn't register as something concerning. He could still breathe, right?

"You're avoiding answering the questions," I told him, aware of how his gaze swept over the guys and kept coming back to me.

"Emmy," he said, his voice dropping in pitch. "Sweetheart…"

Yeah, I didn't like that nickname any more than I did Princess.

"Let's talk," he said, trying to steady his breathing. Sweat had already soaked through his stained shirt and it seemed to be soaking through him now. The sour smell was cloying with the combination of body odor and his favorite cologne. Maybe it was on his shirt somewhere. It would have to be to linger this long.

None of that mattered. He was afraid. Genuine fear lurked in his eyes. The difference in his reaction to Mom's couldn't be more apparent.

"Please, Princess—"

"Don't call me that," I said before the guys could. Though Jasper's knuckles went white and Liam's expression bordered on murder face. I didn't dare look at anyone else. "Especially if that's how you intend to plead your case."

The shift in his expression was a lot harder to read. Confusion? Surprise? Irritation? I wasn't sure what he was thinking.

"What happened to you?" Turning the question on me. "Brad said you've been having some issues, though this is— dangerously close to delusional."

I closed my eyes, but the sudden grunt of pain as the chair crashed over had me opening them again. Daddy was on the floor. Blood leaked from his nose as Jasper and Vaughn, this time, hauled him up. Liam flexed his hand as he glared at him.

"Daddy—" No, that wasn't getting us anywhere; honestly, he'd already answered my questions. Did I want to make him say it aloud? "Mr. Sharpe."

His wild-eyed gaze bounced up to mine. Once upon a time, the evident anger reflecting in there would have made me flinch. "I'm Daddy…"

"Not anymore," I informed him. "You're fast on your way to being a total stranger, Mr. Sharpe."

"What the hell happened to you?" Was he that delusional? Or was he really that good of an actor? "What happened to my sweet girl?"

"Why don't you tell me?"

There.

The moment I asked the question, his gaze slid away.

"Yeah, you knew."

Milo was already moving. I expected it and I didn't look away. He knocked my father over and right out of the chair.

The man hit the ground with a grunt and a crack of something. A rib, maybe? His wrist?

I could perform with cracked ribs.

He'd survive.

The air around Milo seemed to vibrate with the same rage circling everyone else. At my sigh, Freddie let go of my hand and slid an arm around me before catching my hand in his free one.

"Time to go?" The question was so soft I doubted anyone else heard it.

I shook my head once. Not quite yet. Beyond Milo, Liam watched my father with cold eyes. The emptiness there was not something I enjoyed seeing, particularly when he was as far from cold as you could get.

At the same time, I recognized the rage. How could I not? It practically peppered the air around us. With the weight of Freddie's arm grounding me, I watched the man who'd adopted me struggle to try and sit up. He couldn't quite get his feet under him or his arms.

Realization seemed to hit him, and he considered crawling, but Vaughn moved to block him. Everywhere he twisted, the Vandals were right there. We weren't letting him go.

Finally, he wrenched himself around to stare up at Milo then past him to me. "What do you want to get me out of here?"

Behind me, Mickey let out a low snort. "Pathetic piece of shit."

I couldn't have said it better. Honestly, why had I ever idolized him? Too stupid to know better? Or maybe I had. It was why I had tried to stay away more. It wasn't just my uncle I avoided, but all of them.

The mother who left me with her abuser.

The father who didn't care...

"What did you get when you gave me to him?"

The temperature in the fridge dipped. I felt more than saw Freddie slip the knife out of my pocket. When I put my hand over his, he stopped, but the stillness around us was powerful.

"It—wasn't like that."

Rome shifted to move up next to me while Mickey took a position on the other side of Freddie. Kellan hadn't moved from where he, Liam, Milo, Jasper, and Vaughn formed a circle around my father.

My father.

Guess they both ended up being terrible.

"No?" The faintest of quavers in my voice steadied as Rome settled his hand at the base of my spine. Freddie kept an arm around my shoulder while I held his hand with the knife and Rome was right there with us. "What was it like then?"

My father shot a look at the circle around him, hesitation written all over his face. Or maybe he realized that he wasn't going to leave this room. I searched inside me for some sense of sadness or grief. But it wasn't there...

"Answer her question," Jasper said in a bored tone. "She's been exceptionally polite, and you're annoying me."

I didn't quite smile at his description, but it helped.

"Sweetheart," my father—no, Sharpe said as he struggled to sit up. His hands were still bound together and so were his feet. The only restraints Milo had broken were the ones keeping my father to the chair. "Brad—Brad's a bastard. I know that. He's...also very manipulative."

"Fuck off with your excuses," Milo said. "And answer her fucking question."

"I'm working on it," Sharpe spat out. "She needs to understand what was happening."

"Excuse me," Kellan said, reaching forward to seize Sharpe's bound wrists. "Left or right hand?"

"What?"

"Right," I supplied, and Kellan flashed me a smile.

"Thank you, Sparrow."

"Why do you—" Sharpe's next words broke off on a scream as Kellan broke the index finger on his right hand.

"I'm going to break a finger each time you open your mouth and don't answer her question." Kellan's calmness wrapped around me, and I leaned back, resting against Freddie and Rome.

"You son of a bi—" He ended up screaming again as Kellan broke his middle finger.

"You have eight more, and I have time," Kellan told him. "Answer her question."

It took two more fingers, screams that turned his voice ragged, and the distinct stink of urine before he sobbed, "What was the fucking question?"

I gave Freddie's hand a squeeze before taking a step forward. His and Rome's contact fell away, but they didn't retreat. They had my back. With care, I squatted down so I was on eye level with my father.

No matter how often he tried, there was nowhere safe for him to look, so I waited for him to focus on me. Tears were wet on his red face, and there were definite flickers of pain. His right hand was mangled.

They could probably fix it.

Mickey knew how. Not that I intended to ask him for that.

"What did he give you for me?" I didn't raise my voice. I didn't let the tears out. I was pretty sure the trembling inside didn't communicate to my voice.

Twice he opened his mouth, and both times he closed it without saying anything.

"I know you want to lie—whether it's to yourself or to me, I don't care. Just—tell me. It can't be any worse than everything else I endured." The truth in that statement chipped away at a shackle I hadn't even realized was present.

The past chained me as effectively as my uncle had. The past. Their choices. My own in the effort to survive. That was then. This was now.

"I didn't know why he wanted you," Sharpe said slowly. "I've never been good with money—but then you know that."

"You're a gambler," I said without recrimination or much of anything.

"A bad one," he said. "That week...that week he assaulted your mother, that was to punish me for losing two lucrative contracts because I was gambling." He sniffed. "He sent me to try and fix it, but I was pretty sure he knew I'd fail..."

I waited.

"He showed me the tapes when I got back. I took from him so he took from me." Another sniff. "She didn't tell me..." He shot me a teary look. "We never spoke of it, and after that...I made sure to take her with me when I had trips, or I made sure she was off on her own..."

"You want a fucking medal for not leaving your wife with her rapist?" Liam said. "You should have nailed his dick to the floor."

"Then set it on fire," Freddie supplied.

"After you skinned him alive," Jasper offered up.

"You don't know him," my father said, cradling his broken hand. "I thought...I thought since she never said anything that maybe it hadn't been as bad as it looked. Then—she lost the baby and...I was grateful." Guilt filled his expression. "I didn't want her to have his child, and I had no idea if it was mine."

I was going to throw up.

"It was better, you know...he would be a terrible father." He looked right at me, as if begging me to understand.

"I had an abortion when I was sixteen. I'm very well aware of how bad a parent he would have been."

His face drained of all color. "Emersyn..."

"No," I said, shaking my head. "Don't tell me how sorry you are—you're not. You didn't protect Mom. You didn't protect me. You let him use her for your mistakes—what mistakes did you make that I was payment for?"

A sob came out of him, snotty and pained, and I felt... numb.

"He wanted a little girl...someone of his own to love, and he didn't want a wife or any of the baggage. When Moira couldn't have kids...she was broken about it. He suggested that we adopt...that it would be a child for all of us." Head down, he sobbed harder. "He loved you so much and was always so proud of you...I never thought..."

He didn't look away before those last two sentences. "Can you break the pinky on his left hand for me?"

I honestly didn't know who I was asking. Liam ripped his left arm back and Kellan snapped it in a move so smooth it looked like they'd rehearsed. My father shrieked.

"I told you..."

"Lies. Those last two sentences were lies."

"He did love you," my father argued, and I shook my head.

"That was never love. Now, the part about you never thought? You want to try that again?"

"Index finger or ring finger, Hellspawn?"

"Index. He doesn't deserve the ring finger." He still wore his wedding band.

Kellan reached for the index finger, and my father shrieked. "Don't—I knew, okay. I saw...when you were five, and he started insisting on the sleepovers. I saw it....and he told me I had two choices. We adopted you together, where you were his as much as you were mine, and if I fought him on it, he would cut me off. Let my creditors come for me—so they'd have destroyed me, and then he would still have had you—and your mother. At least...if I were around, I could protect you..."

"Wow," Freddie said, elongating the word. "You're a real piece of shit. You sold her for a hit—and you just let him keep her so he'd keep funding your addiction."

"It wasn't supposed to be like that...you left, you went to the show. You stayed away..."

Was that supposed to make it better?

"I'm sorry," he whispered, crying. "I'm so fucking sorry."

I started to rise when Rome held his hand out to me. I slid my fingers over his palm and he helped me to my feet.

"Any more questions, Dove?" Vaughn asked, and the rough sympathy in his eyes buoyed me. Because there was also pride in them. Pride and understanding.

"No," I said slowly. "Nothing I really care about. I know you guys have questions...including where Uncle Fuck-bucket is right now—"

"Emersyn!" Sharpe lunged toward me, except he didn't make it halfway to his feet before Liam kicked him hard. The blow sent him face-first into the concrete.

"You were saying, Hellspawn?"

"Make sure Mom gets to see him before you're done. She deserves some closure." And I needed to get out of this room. Rome tugged me to him, and I closed my eyes as he wrapped me up in a hug. "Can we go now?" My voice was low, but I wasn't sure I could stop the trembling anymore.

Knuckles touched down my spine, and Kellan kissed the back of my head. "We got this. Go, let Rome look after you."

Curled up tight to Rome, I trusted him to guide me toward the door, pausing only to brush a kiss to Freddie's cheek and another to Mickey's.

Liam, Milo, Jasper, and Vaughn were too close to my so-called father. I didn't want to be that close to him.

"Emersyn!" Sharpe yelled. "Emersyn!"

I didn't look back, and whatever he screamed next came out far more pained, but the door closing cut it off. Rome picked me up to carry me out of the office. He didn't say anything as I buried my face against his neck.

Words weren't what I needed right now.

# CHAPTER 26

*JASPER*

$\mathcal{N}$o one moved while Rome walked Swan out. I wasn't the only one tracking their passage. Her head was up and her shoulders back, despite trembling with every attempt she made to cover it.

When she couldn't cover anymore, we did. Rome moved her as Milo shifted his stance to block Sharpe's view, even as the sad sack of shit kept screaming her name. No one said a word as bloody spittle flew from his mouth.

"Godda—" He didn't get to finish his bellow as Kellan made a cutting motion with his hand. We surged forward. Milo, me, and Liam hauled Sharpe to his feet. We were less than gentle.

Vaughn lugged the chains down and moved to get the shackles on his wrists. All at once, Sharpe seemed to finally grasp how precarious his situation was. He tried to kick at Milo, so I wrenched his arms a little harder. Once he was locked in, we towed the chains up until he dangled from his wrists.

There was a certain point where your feet were just barely under you. When you could almost balance on your toes, except you had no steady foundation. The rest of your weight would hang from your wrists while dragging at your shoulders. If you could maintain a specific posture, you relieved the pressure on your upper body only to increase the pain in your feet and ankles.

Mentally and physically exhausting. As the door to the fridge closed, it echoed in the quiet. By unspoken agreement, we swapped places as Doc took point, and he didn't slow down as he ripped the man's shirt open and shredded it.

New bruises littered his chest and arms. Someone hadn't been gentle in how they bound him and transported him. The faint sound of labored breath—

Sharpe cried out as Doc tested his ribs. The moment he found one cracked, he applied fresh pressure and the man flinched, trying to escape the contact. Not that he could go far. He tried to grab at the chain with his mangled hand and shrieked out another cry.

"This is going to get much worse for you," Doc informed him, his voice sounding clinically detached.

"What do you want?" the man practically wept.

"About sixteen years of pure torture," Milo informed him in a voice so chilling it was hot. "I want you to experience every ounce of her terror and discomfort. I want you to feel the humiliating pain and the knowledge that nothing you do will stop what is about to happen to you. That no matter if there is even one single person out there who cares about you, they aren't coming. They are *never* coming, because you are a worthless piece of shit."

"I want dates, I want names, and I want locations," Kellan

informed him as Doc moved to a medical bag we'd set up on the side table. Freddie didn't move at all. He just watched Sharpe with empty, cool eyes as his knife danced over his fingers.

"You're going to give us the information," Liam informed him as he snapped a couple of photographs with his phone. "The only thing to be determined is how long you think you can hold out on giving it to us and how much pain you need to suffer to get there."

"Personally," Vaughn said, his tone as nonchalant even if he was not. "I'm good if it takes a while. We have the time. We also have a solid idea of how much Dove has suffered."

"We do," I said, more to myself than to him. "Let's start this way..." I moved to where Doc was pulling out a scalpel, some clamps, and a series of electrodes.

Yeah, those all looked very uncomfortable. I approved. I snagged a black sack and dragged it over his head. Frankly, I didn't want to look at his fucking face when I wasn't able to just start with breaking the bones in his feet and working my way up.

The sad fact was, we actually needed information from this son of a bitch. I caught Milo's gaze and the barely banked fury flickering in his eyes. There was a stillness in the room, like one spark, and we'd all go up in flames.

Fuck, we all had gone up in flames. We couldn't undo what had been done to her. We couldn't erase the past. The scars were there, inside and out.

We could get vengeance to assuage the loss of her innocence and her freedom. We could seek retribution for the cruelty visited on her repeatedly. It started with that fucker from her dance company, and it wouldn't end until everyone who ever hurt her paid for it.

Kellan cleared his throat and put out his fist. One by one, we all did the same—including Doc. It took four rounds, but we determined the order. We each had a question and a punishment in mind.

The verbal gasping and complaints from under the hood had Liam ripping off a strip of duct tape. So I dragged the fabric upward.

"Just ask the questions."

"Don't worry," Liam told him as he slapped the duct tape over his mouth. The silence was a little blissful. "We will, but you don't make the rules here. You only think you're willing to help right now."

I yanked the cover back over his head. I really didn't want to look at the son of a bitch. Doc moved over to where he was and began to apply the electrodes. His expression had emptied of all emotion after our girl left.

It could be said for all of us. We didn't have to keep anything in reserve right now, for we finally had someone we could unleash our grief and pain on as well. Retribution for his failure to protect the baby he'd taken from all of us.

"You know," Milo said in an undertone next to me. "I keep thinking what it would have been like if I'd fought back against her adoption. If I'd pushed to keep her with me..."

"Don't do that," Kellan said in an equally soft tone. "We can't change it, and what you were trying to do—what Ms. Stephanie tried to do—was put Sparrow first. We didn't know. I wish to fuck we had so we could have acted sooner."

"Only we didn't," I said, catching the lifeline Kellan had thrown to Milo. Grasping it in both hands, I hauled us toward the shore. "We have her now. We'll protect her now. We'll get her the pound of flesh she is owed."

"I know," Milo said, not even a flicker of a smile on his face. "We will...and at the same time, I'm imagining Ivy here, growing up with us to look after her *all* the time."

"We'd have beaten up a lot more people," Vaughn said, and Liam actually laughed.

"That would have been one of the good parts."

But would she have grown up as our baby sister in that scenario? Who would she have been? Would we have smothered her to keep her safe? Fuck knew, we'd have ripped the eyeballs out of anyone who looked at her the wrong way.

"Wouldn't be the same," Freddie said, his voice tight. Although he wasn't pale or shaky. He also looked focused. I wasn't the only one keeping an eye on him. "She wouldn't be. Don't know if she would feel better or not. But I like Boo-Boo as she is, even if I don't like what she lived through."

"Agreed," Doc said, then stepped back and picked up a device. He adjusted something on it and depressed a button. Sharpe let out a squeal of sound as his whole body convulsed. "Little high on the voltage."

He nudged the dial one degree and I had yet to determine if it was up or down. When he depressed the button this time, Sharpe's whole body arched at the voltage hitting him. He was shaking when Doc let go of the control.

Holding it up to all of us, he said, "Warning ahead of time, and everyone else hands off."

Sharpe let out a low sobbing moan that the tape muffled. Kellan looked at his watch before he focused on each of us. "Split it up. We're going to do this in shifts. No one stays if their temper starts to go."

"You keeping watch?" I checked because as much as I wanted to kill this son of a bitch, I wanted him to suffer. We kept Arlington for weeks until he was begging to die.

I was fine with that being the outcome for this asshole as well. We had the time to do it right, but first…

"Yes," Kellan said. "So everyone else not on deck, take a break and walk it off."

I wasn't the only one who glanced at Liam. He rolled his eyes. "I'm fine."

"Me too," Freddie said before we could suggest otherwise.

Of all of us, Vaughn and Kellan were likely the only two as calm as they actually appeared.

Finally, I focused on Milo and Doc.

"I'm not leaving," Milo said. "But I won't touch him until we have answers..."

I could respect that. "Don't worry, brother, I got your back. Oh. We need to get something to cauterize his hand before we're done."

"I got it," Doc said, arms folded as he faced Sharpe. Silence rippled around us in a circle. He actually won the first question, his attention to the man narrowing as if he were weighing which option he would explore first. Then he dropped his gaze to his feet. "Right... Vaughn, you mind gripping the leg for me?"

"Right or left?" Vaughn asked.

"Dealer's choice," Doc told him as he retrieved a scalpel from the tools.

Vaughn gripped Sharpe's right leg. The man immediately started to thrash and kick out with his left as he tried to pull back. Rather than get upset or look even remotely over-worked about it, Vaughn just slammed his elbow into Sharpe's kidney. He let out a muffled grunt and pissed himself.

Again.

The smell was gonna get worse before it got better. Locking his hand around Sharpe's ankle, Vaughn wrenched his foot upwards. At least he didn't try to bend his knee in the other direction.

"Where is your brother?" Doc asked. Simple. Straightforward. Direct.

The muffled response was unintelligible.

"Want to try that again?" Doc said.

Sharpe struggled, but Vaughn kept his leg in place. The

muffled grunting was more shrill sounds and insults in between the sobs than it was worthwhile.

"Right." He cut a slice right down the middle of the guy's foot. I didn't wince, but fuck, that looked painful. The screaming from behind the duct tape said it felt as bad as it sounded.

Vaughn let him go and backed off as he tried to thrash. While Sharpe couldn't balance very well, he did try to extend his foot, opened the cut, and added to the discomfort.

"Nice," I said after a moment. It was simple yet effective.

Doc just shot me a droll look. Folding my arms, I shrugged. I was allowed to enjoy the work, but I got it. Not the time. I'd save my compliments for later.

"Want another go, or are we moving around the circle?" Kellan asked.

"We can come back to my question." Doc nodded to me, and I cracked my knuckles. I had the second question.

I moved up next to our prisoner and ignored the blood smear on the floor. We really were just getting started.

"So, Mr. Sharpe," I said, keeping my tone polite. "You insisted that you tried to protect her. You couldn't answer her question earlier, so let me ask you again. At what point in her life did you *ever* actually protect her?"

A groan was the only sound from under the hood.

"I don't think he gets this game," I said to Kellan. "Do we need to explain the rules to him again?"

Please say yes.

"Give him a life lesson. I don't mind taking my time, but if he needs to understand how much pain we can inflict, let's go ahead and give him a demonstration."

Milo shifted his gaze to the side. Socks and fruit. We needed to keep him alive long enough to answer everything and suffer. So, we started with what hurt but didn't do as much damage as it felt like.

I struck first, but Freddie's blow landed a split second after mine, and Milo's caught him from the front. Liam and Vaughn were quick to join in.

Sharpe had pissed himself for a third time, though I remained content to deliver the beating.

For. Now.

# CHAPTER 27

VAUGHN

Forty-five minutes in, Sharpe passed out from the pain. Doc woke him with smelling salts. He didn't make it another hour before collapsing again. Not all of the patches that Doc put on him were for shock treatments. He actually had two cardiac monitors on.

"His pulse is fast but within range," Doc said as he hooked up an IV for fluids. "We should probably give him a few hours, then start again."

"No, if we wait a few hours, he might dig in. He's already wavering. The only thing keeping him from telling us everything is he's afraid of his brother, " Milo said.

I'd caught that too. "Perhaps we bring Moira down here?"

Jasper grimaced. "We should save her for a final coup de grâce. Once we crack him, *then* we bring her in."

Freddie spun his knife around on the edge of his fingers. "Didn't Rome say he was on the phone with the fuckbucket when we got him?"

"Yes," Kellan answered as he twisted open a bottle of water. "Turned over all the electronics to Alphabet. They already know where we are, so tracking us isn't a concern. At the same time, we need the data off of it."

"He's trying to track the numbers back, but the other phone is off." Of course, Doc had spoken to them. Made sense. Honestly, I wasn't sure what to think about Doc's team personally. Professionally? They were solid. That and Doc trusted them, so that was enough for me.

"I was kind of hoping we could trace him that way," Freddie said, still observing Sharpe as he spun his knife.

"He won't be anywhere they own," Liam said. "He's been in hiding since we got Hellspawn back." Then, he cut a look at Sharpe. "He's been sending this asshole out to do appearances. Meanwhile, they dump the wife in a facility and keep her drugged."

"Leverage?" Doc asked, but even as he formed the word, he appeared to be shaking his head. "No, that would be too direct."

"Yeah, he didn't seem that broken up about her," Milo said. "It could be an act, but we don't know anything for sure."

"Oh, we know some things," Jasper said as he paced the room and stretched. "He's a sack of shit for one."

This was true. "If he isn't hiding at any of his properties, then perhaps something that's in the company name or owned by Moira."

That tugged a thread that pulled the attention in the fridge to him.

"Why else lock her down?" I asked. "He wanted her drugged, insensible, and out of sight. If you wanted to hide in plain sight, you hide where people aren't looking for you…"

Kellan scratched his jaw thoughtfully before glancing at Doc. "Let's ask them to add Moira Sharpe to their searches."

"Yep."

We gave Sharpe another thirty minutes to recoup. After Doc removed the IV, Milo picked up the hose. Icy spray was never a fun way to wake up.

He coughed and sputtered, then groaned as his pains hit. Yeah, I was fine with him suffering. It was my turn to ask him a question. Since we hadn't gotten any actionable answers yet, we would keep going around in a circle until we were back to the beginning.

Stripping the hood off, I studied the man dangling from the chains. He didn't seem remotely intimidating *before* we brought him in. Now?

Pathetic seemed too good a word for him. Breathing hard through his nose, he blinked at the brightness around him and then stared at me. I said nothing, just studied him. This man and his brother were responsible for all the deaths at the tattoo shop.

They were the ones who got Lauren burned. She was still in the hospital, suffering from second-degree burns on one of her legs and smoke inhalation. I'd only made it to the hospital twice to check on her.

On the second visit, she mentioned that someone had paid her medical bills. I didn't have to ask who that was. Liam was still looking after everyone, even while he mourned *his* father.

Then there was this asshole.

Sharpe stared at me then made some guttural sounds behind the tape. Twice more he attempted it. While the words didn't translate, the tone did.

"Yeah, you're still not ready to talk." There was too much defiance in him lingering. Not that he possessed an ounce of his daughter's spirit. Hell, he didn't really deserve to call Dove his daughter. She was so much more than him.

Pivoting, I went to the table and picked up the butane

torch. It was designed for cooking, and what I intended to do definitely fell into a similar category.

That said, I turned so he could see what I was doing as I fired up the torch. I studied the blue flame shooting from the tip before glimpsing at Sharpe.

He'd blanched, what little color he had left melting away.

"You're scared, aren't you?" I asked him. "Worried about what I'm going to do with this. Horrified that no one will take the tape off to let you talk. Worried we'll never hear anything but your screams. If you think we don't give a fuck about those, you're right."

I gave it a moment to let the words sink in before I moved closer. He wanted to lean away from the heat rolling off the torch. Unfortunately for him, he didn't have very far to go. He struggled with getting his feet under him, only that just opened up the cuts on the bottom of his feet—we'd sliced both by now.

"The thing is," I continued as I invaded his space. "You're not ready to talk yet. You think this is hell right now. How long will it take you to realize it's only been a few hours like this, and Dove spent *years* chained, gagged, and tortured. Where were you?"

I canted my head.

"What was it you said? Right...you were there to try and protect her. Only, you didn't protect her. Do something for me. Think about all the times you sat across from her at a meal after your brother put his hands on her. Think about all the nights you left her with him, aware of what he was going to do. Think about all the times she had to return to a traveling show bruised, battered, and brutalized. Then you think about how many years she had to do that for..."

I brought the torch to his side, a glancing blow, though right where the skin on his torso stretched. His screams climbed even if I didn't keep the heat there. It didn't take the torch long, but I'd managed to burn the beginnings of a letter.

Studying the torch for a moment, I looked back at him.

"You know, I gave her both the tattoos she's wearing right now." I kept it conversational. "She didn't even flinch when the needle was on her skin. Determined and courageous, but most of all...she survived. I already know you won't. But keep telling yourself otherwise."

I flicked the torch on against his other side, and the stretch of his mouth as he screamed pulled some of the tape loose.

"Yeah, you keep telling yourself that. It means we get all the time in the world with you. I'm planning to enjoy it."

Not that he caught the last few words, he'd already pissed himself and passed out again.

"Is it me, or should we stop giving him IVs?" Freddie asked. "Cause the pissing is getting old."

Kellan shook his head. "This is going to take time. Bag him up and lock him down. We'll give him time to wake up alone and hurting. Then come see him again."

I didn't want to leave him there just dangling. Waking him up and taking him apart, joint by joint, was on my list of things to do. Except Kellan was right.

Freddie didn't even argue. I had to commend him on holding his temper in check. It would be easy for him to cut the man up. But he didn't.

Not yet.

As it was, we cleaned up and ripped the tape off his face in case he decided to vomit. No one wanted him to off himself that way without us. Once the bag was back on his head, we were out.

I left Kellan and Milo talking to Liam while I headed back to the clubhouse. Freddie and Jasper weren't far behind me. I thought Doc was coming with, but he moved to talk to his guys.

Pausing at the door, I watched them. I still couldn't wrap my head around the idea that Ms. Stephanie was gone. I honestly wasn't sure how any of us were up and functioning —we had no choice.

Dove needed us, and she'd been in this fight her whole life. As much as she wanted to get away from her uncle, she wasn't abandoning us to do it. Not that it was ever a thought in my mind.

"He'll be okay," Jasper said, following my gaze. "We'll all get through this, just like we have everything else."

"Who are you, and what did you do with Hawk?" I asked, eyeing him. "When did you become Mr. Positivity?"

"The day she said yes," he told me, and really—how the fuck did you argue with that?

Inside the clubhouse, Rome and Dove weren't downstairs, so I made coffee and Jasper put together sandwiches. I checked for any bloodstains on me before we headed up.

The others hadn't returned yet, and I wouldn't fault them. They needed a moment; Milo probably more than the rest of us. When we got to the suite, it was dark in the living room, but the running lights around the ceiling were on, as was the television.

Dove was curled up in Rome's lap, and a movie was playing on the screen. It was one of the Fast and Furious ones. Five, maybe.

"How is she?" Freddie asked as he settled on the sofa near them.

"Exhausted but strong," Rome said. "She insisted on seeing her mother."

I grimaced, and so did Jasper. "How'd that go?" He yanked off his shoes before he stood up.

Rome just shrugged. "Lots of tears, her mother's, and anger, Starling's."

Brushing the hair away from her face, I asked, "You good, or do you need to move?"

"I'm good," Rome said, and Freddie shifted to sit next to him and passed Rome a coffee.

"I'm grabbing a shower," Jasper said. "Be out in a few."

That was not a bad idea.

Thirty minutes later, we were sprawled on the sofa when Liam and Doc made their way up. Kellan and Milo were still downstairs. Doc disappeared into Dove's room for a shower, and Liam sprawled in a chair where he could keep an eye on her and the movie.

It was what we were all doing. We finished the food, switched to the next movie, and Doc took over the other chair when Kellan came in.

"Jas?"

Jasper cut a look at him.

"Can you handle first watch?"

"Yep," he said, rising, then bumping my shoulder.

"Four hours, then Vaughn will relieve you."

I gave him a thumbs-up before I stretched back and closed my eyes. If I had four hours, I needed to take advantage of it.

"I'm showering, then we put her to bed," Kellan continued.

"Dibs," Liam said before anyone else could, and I chuckled as Doc grumbled.

"As long as she isn't alone." Kellan sounded tired.

Slitting an eye open, I studied him. "Hit the hay. You need sleep. We're not starting on him again until tomorrow, right?"

"Right."

"Then sleep."

Kel nodded. Freddie was already asleep, and Doc didn't look far off. No one had made any moves to put Dove to bed yet. Liam waited for Milo to join us before he rose and Rome surrendered her to his brother.

After he carried her into her room, Milo sank into the chair Liam had abandoned.

"Doc's friends have watch on the warehouse. The new cameras are working. Everyone who can sleep should." Kellan hadn't come back out, so hopefully, he already was.

"Yeah," Doc said. "Everyone who can."

He cut a look to Rome and me. "Go sleep. I'll nudge you in four hours. Then crash myself."

Worked for me. I shoved off the sofa and headed for my room. To absolutely no one's surprise, Rome went for Dove's room.

Where she slept was usually where he did.

I didn't bother to get undressed, just fell back on the bed. Four hours. My internal clock could handle that.

That was at least eight to twelve before we went to see Sharpe again.

The man was going to shit himself.

Good.

# CHAPTER 28

*EMERSYN*

*W*armth enveloped me. A hand on my back and another on my ass registered, as awareness swept aside the fog of sleep. Twin scents of sandalwood with hints of rosewood and amber tickled my nostril. The thump of a steady heartbeat beneath my ear and hard muscle pressed to my cheek.

Liam.

I rubbed my cheek against him slowly. Hopefully, I hadn't drooled. When it was just Rome, I always woke up with him wrapped around me, cradling me like he would his bear. I loved that bear.

The trickle of thoughts split to follow both mental paths, only at the same time, I tugged my attention from those to Liam. Somehow, Liam always pulled me over him, draping me like I was his personal blanket.

Lifting my head slowly, I blinked to let my eyes focus on the near gloom of the room. There was a night light in the corner, the soft blue light hardly likely to disturb our sleep. Yet it offered just enough illumination where I could make out the line of Liam's jaw. He had one arm curled beneath his head, the other wrapped around me with his hand on my ass.

The other hand on my back belonged to Rome. Turning my head a fraction, I smiled at where Rome slept on his side. He angled toward us, the weight of his hand a steady comfort. I'd gone to sleep in his lap, all the while trying to wrestle my recalcitrant emotions back into their box.

Not that I had much success. I'd hoped so much that my father hadn't known. That we'd see shock or surprise. Even if he hadn't expressed *those* emotions, where was the disgust or sadness? He discussed Mom's rape, like it was an unfortunate punishment for *him* and the miscarriage as a relief.

Going to see Mom after probably hadn't been my brightest move. She was angry and upset that Dad was here. Angrier that I wouldn't let her see him, not yet. When she said she wanted to go, I told her we needed to wait.

The conversation devolved into tears and recrimination. It might have gotten even worse if Rome hadn't told her no, she didn't get to leave until it was safe and to stop harassing me. Then ushered me out.

Hard to harass me if I wasn't in there. Once back in the suite, I had difficulty not thinking about what the guys were doing. I didn't care if they were torturing my father. I *knew* he deserved it. At the same time, he was still the father I'd *protected* from my uncle.

I'd protected them both, or thought I was, and what had they done?

"Hey," a soft voice in the dark said, and I lifted my lashes to meet the concern in Liam's eyes as a tear tracked down my cheek.

"Hi." The word came out more of a croak, and I sniffled.

With care, Liam dragged his hand up my back to my face, then he swiped away the tear. "I didn't mean to wake you."

"Don't care, Hellspawn. If you're crying, you better fucking wake me up." The ferocious statement rippled over me like a cold shiver, yet nothing about it was cold. Nuzzling his jaw, I tried to surreptitiously check my breath. It was early, and I didn't want to—

He didn't wait for me to worry about morning breath or not. Instead, he fisted my hair, the pull lighting up my scalp. The pain chased away the tears even as goosebumps spread over my skin. My nipples stiffened where they rested against his bare chest.

A hum of sound from Rome drifted through me even as Liam's mouth crashed into mine. I sighed as heat ignited, an icy fire spilling into my blood and raging through the crevices that spiderwebbed through my aching soul. I stretched out a hand to Rome as Liam sucked against my tongue. His fierce grip on my hair kept me right where I wanted to be.

Rome pressed a kiss to my shoulder, and my nipples tightened where they kept rubbing against Liam's chest. His tongue tangled with mine. Another tear slipped free, but I ignored it as I chased the promise of peace and passion in Liam's arms.

Sighing against his mouth, I ground my hips down to his. The sweet heat of his erection was right there. It slid between my labia. A groan vibrated through me. Whether it was his, mine, or possibly even Rome's, I didn't know. Maybe it was all of us.

"Hellspawn—" Liam said, tugging my hair to pull my head back so he could study me.

"I want you," I said, simple as that. "Both of you." All of you. Twisting, I glanced at Rome. It seemed like weeks had passed rather than hours since I'd curled up in his lap.

He dipped his head, then kissed me. Open-mouthed, wet, and just as demanding as it was giving. I could drown in Rome so effortlessly. I could drown in Liam. I wanted to drown in both of them.

Something white-hot and desperate flashed through me as Liam slid his hands down to my hips. He lifted even as I wrapped my fingers around his cock. Rome plunged his tongue against mine as I guided Liam into the perfect angle.

Then he thrust upward and I cried out. Rome cupped my breast and released me to Liam's kiss. They were a fever, and it was taking over everything. The bed shifted and moved as Liam urged me to ride him.

He rubbed a slow circle against my ass before slapping one cheek, and I clenched around him. "Fuck," Liam exhaled. "Just like that, Hellspawn." He drove me rather mad by alternating between rubbing the heat in and slapping my ass. Then Rome was back—where had he gone?

I lifted my head to find him spreading lube onto his fingers before drizzling more against my ass. The warmed liquid added yet another layer to the sensations rolling over me.

"You remember what I told you?" Liam asked as he held me still, pushed so deep into me it was almost all I could feel.

"Yes," Rome said, even as Liam spread my asscheeks for me. Then he began to tease my anus, and heat swept up from the base of my spine to warm my face and chest. "Slowly, and carefully."

"Lots of lube."

"I know how to work with my hands," Rome told him, easing one finger into me. There was something utterly delightful about being discussed like this. "Kiss Starling."

Liam snorted and I couldn't stifle the giggles escaping me. I caught Liam's faint smirk and the barest hint of a wink as he nodded over my shoulder. Twisting a little, I found Rome studying my ass with such concentration it wound me up inside.

When he added a second finger, the sweet stretch of the burn had me gasping softly. Darting his gaze up to meet mine, Rome seemed to search my face.

"It feels good," I promised him. "The burn...I can feel you." I flexed around Liam. He let out a little hiss of air, or maybe it was a laugh. Either way, it earned me a pinch and what amounted to an indulgent smile. Rome leaned in and kissed me again as he scissored his fingers. At the same time, Liam leaned up to suck one of my nipples against his teeth.

I forgot how to breathe, not that they were giving me much time to actually do that. Seriously, oxygen was over-rated. I clenched around Liam's cock and reached behind me to stroke Rome's. I wanted to twist, to rotate my hips while I ground against Liam and feel Rome at the same time.

Between them, they kept me pinned until Rome added a third finger and Liam pressed his finger in as well.

"Fuck," I swore all over again. It was my turn to pant. "Too much..."

"You can take us," Liam soothed even as Rome bit down on my shoulder. The sharpness of his teeth contrasted with the burn of their stretch. I wanted to push back and press down at once.

Even as he kept me still, Liam thrust upward and ground his pelvis to mine. It sent sparks through my system at the pressure on my clit. Rome stroked my back with his free hand, then tugged my hair so I'd turn to him for another kiss.

Over his shoulder, I locked gazes with Freddie, who was half-sitting up in the armchair in the corner. At some point, he must have come in here to sleep. His eyes were open, and his expression intense.

"Hey, Boo-Boo," he said, his voice a husky whisper that added another caress to my senses. Surprise flickered through me. Rome nipped my lip but turned his head to follow my gaze. Liam's attention shifted, and we were trapped in the most sensual form of twister I'd ever played.

"Hey," I said, a smile pulling at my lips. "You okay?"

"Yeah," he said slowly, leaning forward. "You want me to go?"

I licked my lips, aware of the twins' full attention. They weren't surprised, so they must have known he was in there. "Only if you need or want to—I like having you here."

His expression shifted, and there was a hint of a sly smile on his lips, which thrilled me. "You've already got that pretty pussy stuffed."

I giggled, and Liam groaned as I clamped down on him. "Yes, I do, and I'm about to be the very happy filling in a twin sandwich."

That got me another sharp slap to the ass, courtesy of Liam, and a huff of laughter from Rome.

"Feel good?" The soft question from Freddie turned me all kinds of inside out. More because the flirty smile and playfulness couldn't quite mask the worry.

"So good," I promised. "They never hurt me."

"And we wouldn't," Rome said, even as Liam nodded.

"That said, Freddie, my man, you want to stay, you stay. But we're going back to fucking our girl now. Hellspawn, eyes on me."

The order was impossible to refuse, but I blew Freddie a kiss before looking down at Liam.

"Good girl," he said. "Rome, stop fucking her with your fingers because I need to move."

The demand held just a whisper of a plea, and I swooped down to kiss Liam. Those words were calm, practical, and in charge, precisely what Freddie needed to hear. As Rome shifted behind me, their fingers were out of my ass, and he replaced them with his dick.

"Go slow," Liam ordered in between kisses. "Relax, Hellspawn. Let him fuck into you with the dick he dedicated to you."

That sent another trill of heat through my system. The burn of Rome sliding into me, combined with Liam's hot kisses, edged me higher. I carded my fingers through Liam's hair even as I reached back for Rome, and then they were both inside me as deep as they could go.

A low keening note escaped as they began to rock. I rolled my hips, savoring the glorious burn of Rome in my ass and Liam thrusting into my cunt. I twisted up to kiss Rome and then back to Liam. They passed my kisses back and forth between them. We were all panting, and in between kisses, I caught Freddie's hot eyes on me.

Rome and Liam's hands were everywhere, adjusting me, balancing me, and desire turned incandescent. They alternated between gentle strokes and fierce thrusts. My control was slipping. At the first touch of Liam's fingers to my clit, pleasure fired along my nerves.

Liam's concentration seemed to slip and Rome shifted his angle, every thrust driving me onto Liam. My vision blurred as everything unraveled. The coiled loops of tension detonated, and a keening cry broke out of me. Liam came with me, the heat of his release sparking another firestorm, even as Rome managed a couple more thrusts before he came.

The heat of their release filled me, and I sagged against Liam's chest as Rome settled against my back. The aftershocks seemed to keep pulling them into my body as I felt every delicious inch of them. Rome kissed a path across my shoulders as Liam nibbled kisses against my throat.

Eyes open, I looked at Freddie again. His stare bored into my soul. He was stroking his cock through his pants, and I wished it was me doing it for him. "Are you going to come?" I asked in a wrecked voice, but I was too full and hot with the twins to care.

"No," Freddie said slowly. "I'm saving that."

Really?

He never looked away from me as he kept stroking his dick, and I grinned.

"It would be my pleasure."

That earned me a bite from Liam and a laugh from Rome as he eased upward. We were all groaning. I was stretched and sore in all the right places. It took a bit of adjusting, but once Rome was up, Liam helped roll me over so he could slide out. From the cum sticking to my thighs and dribbling out of my ass, I was a mess.

"Hey, Boo-Boo," Freddie said after Liam bent to kiss me before heading into the bathroom. Rome was already back with a warm washcloth.

"Hmm?"

"Spread your legs just a little wider."

I dropped my knees into a butterfly pose so that he could see my pussy. His sigh pulled another laugh from me.

"Yeah, still got the prettiest pussy I've ever seen."

He'd stayed, and there was no sign of discomfort or fear or even upset. He'd stayed and watched, and I kind of wanted to go over and help him with the erection tenting his pants. At the same time, I didn't want to push.

"You know," I said. "You can always come over here and come on me if you want."

Rome huffed a laugh as he swiped the washcloth between my thighs.

"Maybe later?" Freddie said, just the barest hint of shyness there.

I let him off the hook immediately. "It's a date...whenever you want."

"Awesome," Liam said as he came out of the bathroom.

"C'mere, Hellspawn. Shower time." He glanced at Rome. "You can get your own."

He snorted but kissed my fingers as I stroked his face on the way past. I paused near Freddie and pressed a kiss to the top of his head. He brushed his pinky to mine and I hooked them together, a pinky hug.

"I'm okay," Freddie promised. "You want coffee?"

"I would love coffee." I was still a little worried about him.

"I'll get it. Go shower. Make him eat you out or something and think of me..."

"Fuck you, Freddie," Liam said, a laugh in his voice.

Chuckling, Freddie squeezed my finger once, then let me go. I drifted over to Liam but tracked Freddie as he slid out of my room, followed by Rome.

"Rome will look after him," Liam said, pulling me back against him. I closed my eyes and rested on his strength. "That was a big step for him."

It definitely was. "Thank you for not minding," I whispered.

He gave me a wordless kiss and then tugged me into the shower.

# CHAPTER 29

*FREDDIE*

Sharpe was unconscious...again. Doc had him hooked up to another IV, and we'd hosed the guy down 'cause he stank. One upside to the refurbished fridge, the drainage was a lot better.

"Spit it out before you choke on it," Doc said as he glanced over at me from where he was going through his medical bag. He'd removed the shock pads and added new ones after we cleaned him up.

He'd also given him a vitamin shot, which I thought was weird, but no one asked me, so—whatever. We weren't letting the fucker die.

"I don't get it," I said, dancing the knife on my fingertips. "He has no pain tolerance that I can identify. If we bruise him, he collapses and snivels more than I did when I was seven."

"So why isn't he just breaking?" Doc asked, and I sighed.

"Yes."

Unscrewing the top off a water bottle, Doc shook his head. "We need to find the leverage he can't withstand. Everyone has a breaking point, a place where the right amount of pressure cracks them open. Not so easy with this guy, even if he is weak."

"You think he's more afraid of his brother." I'd been trying to reconcile all of this. At least my abusers never pretended to be family. Their abuse wasn't about their pleasure but their pocketbooks. Sure, they probably had some sick fucks who enjoyed it—but I'd never had someone I *cared* about do that to me.

Watching her watch him when she'd been hoping he'd throw her a bone—even an ounce of regret or remorse, and she might even have forgiven him—had been hell. I wanted to skin him alive for the wounds he'd inflicted.

I didn't think anything could erase her pain. The day she confessed her secret in Pinetree, her darkness had a name. The same darkness haunting her also haunted me. She fought back. She rose above the shit they tried to drown her in, even if they dressed it up in fancy clothes and hung jewelry on it.

"I know he is," Doc said without an ounce of irony or pity. "What kind of man lets his wife's rapist go on to become his daughter's abuser too?"

"I almost hope he is terrified of him," I said, even though I didn't think he was.

Doc eyed me before taking another long drink. We had another round of questioning. Kel and Milo were talking to Doc's team. They had a possible lead on Bradley Sharpe. Better to make sure we pulled on all the threads.

"You don't think he is?"

I shook my head, then glanced at my phone. "He has to know we're going to kill him. Obviously. So how does fear of his brother compete with that?"

Doc frowned.

"See, I think he knew more than he said he did." It wasn't fear or regret—it was guilt coloring everything he did. "I think he knew exactly what his brother was doing every step of the way and allowed it to happen."

We both looked at the man hanging there.

"You don't tell the people who value Boo-Boo the way we do the truth, because what we'd do is a thousand times worse than what we're already doing."

"Or he's convinced his brother will come for him," Doc suggested, though it didn't seem like he believed that idea any more than I did.

I had an idea. So I touched my nose then pointed to the door. Doc nodded and checked on the IV and the restraints before following me to the fridge door. Once we were in the office, he raised his brows.

"We need to bribe him," I said, and it flew against everything I wanted to do. "Convince him we'll let him go…or whatever, as long as he tells us where his brother is and helps us get to him."

Frowning, Doc folded his arms. While he didn't reject the idea immediately, he didn't look terribly enthusiastic. "He's already had dealings with all of us. That's not going to work."

I hated myself. "It will if Boo-Boo does it."

He gave a little jerk as he straightened. "We are not—" Then he cut himself off. "Fuck."

"Yeah," I said. "I'm not a fan. Except the longer Sharpe stays where we can't find him, the more opportunities he has to come after us." To come after her.

Hands on his hips, Doc began to pace. There was a stiffness to his steps that only showed up when he hadn't had time to do his stretches. I should probably annoy him with a reminder, but being clean, sober, *and* responsible kind of maxed out my card at the moment.

Not to mention, I'd already suggested one unpleasant idea. "Run it by Kel," Doc said finally. "I don't like it, and I don't want to ask Little Bit to do it, but she does have the right to make that call."

"If Kel agrees." I didn't miss the fact we were passing the buck on.

"Yeah." Doc glanced back at the fridge. "I wish we trusted her mother."

I didn't say anything. Didn't have to. We couldn't trust her mother to do or say what we needed. Boo-Boo? She could follow a plan, but...

I really wish I hadn't thought of this.

"I'll go find Kel," I said. "You good here?"

Doc waved me away, and I headed back out into the warehouse. Kel and Milo were talking to Alphabet in the kitchen. The smell of lasagna and garlic bread filled the air.

Score, Kel was in a mood to cook.

"I've checked all properties in the name of Sharpe, corporate and personal. I also checked for any under the name of Emersyn Sharpe. She has quite a bit, by the way." Alphabet twirled a pencil. It was severely chewed around the eraser and had toothmarks along the body.

Those were easily explained by how he put the pencil between his teeth to type on the laptop. "The tricky thing is," he said around the pencil. "Most of the properties are hotels, office buildings, and condos in more than a few places. It's—an odd assortment. There are also some links to foreign investment accounts, including a group out of Colombia. Those people are bad news."

"Boo-Boo has investment accounts with a cartel?" How did that happen?

"I don't think they are hers exactly, but there are investments in *her* name. So—"

"You think the reason we can't find him is that he's using criminal resources to hide."

"More than likely. Man probably has friends. People who will hide him, and he's loaded, not like he can't afford it."

"Can you track the money?" Kellan asked.

"I'm working on that," Alphabet said. "But it's not as simple as it looks—they have an unhealthy web of accounts, trusts, and shells. I'll get there, but maybe not before we track this guy down another way."

I grabbed a bottle of water out as they swapped back and forth a few more ideas. The smell of the food made my mouth water, even if the conversation killed my appetite. Milo said he was walking Alphabet out, and I only half-listened to them going.

"What's up?" Kellan asked, and I dragged my attention to him.

He leaned against the counter, shirt sleeves rolled up and his tie undone.

"Why are you wearing a tie?"

"Had to go to the bank this morning," he answered easily enough. "Now you."

The bank. "I did not have to go to the bank. Why did you have to go to the bank?"

Shaking his head, Kellan said, "The shop. I'm looking at loans for rebuilding. Insurance will only cover so much, and they won't cover anything until the arson investigation is done."

"Huh." I hadn't even thought about that. "Did you own the shop?"

"I had an interest in it and was planning to buy it." The patience in his tone tweaked me.

"Man, I gotta stay sober longer. I missed all kinds of shit getting high." It was only a little bit of a joke. As it was, Kel gave me a faint smile.

"Staying sober sounds like a plan. Now, tell me what's eating at you."

"Right," I said, then took another long drink. My stomach growled, and I was tempted to ask about food but Kel was staring at me. "I had an idea. I don't like the idea. Only I told Doc, and we both think it might work. Well, Doc didn't say he thought it would work, but he also didn't disagree."

I drained the water bottle.

"It has to do with Sparrow," Kellan said on a sigh.

"I think—torture is only going to get us so far. I *think* he's more afraid of us than of his brother..." So I told Kellan what I'd mentioned to Doc. "It's a guess, but I think it's an option we might want to give Boo-Boo. For the record, I don't like being the one who came up with it."

I didn't want her to ever have to see anyone in her family again if she didn't want to see them. Kellan scrubbed his hands over his face.

"Let me think about it," he said. "We could still squeeze the location out and not have to make her deal with that."

I hoped so.

I seriously hoped so.

"Okay, that said, I have a question—like, when is that food gonna be ready?"

"That's your question?" He looked somewhat amused. "Maybe thirty minutes. Needs to cool."

"No, my question—" I held up a finger and moved to the door, then scanned the hall before walking over to the new bar that overlooked the living room.

Just wanted to make sure we were alone.

"Okay," I said. "Normally, I'd ask Jas, but right now you're calling the shots, so...I asked Boo-Boo out on a date."

"Good for you," Kellan said with a grin.

"Yeah, but—can I actually take her out right now? The

whole idea was for us to be...you know, normal and do normal things people our age do."

"What are normal things people your *age* do?" The droll response made me laugh.

"Fuck if I know, I just thought...I like her, Kel. I like her a lot, and I want to do something nice for her." Wanted it to be a fun date, one she could enjoy.

Something she would remember, and maybe...it would lead to other things. I hadn't expected the openness about her sexuality or enjoyment, but watching her with the twins had been somewhat of a revelation.

"I've fucked girls. I've never dated them." Even then, what I did definitely didn't look at all like what she was doing with them. "Boo-Boo's not like them."

"No," Kellan said. "She's not. She's worth it, though."

"You don't have to tell me that. I feel kind of selfish, but with everything going on, I don't want to forget that I asked her out." Did that make me an asshole?

"Be selfish with her," Kellan said, and that shocked the shit out of me.

"What?"

"Be selfish with her. You deserve some happiness. She deserves it too. We're juggling a lot right now. However we've got clear targets for a change. And sooner or later, we're going to kill that son of a bitch, which will clear many of our problems out of the way. Then we're going to be here with our lives. That doesn't mean everything stops."

"But, the go out and be normal date can wait..."

"So do a simpler date. A picnic in the dance studio, a private movie in your room. The point of a date is to spend time together. Everything else is noise."

I turned that over in my head. "Thanks, Kel."

"No problem." The door to the clubhouse opened and

Kellan glanced at his watch. "That's Doc. Go call everyone else down for dinner. Clean up if you need to."

"I want one of the corner pieces," I said and made a shape. "About this big."

He chuckled and waved me off. "You'll get what you get." Then his phone rang and, I caught his, "Traschel," as he answered it. I left him to deal with that, passing Doc on my way to the stairs.

Movies or a picnic.

Would a dance lesson be a date?

Yeah, we needed to find the fuckbucket and off him. I wanted her life back so we could figure out this dating thing. It would be way more fun with that asshole dead.

Way more.

# CHAPTER 30

*KELLAN*

uilt was a living, breathing monster slithering through my veins. The shop burning down was one thing. Had I intended to buy it outright? Yes. While I could afford to wait and get the money together, the insurance wasn't going to cover all of Terry's losses. I didn't think it would be enough to do more than pay down his debt.

The loan would let me buy him out. Then I could work on putting together the resources to rebuild it. The guys would help. Liam had already offered to finance the shop, yet we were already a drain on his resources. We might become more of one before this was over.

War was expensive.

Scrubbing a hand over my face, I tabbed through the screens on the laptop until I reached the expense and budget sheet. The trucking company was barely turning a profit, but it was there. Increased security, upgrades, and doubling up on the teams to provide backup was sucking up a lot of funding.

We had maybe three months before the bleeding took us into the red. Flipping to the next income chart, I frowned. Vaughn would need to replace his equipment and set up a new studio, or at least get space in a new one. That would also need to wait until we'd eliminated current threats.

The loan, if I got it, would only grant me about six weeks before we had to start paying on it. That would add more burden. Construction *might* be finished in that time, unless I skipped the location entirely and bought somewhere else.

That wouldn't be fair to Terry.

Fuck.

Depending on the funds and the construction time, trucking would be in the red in a matter of two months rather than three. A soft padding of feet brought my head up and I tracked the sound from the darkened hallway.

The sleepy, rumpled beauty appearing in the doorway tugged a smile from me, even if she should be in bed. It was —I glanced at the clock on the wall—after one in the morning.

"Hey," she murmured, pushing off the doorframe to walk over to me. The t-shirt she had on was one of Vaughn's and it hit her at mid-thigh. From her disheveled hair to her painted toenails, she was adorable.

"Hey," I said, holding out a hand to her. She padded over the tile floor, and rather than pull out a chair for her, I tugged her into sitting on my lap. Turning sideways, she ground that sweet ass against my thigh and curled up to tuck her head on my shoulder. "What are you doing up?"

"Bad dreams," she murmured.

"Why didn't you wake up Liam or Jasper?" They were the last two I'd seen her with, but she gave a little shrug.

"Mickey was sleeping with me, although he got up at

some point and left." She rubbed a slow circle against my chest.

I sighed, then brushed a kiss to her forehead. He hadn't come down, but there were other rooms upstairs. Doc's issues weren't ones he often let us help with. "He probably didn't want to wake you up."

But we needed to remind him that if he was leaving her alone to sleep, he needed to nudge one of us. Rubbing her hip, I cradled her a little closer. "It's okay, I just—I didn't want to go back to sleep after."

"Need to talk about it?" We all suffered from our own bad dreams. Some were just easier than others to deal with.

"It's the same dream I've had before. We were in a car, and you guys were taking me back to my uncle."

I loathed that particular dream. Sliding my hand up to her chin, I nudged her face up so she would look at me. The weariness in her eyes tugged at me. It was that weariness that should never have been present there. She was nineteen, twenty in a few months. She should be going to college, maybe be in a sorority, perhaps partying and beating off frat boys with a stick.

Fuck that, frat boys didn't need to be anywhere near her. At the same time, it was the darkness and the weariness in her eyes that pulled me in. The darkness that shaped her life also made her perfect for us. Her damage made her human, but it also made me angry.

"We will *never* give you to him," I said, holding her gaze. "I'll die first. So would every single one of us."

Pain flickered across her face.

"We're not planning on dying, Sparrow." Resting my hand around her throat, I measured her pulse. It was rabbiting but began to slow as my grip settled into place. "Do you believe me?"

"I do." Zero hesitation marked the response. "But at the

same time—I know what he's already done to all of you. What he'll continue to do, and my father isn't cooperating."

"We'll get the answers we need, one way or another." I rested my forehead on hers. "Freddie had an idea. If we don't make any progress soon, I'll discuss it with you."

Surprise surged in her gaze. "You want me to talk to him?"

"No, I don't want you to do anything except thrive and be happy." That said... "We may need you to talk to him, to sell him a bill of goods and see what he says and does."

"I can do that." Her bravery was forever on display. "Just tell me what you need me to do."

"Not yet," I said. "It's not because I don't think you're capable, for I know you are. But because I'm not willing to ask you to do it—yet."

A frown tightened her forehead. Her pulse continued to even out though, and her eyes drifted half shut. I flexed my fingers lightly against her throat, and she let out a little sigh. My dick was already rousing to the prospect of her ass being so close, but I focused more on her mood than my desire.

"Okay," she conceded. "But whatever it is, if it helps, I'll do it."

Those words cut me right off at the knees. Tightening my fingers around her throat, I nuzzled a kiss to her lips. She opened to me, sweeping her tongue out to greet mine, and I groaned.

"Sparrow," I whispered against her lips. "You are too fucking precious to risk."

"You would never risk me if there was any other choice." It didn't matter how accurate her statement was, I hated even the idea of *not* having a choice.

"I don't know that I could risk you even then," I told her, stroking my thumb against her pulse.

She nuzzled her nose against my jaw. The bristle there

reminded me that I needed to shave, but then she kissed my throat, and I sighed.

"What's wrong?" She laughed softly. "I mean besides, you know, the obvious."

"The obvious is more than enough," I told her. Then, since the laptop was there, I tugged it over and tapped the screen to wake it up. I typed in my password. "I'm working on finances."

She scooted a little against my lap and stared at the screen. I walked her through the different columns for profit, loss, expected payout, and income. By the time I finished, she was chewing on her lower lip.

"I can help," she told me, and I had to resist the urge to pinch her. This was part of why I hadn't brought it up earlier.

"You help me every day by smiling, lifting your chin, flying…"

"Kissing you?" The tease in her smile definitely brightened the darkness lurking in her eyes.

"That always makes the day better," I told her, and when she touched her lips to mine, I deepened the kiss. It held us there, suspended, while she melted against me. Delving deeper into her mouth, I groaned at the taste of her. Since Doc left her bed, maybe I should be the one who took her back to it.

She chuckled against my mouth, sifting her fingers through my hair. "Kellan…"

"Hmm?" I asked, nibbling kisses along her jaw. If she wanted to talk, I could lick and nip a path to her throat. Laughter bubbled up through her as I sucked a little hickey into place over her pulse.

"I can help," she murmured. "I have the money…"

"Sparrow…"

She pressed two fingers to my lips and leaned back. "Kestrel," she said, and it gave me a mild shock to hear that name after so long as Kel or Kellan. I raised my brows, but she didn't retreat. "I'm a vandal too. Remember?"

A sigh escaped.

"I have money—I have a lot of it. Granted, some of it is in trusts but...not all. We can go after my money. If we need more, I can marry one of you and get it released sooner." She paused for a moment, a troubled look floating over her face as she scraped her teeth over her lower lip.

One of us. *Sparrow, you are already ours.* Not that I said it aloud, but the thought was there. Marriage was paperwork. Then again, so was adoption.

"That said...it might help us if I do go after my money," she said slowly, and I almost swore I could hear where she was going.

"That's still dangling you as bait."

"Eh," she said, making a face. "Not really. There are three trusts that I know of...and from what Adam said, there might be more."

There was undoubtedly more.

"One of those trusts was overseen by Mom. All I need is for her to sign off on the request, and then I can file the paperwork. That kicks off the legal process of getting the cash wired to a chosen account of my choosing..."

The more she detailed out the idea, the harder it became to argue.

"That's a financial process, one we could easily turn over to an attorney to front. Granted, all the attorneys I knew worked for Uncle Fuckbucket, but we must know other attorneys."

I frowned.

"Attorneys have the whole client-privilege thing... I would ask Adam, but I haven't heard from him since he turned himself over." That bothered her. Bothered all of us. We knew he was still alive, and Liam mentioned speaking to him once, yet that wasn't enough. "Ezra might know one. I could ask Lainey. She definitely has the resources, and her grandfather has a whole battalion of attorneys—"

She straightened abruptly, and what traces of sleep had been present simply vanished.

"The king."

"No," I snapped the single syllable out, and she blinked. "Absolutely not. I will entertain a lot of choices you make, even if I worry about the long-term effects. The king is another threat and one we have not fully categorized. I haven't forgotten why he recruited Liam to go after Milo. You shouldn't either."

Her eyelashes dipped at the scold in my tone. Maybe I could have lightened it up, but this was a dangerous game and he was a dangerous man.

"You want to help us, I respect that. But..." Now, I wrapped my hand around her throat again and her stiffness eased as she locked her gaze on mine. The unfiltered trust would humble me on my best days. Right now? It put me on my knees for her. "That man is dangerous. We don't know what he wants from you yet, or why he's decided you're a part of this game. Just because he's been quiet doesn't mean he will stay that way..."

She licked her lips. "What if we could pit him against Uncle Fuckbucket?"

"If we could without any chance of you owing that man something or him trying to collect? Fine. Except we can't guarantee that." I reached past her to shut the laptop before standing and taking her with me. She wrapped her legs around my hips, and all at once, the fact she was naked under that shirt registered.

"That's your final answer?" The dare was right there in her voice, and I bit her lower lip as I carried her out of the kitchen and toward the living room. I didn't bother going upstairs.

"On the subject of the King?" I nodded once. "Absolutely. Everything else we're tabling to discuss later. I can see the strategy and the strength of the idea, but I want you for you, Sparrow. We all do. Your money is not a part of that equation." As far as I was concerned, it never would be. She could be as poor as we'd all been in that home, and she would still be far more valuable to me than anything else in the world.

It was the middle of the night, and the clubhouse was quiet. Instead of carrying her upstairs, I settled her on the pool table and when I tugged up her shirt, she let me pull it up and over. I didn't remove it entirely, using it to bind her arms behind her.

Surprise flickered in her eyes. I paused to give her a moment. The air in here was chilly as goosebumps rippled over her skin and her nipples were peaked.

"Good?" I checked. "You will tell me if it's not."

There was no room for error here.

A smile tilted the corners of her lips. "I'm good..."

That trust was back in her eyes.

"But I'm not done trying to help you."

I smoothed my hands down her hips and thighs, then nudged them wide to enjoy the sweet dampness visibly there. Her pussy was all kinds of pink, and a little swollen.

"Do we ever give you a break, Sparrow?" There were six of us, and there would be seven eventually.

She laughed. "More than you might think...I like when I'm sore after all of you." A shudder rippled over her. I drew a finger between her labia, gathering moisture to tease around her clit.

"I don't ever want you to be too sore." Or pained. No pain for her. Not like this. "So you will say when it's too much and let us take care of you."

Instead of acquiescing, she ran her foot up my side to my shoulder, then hooked her leg around me. Even with her arms tied around her back and balancing on her hands, she managed to snare me and drag me forward.

"I will if you will, Kestrel. You will tell me when you need me to take care of you."

Easing two fingers into her, I bit her lower lip before I kissed her. She returned the favor, sucking my lower lip between her teeth. "Yes, ma'am," I murmured. "But first...I'm going to take care of you."

Her sigh as I began to kiss my way down her body made me chuckle.

"This is not the way to win arguments," she scolded on a groan as I grinned, because her hips were arching up to me even as I helped to lay her down. This angle gave me all of the control.

"I'm not arguing," I informed her before I sucked her clit between my teeth. I was also not talking anymore. No, now I was going to take care of both of us.

# CHAPTER 31

*LIAM*

"Jt's late," Ezra said from where he leaned against the railing. The air was damp. Even the briny breeze hitting us carried in more moisture from the ocean. Rain-kissed without the actual rain.

"You were the one who set the time and the place," I told him, more annoyed that we were sneaking around to avoid potential eavesdroppers and spies.

"Technically—" Ezra motioned to his car, and the passenger door opened.

Air whooshed out of me as Adam exited the vehicle. Like us, he was dressed in all black, but it was still a suit. He was also sporting a beard.

"That's new," I said, lifting my chin at him even as I extended my hand.

He clasped it for a firm handshake. "Helps me to blend. I'm still playing dead, after all." The last was a pointed reminder of his status.

"Better than real dead." Dropping back to the railing, I swept the area. It was quiet. Not that someone couldn't observe us, but the place was also closed to the public. "What's going on?"

"Heard about your father," Adam said, and I didn't focus on the spasm of pain those words provoked. That was the problem with waiting around, it gave me too much time to think. So I didn't wait. I moved. I planned. I worked.

Until I could do nothing but wait. The only thing assuaging that ache right now was Hellspawn. Hellspawn, followed by my mirror, kept me grounded and balanced me out.

That and torturing Sharpe were the bright spots in my day.

"Sorry for the loss," Adam continued. "Glad your mom made it. She's going to be all right?"

I shrugged, fighting the urge to fold my arms. I wouldn't show defensiveness here. "She's—grieving. I've got her tucked away for safety until we can deal with Bradley Sharpe."

"That's why I'm here," Adam said, then nodded to Ezra. "We're not fans of Sharpe."

"Never have been," Ezra supplied, as he scanned the area. It was like he was both a part of the conversation and not. "He's a ghoul."

That was a word for him.

"Just keep Hellspawn's friend safe. She worries about Lainey." Particularly right now, with the wagons circling.

"Lainey will be fine," Ezra said in an almost amused tone. "I've been keeping her just fine, and I'll keep her that way."

That earned him a dour look from Adam. Reckless or not, Ezra ignored him.

"Anyway," Adam continued, shifting his weight but not his glare. Ezra's smirk grew defiant. Yeah, I didn't need to try and figure out what was going on between the two of them. Not right now. I already had enough headaches. "Sharpe dropped out of sight a few months ago. He's been almost impossible to track."

I was aware, so I just met Adam's gaze and waited. There was a point there.

"I got information on him from a credible source." He pulled a card out of his pocket and passed it to me.

"Do I get to know the source?" I scanned the card. It didn't offer much. There was a raven in the corner and a single name on the front with a phone number. Not a local area code. The back just read relocation specialist.

"Margareta Waldemar."

The name meant nothing to me.

"Yeah, I didn't know her before, either. However, I have gotten to know her the past few months…"

"Brixton's boss." The bitch who had Rome and Hellspawn taken.

One nod.

"And this?" I looked at the card again, filing the name Margareta Waldemar away. He pronounced the last name with a v sound and a hint of German inflection.

"A broker. They make arrangements for safe havens at a price for a particular clientele."

So—criminal WITSEC, more or less. Great.

"You may not be able to buy them off," Adam warned. "Secrecy and anonymity are part of what is offered. They aren't going to break easy."

But we could torture it out of them. Maybe.

"Where there is a relocator," Adam continued, "there might be a locator who can track them down."

"The Network." We didn't do business with them often. The transport of Sharpe had been one of the first times in a while. The Network had undergone some seismic shifts over the last few months.

"You can trust them, some of them. I know people. He's looking for us right now but also running into dead ends. But for the right price, anyone can be found."

"A bounty."

Adam nodded once. "Then there's the more direct route..."

Ezra slid a look to me. "Go after his money, particularly what he has in Em's name."

I'd already debated that. Although I didn't want Hellspawn having to deal with him any more than necessary.

"If you don't want to go at him straight-on, we can put together the legal paperwork to make it possible for me—"

"Fuck no," I said to Adam, not even letting him finish that thought. "You asked her to marry you, and she said no. Let that go."

"Technically," Ezra said. "She didn't say anything."

I wasn't the only one glaring at him. "What is up with you?"

"Nothing," Ezra said, folding his arms. Then as if to debunk that particular answer, he said, "We've been in a holding pattern for a while, and King went quiet."

King. Not *the* king, just king. Julius King had a lot of explaining to do. But fuck, he had been quiet since that rather colorful dinner.

"I still can't believe we finally have a name for that asshole, and there's literally *nothing* out there on him." Adam's frustration echoed my own.

Pinching the bridge of my nose, I slid the card into my back pocket and sighed. With all the chaos, I hadn't genuinely given two shits about King or his plans. The fact he went quiet worked in my favor.

Problem one: if he was quiet, what was he up to? Problem

two: he already expressed an interest in Hellspawn and her fortune. Problem three: he wanted Hellspawn as part of the Royals.

"Been a little busy," I said. "So we haven't spent as much time dealing with him as we probably should." That said... "Sharpe has to come first. Those attacks came from him. We took her mother out of a facility, and we're keeping Hellspawn from him."

The sick son of a bitch lashed out. We should have expected retaliation. Only, he'd been circumspect since we'd retrieved Hellspawn. Like most bullies, he'd gone into his hole to nurse his wounds.

Probably looking for alternatives. Either he'd dropped off the radar. Now, securely out of sight, he was attacking. The coordination of the last attack made every part of it deliberate. If we hadn't been armed and at least somewhat on guard...

Didn't matter, we still paid too high of a cost.

At the same time, the uncle's endgame seemed murky at best. Clearly, he wanted her back. Only they hadn't hesitated in the slightest to put Hellspawn in the middle of the firefight either. If that truck had hit my car, she could have been hurt.

The explosions could have hurt her. The firefight *after* could have hurt her. Some dumb son of a bitch grabbing at her in an alley *had* almost hurt her.

"He's delivered two messages through his subordinates that basically stated the same thing. We took from him, so he will take from us. Hurting Lainey could come into that equation if he wants to force Hellspawn's hand."

Adam's whole demeanor darkened. For all of his flippant and careless attitude, Ezra turned to stone.

"I have security on her," Ezra said. "Including a personal bodyguard that goes wherever she goes."

"How the fuck did you get her to agree to that?" Adam glared at Ezra.

"It was that, or she went back to the island." If Adam's glare bothered him, Ezra didn't show it. "I don't have time for this shit. You've fucked off with this power broker, and Liam's tied up with Emersyn and their little gang."

I ignored that last dig.

"That leaves Lainey to me. So *I* am taking care of her. You don't like it? Too. Fucking. Bad."

The animosity swelled up between them like a violent summer storm. "Trouble in paradise, boys?"

All that antagonism was then directed at me. "Definitely not paradise," Adam stated.

"Speak for yourself," Ezra drawled with a smirk. "I was definitely in paradise on the island. Should probably just steal her back there until you two are—"

Adam's fist slammed into Ezra's jaw. The clack of his teeth together actually sounded painful. The blow staggered the other man, and he put a hand to his face as he fought to stay on his feet.

"Mother fucking asshole," Ezra spat out blood and glared at Adam. "What the fuck was that for?"

"You know what." The frigid tone sliced through the air like an axe. With the antipathy crackling between them, I half-expected Ezra to lunge at Adam—except he didn't. He just rubbed at his jaw and paced away a few steps.

"I didn't fucking tell you to fall on your sword," Ezra stated, the wintry notes frosting every syllable. "That was your call. You don't like the results. I'll repeat what I already said, too fucking bad. I'll be in the car."

He cut a look toward me.

"O'Connell."

"Graham."

Then he stalked off without a look back. Adam didn't

watch him go. Instead, he focused his glare across the water. "Marry her," Adam said abruptly. "Marry her and shield her behind your name. Then move the accounts. Drain them. It will pull him out faster than anything."

"I think I'll find another reason to marry her, but thanks for the advice."

"Marriage is a transaction," Adam told me flatly. "It offers protection and access. This is a win for both of you."

"I'm starting to think I get why Ezra isn't interested in your advice."

That didn't even get me a smile. "As long as she is vulnerable," Adam said. "There's a chance for someone else to swoop in. Do I think she's only a piece on the board? No. However, it doesn't mean she *isn't* one, and a valuable one at that. From what Ezra said, King wants to make use of her connections and her accounts. He may be planning to use her to access and take over Sharpe's corporate holdings."

Irritation scraped through me.

"Do I like it? No. But the simple fact is, she's a Sharpe. She's their only heir. Unless he's changed things recently— she is the key. So...lock it down, or you may end up being stuck watching everyone else have what you want because they are where you want to be."

Shaking my head, I raked the hair back from my forehead. "You want out—get out. We'll make it happen."

"No," Adam said, his expression unchanged. "I'm where I can do the most good right now. The minute this Julius King finds out that not only am I not dead, but I'm in bed with someone who wants to destroy him? It won't go well for any of us, and we need to be ready for that battle."

He didn't have to necessarily point out that we weren't ready right now, because we absolutely weren't.

Fuck.

"And if it costs you...?"

The only answer he gave was a shrug. "It has already cost me. At this point…"

Been there.

"I do have a question for you," Adam said.

"Ask. No promises that I'll answer."

He didn't say anything at first, pausing only to glance back at the car where Ezra sat in the driver's seat, *not* looking at us.

"When we approached you at school…"

"I'd been waiting for it," I said, and he turned his gaze back to me. "Yes, I had an idea of who you were and that you were involved."

"Because of Hardigan." It wasn't a question, and the dead neutral tone gave nothing away.

"Yes."

He exhaled a long breath. "So, your loyalty has always been to the Vandals."

"You earned my loyalty, too—both of you did. Even when Ezra is being a shithead."

A faint smirk touched his lips. "I got that when you didn't kill me."

"You're welcome."

He snorted, then faced me. "Hardigan."

Guarding my expression, I waited. "What about him?"

"Do you trust him?" Not the question I expected.

"With my life." Nevertheless, because he may not understand just that, I added, "With Rome's life.

That earned a frown and a glint of surprise. But he said nothing before glancing back at the water.

"Why?" I would have thought it was apparent that Milo, like the other Vandals, was my family and I trusted them with everything.

"I don't know Hardigan, and he's—" He glanced at the car,

then shook his head. "You know what, never mind. Is he still working on that job for your friend Traschel?"

"Fuck, probably. I don't know. We've been a little busy."

He handed me a card. "Give him this if he is. I'll answer the call."

I studied the card then him. "Is it a trap?"

Adam smirked. "Not at the moment. No promises in the future, though."

Right.

I shook my head. "Adam..."

"Yeah, I know. He's Emersyn's brother. That gives him some leeway, and he's your friend, so that will give him a little more." The pause was significant. "Don't ask me for more than that."

"I'm not asking you for anything," I reminded him. "I meant what I said. You want out, we'll get you out."

"I know—" Adam turned to walk away, glancing back over his shoulder. "That's why I'm willing to give him some latitude."

Then he was at the car and sliding in the passenger side, Ezra flipped me off in a mocking salute, and then they were pulling away and leaving me to look out over the bay.

I gave them time to go before I walked back to my bike. It was faster and more maneuverable. The ride back to the clubhouse passed in silence. It was late, and I didn't run into a lot of traffic. Made it easy to spot any potential tails.

I was still turning the conversation over when I let myself in and the sound of Hellspawn's moans greeted me. The fact she was spread out on the pool table with Kellan's head between her legs chased away the gloomier thoughts.

Locking up, I headed toward them. "Tagging in to play..."

Kel glanced up, his face slick with her release, and he grinned. "Go keep her mouth busy. I'm enjoying this."

Hellspawn turned those dark eyes on me and reached out

a hand, and the rest of the worries just fell away. They didn't belong here with her.

"My pleasure," I murmured, and she let out a sultry little laugh.

"Mine too," she said, and I grinned.

Hell yes, it would be.

# CHAPTER 32

*EMERSYN*

"*E*xplain to me again why it has to be *you* that marries her." Jasper's expression wasn't frosty so much as fierce as he stared at Liam.

"Because he's already loaded," Vaughn commented, lifting me right out of my seat before he took my spot and then settled me in his lap. I eyed him over the rim of my coffee cup.

"Nicely done." He hadn't spilled a drop.

He winked, then nipped my lower lip before he kissed me gently. "Thank you."

"Actually," Liam said. "It isn't directly related to the money."

"So, it's only indirectly related," Jasper said, arms folded. I wasn't sure if he was truly annoyed or not.

"The point," Kellan said before Liam could offer another explanation. "This is an *option* and an *option* only. Sparrow doesn't have to do a damn thing."

Rome looked at me. "Do you want to marry Liam?"

I blinked. "What?"

"Do you want to marry him?" The simplicity of his question soothed some of the ruffled feathers following the rather blunt announcement over breakfast that Liam and I should go ahead and apply for a marriage license. We could probably sort everything out by the end of the week.

"I don't *not* want to marry him," I admitted. "And I told Kel that I'd marry any of you if it got us access to my trust..."

Freddie squinted at me as Mickey pinched the bridge of his nose.

"Question, Boo-Boo."

Shifting on Vaughn's lap, I glanced at him.

"If this wasn't about money, would you want to get married?"

"Never really saw myself getting married at all." I could be honest about that, and there were more than a few measuring gazes on me. The weight of those assessments pressed in, yet they weren't holding me hostage. "Guys, I never really thought much about my future, but the big wedding and the happily ever after parts were the fantasy we sold with the various shows I did."

Even then, it was all so manufactured.

"Do you want kids?" Milo asked. It was the first time he'd said anything since Liam brought the subject up.

I lifted my shoulders. "I don't know? I don't think I do." That test turning blue filled me with blind terror. "The thought of it scares me."

Liam's scowl deepened as he stared at me, and Vaughn wrapped his arms around my middle and tugged me more firmly against him.

Worry filled Milo's eyes. "Why?"

"I honestly don't want to talk about this right now...I don't have to have a baby to get to my trusts. If we could afford to wait until I'm twenty-five, I wouldn't even worry about getting married."

"You don't have to do anything," Kel said, his tone firm and his gaze steady. "I mean it, Sparrow, don't care what money the Sharpes have. I can take apart Warrick's business. We've been shutting it down and dismantling it. If necessary, I'll sell it for parts."

Even as he said it, the strain showed around his eyes. Kellan wanted nothing to do with that business. But he'd do it to protect all of us.

"Let me ask you this..." I licked my lips. "If I marry Liam, and we get my accounts transferred and drained. I know it won't be an overnight process, but we can at least get it started. If we do that, what changes for all of us?"

"Changes?" Jasper asked. "Nothing. I don't care if he has a legal claim on you or not. You're still *our* girl."

That wasn't entirely true. Whether Jasper recognized it or not, the idea bugged him. Rome shrugged.

"Jasper is right. The only thing that would change is your name."

"And you don't need to get married to change that," Milo grumbled. "It should be Hardigan anyway."

Sharpe.

It had been my name for as long as I could remember. I'd always been Emersyn Sharpe. But being her came with a lot of baggage. No... being *me* came with a lot of baggage. The name came with my uncle, my father...

"I want to change my name, regardless," I said abruptly. "And I don't want to talk about having kids or any of that. There are plenty of kids out there who need a home, a good one, and to be parents like Liam's were. Or parents like Vaughn's mom or Kellan's mother."

I looked at Freddie, then Jasper, and finally at Rome, Liam, and Milo before I looked at Mickey.

"Little Bit, I don't think anyone is focusing on getting you pregnant right now."

"But practice is fun," Jasper admitted. Instead of growling, Milo threw a pillow at Jasper and hit him upside the head.

"Talk about that shit when I'm not around," Milo ordered, and Jasper grinned.

"Nope." He flung the pillow back, and I hid a smile.

"Children," Kellan said in an impatient tone.

"He started it," Jasper muttered, and Liam actually chuckled. The laughter rippled around the room, crackling through the tension, and one by one, they seemed to relax.

"Look," Kellan said as he stood. "We're all getting agitated because we know Sharpe is out there. But if we start *reacting*, we will be playing into his hands. We've taken steps, and we got Moira out for Sparrow. Now we have Sharpe's brother."

Divorcing myself from the idea of Moira and Reginald as my parents, and Uncle Fuckbucket as family, was hard. I still loved Moira...she was still torn up about it all, and at the same time...

"I just want him gone," I said softly. "I don't want him to touch you guys again, or me, or anything in my life."

"He is *never* touching you again," Milo said with a kind of steel that demanded I listen.

"No," Liam said. "We'll cut his hands off."

"We'll start with his fingertips. Then go for the joints," Freddie mused. "Make it really fucking hurt. Did you know you can use a cheese grater on skin? It really sucks."

"Be careful. Telling her about torture turns her on," Jasper warned almost playfully. A laugh bubbled up through me even as Milo glared at him and Kellan shook his head.

Vaughn pressed a kiss just behind my ear. "Dove, I think what we're all trying to say is that we've got this. Not sure why Liam is suddenly putting his foot on the gas pedal."

"Because I want him gone," Liam said, ice underscoring

every word. "More, I want him erased as painfully and brutally as possible. This isn't just about revenge. It's about war and about—"

A rapid fist banged on the door to the clubhouse. The casual attitude shifted. Vaughn rose, and I was behind him, with Freddie sliding up to stand right next to me. Rome moved to my other side as Jasper, Kel, and Milo all headed for the door. Liam and Mickey shifted to be on either side of the entrance to the annex.

The pounding continued as Milo reached for the door. Liam had his gun out and pointed at it. Freddie had his knife out, and Vaughn stood right in front of me. I wanted to look around him, but the tension in the room had stretched so taut it felt like it would snap.

Milo yanked the door open, and Jasper seized the rat who'd been knocking frantically and hauled him inside. "What the hell are you doing in the annex?"

None of the rats were allowed in the clubhouse. The annex was off limits too. They were supposed to call...

"Someone dropped another body on us," JD said, not struggling where Jasper had him by the shirt.

"Fuck," Mickey swore, and he was already heading out the door with Liam, Kellan, and Milo right behind him.

I started forward, except Rome hooked an arm around me and pulled me back.

"Rome—"

"Not yet," he cautioned.

"But that was how Mickey found Ms. Stephanie..."

"Don't think it's a chick this—" JD broke off when Jasper smacked him upside the head.

"Out," he ordered. "We'll be right back," he said over his shoulder to me.

I almost felt bad for JD.

Almost.

I still thought he was creepy, even though I didn't spend time around the rats, and the guys didn't encourage me to be anywhere near them. Still, with the increased number, it was hard to avoid them.

"Doc's gonna be okay, Boo-Boo," Freddie said as he and Vaughn moved to the door. Jasper had closed it behind him, and I was left on the far side of the room, leaning against Rome.

None of us spoke as the silence proved harrowing. My pulse rabbited, sweat beaded along my lip, and agitation seemed to swarm beneath my skin. Rome wrapped his arms more firmly around me, hugging my shoulders. I leaned into the contact.

Then Freddie was there, hooking our pinkies together as he rested his forehead against mine. "Breathe, Boo-Boo."

I was trying, but it was getting harder, and the vise around my chest seemed almost impossible. Not knowing was way worse than knowing.

"Give me an update," Vaughn was saying. "Dove is on the verge of a panic attack—"

No, I wasn't. Was I? Why was it so hard to get a deep breath?

"Right," Vaughn said. "Do we know... So they're following. Okay... Yep... Keep us in the loop... Yeah—I'll tell her... Thanks."

The more I tried to get my breathing under control, the more difficult it became. It was like trying to snorkel with a straw.

"Breathe, Starling," Rome said, his arms banding so tightly around me that it made my whole being feel secure.

"Dove, they're fine. Doc's guys are out there with them and covering. Two of them went after the car that dropped the body. We'll have answers soon, but everyone else is okay."

"Is it someone we know?" I almost didn't want to ask that

question. What if it was someone else important to them? To me? Vaughn still had burns that were healing, so did Rome. Kellan had some bruises and scorched spots.

Everyone had wounds.

"I don't know," Vaughn said. "I don't think they know who it is...this could be a random body dump. Someone trying to frame us."

"You don't believe that."

Freddie didn't move the whole time I spoke, but between him and Rome, the hyperventilating slowed down along with my rapid pulse.

Vaughn sighed. "No, Dove, I don't. However, we can't afford to worry about what-ifs right now. They're handling it, and when they know, we'll know. Kel knows you're worried. Can you try to sit down? Maybe eat something?"

I let out a half-laugh. "I'm not hungry." If anything, what appetite I might have had fled. There were just too many variables.

Liam bringing up the marriage thing again made total sense. Considering he had people looking, Mickey had people looking, and the guys were looking—no one knew where Uncle Fuckbucket was...

I'd been trying to think of all his possible locations. He had a couple of places—an apartment in the city and another down on the coast. They were his "retreats." I'd only ever accompanied him a couple of times.

"Better?" Freddie asked as I finally started taking deeper breaths.

"Working on it," I told him. "I promise."

"You're safe," Rome said, and honestly, I needed to hear that. I needed the hug he wrapped around me. I needed Freddie's nearness and support. I needed Vaughn's soothing, sweet croon that just washed away so much darkness.

"I know," I said softly, with a little more strength. "I know I am...I'm always safe with you guys."

Rome kissed the shell of my ear, and some tension bled out of me.

"So," Freddie said. "Would now be a good time to discuss date options?"

His smile was so damn playful, I couldn't help smiling at him. "Good time? Probably not. But let's do it anyway."

"Painting is a good date," Rome suggested as he eased up on his tight hug. I tilted my head back to look up at him.

"Yes, it is." It was a very fun date.

"You put her butt print on the wall," Freddie said. "That's not a date."

"Um, actually, pretty sure *I* put my butt print there. Rome just helped."

All three stared at me for a moment, then Freddie's serious expression cracked as he laughed. Vaughn chuckled, and Rome smiled. A little more relief trickled in.

"Right, date. What do you want to do?"

"Been thinking about that," Freddie said, but before he could continue, my phone rang.

Rome loosened his grip further so I could pull out my phone. I didn't recognize the number, but the fact the phone suggested it might be Julius King froze me in place.

This wasn't the phone he'd given Liam for me. He shouldn't even have this number...

# CHAPTER 33

*EMERSYN*

*L*iam vibrated with barely suppressed rage. Rome was in the passenger seat next to him, and no amount of snarling from Liam had dissuaded Rome from accompanying us after I presented the message from the king.

Restlessness exploded within the clubhouse when the guys came back in and Mickey scanned the message. "Why don't we have a photo of this son of a bitch?"

I shrugged. "The only time I met him, I didn't think asking for a selfie was a good idea." Despite the flippant comment, I was in no way feeling remotely blasé about the subject.

"Wasn't yelling at you, Little Bit," he said, some of the saltiness in his tone lessening. "But you met him—" He cut his glance between Liam and me. "What did he look like?"

"Six foot, maybe six-two," Liam said.

"I'd say just under two hundred pounds." It was a guess,

since the guy had been built under that suit. He hadn't been able to hide his frame, no matter how expensive or well-cut the tailoring had been.

"Dark hair," Liam supplied.

"Hints of silver here and there. I think he colors it." That could also be a guess. "Dark eyes. Mid-fifties? Maybe older?" He seemed around my uncle's age.

"Clean-shaven," Liam continued, then eyed me. "You think he colors his hair?"

"Maybe," I said. "I know a lot of older gentlemen in some circles do that to keep their youthful appearance."

Mickey snorted. "We need a picture of him, especially because Alphabet has turned up fuck all on Julius King."

"What are the chances it's not his name?" Milo asked, and since there was as much likelihood of that as anything else, I wasn't the only one shrugging.

"Maybe I can get a picture when I go to see him."

Liam spun around and *glared* at me. The very real anger and irritation in his gaze buoyed my mood. "Hellspawn..."

"Yes?" I grinned, and his impatient huff made me smile a little broader.

"What am I going to do with you?" He might have groaned and glared, but there was also a hint of a smile as he dragged me close.

"I'd say anything you want," I told him as he shook his head. "Except Milo is here. You know he gets kind of touchy about it."

"Brat," my brother grumbled. Even as laughter threaded through Liam, he tightened his grip around me. He hated this. We all did.

I wasn't a fan, either. Nevertheless, if we could use Julius King, and it could protect them, then I was all for it. Not that I intended on trusting the man. He'd already wanted Adam

306

dead for asking me to marry him. I didn't want him to hear one word about Liam's rather abrupt announcement.

Ten minutes later, the argument shifted to the body dump. It hadn't been anyone we knew. The guys got photos, fingerprints, and then Mickey's guys removed him. There was nothing to be done for him. The guy had been dead way before they even dropped him.

On some level, the idea that it was a guy relieved me. Only—what if it were Adam or Ezra? Liam had said it wasn't either of them. While the face had been unidentifiable, he knew each man's tattoos on their arms, which were not present on the body dump.

So, for now, we had to wait on that. Meanwhile, Julius King wanted to see me as soon as possible. That afternoon, non-negotiable. Which was how I found myself sitting in the back of Liam's SUV with Rome riding shotgun and a car with Kel and Vaughn following us. Milo wanted in on it, but even Kellan had nixed the idea as Liam objected.

"Vaughn and I can go for the money shot and see if we can get a photograph of this guy. We can't afford for you to be seen there." The even tone Kel used was hard to argue with, not that Milo had cared for it.

"We have more questions for Sharpe," Mickey said, and then there was also my mother.

So we split up, four of them going with me and the other four staying behind.

When I leaned forward to put my hand on Rome's shoulder, he glanced back at me. The weight of his gaze held the kind of quiet confidence I really needed at the moment.

"We have him," I promised because whether Liam liked it or not, we all worried about him too.

"Yes," Rome said. "Even if he's an asshole."

"Bite me," Liam commented without an ounce of heat.

"Not while you're driving," I retorted, and he cut a look at me via the rearview mirror.

"You really do want a spanking, don't you?" The fact desire licked along the teasing words pleased me enormously.

"I won't tell you no."

"Just not while I'm driving," he commented, and Rome reached up to cover my hand on his shoulder.

"Exactly."

Shaking his head, Liam said, "You really are a brat."

"I know." I kind of liked it. "However, you get what you get when you nickname me hellspawn."

Rome chuckled, and a grin flashed over Liam's face. "Good point. Doesn't hurt that I enjoy your sassiness."

"You enjoy it?" I put my free hand to my chest. "Shocked."

He just snorted, but it helped to alleviate another band of tension around us. Not that the relief lasted for long. We'd left Braxton Harbor, the drive taking us almost two hours north toward Rosewood.

The landscape and scenery changed on the highway. More than once, I glanced back to check on Kellan and Vaughn. I'd also sent a message to Lainey asking her about Julius King and if the name was familiar to her.

She hadn't answered yet, but I would give her some time. A lot was going on with her and the minute I was free of lockdown, she was my next stop. I refused to bring trouble to her door—especially with the kind of life and death threats my uncle had been sending after us.

"We're ten minutes out," Liam warned. "We have reservations at the Rosewood Garden Club."

I wrinkled my nose and then glanced down at my clothes. "I'm not really dressed for a garden club."

"We're gonna change when we get there, Hellspawn. Don't worry."

I wasn't, except—"Are Kellan and Vaughn going to be able to get in?"

"Let them worry about that," Liam advised. "This is really not our first job dancing the line between the one-percenters and ourselves."

Ourselves.

Liam and I both qualified as one-percenters. Neither of us truly identified as them, in any case. The only thing I'd ever wanted from the money was freedom from the people who put the money in the trust in the first place.

When we reached the club, Liam let the valet park the car. I didn't say anything, trusting all of them to have a plan. As it was, irritation and jumpiness kept me on edge. The man who greeted us wasn't just some useless middleman. He also knew Liam.

"Mr. O'Connell, a suite has been prepared for you as well as a clothing selection in the usual sizes. More were also sent for your guests."

"Thanks, Carson," Liam said as he shook his hand. Then we were whisked to a set of private rooms where there were indeed racks of clothing.

"If you'll follow me, Miss…" Carson said to me, but Liam caught my hand and yanked me back and toward Rome.

"She'll be changing with us. Just bring her clothes here."

"Of course." No arguments, not even an ounce of side-eye. He stepped out, and within a moment later, a rack of clothes was delivered. I stared at them before glancing at Liam.

"Sorry, Hellspawn. I know you're not a fan. I promise I'll even help you burn them after this."

The corners of my lips quirked. "No, but this is different…" I scanned the clothes. "Did you pick any of these out?"

His expression darkened. "No, but they were probably sent over from the store. I said we were going to need stuff."

He was so tense. By contrast, Rome seemed to be more relaxed. He was here just to look after Liam and me and didn't give a damn about the rest. There was something to be said for that attitude.

"Want to pick out something for me now?" The offer was easily made, and Liam was *not* Fuckbucket and would *never* be him.

His whole demeanor transformed at the offer. "Really?"

I caught Rome's eye, and he smiled with a little nod. "He likes picking out clothes."

"I had kind of noticed," I murmured.

"I'm ignoring both of you because, yes, Hellspawn, just this once, I'd like to pick out your clothes." The offer did what I wanted it to do. It alleviated some of the darkness swirling around him.

While we didn't have much time to waste, he checked the different outfits hanging on the rack and picked out a cross-halter, dark blue midi dress with slits that went to my thigh. He added a couple of bangles and a pair of simple ballet flats.

"Not a lot of jewelry in this selection, but you don't wear much," was his only comment. I didn't miss Rome picking out a dress shirt that matched my dress, nor how Liam picked out something similar as well. Not worrying about privacy, I stripped and got dressed in short order. Afterward, I styled my hair into a simple chignon before adding the bangles to my wrists.

I also got to enjoy them changing. I'd never seen them in nearly matching outfits before. Yet, it didn't matter. Even with similar haircuts and Liam's lack of facial bruising, I could still tell them apart. Thankfully, they didn't complain when I asked for a picture of them like that.

"Planning to annoy King by making him guess which one of you is which?"

Liam actually laughed, but Rome held out his hand to me as he said, "I wouldn't mind if it annoyed him."

Me neither, for my part. I couldn't strap a gun on with this outfit, but it did fit in a purse I could carry. Liam had his guns, and Rome wore one. They both had jackets on to cover the holsters.

Twenty minutes after arriving, we were ready to head out and meet the King. I walked between them as Carson guided us into the private dining room—private being a bit of a subjective term, considering the scattered tables throughout the room.

Julius King rose as we approached. Amusement creased his face as he set his napkin aside. "One of these days, Bishop, you're going to learn to listen."

"Not today," Liam said, pulling out a chair for me. "We've had a few issues..."

"So I heard," King said as he flicked a gaze over me and then Rome before focusing on me again. "Mr. Cleary, I've heard a great deal about you over the years."

Rome said nothing, and King actually looked amused.

Shaking his head, King refocused on Liam. "Have a seat, all of you. Then tell me about your father and what you need."

Stillness rippled over Liam, holding him rigid.

"Yes, I heard. While I think you should have told me, I'll grant you an exception since you were grieving."

"And you want to know because...?"

"Someone attacks you, they are attacking me." King's expression turned cold and unfriendly. "I don't let people who attack me go."

# CHAPTER 34

*ROME*

The king was not that regal or impressive. His suit was expensive, but his hands were rough. His nose had been broken before. Maybe more than once. The facial features weren't totally symmetrical. Not unusual because people didn't always have proportional features.

The meal featured several rich foods, none of which appealed to me. Manners dictated that I, at least, attempted to take bites. Rearranging the food to give the impression that I was eating, I tracked Julius King's movements, attitudes, glances, and the subtle shifts in his demeanor. As calm as he appeared, it was an act.

He'd revealed *some* of his mood when he established that an attack on Liam was an attack on him. But I didn't like the way King looked at Starling. I couldn't interpret it. Not possession. Not coveting. Just—not right. Too familiar, maybe. It irked.

As it was, my other half's manner grew more combative.

"If you were going to help, maybe you should have done something sooner."

"Maybe you should have informed me of what was happening rather than leaving it for me to discover on my own. One would think you don't trust me, Bishop."

"I don't," Liam stated in a glacial tone. "First rule of business, trust must be earned."

Instead of offense, the man in question looked thoughtful as he leaned back. "And I have not earned your trust?"

"No." My mirror didn't sugarcoat or sanitize his opinion. "You kept your identity and name secret for almost a decade since recruiting me. In that time, you've had me do how many jobs? No explanations, just instructions. You put me through my paces, yet what exactly have you done to prove to me that you are trustworthy?"

Starling tracked the conversation between them as I did. She was across from King, with Liam and I taking the seats across from each other and nearer to him. Liam had even angled his chair so he could be out of it and attacking King before he knew what hit him.

For all that my other half could play the part of wealthy heir—pain, sharp and sad, spasmed in my chest. Liam flicked a look at me, and for a moment, it was all there in his eyes. The loss. The pain. The fury. He wasn't the *heir* any longer. Jonathon O'Connell, a man Liam had as much chosen to be his father as the man had chosen Liam for a son, was dead.

Mary O'Connell was hurting and lost. Her heart broken as much as Liam's, perhaps more. The couple had only ever wanted to love Liam. They wanted to love me too, but I hadn't needed them the way he had. Still...

It was all there in my mirror's eyes. His pain would always be mine. Just as mine was his. Understanding crystalized in his gaze, and he nodded once. Then we both looked at King again.

"I controlled the game," was all King said, his tone and demeanor far milder than I would have expected. "I controlled it, and I invited you to play. You proved yourself capable. In some ways, you were already adept, but in others —" He shrugged. "You weren't ready for the task ahead of you. Now you are."

"What task?" Starling asked before Liam could say a word, and he cut his glance at her. She stared right at King, an open challenge in her expression. Starling's pure defiance added a sparkle to her eyes.

"He has his tasks," King told her. "And you will have yours."

"No," she said, and that had Liam shifting. I palmed a knife because if Starling wanted to provoke the fight, I would end it for her.

"No?" King probably hadn't heard that word very often.

"No, I will not have *tasks,* and Liam will not have them *either.* You want to treat him like a servant, a player in your so-called game. It doesn't mean either of us has to play." She picked up the wine glass she'd been nursing and drained it all before leaning back in her seat. "Frankly, nothing you've done has benefited Liam or me, for that matter. So, if you want us to continue to 'play' whatever this sordid little game of yours is—I think *you* need to earn that privilege."

Liam cut his gaze back to King, but I hadn't moved mine. I could see my other half in my periphery. The danger present at this meal had just escalated. King's expression chilled to ice. Nothing moved in his eyes or his manner as he glowered at her.

"I see," he said. Those two words carried tremendous weight. He motioned to her glass. "Another?"

"No, thank you." Starling betrayed nothing with those three words.

"Tell me, Bishop," King said as he turned his attention to Liam. "Do you believe I need to *earn* that privilege?"

"Yes," Liam replied without hesitation. "Hellspawn has a point. You have not done a damn thing for me."

"That you're aware of," King stated, as though questioning the possibility. What did he know that we didn't?

"It only really matters if I know," Liam stated, setting his silverware aside and wiping the corners of his mouth with the napkin. "Otherwise, what was done was charity or a gift. One doesn't expect either of those to be repaid."

King stared at him for a long moment, his expression unreadable. "Or it could be an act of forgiveness despite multiple failures."

Liam and King locked gazes, except it was Starling who snorted. "It could also just be another manipulation in a long line of them. Telling someone they should be grateful for something tangible or not is not respect, affection... or even trust. It's control."

King snapped his gaze to her. The wobble in her voice, the faint tremor in her hands—I doubted they were audible or visible to anyone else. Although Liam heard what I did, his jaw tightening as a muscle jumped in his cheek.

Starling's uncle had used his power over her to dictate the terms, to manipulate and control her. He'd used it to *hurt* her and had for so long he convinced her she couldn't tell anyone.

She couldn't get help. She couldn't seek out escape. She'd been trapped in the cage of lies he'd constructed around her and locked in by her parents. The more I thought about it, the more I wanted to go back to the clubhouse and beat the answers out of her father. There were ways to extract the truth...

"Speaking from experience?" King asked.

"She doesn't have to answer that," Liam said, putting his

hand on hers as if to ensure she listened. "In fact, we don't have to answer anything. You want to make this a more equitable arrangement, we'll consider entertaining your thoughts on various subjects. But I'm with Hellspawn..."

King placed his silverware down then leaned back in the chair, steepling his fingers as he studied them. Not once did he glance at me. I was okay with him dismissing me. I preferred the angle of observer rather than engaged.

"Let's clarify this position you're taking, Liam." The use of my brother's name seemed a tell, only for what, I wasn't sure. As it was, my mirror didn't react.

"Feel free," was his only response.

"You have duties and obligations..."

"No," Liam said, his hand flexing around Starling's. "I have tasks and assignments. A duty is a moral or legal obligation, an implied responsibility. Obligations are pretty much the same thing."

A chuckle escaped the man, and the humor in his expression was unsettling. "Very well, then you have tasks and assignments. Ones, I will remind you, that you accepted and performed. The contract, implied or explicit, exists through your actions and consequences."

"Not my problem," my mirror said. "Unless you decide to make it my problem. I once warned you what would happen if you made me an enemy."

"And I have never gone after your brother. I'm not even addressing him, though he is seated at this table, and *you* invited him to join us." Spreading his hands, King seemed to ask what else he wanted?

"No, you decided to involve my *girlfriend*."

"No," King said with another chuckle. "*You* did that by making her important. She's leverage. As much as your brother is, if not more. *You* put her in that position." He transferred his attention to Starling. "Emersyn can handle it, can't you?"

She shrugged, nowhere near as careless as she tried to appear. "I can do a lot of things. Doesn't mean I want to do them."

"Noted," he said, then exhaled as he picked up his glass. For a moment, he swirled the alcohol around in it as he studied both of them. No emotions were on display as he weighed his next move or response.

The silence elongated to the point the tension grew palpable. Even the air seemed to buzz like a power line had been downed and it danced and sparked between all of us.

This hadn't been my mirror's plan. Starling changed the game. Right call? Maybe.

I wanted it to be.

Liam had played this game for a decade or more, dancing to this man's whims, from brutal fights to sometimes executions. I wanted him free. Starling was on my side.

Our side.

"Then let us open negotiations. If you want this seat at a more level table, I can acknowledge you have earned the right to demand it."

The concession seemed almost too good to be true.

"Thanks for your permission," Liam stated in a droll, almost dry tone. "Wasn't asking."

"I'm aware. You have demanded it, and you don't give a damn about my thoughts on the subject. However..." His gaze cut to Emersyn again. "You want something from me, and that means I am in a position to negotiate."

Exhaling, my mirror picked up his drink. It was the first signal that the conversation traveled in the direction he wanted it to go.

"The question is—*what* do you want?" King swallowed a

mouthful of alcohol before setting the glass aside. "Or perhaps, more fitting, what do you *need* from me?"

Move.

Countermove.

Concession.

Negotiation.

The moment stretched out again as my mirror and the King stared at each other. The locked battle of wills seemed intensely private. The metal of the knife warmed in my palm as I waited for the final resolution. There were three exits from the dining room. Two are more accessible than the third. One is safer than the other of those two accessible ones.

If we had to get out of here, we could. One of us to get Starling out, the other to cover our escape. I didn't have to look at my other half to know he understood all of those steps as well as I did.

The stare-off lasted long enough that the waitstaff came by to see if we needed anything more. Neither King nor Liam answered, but Starling said, "No, I believe we have everything we need for the moment."

It was the moment that broke through the contest of wills. Both men looked at her, and King nodded.

"You want me to prove something to you," King said abruptly. "Name the task."

When Liam would have opened his mouth, the King raised a hand and shook his head.

"Your girlfriend threw down the gauntlet, Bishop. I will allow Emersyn to demand the boon." His expression sobered from mock amusement to deadly serious. "Have a care with what you ask for, Emersyn. I am a man of my word."

The tension snapped taut once more, and Liam flicked a glimpse at me. The unspoken *watch him* resonated plainly. I nodded. Then, and only then, did he glance at Starling.

From this angle, I couldn't make out that silent conversation. I could only hope their connection had deepened enough for them to understand each other.

"My uncle," Emersyn said abruptly, and I didn't smile. Because that was perfect.

"What about him?"

"I want to know where he is and how to get to him." The request seemed simple, almost too simple.

"Would you like me to just execute the problem?" Challenge offered.

"*If* I wanted you to do that," she countered. "I would have asked for that. Accurate location and possible access points are what I want right now."

King rubbed his jaw. "I'm surprised you didn't ask for protection for your brother."

"My brother can take care of himself," she said, tone tart, sharp, and confident.

The older man actually chuckled. "I do like you. Smart-mouthed, sassy, and full of piss and vinegar."

"Also taken," Liam informed him.

King shook his head. "Don't remind me. Now—I will find the uncle. I will get you the information. What does that get me?"

"An opportunity to negotiate my continued goodwill and service." Liam was too swift to answer that.

"Maybe," Starling countered, and she put her hand over Liam's.

"Not giving an inch, are you?" King seemed more puzzled now than just fascinated.

"No." Her flat tone pulled a smile from me. My mirror as well, even though his vanished nearly as soon as it had formed.

"Very well." Tension threaded his amusement. He was indulging them, not finding it nearly as funny anymore. We weren't backing down. The rules had changed. "I will find your uncle and information on how to reach him. Then we will talk again, you and I," he said to her before he glanced at Liam. "As for you, Bishop...don't test me again."

"Then don't fuck this up," Liam said, as he rose smoothly and pushed back the chair. He held out a hand to Starling. I was on my feet a split-second before she was. King rose as well. Only his manner was more observational than aggressive.

"My sympathies for your loss," King said. "When you have the person or persons responsible... let me know. Or if you require assistance. As I said, an attack on you is an attack on me."

That carried an echo of a warning. I waited for Liam to lead Starling from the table before I moved to follow them.

"Rome?" the man said, and I spared him a fleeting stare. "Look after them."

I snorted. I had no other response for him. We were on the highway ten minutes later, and Liam had Kellan on the phone.

"We didn't get close enough," he said, aggravation in his tone. "The security there was impressive."

"I have it," I said before Liam could respond. I already had a sketchbook open and a pencil going. It would take me some time, but I'd memorized Julius King's face.

"We're right behind you," Kellan said, and Liam nodded before ending the call.

"Hellspawn..." He dragged in a deep breath, and I peeked up from my sketch.

"Do I owe you an apology?" The question in her voice demanded we reassure her.

"No," my mirror said, his grumpy tone more from concern and fear than anger. "But next time, warn a guy if you're going to wave a red flag at a bull."

"I didn't like how he spoke to you," she answered, and I went back to my sketch. No, I didn't like how he spoke to Liam either. My other half just grunted.

But he didn't argue.

"And I wanted to see what he would do..." She sighed. "I don't know why he's so interested in me one minute, and so annoyed the next."

"You have talent, Hellspawn," Liam said, amusement curving around the words. "You could test a saint."

"Good thing you aren't one, then."

I chuckled, and a moment later Liam joined me.

Yes, the eyes were shaping up nicely. Hopefully, I'd have a mostly finished sketch by the time we got back.

Julius King wasn't going to be a mystery for us anymore.

Or a threat to Milo, Liam, *or* Starling.

# CHAPTER 35

*EMERSYN*

*W*hen I slipped into my room for a shower, I wasn't expecting Rome to wrap an arm around my waist or to twirl me around. I barely parted my lips on a gasp, and he was there, claiming my mouth in a fierce kiss. Slow, deep, and demanding, he swept his tongue in even as he pressed a thigh between my legs. The weight of him sandwiching me against the door was so damn delicious.

It chased away the chill from dinner, from the tension in the car on our way back. It erased the lingering questions and doubts that always popped up when I browsed the fridge or peeked down the hall to where my mother was being kept. There was no coloring between the lines on that one. She was as much a prisoner as my father at the moment, save she was in better accommodations.

Rome slid a hand in my hair while his other glided down my skirt, pushing it up. The warmth of his palm, coupled with the gentle tug, lit me up. He spread teasing kisses along my jaw as I arched my hips to grind against his thigh.

He flexed his thigh. Rome's build was as tight and rugged as Liam's. The work he did, the places he climbed to paint— the fact he could fly. A dizzying sense of joy invaded me as he flexed those muscles again. Fuck, that felt so good. He tugged my hair to tilt my head back, and I melted with him as he kissed a path down my throat.

"Need you, Starling."

With care, he pushed my dress upward. I tried to help, but all I succeeded in doing was putting more pressure on my clit where I rode his thigh. My panties were soaked and my nipples strained.

"You feel so good," he muttered, need drenching his voice, darkening it. Liam echoed there. I dragged my eyes open, needing to see him. His lips softened into a sinful smile and heat flushed through my system.

I pushed my hands under his shirt. He'd changed after returning. T-shirt and sweats, comfortable clothing versus what we'd been wearing. He had to let me go when I pushed the shirt upward, stripping it off and throwing it aside. Impatience, not something I was used to in Rome, marked his every movement. The ripple of muscle his action revealed sent another bolt of lust through me.

Lust and appreciation. Rome was beautiful. They all were. Rough. Thick. Lean. Tatted. Clean skinned. Scarred. Smooth. They were all so damn gorgeous. So warm.

Safe.

Leaning forward, I traced my tongue over the outline of the swirling ink pattern. A magical path that let me venture into his world where he saw it through this vibrant lens. Scraping my teeth over his flat nipple, I teased my nails against his back. Then he was dragging my dress up and over.

It vanished somewhere behind him and then it was just us. I ached for him as a low sound escaped his throat and he gathered my wrists into one hand and pinned them to the door above my head. There was something hot and electric in his expression. His gaze was a caress all its own as he stared at me.

Suddenly, I wished I was naked and then he stole another kiss, his mouth locking over mine until the only oxygen I got was what he allowed me to have. His panting breaths were just as broken as my own, and I wanted *more.*

His palms were hot on my skin. Something snapped, the elastic biting against my flesh. It was gone.

"You broke my bra," I whispered in between harsh breaths.

"Yes," he said, devouring my mouth. "It was in the way." Then he was cupping my breasts and I didn't give a damn about the fabric.

He sucked my lower lip between his teeth. Everything in me was going hot and laxed. The rip of my panties made me chuckle. The firm twist and pinch of his thumbs and forefingers on my nipples sent hot, wanton pulses to my cunt.

Drunk on the feel of him, I rocked on his thigh as I tugged his sweats down. The hot length of his cock filled my palm. A low sound escaped him as he laved kisses along my throat and I gave him a long slow stroke.

The velvet skin, strong and corded with the veins popping below and moisture gathering on the tip, was as inviting to me as the mixture of desperate sweetness and molten, hungry kisses he drowned me in.

"I want you," I told him on a gasp, and Rome lifted his head.

"Want you too," he promised in the same desperate tone I was feeling. He lifted me right up, and I kept my hand on his dick, angling him so he filled me with one thrust.

The pressure shoved all the air out of my lungs. Arching my hips, I locked my thighs on his hips, freeing his hands as I crossed my ankles behind his ass.

He angled his mouth to mine, the kiss deepening as he thrust his tongue in a motion that mimicked his cock. Rotating my hips, I rocked with him and kept adding twists to every thrust. The angle kept him stroking the right spot with every push.

This close, his skin was like the perfect balm and torture for my nipples. I swore stars began to spark in my vision when he ground me against him with every deeper drive. Nails in his shoulders, I clung to him as we dueled and danced with our tongues. The desperation only seemed to grow more intense. Every brush of his skin on mine sent me up in flames.

It wasn't until the tension snapped abruptly and I came in a rush that I even understood how close I'd been. I clung to him as he worked me through that orgasm, the piston of his hips maintaining their speed. His mouth abandoned mine and then he bit down on the juncture between my shoulder and neck.

The pain was sharp, bright and intense. It slammed me into another orgasm that robbed me of breath even as I cried out. Rome came in a blazingly hot rush, the liquid fire filling me up as we staggered back toward the bed.

When he sat abruptly, we both let out a low cry. Harsh breaths filled the air as he held onto me and I wrapped around him. Somewhere the sound of a door opening registered, and I lifted my head to find Mickey staring at us.

"You sharing, Rome?"

Rome chuckled a low, deliciously deviant sound that I suddenly wanted more of from him. "Do you want Doc, Starling?"

I didn't think it was possible to go from wildly satisfied to shockingly hungry all over again. "Can Rome stay?" The question came out shakier than I intended, but Doc speared me with a look so intense, I swore I could feel him filling me even as Rome softened. He slipped out of me and I wanted to weep a little.

Mickey closed the door behind him and locked it. Then he had his pants open. "You can have anything you want," Mickey promised. There was a madness in his eyes that I understood. I urged Rome to lie down and kissed a path down him as I eased toward the edge of the bed.

A warm hand caressed my ass, and Mickey pressed a kiss to my spine. "Fast or slow, Little Bit?"

That need twisted up inside me. I wanted both. "Fast now...slow later?"

His chuckle echoed Rome's with the dark pleasure threading throughout it.

"Anything you want," he said, and his hands bit into my thighs, half-lifting me as I began to swallow Rome's softened cock. Then Mickey thrust into me hard and furious.

Still quivering from my earlier orgasms, I reveled at the brute force of it and pushed back to meet him as he fucked me right through Rome's cum.

Dazzled and delighted, I sucked harder, bobbing my head as Rome began to stiffen. When Micky fisted my hair, everything went lax and easy. Then he began to move my head, controlling how I swallowed Rome, even as he fucked me harder.

There was an edge of pain to every thrust. Nevertheless, I wanted that pain, needed it. I could feel Mickey's cock, so deep inside me that I wanted to keep him there. I wanted to keep all of them there, nestled safe and warm, where we could have each other always.

"That's my girl," Mickey murmured, the words a slow caress that seemed to tickle my clit. "Open your eyes and look at Rome—look at what you do to him—to us."

I hadn't even realized my eyes had fallen shut. I lifted my lashes and stared along the length of Rome, over the ivy peeking out from his tattoos and the scattering of birds to where he stared at me with dilated eyes and a stunned expression.

Delight curved through me even as Mickey's pace drove me relentlessly toward another orgasm. I wanted to come so bad, but not before I got Rome there again. Mickey's hot hands were stroking my back and my ass when he wasn't controlling my head.

Loose-limbed and replete, I rode the wave as Rome began to thrust. The bump of his cock in my throat added to the dizzying joy as I lost the ability to breathe intermittently.

I fucking wished for Kellan's hand on my throat. Just imagining it sent me over the edge as Rome came in a hot spurt, and Mickey's own pace stuttered. I was a soaking mess when he finished, it leaked down my thighs, and I gasped with laughter when Mickey dragged me up to lay on the bed.

He vanished only to come back with a warm washcloth. Rome wrapped his arms around me to keep me still as Mickey cleaned me up. I was almost too sensitive when he cupped my cunt. The problem was, Mickey was still dressed.

"How are you doing, Little Bit?" he asked in a rough voice as he stroked my thighs. Despite the buttery consistency of my muscles, a shudder worked through me. Hot and cold collided as my nipples tightened. The rough stroke of his hands was too much and not enough.

"I feel good," I admitted and he smiled.

"Yeah?"

I rubbed my cheek against Rome's jaw, curling one hand

over his where he held me and then stretching my other hand toward Mickey. "Oh yeah," I whispered. "I came in here to shower."

He chuckled. "You can shower... in a little while."

I wanted to say all right, but he pressed my thighs apart, and then his mouth was on my cunt. I almost bolted upright if it wasn't for Rome nuzzling kisses and massaging my breasts. They were everywhere, and I forgot how to string thoughts together as Mickey devoured me.

The third time I came on his face, there was a knock on the door and a laugh bubbled out of me.

"Ten more minutes," Jasper called. "Then we're breaking in. You guys gotta learn to share."

Rome glanced at me and then down at Mickey. "We are sharing," he called. "All full now."

As if to prove his point, Mickey moved and Rome took his place. The first time he pushed into me, another orgasm rattled over me and I shook.

"You can take more," Mickey whispered, nipping my ear before he shifted to brush his cock to my lips.

Yes, yes, I could.

Laughter carried through the door.

"Give a shout if you need a rescue, Sparrow," Kellan called, but there was so much humor in his voice I wanted to smile, although I also didn't want to let go of Mickey's cock.

What would it be like to have all of them... at once or one after the other.

Was that even possible?

Would I be able to walk?

Between the thrust of Rome's tongue and the push of Mickey's cock, I lost the thread of it. But I'd come back to it.

To them.

If I wanted to know...

They'd help me.

And the unsteady sensation burst as I came again under the sensual assault, and the world kaleidoscoped.

By the time I made it to the shower, Mickey had to take it with me. Boneless and sated, I floated on a haze of pleasure.

# CHAPTER 36

*EMERSYN*

*a* strangled sound had me snapping my eyes open. The hint of lights around the ceiling offered gloomy illumination to chase away the shadows but not so bright as to keep anyone awake. I was still boneless and more than gloriously sore. The sensual aches were right there waiting for me.

Warmth pressed against me, the steady thrum of a pulse under my hand. Smothering a yawn, I let my head drift back down to pillow against the muscle of Mickey's chest when a sound erupted from him again. It was like a low, smothered cry swallowed in his sleep. If not for the vibration of his chest, I'd almost have thought it came from somewhere else.

I pushed up and set a hand on his chest, only he had his hand around my throat and pitched over on my back before I could do or say anything. Adrenaline surged through me, erasing any trace of sleep. The flex of his hand tightened a fraction. He wasn't strangling me, but he wasn't awake either. His eyes were open but almost blank.

Another sound escaped him, tortured and pained. The sound was so primal, tears sparked in my eyes. The heavy weight of him pressed me into the bed and his hand tightened but it was like a twitch of the muscles in his fingers—a reflex. A release and regathering of tension kept me still.

"Mickey—" I couldn't finish the word as he closed his hand, cutting off my oxygen. I flattened a hand to his chest. Fear skated through me. Not for me. For him. I didn't push him away, rubbing a slow circle against his breastbone. The contrasting textures between smooth and scarred skin grounding me.

He shuddered, his whole body jerking as his head snapped up, and then he blinked. Spots danced in front of my eyes.

"Fuck…" His hand opened and I sucked in air desperately even as Mickey threw himself off the bed. He slammed into the wall.

The world swam as I inhaled more air in me. I tried to call out to him, except the words weren't coming out and the door slammed open. Jasper, with Vaughn only a half-step behind him, was just there.

Mickey didn't wait for them to say anything, he bolted, shoving past them.

"Wait…" It was hard to talk. He hadn't crushed my throat, but I still had some trouble getting everything working.

"Go," Vaughn told Jasper, and Jasper cut a look at me then nodded before taking off after Mickey. Vaughn was in the room, scooping me right out of the bed. Sounds erupted from the sitting room as doors opened.

An alarm cut through the building. Mickey hadn't deactivated it before going out. Tears pooled in my eyes as Vaughn set me on the bathroom counter.

"Shhh," he crooned, touching two fingers to my chin and nudging my head up. "He's going to be fine, Dove."

"What happened?" Kellan asked, his blue eyes fierce and locked on me.

"Bad dream," I managed as a hateful tear escaped.

"Bruised," Vaughn said. "We should probably grab one of the ice packs—"

"I'll get it," Freddie said. Dammit, everyone was awake.

"Mickey?"

"Will be fine," Kellan said. The confidence he projected with those three words helped. "Right now, I need to know how you are?"

"He didn't hurt me."

Vaughn's gaze held some doubt while Freddie was already back with the ice pack. Rome was just behind them, silent and wary. Liam and Milo were absent. Maybe they'd gone with Jasper to catch up to Mickey. I didn't even care that I was naked. Freddie's gaze was pinned to mine as he held out the ice pack.

"Boo-Boo, the red marks on your neck say otherwise."

"So does your voice," Kellan added, but then he raised a hand. "But I get it. You don't think he was trying to hurt *you*."

No, he definitely hadn't been trying to hurt me at all. "He was dreaming." As pained as he sounded, though... it was a nightmare.

I'd woken up alone a few times after going to bed with Mickey. He didn't trust himself or his dreams. Most of the time, he waited for me to go to sleep and then would leave. Tonight...he'd stayed.

Vaughn wrapped the ice pack around my neck. "He didn't want to hurt me," I assured Vaughn, and his eyes softened, their topaz hue seeming even more magical.

"I know he didn't, Dove. Doc would never hurt you willingly."

333

Tracking my gaze to Kellan and then Freddie, I searched for any disagreement. But all Kellan said was, "Are you bruised anywhere else?"

"No." I folded my arms because the combination of marble countertop, ice pack, and nudity made for hard nipples and shivers. "He pinned me, but he wasn't trying to hurt me. He didn't even say anything, just—sounds." Wounded sounds. They hurt to hear.

Had he been dreaming about Ms. Stephanie? The firefight where he was wounded? His wounds? I had no idea, but there was no mistaking the pain and the *loss* in those guttural sounds.

"Then I said his name..." I lifted my shoulders. I really didn't know what else to say or to do. I hated that Mickey was going through this.

"Think you can go back to sleep?" Kellan asked. "And before you say you want to go find Doc, I think you should let Jasper and Milo talk him down first. There's gonna be a lot of self-loathing he needs to deal with."

I hated that.

"He may not be ready to see you yet, Boo-Boo," Freddie told me. "C'mon, I'll stay with you. I can slip out if he comes back."

"Vaughn?"

"I'll go help find him," he murmured, pressing his palm to my cheek. I leaned into the contact, and he touched his lips to my forehead. "Try to sleep, Dove. Let Freddie look after you, okay?"

I nodded.

I slid off the counter, and Kellan caught me in a one-armed hug and I wrapped my arms around him. He didn't say anything, just held me, and then Rome was there. Buffering and surrounding me in their affection.

It was only after they left, leaving me with Freddie, that I debated getting a shirt. Instead of grabbing one, I glanced at him in his t-shirt and shorts. He parked it on the edge of my bed and stared at me with a kind of open appreciation.

"Do I need to put a shirt on?" I didn't want him to be uncomfortable.

"If you want," he said, a hint of a smile on his lips. "You still have the prettiest pussy I've ever seen."

A soft laugh escaped me as I shook my head. "The first time you met me, I was naked."

"Yep," Freddie said, then patted the bed. "You look great naked, Boo-Boo. I say you can be naked whenever you want."

The open affection and acceptance there nudged me into motion. Freddie held out a hand, and I slid onto his lap rather than the bed and he wrapped me up in the best hug.

Tucking my face against his throat, I sighed as he ran his hand up and down my back. "Is this okay?" I asked.

"I got you, Boo-Boo." The swift response sparked fresh tears.

I hated it when any of them were hurting. I hated the idea of them hurting at *all* or for any reason. Freddie murmured a litany of nonsense. I barely understood him, even as I swore I was soaking his shirt with the tears escaping me.

"I'm here," he repeated, those two words breaking off from the rest. "Doc is gonna be okay, and so are you."

Time lost meaning as I curled into him. Eventually, he coaxed me into the bed and slid under the covers. Freddie eased over to me and slid an arm around me.

"This okay?"

I nodded, settling against him as he dragged the blankets up.

"Goddamn, Boo-Boo. Your feet are freezing."

Despite the complaint, he didn't pull away, just snared me closer until my back was firm against his chest. Freddie radiated heat. It didn't take long for the shivers to fade in the cocoon he'd created around me.

The placement of his hands though, made me giggle. The first one escaped, and Freddie lifted his head. "Shh, you're supposed to be sleeping."

Pressing my lips together didn't keep the sound from slipping out. He gave me a gentle squeeze. He had one hand on my side and the other on my ribs just below my breasts. The warmth of his fingers against my chilly flesh made me sigh.

But when he tightened his grip, I giggled all over again. Huffs of his breath feathered over my shoulder as he chuckled. Then he pressed his lips to my shoulder.

"You're killing me," he muttered a moment before curling his fingers against my ribs. The featherlight brush of sensation had me wiggling all over again. I was trying to be still for him, and he was tickling me.

Half-twisting to look over my shoulder, I clenched at the press of his erection through his shorts. I couldn't quite make out his eyes in the dark, but Freddie pressed a kiss to my nose.

"Sorry," I whispered, and it was his turn to laugh as he ran his fingers over my ribs, and then laughter spilled out of me.

"No, you're not," he countered. However the grin in his words pulled another smile from me, and when he went to tickle for real, a squeal escaped. "Shh," he cautioned, but his smile made a lie out of the word even as he chuckled.

With light-fingered grace, he teased his hands up and down my sides until I was breathless with laughter. What started out as cuddles and tickles swiftly turned into wrestling. I managed to get my legs around him and then flipped him onto his back.

An *oof* escaped him as I stared down at his face. My

cheeks ached from grinning and Freddie snickered. "Boo-Boo is a badass."

I flicked his nose. "And don't you forget it."

The mood turned electric. One moment we were playing the next, he surged upward and his mouth was on mine. The whole world went on a tilt-a-whirl as his lips teased mine apart before he traced his tongue lightly over my teeth in search of my tongue.

My arms wrapped around him, and I drank in his nearness and the taste of his kiss as he nibbled and sucked against my mouth. Teasing and playful one moment, heartfelt and passionate in the next. The rub of his shirt against my breasts was a tease but one I found myself craving.

Just like I did his nearness. Kissing Freddie offered a balm to my system that was equal parts soothing and sensual. We tumbled over to our sides and I fought the need to roll my hips. The only thing keeping us apart was his shorts. When he sucked against my lower lip, I fisted his hair.

The locks of golden blond tumbled around my fingers, soft and silky. I'd never really gotten to play with his hair before, and I licked at his lips as I teased my fingers along his scalp.

Tension threaded his arms when he lifted his head and I loosened my grip. Instead of pulling away, Freddie teased his nose to mine. "You feel good, Boo-Boo."

"That's the nakedness."

The corners of his mouth twitched. I couldn't see his eyes in the shadows, but the shape of his mouth, the gleam of his teeth—they were right there. "Maybe." He ran his hands over my back, slow, stroking motions that made me want to stretch like a cat.

When his thumbs dug into a particularly stubborn muscle, I arched, and a hum of sound escaped me.

"Like that?" There was no mistaking the excitement invading his tone.

Then he hit another stubborn knot that I hadn't realized was there. The pain twisted into pleasure as he worked it free. "Yes," I groaned. He slid away from me and rubbed my back in a slow circle when I let out a complaining sound.

"Roll over, Boo-Boo."

I didn't wait to ask him why. I just rolled onto my back, and he essentially tweaked my nipple once—a light, brushing contact that was hilarious and teasing all at once.

"Other side."

"Fine," I huffed with a mock sigh and rolled my eyes. As soon as I was on my tummy, he rubbed his hands together and then settled both on my back. The even pressure spread warmth through my system, eradicating the stiffness and the unease.

The boneless river I'd floated on earlier surged up to drag me along as he started with my shoulders and then moved his way down along my spine. I wasn't sure what he'd do when he got to my glutes, but the concentrated effort had me groaning.

"Boo-Boo…"

"Hmm."

"I'm going to take my clothes off."

Despite the languid sensations his massage triggered in my limbs, I didn't miss the words or what they meant. "Okay. Will you tell me what is okay for you?"

"Yes." He pressed a kiss to my shoulder and then moved away. The bed shifted as he climbed off and when it depressed again, the warmth of his skin was against mine as he lightly straddled my ass. His cock lay against me, hot and hard.

When he didn't comment on it, however, I just reveled in the fact he could touch me.

"This okay?" Always checking. Adoration fountained up within me.

"I like it," I promised, then gave a slight clench of my ass to tease his cock. "How about you?"

He gave a shuddering laugh. "Tempting, Boo-Boo. I want —I want to touch you, but not have you touch me yet. Is that okay?"

Lifting my head, I twisted just enough to look over my shoulder at him. "Freddie, you can do anything you want. I trust you. If you need me to not touch you right now, I can wait."

Anticipation coiled tightly in my stomach, and Freddie's smile dazzled in the darkness.

"You make me think it's all going to be okay," he said as he rocked his hips and began to rub up against my ass. "That *I* can be okay."

I didn't tell him he could be. He had to believe it for himself.

"That it's okay to want the things with you that I want, even as—"

I held my breath as he settled his full weight against my back. The contact was overwhelming, leaving me aching for more since he was still rubbing his dick against my ass.

"Promise me something," he whispered against my ear.

"Anything I can," I told him, fighting every instinct to roll over and just hug him. He wanted to touch and not the other way around. The pulse of his cock was so hot against my skin, and my cunt was clenching around emptiness.

"If this is ever too much or I do something you don't like —tell me? Doc's gonna be kicking his own ass because he might have hurt you. I never want to hurt you, either."

He didn't have to tell me that. I knew it in my soul. Just as I knew Mickey hadn't meant to hurt me, and honestly, he really hadn't. He'd scared himself and I hated that more than anything.

"Freddie," I said without hesitation. "Anything you want will be okay by me—but I promise. I'll tell you if I don't like something or it makes me uncomfortable."

The soft rub of his cheek to mine had me sighing.

"Will you promise me the same thing?"

"Yes, Boo-Boo. This feels good—just holding you." I heard the rest of the sentence. Holding me and feeling me. Because, I craved the same thing. More contact.

Just more.

He pressed his lips in light kisses along my jaw before sliding his hand down to my hip. When he held me still and rocked against my ass, I closed my eyes. It was the most sensual torture—even more when his breath began to speed up.

"Come for me, Freddie," I whispered. "I want to feel you come all over me."

The first spurt hit my lower back and then my ass. Another jerked out of him as he pushed upward and it hit right between my shoulder blades.

The sound of his hand on his dick as he nudged my legs apart had me tilting my ass upward and then he came on my cunt. Not pressing into me, he traced it up and down against my labia and then down to my clit. Hot and sticky cum slid over me.

I shuddered just from the image. More from how Freddie let out little sighs. He traced his finger over the cum, then dragged it down on his fingers to push into me, and I clenched on his hand.

He fucked me gently, thrusting his fingers in to the knuckle, only pulling his hand away to gather more cum. But he kept up the rhythmic pushes, and when his thumb began to work my clit, I rocked with him.

My orgasm was right there, even as we lazily circled it, and I savored every brush of his skin on mine. How his fingers scissored or gained in force. I relished the fact that he fucked me with his hand.

"Want to come?" he whispered.

"Please," I answered in the same low voice, and the pressure intensified along with the force. Now my nipples rocked against the sheets, adding another layer to the sweet torment.

Then I was coming, my head back as I cried out, and Freddie kissed me. All teeth and tongue, he devoured the sound and was right there to stroke me down as I shuddered and trembled.

He didn't leave me even after, just wrapping me up tight. Our skin was tacky and would be a mess in a few hours. But that was what showers were for. I wasn't leaving him. When he wrapped a hand over my breast, cupping it firmly, I sighed.

"Yes," I answered his unspoken question. "That is perfect."

"Good," he said. "Me too."

# CHAPTER 37

DOC

*I*'d barely slammed open the door to my truck, when Jasper slammed it closed. Jerking around, I stared at him. Milo was three steps behind him and Liam was following right behind him.

"Not the time for this, boys," I warned. Right now, I needed distance between Little Bit and me. Distance to not see my hands around her throat. Distance to not see what could have happened if I hadn't woken up.

"You're not going anywhere, Mickey," Milo told me as he boxed me in. Jasper leaned back against the truck door, arms folded. Liam met my stare without flinching.

Opening and closing my hands, I fought the urge to strike out. I almost wished Bones or Voodoo were here. They'd both give me a solid fight if I asked for it.

"This isn't the time…" I said slowly.

"No," Liam commented, arms folded. The fact they were all in various states of sleepwear wasn't lost on me. The air out in the warehouse was almost too cold against my skin. I'd only had on a pair of sweats. I didn't even remember dragging them on.

"Boys—"

"Guys," Milo corrected. "Ten years ago, you could get away with that *boys* bullshit. None of us are kids anymore." There was something flat in his eyes that refused to let me go. "We haven't been for a long time."

Fuck.

Hands on my hips, I backed off a step or two and stared down at my feet. The burn scars feathered over the top of one foot. You could see the elements from one of my boots that had scored deeper than others there.

Even as the presence of those scars registered, the history of them, and the memories of receiving them—nausea swam through me. I dropped my hands to my thighs as I bent over and tried to slow the race of my heart.

A hand came to rest on my shoulder. "We got you," Milo said.

"I had my hands on her throat." They should be killing me.

"If I thought for an instant you wanted your hands there," Jasper said in a rock-steady voice, "I'd cut them off for you."

I jerked my gaze up to lock on his. Jasper, who'd been furious with me for years and more than willing to put a bullet in me, had a kind of rough compassion in his eyes.

The urge to rail at him died, unspoken. If he wanted to protect Little Bit, I needed to never sleep with her again. I hadn't meant to fall asleep in the first place. I knew better. My dreams could be dark fucking places.

Milo's grip on my shoulder was like steel. The kids shouldn't be the ones holding me up. The door to the clubhouse opened, and Vaughn strode out with Kellan a few steps behind him.

When Rome appeared, I had to fight the urge to shake Milo off. "Where is Little Bit?"

"She's with Freddie," Kellan said. "He's got her. How are you?"

I frowned. Freddie wasn't always in the best headspace...

"He's fine with her," Rome said. "He wouldn't have stayed if he wasn't." While no judgment echoed in his tone, it resonated within me, nevertheless. I shouldn't have stayed with her.

"Do you need to talk about it?" Milo asked, and I shook my head.

"I've done all the talk therapy I ever intend to do," I told him. When I took a step, he let me go and I paced away from them in the warehouse. The colder air helped settle my nerves. The movement helped too. I needed to walk, to try and shake off the dregs of that dream. "Not much to be done for it except to try and shake it off."

I didn't expect there to be any comments, and they didn't surprise me by making any, either. But it wasn't hard to read the doubt in their expressions. Liam folded his arms, his eyes narrowing as he studied me. I read the assessment in his manner.

Could he take me down? Probably. But only if I didn't see him coming. Of all of them, he was the most dangerous when it came to hand-to-hand. Jasper was still too volatile; he led with his temper. Kel, on the other hand?

He'd just shoot me. I appreciated that. Milo and Vaughn were the more unpredictable ones...

"If you want to keep seeing Starling, then be uncomfortable and talk." Speaking of unpredictable.

I cut a look at Rome, yet he didn't flinch.

"She's worth it."

"You don't have to tell me that," I said, fighting to keep my temper and voice level in check. I got where he was coming from.

Rome shrugged. "Yes, I do. You don't trust us with your pain."

That stopped me dead in my tracks, and I pivoted to face them. They each met my gaze evenly. Kel stood there in pajama pants and a t-shirt, hands in his pockets like he was wearing one of his suits. Milo was dressed similarly, only his arms were folded. We were all dressed for bed in some fashion. It was two—fuck, it was three in the morning.

The time when the wolves were at the door. Fuck knew they were always at my door. I wanted to deny the charge. To tell them it wasn't about trust. That would be a lie. I didn't even talk to my team about this. I trusted them with my life, and they trusted me with theirs.

Except we didn't *talk*.

"Do you trust Hellspawn?" Liam's question set me back on my heels.

"I trust her." Those words came effortlessly. "But telling her this…" Even if I *had* told her about the injuries, the hospital, and the time in recovery. I had told her, and it didn't change a damn thing in her eyes. When she looked at me, it wasn't with pity but a rough sympathy. The kind one survivor had for another.

"Telling her this?" Jasper prompted, with the kind of patience I didn't expect. "Pretty sure she already knows, Doc."

Sighing, I shook my head. As soon as I'd recognized my hand around her throat, I bolted. Distance between Little Bit and me was vital to keeping her safe in the immediate aftermath.

"Fuck." I needed to go back in there and apologize.

"Give her till morning," Kellan said. "She knows you didn't mean it."

I spared him a look. How could she possibly...

"Because she knows, Doc," Vaughn said, arms folded. His posture was a lot more relaxed than mine. "She wanted to come after you, and we told her to give you time. Freddie has her, and she's safe with him. We're all right here."

"Did I hurt her?" Asking that question cost me everything.

"Bruised, lightly," Kellan answered in an even tone I didn't deserve. Goddammit, Little Bit didn't need to deal with my damage.

"We're all broken, Doc," Rome said. "Starling knows."

"Broken isn't bad," I muttered, the echo of Little Bit repeating that not too long ago resonated with me.

"Yep," Liam said. "We're all fucked up in our own ways."

"Some of us are a lot fucked up," Milo admitted.

"Some of us aren't," Jasper countered, and I wasn't the only one who flipped him off. Rough laughter dislodged the boulder on my chest.

"Jas," Liam said in the driest of tones. "They haven't come up with the word for you yet."

"Makes me unique then, doesn't it?" The snark he volleyed back put a real smile on my face. Jasper and Liam used to be tight. Not like he was with Milo, but close enough. The fissure between them had gone too deep for far too long.

"Unique is not another word for cool or awesome." Liam rolled his eyes, even if his smile hinted at sardonic humor.

"Nope," Jasper countered. "It means one of a kind..."

"Anyway," Kellan said, emphasizing the word with a shake of his head. "The point is—we've all got our issues. If you want to learn to sleep in there with Sparrow, one of us will start sleeping there too—until you have it under control."

Except... "I might never have it under control. I've had these nightmares since the ambush." Nightmares. Night terrors, really. Flashbacks. PTSD. "Happened in the field. In the hospital. In counseling."

I shrugged.

It was one of the reasons.

"Then it can't hurt to try 'cause you want to be there, or you wouldn't have fallen asleep tonight." The absolute certainty in Kellan's voice slashed through me. Level-headed, even, and grounded.

"Ms. Stephanie—" Jasper broke off for a moment, and the punch of grief slammed into me. Slammed into all of us, honestly. I wasn't the only one sucking in a deep breath. "Ms. Stephanie," Jasper said again, "always said that talking it out wasn't an easy fix. It wasn't a painless fix. Sometimes, it wasn't a fix at all. But it did work. You just had to be willing…"

"…to put in the work," I said in the same breath as Vaughn, Milo, and Kellan. "Yeah, she believed that you could do anything if you invested yourself in it."

"So invest yourself in us, Doc," Liam suggested. "No one here is going to judge."

"I would," Jasper volunteered, ignoring the exasperated looks thrown his way. "I said I *would*, except—my glass house has enough cracks in it that I'd rather just try to understand."

"Fuck my life," Liam muttered. "Who are you, and what did you do with Hawk?"

"I've matured," Jasper informed him. "Maybe that's gonna be an acquired taste for you."

A real, if reluctant, chuckle escaped me. Milo, however, laughed for real. So did Kellan. Pretty sure Vaughn was chuckling as he muttered, "Bullshit."

That set Liam off. Shaking my head, I stared at the fridge. What mirth filtered through me sobered. "Any luck with that prick?"

"No," Milo said. "He has no pain tolerance."

"None," Liam agreed. "But he's more afraid of his brother than he is of us."

"We could take the wife in there," Kellan said. "But that's a card we're only going to get to play once. If he couldn't fight for his abused wife, *then*, I don't expect that will have changed all these years later."

Thoughts of violence drifted through me. Thoughts and ideas.

"How long of a break has he had this time?"

Liam glanced at his watch. "Twenty-four hours, no food, no water, and no relief from the music blasting or how we hoisted his arms."

He'd need hydration soon. "It's not talking..."

"But it is therapeutic." Milo nodded, then paused to glimpse at Kellan. I spared them both a look. Far too used to leading, Milo still struggled now and then when it came to deferring. At the same time, the role fits Kellan, and I understood why everyone adapted—even Milo—swiftly. "Thoughts?"

"It's almost four in the morning. Clothes. Coffee. Then carnage."

The others filtered back inside, but Milo and Jasper lingered with me. When it was just the three of us, I glanced at them. "Thank you."

"Don't mention it," Jasper said. "Really—being the one who gets to knock some sense into you for a change was a thrill." His grin was both cocky and amused. Little shit.

Milo gave it a beat while Jasper slipped inside then looked at me. "You good?"

"Nope," I said. "But I'm back on dry land again instead of wading in the weeds."

"Might be all you can get."

I studied him. Milo hadn't said a word about me dating— was that what we were doing? It felt like a lot more—his sister. Reconciling Little Bit with his Ivy didn't always register in my brain, and at the same time...fuck, I was a little under twice her age. You'd think I had more sense.

The hell of it was. I didn't want to let her go, for anything.

"I guess. But I'm going to push for more," I said. "She deserves better."

"Keep her in the loop," Milo told me in all seriousness. "She's tough, my baby sister. Tougher than I could have ever imagined. Trust that."

I would.

"Okay, clothes, coffee, and carnage. I really need to hurt something. Her piece of shit father will have to do for the moment."

It took me a few minutes to grab some clothes when I got upstairs. I avoided Little Bit's bedroom more to let her and Freddie sleep if they'd managed to get back there than because I didn't want to see her.

When she got up later in the morning, I would apologize, and by then, I'd have a game plan too. I followed the sound of the voices downstairs to the kitchen, where Liam worked as a barista. I was fine with plain black coffee, but there was some comfort in these drinks.

Rome was at the table, a cup of coffee steaming next to him as he sketched. Someone had found a handful of mismatched chairs to replace the ones Milo had destroyed. I dragged one out and then frowned as I caught sight of what Rome was sketching.

"You want coffee, Doc?" Liam asked, but I only half-nodded.

"Yeah—Rome, why are you sketching him?" Because that was a face I would never forget. The last place I expected to see it was here.

"Sketching who?" Vaughn leaned over to look at the image. "Who is that?"

"Julius King," Rome said. "I'm sketching a picture for us."

"Seriously?" Kellan joined us then Jasper crowded in. Liam glanced at the sketch and nodded.

"That's him. The jaw is a little more angular. Harsher. But that could just be my opinion of him."

"What's wrong, Doc?" Milo asked as he walked in. He'd thrown himself through a shower. I cut a look at him. His whole expression blanked as he caught his first look at *Julius King*. "Why the fuck are you drawing him?"

The tension in his voice cut through the room. Liam shot Milo a look. "That's the king."

The king.

The son of a bitch who'd put a contract out on Milo.

Who'd recruited Liam to hunt the Vandals.

To be his inside man.

The king, who'd wanted a piece of Little Bit. Wanted her to work for him...

"Don't care what he's calling himself now, but that's Jeff Hardigan," I said into the silence as their confused looks focused on me and then jerked to Milo.

Milo's expression betrayed no emotion. "My father."

# CHAPTER 38

*O*ur father.

Milo's face had been cast in stone since Freddie and I found them all gathered in the kitchen. Their conversation had broken off the moment I came in. Tension collected in the room, swelling with all the things they weren't saying.

Worry for Mickey flooded me, but he opened his arms as soon as I turned to him. I wrapped around him as I slid into his lap. The soft rasp of his cheek against my hair made me sigh. "I'm sorry, Little Bit," he murmured against my ear, and I hugged him tighter. Only when I pulled back did he study my throat.

I'd seen the faint marks in the bathroom. They weren't that bad, truthfully. The ice had helped to fade some of it, but he hadn't crushed anything. "I'm okay," I assured.

His eyes darkened and I rested my forehead on his. I needed him to believe me. I wasn't sure how to help him right now, but we would figure this out.

"I'm sorry, Little Bit." He pressed a kiss to the side of my head. "I'm going to work on it. I promise."

"I'll help," I said. "If I can."

"You help me every goddamn day." Then he traced his fingers against my throat. "I am sorry."

Tears burned in my eyes for the tragedy in his voice. But also because no one had ever apologized for actually hurting me before—then again, everyone else who'd done it hadn't cared if they hurt me.

"Thank you." I caught his hand and kissed his palm.

"So..." Freddie elongated the syllable, pulling my attention toward him and the rest of the room. The silence had weight. "What did we miss?"

He winked when his gaze collided with mine, but I understood what he meant. The guys were all strung out and a little too sober. Rome turned the sketch he'd drawn toward me and I skimmed it.

"Oh. You drew the King."

"So, he is the man you had dinner with a few nights ago?" Milo asked.

"Yes. The same one we had to meet a few weeks ago with Ezra. The king." I wrinkled my nose. I got the joke. His name was Julius King—so taking the name "The king" was more than a little ostentatious. Then again, after meeting the man, he seemed to live up to all that arrogance.

Milo's scowl deepened, and the temperature in the room shifted. Even Mickey let out a ragged breath.

"What happened?"

I twisted in Mickey's lap and then stood up. Kellan and Liam were grimmer than I'd ever seen them. Jasper and Vaughn looked more disturbed than angry. Rome seemed more thoughtful, but Milo—he was furious.

"Milo?"

Mickey caught my hand, squeezing gently, but no one

else was saying anything. *Everyone* was looking at Milo. Fear plummeted through me.

"Is it Lainey?"

He jerked his head up. "No, Ivy, Mayhem is fine—as far as I know."

Relief cut through me like it severed all my strings. "Then what?"

"That man..." Milo said, nodding to Rome's sketch. "He might be calling himself Julius King now—for all I fucking know, maybe he changed his name legally. But that's *not* his name."

Ice slicked over my spine at the frost in Milo's tone. Worse was the barren wasteland in his eyes when he locked his gaze on me.

"Take a long look at him. Memorize his face. Then *never* go near him again."

Beyond the obvious... "Who is he?"

"His real name is Jeff," Mickey said quietly. "Jeff Hardigan."

"He's the son of a bitch who dumped us," Milo said, and the hostility edging every single word sent goosebumps racing over my skin. I jerked my gaze from Milo to the sketch again. Rome had always been a truly gifted artist. He'd captured the arrogance in King, as well as the harsher elements of his personality: the abrasiveness and the way he had of staring right through a person.

This was our father?

I cut a look toward Milo again. Only he wasn't staring at me, but at the sketch. "Our father tried to have you killed?"

*Why?*

"That's not all he did, Ivy." The dead notes in his tone pulled at me. "However, you don't need to worry about him. You will *never* go near him again."

Except... I tracked my gaze to Liam. We'd thrown a

gauntlet down at King. He gave me the barest head shake. Not a discussion for now.

All I wanted was to do something that would make it all better for Milo, I just had no idea *what*. Releasing Mickey's hand, I folded my arms. Milo might not want a hug. I dismissed that thought a second later and simply went to my brother.

He gave a little jolt when I wrapped my arms around him. Closing his own arms around me, he pulled me in close.

"I'm okay, Ivy." There was no way that was the truth. It might be what he wanted me to believe. But how could he be okay? I wasn't okay, and I had no memories of the man.

Leaning into Milo, I considered my two encounters with The king. The handful of conversations around him. The threats—

"He wanted Adam killed because Adam asked me to marry him."

The initial horror at the suggestion seemed almost violently magnified. Cold sheathed my spine, then cracked as realization shivered through my whole system.

"He said as much that day..."

"It's going to be fine, Hellspawn. Whether he wanted Adam dead or not is irrelevant. Adam is alive." Not even Liam's reasoning helped lift the unease invading every one of my cells.

I wished I had shared that certainty. How could it all be okay? "He wanted you dead..." That was what they'd all said. Pulling back from Milo, I scanned my gaze over them and then back. "Why is all of this happening now?"

"It's not just happening now," Kellan answered, and I twisted to meet his calm eyes.

No—they weren't calm. They were steely, focused. When he held out his hand to me, I gave Milo a squeeze and then went to Kel.

He settled me under his arm, and I shivered even as I burrowed into the side of him. "It's been happening for years. It's coming to a head now—partially because we're together."

Because I was here, bringing my past with me. Now our past—Milo's and mine—was also invading.

"It's also because we're peeling back the facade. We're digging into all the lies, all the half-truths, and all the secrets. We're talking. We're not letting anyone else tell us what is true or not, anymore. We're figuring this out—*together*." He swung his stare around to look at all the guys before focusing on me began. "No one is on their own. We're stronger together."

It was hard to deny the confidence in his eyes. His strength and determination buoyed me. At the same time, I had more questions than answers.

"Come on, Ivy, come, sit down and eat. We have a lot to get through today." As much as I adored Milo, I had to worry about how tired he sounded right now.

Who could blame him? I was exhausted. My mother was upstairs, and my father was in the fridge – wait, my adoptive father was in the fridge. My biological father? I glanced back at the sketch Rome drew. The accuracy of his depiction was unsettling.

I sat for a meal with him. I stood in a room alone with him while he seemed to assess me before Liam and Ezra charged in. He wanted something from me, that much had been clear from the beginning.

What did he want? Was it my money? Was it the Sharpe money? Was it something else entirely? Was this why he wanted me to become a so-called Royal?

I was so fucking sick of the lies.

I was sick of feeling like the whole world had conspired against all of us.

The guys hustled for food, and I let Vaughn coax me back

over to the table. He sandwiched me into a seat between him and Freddie. Muted conversation surrounded me. Everywhere I looked, I caught the same questions in their eyes.

Yet, everyone, Freddie included, fought for a sense of normalcy at the table. Following along wasn't hard. Nevertheless, I also couldn't distract myself. In the past, the wall of nothingness had become my defense against the world.

No one knew me. Not really. The closest I came to anyone seeing *me* had been Lainey. Bless her for never giving up on me, but the long separations helped me keep that barrier in place. A barrier that hid all my dark and dirty secrets—no, not mine. Fuckbucket's. The stain of them discolored everything, fouling the very air around me, and I'd hidden from it as much as I'd hidden it from the world.

Now, another lie had been peeled open. "Could he know —who I am?"

The question spilled out of me, killing the conversation around the table. One by one, the guys exhaled long breaths or just appeared thoughtful. Had they already discussed this? When I shot Freddie a questioning look, he shook his head.

I almost wished we could retreat back to the cocoon of warmth we'd woken in this morning. We'd showered—separately—but Freddie sat in the bathroom while I showered, and I'd stuck around for him when he asked.

Scars had been visible on his skin, though I refused to stare at them or make him uncomfortable. He was letting me see him, entrusting himself to me. I wouldn't give him any cause to regret that vulnerability.

"You look like Mom," Milo admitted. "He'd have to be even more of a cold-souled bastard than I think he is to not recognize you."

Oh, that grated. I wanted to slap the shit out of him. Beneath the veneer of gruffness and genuine anger was a core of hurt. Jeff Hardigan, Julius King, or whatever his name was, had injured my brother. Wounded all of them in his attempts to cut Milo out and assassinate him.

Was he the reason Milo went to prison? That just added more salt to the ire brewing in my soul. Anger kindled deep inside, the fire fueling me as the guys sought to talk around the revelations boiling in the center of everything.

"I need to see my mother," I said, pulling out my phone to snap a picture of the sketch. "I have questions. Then I want to see Sharpe."

Not Daddy. Not my father. Not even Moira's husband. Sharpe. I needed the distance. I was halfway up the stairs before Milo and Kellan caught up to me.

Static buzzed through me as I used the key to unlock the door. They'd discussed putting a keypad to secure the lock, but frankly, I didn't want Moira to be here that long.

The smell of coffee and food hit me as I opened the door. The guys had fed her. The belated knowledge flooded me with affection for my guys. They were looking after her, even when I had a hard time just thinking about her.

She was already on her feet as I stepped inside with my shadows. I zeroed in on her appearance. She wasn't dressed up or even wearing cosmetics. If anything, her casual attire of yoga pants, tunic blouse, and lightly brushed hair made me smile a little.

More approachable and warm. More like the woman who would steal me away for fun weekends or stories. All the times she "pretended" we were running away—they weren't necessarily a pretense, were they?

"Emersyn," she said, and the relief in her eyes sent guilt raking over my heart.

"Mom," I said, narrowing the space between us while keeping the sofa there as a barrier. "Hong Kong—Singapore…Monte Carlo…" I licked my lips. "Were you really running away? Or were you just taking me to punish Uncle Fuckbucket?"

She didn't even attempt to cover her wince. "I wanted to run away...sometimes I even convinced myself I could. They always tracked us down...always pulled me back in. More than once, Bradley—" Her nose wrinkled in distaste. "Fuckbucket warned me that if I didn't obey, he would take you permanently, cut me off without a dime or access. I kept...I want to tell you I kept fighting, but it was hard, baby. How far could I go before I couldn't get to you at all?"

I searched for sympathy. On some level, I wanted to feel it for her. I wanted to offer her some semblance of comfort. Maybe someday, but I didn't have it in me right now. "We'll never know."

Even though she didn't flinch, she did cut her gaze to Milo and Kellan before peering back at me. "I'm sorry."

"I know." Truthfully, I believed her. She wasn't perfect, and she'd also suffered. I wished—I wished for many things, but we weren't getting that now. So, there was only one way to go. "I have two questions and need honest and straightforward answers."

Mom squared her shoulders. "I'm ready."

"Do you know this man?" I held out my phone with the sketch of Julius King. She circled the sofa to get a better look.

A frown tightened her brow. "He seems familiar...like..." She shook her head. "I feel like I've seen him, but I don't know where. I've met so many people over the years. Do you have a better picture of him?"

"No," I said, then clicked away the picture. Kellan and Milo said nothing, since they were allowing me to do this my way.

Hopefully, they would agree with this next part.

"Do you want to see Dad?"

Stunned silence greeted the question. "What?"

"Dad," I repeated. "He's here. Do you want to see him?"

The fact she almost recoiled made me feel better than anything else. "Baby, you need to be careful of him."

I already knew that. I already knew what he'd done about her being hurt. The same thing he'd done about me.

Absolutely nothing.

Her throat convulsed. "Em…"

"I know, Mom. If I could not ask you, I wouldn't. However, I need your help…"

Her chin came up and her eyes flashed. She met and held my gaze for a long moment, then nodded. "Tell me what I can do."

"I need you to talk to him. We need to know where Fuckbucket is right now…and I need to know how my trusts are set up."

We needed *everything*.

# CHAPTER 39

*EMERSYN*

uiding Moira out of her room, I caught Kellan's measured look. Except when I raised my eyebrows, he only nodded. Milo had gone ahead while Kellan walked with us. When I'd offered Mom my arm, her relief had been profound as she threaded her arm through mine.

Downstairs, Freddie waited with Rome and Vaughn. Mickey, Milo, Jasper, and Liam were conspicuous in their absence. They were probably trying to make the fridge palatable.

I hadn't been back to see him since the first day. Mom studied each of them as we moved through the room. I paused to glance at Kellan. "Do we need to give them a few minutes?"

He shook his head. "No, but I should warn you, Mrs. Sharpe…"

"Moira," she said. "Please. I don't want to be any kind of Sharpe anymore…"

I clutched her arm. Honestly, I was right there with her on that. Sharpe had been my performance name because Uncle Fuckbucket wanted to own me everywhere.

No more.

But I would deal with that later. Right now, I needed to focus on Mom.

"Very well, Moira," Kellan said in an even tone. "Sparrow needs you to ask your husband some questions. Despite our very persuasive efforts, he has resisted answering questions regarding his brother."

Mom's eyes narrowed at that announcement. "You just want to know where—" She spared me a look. "You just want to know where Fuckbucket is."

To be honest, it entertained me when she called him that. "Yes. He won't talk about him as far as we've tried. He's made excuses, but nothing else…"

She swallowed, her eyes damp, but the tears didn't slip free. As her chin lifted, she seemed to be schooling her features. I recognized that look. She was girding herself for what came next.

"Where was he when you found him?"

"Vegas," Rome said. "He had bodyguards with him. We removed him from them then brought him here."

Distaste creased her features. "Gambling has always been his vice." She sighed, then glanced at me. "You wanted to know about your trusts?"

I nodded. "Now or later, but I need to know."

"You've never cared about the money before." She wasn't wrong.

"I don't, except…"

"Money is power."

I nodded once.

"You would have received access to twenty-five percent on your eighteenth birthday. It would have been automatic and dropped into your private accounts." She released me to smooth her hair. "The rest vests over the next decade."

"If I get married?"

Her eyes narrowed, and she glanced at the guys then back to me. "Yes. You would receive a sizable chunk...though you won't have to share it with anyone if you wait for twenty-five."

"Sizable...how sizable?"

"Seventy-five percent. The final will vest on your twenty-eighth birthday or when you have a child. There's a considerable secondary trust that will pass straight to your children. We set it up the day we adopted you..."

For a moment, her voice wobbled, and she had to close her eyes to try and regain her breath.

"We—we didn't want you to ever have to worry about anything. So, we set up a secondary trust for your children. Nothing about it is contingent on who you marry, or even if you do...it was always there for you. A golden parachute."

An escape route.

"Who controls the trusts?" Kellan asked. "Sharpe? Your husband?"

"No," Mom said with a shake of her head. "The point of the trusts is independence and support. Bradley craved control, yet to keep the tax burden offset and manageable, it went to a financial manager. He would handle everything as a neutral third party."

"Meaning Fuckbucket can't undo it."

"No," she said, though her tone didn't sound as confident. "I imagine he still exercises some control through notifications..."

"Which account of mine would they have deposited that twenty-five percent in?"

"Your account," Mom said. "The one we set up for you when you started performing. All of your money has been deposited. You have your own financial advisor, baby. He should have been sending you reports..."

Right. When would I have seen those? Before the Vandals took me, I was still legally a minor and had been barely eighteen. "I'm going to have to make some calls."

"I'll help you," Mom told me, except Kellan's expression grew increasingly grim as the conversation continued.

"Let's investigate this after," he said. "You're going to need an attorney. One we can trust."

"Liam will know someone."

Rome nodded at that assessment, and Kellan sighed. "Sparrow? Stay with me a moment while the guys escort Moira?"

"I'll be right with you," I told her. "Don't go in until I'm there." I squeezed her arm, and she gave Kellan a long studying look before Vaughn motioned for her to follow him. Freddie squeezed my pinky before he and Rome escorted Mom out.

She looked unnerved, then again, why wouldn't she be? She didn't know them as I did. Didn't know they wouldn't hurt her unless she posed a threat. Honestly, I didn't think they'd hurt her even then unless I said something.

They'd restrain her, in any case.

That was enough for now.

When the door closed, I faced Kellan. He studied me, hands in his pockets and head tilted. It had been a while since he looked at me like this. "What are you hoping to accomplish with taking her out there?"

I didn't answer immediately or dismiss the question. Instead, I turned it over in my head. "I want the truth...but I need closure, and so does she."

He gave me a slow nod. "You know you might not get either?"

I lifted my shoulders. "I have to try. I can't—-I can't take these lies anymore. Parents who wanted me for someone else. A father who abandoned me but now wants me for something? The same people are trying to hurt all of you...*have* hurt you. Hurt me. Sent Milo to prison."

No, I had to do something.

"I wish I had the answers for you, Sparrow."

"Me too. But for the first time...there's a light at the end of the tunnel. A place where we get everything we want and live in a world we make for ourselves." I spread my arms. "I know it won't always be easy. If you'd asked me two years ago, would I embrace a relationship with so many lovers that accepted me *with* so many others? Honestly, I'd probably have laughed in your face and then run to hide with security."

"But we do accept you with everyone else," Kellan said. "You know that, right?"

"I do," I promised him, then closed the distance between us. As soon as I was there, he hooked an arm around me and dragged me to him. "I love you. I love all of you so damn much."

His smile gentled. "I love you too, Sparrow. We all do. So no matter what happens, we do this together."

"Even if together means I stay behind while you take on the bad guys?"

"Even if," he agreed. "Trust me—when the time comes to pull the trigger, you will have that say. We will extract the punishment for you and the vengeance, but we aren't taking it from you."

A shiver raced up my spine. "And when they are gone...?"

"Sky's the limit, little bird. Head up, wings out."

I pushed up on my toes, and Kellan met me with a heart-wrenching, sweet kiss. His lips massaged mine apart even as he swept his tongue in to tangle with my own. A sigh escaped me as I sank into his kiss. When he lifted me, I wrapped my arms around him to hold on.

Never letting go.

I was *never* letting any of them go again. "We can do this, right?"

"Yes," he said without hesitation. When he shifted to wrap his fingers around my throat, he paused to study the marks there. They weren't that bad. Thankfully, Mom hadn't noticed them or if she had, she hadn't said a word. "We can do this. Trust me?"

"Yes." Even if I knew the answer, I needed to ask. "You trust me?"

"Absolutely, Sparrow. But—" He lifted his chin, watching me with absolute calm as he massaged my neck. His touch was infinitely gentle as he avoided the bruises. "When we get in there if I say go—you go, understood?"

"Protect Mom?"

"I will do my best, but you come first. If he loses it, which he might when she walks in there, I want you to take that step out."

Sucking in a deep breath, I fought the shudder rocking my whole system. "Then I'll go if you say to."

He closed his eyes and rested his forehead on mine. "You are a fucking miracle, Sparrow. Never forget it."

The kiss he pressed to my lips was both hungry and sweet. Longing unfolded within me. I just wanted—everything. There was no *just* about it. I wanted everything with them. With *my* Vandals.

When he set me back on my feet, he traced his fingers over my throat. "Don't worry about Doc. We've got him too."

"I knew that...and I have Freddie."

His grin grew. "Yeah?"

I nodded. "We'll take care of each other."

"Damn right, we will." Tucking me under his arm, he

headed for the door. "Now for the unpleasant part of the day."

Mom stood with the guys in the office. Well, she sat there. Someone had given her a cup of coffee. She sat at the desk with the cup cradled in her hands. I wasn't sure if she was hugging it for warmth or comfort.

Her expression lifted as I stepped in with Kellan. "This place is larger than I expected," she admitted.

"They're full of charm and secrets," I told her.

"Are they?" Mom glanced at me and then at the guys. "Maybe sometime you can tell me about them?"

"Maybe," I hedged. I wasn't sure what I wanted to promise her. "Are you ready to do this?" Was I?

Now that we were here, my heart was racing and my palms were sweaty. Kellan's measured look grounded me, and Freddie hooking his pinky to mine as he planted himself at my side, helped. Rome straightened from where he and Vaughn guarded the door to the fridge itself.

She nodded as she stood. It took her a moment to compose herself, but I recognized the steel in her manner as she schooled her features into something mild and disinterested. All emotions needed to be compartmentalized and tucked away. The best way to control a situation was to control your reactions.

"Let's see Reginald and whether he can continue lying with me right there." The barest hint of nerves wavered in her voice, and I held out my hand to her. She clasped it once. "I've got this, baby. Trust me…"

I genuinely wanted to. Glancing first to Vaughn, then Rome, and then Freddie before I met Kellan's steady gaze. "We're ready."

"Keep your distance when we're in there, Moira. I can't promise he'll be in the best of moods, but I can tell you he won't lay a finger on either of you."

The reassurance seemed to buoy Mom, but she held onto her coffee in a white-knuckled grip. Rome opened the fridge door, and Vaughn went through first, followed by Freddie. Mom and I were next, with Rome and Kellan right behind us.

The smell was pretty atrocious. The fridge was wet since they'd hosed it down—they'd hosed Sharpe down too. He hung from two chains, though his feet were flat on the floor. He'd lost weight and there was something almost hollow about his face and chest.

Thankfully, someone had dragged pants onto him. Although, like him, they were soaked.

"He looks…" Mom said slowly, no amount of manners burying the disgust in her voice or her expression.

All at once, he jerked his head up. "Moira." Ragged didn't begin to describe his voice. He sported a beard. Never, in all my life, had I seen him with a beard. It was scraggly, salt and pepper. His hair was showing more silver than it had before.

It was difficult to be away from your beauty regimen.

"Reginald," Mom said. Mickey and Liam weren't standing that far from him. There was an IV in Sharpe's arm, and two huge bags of saline hung nearby. "What have you done to yourself?"

"Me?" he demanded in a harsh voice before coughing. It neutered him as any threat, that wet, thready cough. It shook his whole body, and when he spat out blood, I couldn't disguise my own grimace.

Mom didn't try. "Yes, you," she said, moving a few steps forward. "You're protecting your brother—*again*."

"It's not like that…"

"No?" She raised her eyebrows. "This is *much* worse. What you let him do to me was one thing…how could you let him do it to Emersyn?"

"I didn't *let* him do anything. He controls—"

"Yes, yes, I've heard your excuses about how he controls

the money. Nonetheless, you had been in a position to oust him. Instead, you let him make all the decisions—"

"I don't have a choice, Moira. If I fought him, he would have taken you *again*. I don't have the shares in the company or support on the board." The last came out a snivel. "He has everything…"

"Because of your gambling," I said. It was a guess, yet somehow I suspected it was the right one. He closed his eyes.

"Baby—"

Liam's fist landed against his kidney and Sharpe's whole body contorted as he began to cough up blood.

"You keep your endearments to yourself," Liam informed him. "Do it again, and I'll start ripping out your teeth—then your tongue."

Sharpe coughed as he struggled to pull in a breath. Mom shot a glance at Liam then at me. I lifted my shoulders. I wasn't going to complain about their tactics.

"We've given him plenty of opportunities," I told her, ignoring the man I'd called Dad and Daddy for most of my life. "He would rather protect Fuckbucket, than us."

Mom met my gaze, her expression tense, then she looked at him again. This time she took another two steps forward and flung the contents of her coffee cup at his abdomen and pants. The coffee had still been steaming.

He let out a shriek as the hot coffee made contact.

"Do I have your attention, Reginald?" she demanded. "Where is he? Where would he go to hide? For once in our miserable marriage, put us first and not him." A sob caught in her throat. "Please. Put Em first…you promised me a family, and then you sacrificed us to him."

He stared at her, pain on his face and agony in his eyes. This really hurt him.

On some primitive level, I was fine with it. When Freddie ghosted up next to me and pressed his knife into my hand, I pulled my gaze off of them and found a smile just for him.

"When you're ready," he said.

When I was ready... Reginald Sharpe was going to die, and Fuckbucket was next.

Calm invaded me, sliding through my veins like a soothing salve for my soul. When I leaned into Freddie, he wrapped an arm around my shoulders, and we stared at Reginald Sharpe as Mom glared at him.

She was shaking.

But then, so was I.

Sharpe still broke first.

Thank fuck.

"He's—he's got a place he prefers...Adirondacks..."

# CHAPTER 40

*EMERSYN*

*A*dirondacks? No. It wasn't until after we'd finished questioning him—well, after Mom finished with him—that I let myself process the revelations he'd made.

Standing in the warehouse, Mom stared sightlessly at one of the trucks. Bewildered and a little lost, she made my heart hurt. The others filed out, but I heard a pained yelp before the door closed fully.

So did Mom if her flinch was anything to go by. "What's going to happen to him?" she asked, not looking at me or anyone else.

"He's going to disappear," Milo said steadily. "He was playing the high stakes in Vegas, on a bender, and then he went missing. It could take seven years for you to have him declared dead. You may want to wait a few months before you report him missing. We'll have to see about that."

"We spent a lot of time apart," she said, pivoting slowly to look at Milo. "The last few years, it was just easier to avoid him rather than see him. I had no idea how much I hated him until just now."

My heart ached for her. "You won't have to see him again." I wouldn't have asked her this time if I hadn't needed the answers.

"No, but I don't—I can't see Bra—" Distaste twisted her mouth. "Fuckbucket going to the Adirondacks. It's far too *quaint* for him."

I didn't disagree.

"Ivy?" Milo nudged me quietly, and I glanced up at him.

"She's right...nothing about the Adirondacks would appeal to him. They're neat, but he's caviar and champagne with expensive bourbon and maids who give him blowjobs on command. He wouldn't—"

He wouldn't go to the mountains when he had yachts.

"Hans Sachs."

Mom straightened. "He's on the Hans Sachs? If he's there, we might never find him..."

Bile burned in the back of my throat. Awareness of the guys swarmed over me. They were paying attention to every word, every nuance. "Mom, do you want to go lay down for a bit?"

"I'm not going to break," she countered, anger sparking in her eyes. It was the first real sign of her spirit I'd seen since they'd brought her in. "If you're going after him, you're not doing it without me." The ferocity in those last few words made my eyes burn.

"I need *you* to be okay and seeing—Sharpe was a lot." I wasn't quite braced for her to throw herself at me, but I met her hug and held her tight. "I'm going to be okay, Mom. But I can't afford to worry about you right now. We will figure this out...both your situation and this one."

It took some coaxing, but she finally let me take her upstairs. When it was just the two of us in her room though, she studied me with a critical eye.

"Emersyn... these men you've found. They're dangerous."

"I know." I met her gaze without hesitation. "It's part of their charm."

"I'm serious." Worry filtered through her eyes. "Are you sure you can trust them?"

An image of Kellan tackling me away from the speeding car in the garage flashed through my head. He hadn't hesitated.

Taking her hands, I tugged her over to the sofa and urged her to sit before I slid onto it to face her. "I know I can trust them. When I was in trouble, they took me."

That night in the alley, Eric had been furious. He slammed me into the wall and hit my head. If not for Vaughn intervening—then the guys coming to help...

"They punished the person hurting me and they took care of me. When bounty hunters tried to steal me back, they protected me."

Rome never slowed down when he found me fighting the guy in the kitchen at the shop. Nor had he when those guys came at me in the park.

"When I was stupid enough to return to Fuckbucket to protect them, *they* followed me. *They* got me out of Pinetree. *They* have protected me over and over and over again. There is *nothing* they have to prove to me."

Mom stared at me, worry glittering in her eyes. "You've had such a hard life... *This...*" She motioned to the room or maybe the warehouse. "This is not anything I would have imagined for you. Nor wanted for you, but the life I gave you wasn't what I wanted you to have either."

Misery lived in her eyes.

"Baby…"

"I know, Mom." Then I reached out to hug her. She closed her arms around me fiercely. "Neither of us deserved that life. So, no more. For you or for me." Her shudder echoed in my soul. "We're going to get through this. We will build the lives we want—me *and* you."

I pulled back to meet her tear-filled eyes.

"Trust me?"

"You truly trust those men?"

"Yes. They're my family." I didn't back off on it even when she cringed. "If you let them, they might be your family someday too." I wouldn't sugarcoat or lie to her about this. "Trust takes time."

With a light hand, she cupped my cheek. "And forgiveness?"

"We're not there yet," I said, trying to be honest. "I want to get there, however. So maybe that will take time too."

"Take all the time you need, Baby. If you need something from me, say the word. I'll do it."

I believed her. "I wish we'd been able to talk like this before…"

"Me too," she admitted. "You've always been the strong one, though. For all that I hate for them, I can't regret having you in my life."

I wasn't there yet either, but maybe soon. Maybe never. I hugged her again, then pulled away. "I may be gone for a bit. We'll make sure you're looked after."

When all was said and done, I'd look into getting her a place and setting her up.

"I'll be fine. You look after *you*."

When the Sharpes were gone. When we erased them from the board, we would have some breathing room. Then we could deal with Julius King. But my guys were getting their future, and Mom…she deserved one too. A future and time for me to forgive her so we could build that relationship.

I wanted to say more, but the words just weren't there. Only Milo was waiting when I let myself out. He locked the door and then gave me a rough hug.

"You okay?" he asked in a gruff voice that was somehow comforting in its abrasive bluntness. Or maybe I was just used to him.

"No," I said, with a slow shake of my head. "But I'm getting there." I peeked back at the locked door.

"She's tough," he said. "I wasn't sure until she walked into the fridge. But she can handle this—even the ugly stuff."

I didn't snort, because I thought that too. "I don't know if I can ever forgive her." I wanted to—maybe that was enough?

"Ivy, she's not going to ever forgive herself. Even if you somehow manage it. I want to hate her on your behalf. For a little while there...I did." He stared at the door for a long moment. "She left a defenseless child with her rapist. No excuse will ever justify that to me. None."

I swallowed.

"But that woman also loves you and wants to fight for you —and that's worth so much. We didn't win the lottery with our parents, biological or adoptive."

"You think there's hope for her?" I studied him, and he lifted his shoulders in a shrug.

"I think she cares. That's a start. Everything else, we'll tackle as we go along. I got you. We all do."

A smile pulled at my mouth. "You're a big ol' teddy bear. You know that?" A teddy bear with teeth and a ferocious temper, but a teddy bear nonetheless.

"That's our secret." He booped my nose. "Now, let's go settle all your boyfriends down because none of them wanted to wait downstairs."

My boyfriends.

"I love our family," I told him, and he gave me a one-armed hug before pressing a kiss to the top of my head.

"Me too—but that's our secret too."

I mimed zipping my lips, and he winked.

\* \* \*

DESPITE GETTING THE INFO WE WANTED, FINDING THE YACHT named the Hans Sachs took a lot of work. I'd forgotten about the damn boat. Even so, I'd put it out of my mind. I'd only ever been on it once.

For my birthday, when he decided I was ready for *more*. Just the name of it sent ice shivering over my skin. I couldn't focus on that part. Liam made calls to his security people, his investigators, and finally, his attorneys.

He had people. A lot of them. None of it seemed to settle him down. Jasper and Vaughn played pool, but the game was more like something for them to do with their hands as conversation circled in the room.

Mickey was on the phone with Alphabet. His guys were sticking close, but with everyone here they didn't need to be so vigilant at the warehouse. I remembered three possible ports where the Hans Sachs might be moored. None of them were anywhere near Braxton Harbor.

"We're going to have to rethink how we're doing this," Kellan said.

"We need a plan, period," Jasper said as he polished the end of the cue. "We're already stretched thin. We need to send Moira somewhere else."

That suggestion was both a relief and a concern. I wanted her safe, but I needed the distance. "What options do we have for that? She said I have money in my accounts...I can definitely move some around."

"I have it," Liam told me. "I will arrange a security detail for her as I have for my mom. Then we'll set her up somewhere safe. Maybe find her a real doctor instead of some fucking quack to work with her."

"Thank you." I honestly had no other profound words for the gratitude surging through me. Liam had so much on his plate already. He winked as he put the phone back to his ear and paced away.

"Okay, so we ditch Mama Sharpe, and we gut Daddy Sharpe," Freddie said.

"Freddie," Mickey said, but I reached over to catch Freddie's hand and squeezed it.

"It's okay, he's right...and I don't have a problem with it." No matter how much I wanted to make things work with Mom, I didn't and couldn't with Sharpe himself. I'd rather mourn who he could have been than worry about him now.

"Good," Kellan said as he leaned back in the chair. "What bothers me is we will have to split up to do this. We're stronger as a unit, but we're also a lot of people—not all of us need to be on this hunt."

"Are we rushing it, though?" Vaughn asked. "We're thinking he might be on a boat, but we don't have anything concrete that says he is."

Which was a problem. "We don't have any evidence he isn't. We've not found him at any of the properties the family owns or corporate holdings. Wherever he is, he's staying out of sight. Not even The king has come through on that challenge."

"Granted, we only gave it to him a few days ago," Liam said, folding his arms. "However, this is a man who likes to know things. He prides himself on knowing the answers to any questions before they're asked."

"He also said an attack on you is an attack on him." That

was a twisted fact considering his own attacks on our family. I still couldn't wrap my mind around the idea that he was my biological father.

I didn't think I even wanted to try and process it.

"That's why I believe we'll have to play this game out to the bitter end." Kellan shook his head and then looked at me. "How adamant are you about not going into hiding?"

Everything in me resisted that idea. Except... "Do you need me to? To hide? To be out of sight?"

His eyes softened. "Sparrow, I need you to be safe. If we split our resources, I want you in a secure location. I'd say here, but they know where here is, and Doc's friends..."

Mickey's friends could shelter me on the move. That discussion had already come up more than once.

"So I hide while you guys take all the risks?" Couldn't say I was a fan.

"Measured risks," Jasper told me. "We can save the crazy shit for when you're back with us."

The look Kellan gave him was so damn unfriendly, I burst out laughing. Freddie snorted, but no one disagreed.

I loathed this plan.

"I'll make sure you get to where you're going," Milo said. "One of us should be with her."

"If you want," Kellan said. "I'm not going to argue."

Milo just shook his head, but I caught Liam and Jasper's nods of approval. They'd set Milo up. They wanted *him* out of the line of fire too.

"It's okay, big brother," I told him. "I'll watch your back."

He chuckled, but a hint of a smile touched Rome's lips and Mickey seemed to relax. Right, they wanted me and Milo both safe. I could do that. I could go *hide* if it meant protecting Milo. I hated leaving them, but if I stayed, so would Milo. The threat against him was very real.

"Okay," I said. "Tell me the plan. What can I do—or better —what do you need me to do?"

Because I wanted this over and done with. I wanted my freedom and theirs.

Frankly, I didn't care who we had to kill to make it happen.

# CHAPTER 41

DOC

"Just remember," I told Milo. "The guys are going to be waiting for you out at the old Forty-Two Saloon in Lisbon. Just head there. They've already picked the location for the two of you to hunker down. We debated having them come in, but the more distance we put between the car swaps, the better."

"I got it," he said, shaking his head. "Feels all James Bond. Leave here in one car, change it for another before we're actually out of the city. Then stop at a place on Route 61 to pick up another car."

"Well, it's only paranoid if someone isn't out to get us." No matter how light I kept it, there was no way to ease the sting of the upcoming separation from Little Bit or the stress of knowing we were sending them into hiding.

It had been a discussion point for days. Little Bit wanted to fight. She didn't want to be sent away, but she was our most vulnerable. That vulnerability put Milo at risk too.

Especially after discovering Jeff's latest maneuvers. I couldn't believe that son of a bitch.

I hadn't even thought of that asshole in over a decade, and he was working an angle that landed his son in jail. Soon as we fucked up the uncle and took that trash out, we'd deal with Jeff.

No more shit from the past coming to touch them—any of them.

"Not sure that makes me feel better," Milo said with a wry shake of his head.

"But it doesn't make you feel worse." I glanced over to where Little Bit was saying goodbye to the guys. We'd been in a flurry of activity in the three days since making the decision. Moira Sharpe had been relocated with a security team to watch her back.

The place Liam secured put her four states away. We'd gotten confirmation earlier in the day that she had arrived on schedule. The relief on Little Bit's face that her mom was safe had only been matched by her relief when her mother had been driven out by Liam's security people.

Julius King had been silent. Through a mutual decision, we were keeping *his* identity under wraps for now. I'd rather call him on his shit right now, but we had enough to deal with in the immediate. So, I put a sock in it *for the moment.* Steph would be proud. Every day I missed her more and, at the same time, I heard her even more clearly.

*"You can only be responsible for yourself, Mickey. Helping others to carry their burdens doesn't mean they get to put them down. It means you lessen the weight but can't take it all on yourself."*

At the time, it had amazed me, because I knew just how much she carried for everyone else. When I called her on it, all she'd done was pat my cheek.

*"Knowing when you can't carry it all is the most difficult part.*

*You have to trust them to help themselves. Although, a little judicious boot to the ass never hurt anyone."*

"You and Little Bit go and pretend this is some kind of vacation. Teach her how to play poker..."

Milo snorted, and I grinned. "Yeah, my little sister is a card shark. I already figured that out."

"Yeah, it was fun when the guys discovered it too."

That earned me a genuine laugh, and I clapped him on the shoulder.

"Let her look after you. She needs to fuss, and she's worried about you."

"I'm worried about her."

That, I got. "We all are...that's why you need to let her fuss."

"She's on her way," Milo warned, and I glanced back to find her strolling toward me. We hadn't had much time to talk since—

"Give me a minute."

His noncommittal sound was answer enough. I met her halfway. When she slid her arms around me, I dragged her closer and kissed the top of her head. "Can I ask you to be good for me and stick close to Milo?" I kept the comment low.

Her laugh was the antidote to the fist in my chest. "You can ask," she said. "Can I ask you to take care of yourself? And to let the guys look after you too?"

I didn't snort or smirk, but the temptation was there. We hadn't discussed what had happened. "I need to apologize to you..."

She pressed her fingers to my lips. "Later," she whispered. "We can talk about all of that later. I'm fine. Even the bruises are mostly gone."

I scraped my teeth over her fingertips as I captured her

hand. "Don't make light of this," I asked carefully. "I never want to be someone who hurts you."

"I know," she said. "We're going to handle it...together, okay?"

"I'd complain about how stubborn you are," I muttered. "But I also know that's how you survived." In what way could I not be grateful for that? "Now, go be good or torture your brother. He might enjoy that."

She laughed for real.

"And we'll keep you in the loop."

"Look after them?" Worry filtered into her eyes.

"Always. And *yes*," I continued before she could. "I'll let them look after me." I'd try anyway. Action. Getting our hands on the piece of shit who abused her would all go a long way toward smoothing over the cracks.

When she pushed upward to hug me, I cradled her close.

"Be safe for me, Little Bit."

"You too."

Then I had to let her go. She blew us a kiss then climbed into the car with Milo. There was a security team escorting them, a shadow car that would follow and then deal with any initial tails.

The plan was solid. We needed to keep the attention on us, which was why we'd split the tasks, with the rats sending a half-dozen out in our cars to get the hell out of Braxton Harbor. Leaving at different times, it was going to stretch the resources of anyone watching us. The local kids Kel had hired worked with the rats to load trucks. Another dozen of Jasper's drivers had already pulled out of here and the truckyard.

More distractions.

They wouldn't all work, although the point of the shell game was to keep them guessing. Maybe if they looked one way, they wouldn't see what we were doing with our free hand.

Liam put her in the car, hands braced on the open window as he spoke to both of them. The others drifted over until we stood in a half-circle. Kellan checked his watch, then whistled. The doors opened as five different cars all started.

Milo and Little Bit were just one more in a series of dark SUVs that pulled out. She would also not be visible in the car, ducking down until they were clear.

"I hate this," Freddie said.

"Me too," Vaughn and Jasper echoed. Liam said nothing as he made his way toward us. Instead, his gaze was on his phone.

"Adam needs a meet," he said before pocketing it. "I told him we needed a couple of days."

Kellan nodded. "I know you want to tell them…"

"We will," Liam said with a wave of his hand. "Just not yet. The king's identity won't mean as much to them. So, I'm not keeping anything life or death from them."

Which was the crux of it.

"How long?" Rome asked, and Liam cut a look at his brother.

"Forty-five minutes, then we start our rollouts."

More distractions. More shells. More peas in motion.

I stared at the doors as they rolled closed. There was something just off about the whole thing. I didn't like having her out of reach. Sending a message to Alphabet, I asked for status updates at least every twenty-four hours.

More would be appreciated.

"Let's go, guys," Kellan said, the crisp command pulling me out of the mental rut where I wasn't here but in that car with them. "The sooner we get Sharpe nailed down, the sooner we bring Sparrow and Milo back home."

"Do we get to kill that fucker in the fridge yet?" Freddie asked, and I wasn't the only one eyeing Kellan.

"It's on the list," was all Kellan said. Then he checked his watch again. "Fifteen minutes, Liam, then make the call."

He nodded. "On it."

I glanced back at the closed doors again. Vaughn patted my shoulder. "C'mon, Doc. The sooner we get this done, the sooner we get her back."

## FREDDIE

After I put the gear in the trunk, I rubbed my hands together. The rats were everywhere right now. Granted, they weren't all rats, and we were supposed to be looking for a new name for them.

Rats didn't exactly inspire confidence. But in my head, they were always going to be rats. I wanted to find Fuck-bucket and castrate him before we did anything else. I wanted him to know what it was like to lose his balls. Man didn't deserve them.

Then I wanted him to suffer and die by inches. Thirteen to fourteen years of hell might begin to even the scales.

Might.

"Hey," Jasper said, bumping my shoulder with his fist. "You good?"

"I got naked with her," I said abruptly, then glanced at Jasper. "And yeah—it was good."

The corners of his mouth twitched, though the measuring look in his eyes told me he got it. "Good."

"I mean, I thought it was kind of great—we haven't really had time since, but…"

"You're going to have time," he said in a steady, confident voice. "You're both going to have the time. We'll damn well steal it if we have to."

"Not like it would be a first," Vaughn said as he passed us by carrying a pair of bags on his way to another car. "We're pretty good at stealing what we need."

"Some of us are," Liam commented as he followed. "Some of us just like to make a lot of noise."

I snorted. "I can do both. I'm talented like that."

Rome paused to shove his two bags at me. "Carry bags, then."

"Yeah, yeah." I grinned, hauling them over toward Jasper's vehicle. I didn't miss the speculative looks from the guys, yet I also didn't feel cornered by them.

Boo-Boo belonged to all of us, and I still couldn't believe I'd gotten to not only hold her while she was naked but let myself be naked with her. I wasn't sure about her touching me yet, not totally, but her absolute willingness to let me touch her—that was fucking everything.

My cock gave a little pulse at the idea of her hand on me, and that—that was pretty cool. Normally, nothing killed an erection faster. I'd managed to fuck others, but I couldn't let them do the same to me.

It was why I'd pressed myself against her back, rubbed myself off on her ass... I thought it would be easier. It was, but even better was when she'd let me play with her and hadn't denied me anything.

Her trust was the sweetest gift.

"Hey," Kellan said, crashing into the fantasy holding me hostage, and I blinked at him. "Take it easy. You with us?"

Yeah... "Hard not to think about her."

"I know. If you're going to struggle, we can send you to them. Might be good for you and Rome both—"

"No," Rome said before I could. Kellan and I both glanced at him. "Freddie needs this." He didn't add that so did he, but it seemed to hang in the air.

He wasn't wrong. I did need this. Returning my attention

to Kellan, I nodded. "He's right. I need this. I need to do this for her."

"We all do," Kel said. "Head in the game, daydream about her later—and before you mouth off, remember, I know just how pretty her pussy is."

"Yep," came the comments from the rest of them. "We all do," Liam said. "Can we save the boner discussions for later? This is hard enough—" He grimaced and I snorted.

"Too easy."

That broke some of the tension, and my grin grew. We had later. We would absolutely have it later and all the days after that.

Probably a good thing Boo-Boo wasn't here right now, 'cause Liam was right; she really did have the prettiest pussy. Next time, I promised her and her pussy in my head. Next time, I'd work on letting her touch me, and maybe...maybe she'd let me eat her out.

That could be fun.

"Freddie," Jasper called. "Get your ass in gear."

"Moving," I said, but I was still grinning. We had a lot to look forward to, and I wanted to try all of it.

Just—one at a time.

Yep.

"Freddie," Vaughn yelled, and I shot him a middle finger, much to Liam's amusement. I picked up the pace. Yeah yeah, think about her pussy later.

# CHAPTER 42

$\mathcal{M}$*ilo*

OPENING MY EYES TOOK REAL EFFORT. IT WAS LIKE MY EYELIDS had grown impossibly heavy, or they'd been glued shut. It was a fucking battle to get them to open. Cool air filtered over my chest.

"I know you can hear me, Princess," a voice said from what seemed like very far away. "Can you hear him?"

Hear wh—the thought didn't complete as something burning hot connected with my back. The smell of scorched flesh and burning hair filled my nostrils even as pain shredded my thoughts.

A shout escaped me even as I clenched my teeth together. Adrenaline flooded my system along with alertness. Whatever had been keeping me out didn't survive the—

The man beside me held out a brand, a simple x-formed metal cross-section heated to flaming orange. I still couldn't quite breathe around the pain.

"You have one minute, Princess. Then I'll burn him again." The man speaking pulled my attention even as details of where we were filtered in.

Outside.

I was chained to something. Head tilting, I studied my wrists—not chained. Tied. Yeah, okay, I needed some focus to get out of those.

My shirt was in tatters, but I still had on jeans and boots. A headache split through my skull. Blood was in my mouth— the taste of it, anyway. Lips cracked. Throat dry. Pain throbbing in my back.

"Again," the man said, and the brand gouged into a second spot on my lower back, right next to the already brutalized flesh. Even with my teeth clenched, the sound escaped as I fought to breathe around the pain.

"How many times do you want me to burn him, Princess? Three? Four? A dozen? I know you're out there—"

I swallowed painfully then leaned over to spit out the blood. "Leave her the fuck alone," I told him as the man in question strolled toward me. I recognized him.

Bradley Sharpe.

Fuckbucket.

Rapist.

Pedophile.

Asshole.

"She's mine," he informed me. "She's always been mine, and if I have to gut every single one of you until I cut away your taint, I will."

"She's not coming back to you," I said, even as I tried to remember how the fuck we ended up here. My last memory was being in the car, Ivy giving me shit as she kept changing what music we were listening to, and then...

"Deluded boy," Sharpe said as he limped around in his too-expensive suit. Whatever aftershave he wore was cloying. "She always comes back to me." He moved behind me. "She loves me—loves what I can do for her." Then he dug his fingers into one of the burns, and I took the chance to twist.

My legs were still free and I got a good kick in that knocked him back. His lackeys were on me, raining down blows with fists and canes. The lashing offered a kind of brutal clarity.

But the fucker was limping.

Worth it.

Too bad he was still breathing.

"She won't come back to you," I told him. "Because she's free, and she's staying that way."

"She always comes back," he said, pulling out a handkerchief to dot at his mouth. "But I am growing impatient..." he called. "It's been months, Princess. I've missed you."

Then the deluded fucker added, "And I know you've missed me. I even forgive you for Reginald. Not that I'm going to miss bailing him out."

He coughed.

"With him gone, it will be the two of us—you and me. Where you belong..."

Rage curled through me, and then there was pain shuttling my thoughts to the side as the brand impacted on my flesh. There was more when it took skin away with it this time.

"Need to reheat it," one of the guys said as I fought for breath. Stay out there, Ivy. Don't you dare come to—wherever the fuck we were.

It was dark, damp, and there was—a gravestone a few feet behind Sharpe. Were we in a cemetery?

"You're hurting my feelings," Sharpe said to the darkness. She didn't answer him. Not even the nightbirds made a sound.

Good girl. Stay down, stay hidden. The guys will come.

If we'd missed our rendezvous, they'd show up.

Doc's guys were out there too.

Just gotta hang—

A grunt of sound pierced the silence, and I jerked my head up. Sharpe had a phone in his hand. Another grunt came from it, and a slap of skin echoed against a far more feminine huff.

"That's it," Sharpe said, only it was from whatever he was watching. "You can take me—oh, your tears are so beautiful, Princess. But I fucking love watching my cock go into you…"

The man watched me for a beat before he held his phone up so I could see him humping away on her. I couldn't see her face, thank fuck. But with the angle changed, I could hear her crying.

I was going to take one of these brands and shove it up his ass…

"So many good times we've shared, Princess. Do you remember the first time I made you come?"

I was going to throw up.

"I recorded it for us…"

Then he switched the video. The sounds were even more disturbing than the first one.

"So many firsts for us…" He let out a sigh. "I don't want to lose you, Princess. I never have…" He snapped his fingers, and the cane lashed across my back. It struck my sides and the burns. I was pretty sure one of my ribs cracked.

The son of a bitch ignored me as he stared at the latest video. Screams were coming from that one.

Her screams.

"So tight at first, but we fixed that," he mused. "Are you still tight, or have you ruined that by spreading your legs for those criminals?"

His expression shifted to something even more furious.

Another scream echoed in the night air, and I jerked my head toward that sound.

Fuck no…

One of the men came striding in with her over their shoulder. She was struggling and landed hard when he dumped her on the ground in front of Sharpe. She didn't hesitate to lash out.

Sharpe was already reaching for her when she hit his knee, and he went down. There was a flash of a knife, but she didn't reach him before one of his goons had her wrist and twisted it viciously behind her.

She dropped the blade as she kept fighting. I went to work twisting my hands to try and loosen the ropes. Blood slicked my skin where they were cutting into it. All I needed was one arm free…

"You break my heart," Sharpe said as he closed the distance to where his men were holding her. It was taking two of them to keep her still. Bastards.

When he put his hand on her face, she spit. The wad struck his cheek, and he backhanded her hard enough that her head rocked.

Fucker.

"Burn him again," Sharpe ordered, and the brand hit the other side of my lower back even as I twisted. I bit my fucking tongue that time.

"Stop it," she screamed, and Sharpe gripped her face tight. His knuckles were white where he dug into her cheeks.

He stared at her, his expression emptying of all emotion. "Do you want me to free him?" He cut a look at me then back to her. "Do you want him to live?"

She didn't answer, and I couldn't see her face, but his face turned into a dark mask as he glared down at her.

"You do…is he one of your lovers too? Has he—"

"You're disgusting," she said. "He's my brother—my family."

"*I* am your family," Sharpe argued. "The only family you will ever need."

"I'd rather be dead."

That declaration actually seemed to rock him. Cold invaded his eyes. "As you wish…"

"Don't you—" I didn't get to finish my statement as a blow slammed into my head. Darkness swarmed me. I fought dropping off; I needed to stay awake. Stay aware.

However, time had to have passed because when I opened my eyes again, Ivy wasn't there. Her scream roused further, and that's when I saw the coffin.

And the grave right behind it. There was a video playing somewhere. Sharpe had it up as he watched it on his phone. The insane son of a bitch truly looked sad as the coffin was lowered.

If not for her actual cries and the sound of her hitting the sides, I might have lost it right there.

"Sir?" one of the men asked.

"Finish it," he said. "She would rather be dead than come back. We'll bury her—then go."

"What about him?"

Sharpe glanced at me.

"Let him watch. Then bring him. You took from me, Hardigan. I don't forgive. You're going to pay for this…for taking her. You gave her up, and you should have left it alone."

The man was insane.

Yet, he stood there the whole time as they used a backhoe to dump dirt into the hole. It took almost no time to fill it in, her cries growing fainter and fainter until the soil muffled them completely.

Sharpe wiped at his face, then pocketed his phone before

accepting his cane. "You and I will have a longer conversation later," he informed me before limping away.

He took most of his bodyguards with him.

"You got him, Ron?"

"Yep," the man who'd been wielding the brand said. The ropes cut abruptly, and I fell. I'd been just off balance enough that I couldn't catch myself. My right shoulder ached like a bitch.

If I had to guess, it was dislocated. Pain littered my flesh from the burns and welts on my back to the bruises striping my ribs.

"Grab his feet," Ron's companion said. I didn't struggle as they hoisted me up. I needed to see.

Two guys—nope, there was the third one. He had lit a cigarette.

"Get your ass over here," Ron complained. "Fucker is heavy."

I didn't try to help them, just went for dead weight. Ron stumbled, swearing as I collapsed into him. He went down, and his friend dropped my feet.

That was all I needed.

I'd been in a couple of yard fights in prison. They weren't like the cage matches Liam favored or even a straight-up fist-fight. They were open brawls. Killing people wasn't always the goal; not all the inmates cared about that.

No, they cared about inflicting pain.

Right now, I had a lot of pain I wanted to inflict. Unfortunately, Ron wasn't going to get near enough of it. Especially since I got my bound wrists around his neck and wrenched it, even as his friend came at me.

I ignored their blows where they struck me, bit into my flesh, or gouged at me. Fists together, I slammed them up into the second guy's jaw. The crack of it was almost satisfying to me, and then the third guy was on me.

Easily my height and weight, he landed his blows with meaty fists that sucked all the breath out of me. We went down in the dirt, twisting, tumbling, and then he let out a harsh grunt as he came up with a knife.

I blocked the first blow, then the second, as we tumbled again. Twisting his grip, we fought for control of it, and then it sank into him, blood—his and mine—soaking my hands as I shoved it up under his ribs.

Once he collapsed, I shoved him off me and stumbled to my feet. It took me a minute to use the knife to try and cut through the heavy layer of rope.

Too long, I glanced over at the tampered earth as I finally slid one of the coils off, and as soon as it was loose, the rest fell away.

On my feet, I staggered toward the plot. Even sucking in air hurt, but I got one foot in front of the other. One of my legs buckled, and I hit my knees. Covering my side with a hand, I grimaced as blood poured between my fingers.

Fuck.

I didn't think he'd gotten me with the knife.

Didn't matter.

Ivy mattered.

Crawling, I barely made it to the dirt. Burrowing my fingers into the earth, I started digging. Spots danced in front of my eyes, but I had to get her out.

"Hang on," I begged her even as my vision tunneled. "I'm coming, Ivy…"

Then everything went black.

\* \* \*

Don't miss Fierce Dancer, the stunning conclusion to the 82nd Street Vandals

# FIERCE DANCER

The dancer.

The victim.

The sister.

I've worn a lot of labels over the years. For as long as I can remember, I wanted to escape. I hid in my dance. I ran away from my life as much as I could. I fought to be somewhere else, even if I couldn't be someone else.

One night, after my partner lashed out at me and I'd been hurt, the Vandals took me and never looked back. They introduced me to a world I had no idea existed and a family so much greater than the one I'd been trying to survive.

I gave myself up once to protect them.

I've fought for them.

I've bled for them.

I've killed for them.

And I'd do it all again if it keeps them safe.

My name is Emersyn Sharpe. I was born Ivy Hardigan. When the Vandals kidnapped me, I had no idea how life-changing it would be or how I would find real love. More, I found my place in this world. To have the future I want, I will finally wage war on the past.

Fierce Dancer is a full-length mature dark, new adult romance with enemies-to-lovers/love-hate themes. The dark romance aspects of this tale continue. Please be aware some situations may be uncomfortable for readers. Trigger warnings can be found in the foreword should you require them. This is a why choose novel, meaning the main character has more than one love interest. This is book nine and the final in the series.

# AFTERWORD

Yeah, I got nothing here for y'all. You knew it would be bad. How bad? Well...clearly, no one knew how bad. Just remember Fierce Dancer is coming and that is the 9th and final book in the series.

Right, you don't care about that so much right now. Back to my corner I go—

xoxo
Heather

Reader group:
facebook.com/groups/heatherspack
Spoiler group:
facebook.com/groups/teammadatheather

# ABOUT HEATHER LONG

I *love* books. Not just a little bit, but a lot. Books were my best friends when I was growing up. Books didn't care if I was new to a town or to a class. They were always there, my trustiest of companions. Until they turned on me and said I had to write them.

I can tell you that my own personal happily ever after included writing books. I've always said that an HEA is a work in progress. It's true in my marriage, my friendships, and in my career. I am constantly nurturing my muse as we dive into new tales, new tropes, new characters and more.

After seventeen years in Texas, we relocated to the Pacific Northwest in search of seasons, new experiences, and new geography. I can't wait to discover what life (and my muse) have in store for me.

Maybe writing was always my destiny and romance my fate. After all, my grandmother wasn't a fan of picture books and used to read me her Harlequin Romance novels.

*Follow Heather & Sign up for her newsletter:*
www.heatherlong.net
TikTok

## ALSO BY HEATHER LONG

**82nd Street Vandals**

Savage Vandal

Vicious Rebel

Ruthless Traitor

Dirty Devil

Brutal Fighter

Dangerous Renegade

Merciless Spy

Reckless Thief

Fierce Dancer

**Always a Marine Series**

Once Her Man, Always Her Man

Retreat Hell! She Just Got Here

Tell It to the Marine

Proud to Serve Her

Her Marine

No Regrets, No Surrender

The Marine Cowboy

The Two and the Proud

A Marine and a Gentleman

Combat Barbie

Whiskey Tango Foxtrot

What Part of Marine Don't You Understand?

A Marine Affair

Marine Ever After

Marine in the Wind

Marine with Benefits

A Marine of Plenty

A Candle for a Marine

Marine under the Mistletoe

Have Yourself a Marine Christmas

Lest Old Marines Be Forgot

Her Marine Bodyguard

Smoke & Marines

### Blue Ivy Prep

Problem Child

Mad Boys

Party Crashers

### Bravo Team Wolf

When Danger Bites

Bitten Under Fire

### Cardinal Sins

Kill Song

First Chorus

High Note

Last Word

### Chance Monroe

Earth Witches Aren't Easy

Plan Witch from Out of Town

Bad Witch Rising

**Her Elite Assets**

Featuring:

Pure Copper

Target: Tungsten

Asset: Arsenic

**Fevered Hearts**

Marshal of Hel Dorado

Brave are the Lonely

Micah & Mrs. Miller

A Fistful of Dreams

Raising Kane

Wanted: Fevered or Alive

Wild and Fevered

The Quick & The Fevered

A Man Called Wyatt

**Going Royal**

Some Like It Royal

Some Like It Scandalous

Some Like It Deadly

Some Like it Secret

Some Like it Easy

Her Marine Prince

Blocked

**Heart of the Nebula**

Queenmaker

Deal Breaker

Throne Taker

**Lone Star Leathernecks**

Semper Fi Cowboy

As You Were, Cowboy

**Magic & Mayhem**

The Witch Singer

Bridget's Witch's Diary

The Witched Away Bride

**Mongrels**

Mongrels, Mischief & Mayhem

**Shackled Souls**

Succubus Chained

Succubus Unchained

Succubus Blessed

Shackled Souls (Omnibus)

**Space Cowboy**

Space Cowboy Survival Guide

**Time Captive**

Paused

Rewind

Fast Forward

**Untouchable**

Rules and Roses

Changes and Chocolates

Keys and Kisses

Whispers and Wishes

Hangovers and Holidays

Brazen and Breathless

Trials and Tiaras

Graduation and Gifts

Defiance and Dedication

Songs and Sweethearts

Legacy and Lovers

Farewells and Forever

**Wolves of Willow Bend**

Wolf at Law

Wolf Bite

Caged Wolf

Wolf Claim

Wolf Next Door

Rogue Wolf

Bayou Wolf

Untamed Wolf

Wolf with Benefits

River Wolf

Single Wicked Wolf

Desert Wolf

Snow Wolf